Elsie Silver is a Canadian author of sassy, sexy, small town romance who loves a good book boyfriend and the strong heroines who bring them to their knees. She lives just outside of Vancouver, British Columbia with her husband, son, and three dogs and has been voraciously reading romance books since before she was probably supposed to.

She loves cooking and trying new foods, traveling, and spending time with her boys—especially outdoors. Elsie has also become a big fan of her quiet five o'clock mornings, which is when most of her writing happens. It's during this time that she can sip a cup of hot coffee and dream up a fictional world full of romantic stories to share with her readers.

www.elsiesilver.com

Heartless
ELSIE SILVER

PIATKUS

PIATKUS

First published in Great Britain in 2023 by Piatkus

16

A CIP catalogue record for this book
is available from the British Library.

ISBN: 978-0-349-43768-2

Printed and bound in Great Britain by Clays Ltd, Elcograf S.p.A.

Papers used by Piatkus are from well-managed forests
and other responsible sources.

Piatkus
An imprint of
Little, Brown Book Group
Carmelite House
50 Victoria Embankment
London EC4Y 0DZ

An Hachette UK Company
www.hachette.co.uk

www.littlebrown.co.uk

For the incredible women who've been my biggest supporters. And for all the women out there who build other women up rather than tearing them down. We're better together.

Sometimes good things fall apart so better things can fall together.

— Marilyn Monroe

1

Cade

Lucy Reid's eyes flutter my way. The look in them is just a *little* too appreciative for my taste.

"Well, I love to do arts and crafts. I do a lot of scrapbooking in my spare time. Knitting. I bet Luke would love to do some knitting. Don't you think, Cade?"

I almost laugh at the way she purrs my name. Also, I'd love to see someone get Luke to sit still long enough to handle two pointy sticks and create something.

She smiles over at Summer now, my little brother's fiancée, before adding, "You know how it is. We all need some sort of feminine hobbies, don't we?"

I hear my dad, Harvey, chuckle from where he's seated in the room's corner. Hiring a nanny has turned into a full-on family affair.

And a full-on nightmare.

Summer's lips roll together, and she offers a small,

fake smile. "Yes, of course." I almost snort. Summer's idea of feminine entertainment is squatting heavy plates at the gym and torturing grown men in the name of "personal training." She's lying through her fucking teeth, but it's possible she's still new enough in town that Lucy doesn't know.

Or maybe Lucy is being a snarky bitch to my future sister.

"Alright." I stand. "Well, thanks. We'll get back to you."

Lucy seems a little taken aback by how swiftly I've changed the conversation, but I've heard and seen all I need to.

And bedside manner isn't my strong suit. I'm more of a rip-the-band-aid off type.

I spin on my heel, drop my chin, and walk out before it's too obvious that I saw her outstretched hand and just didn't care to shake it. Practically stomping to the kitchen, I prop my hands against the butcher block counter that butts up against the window and let my eyes trace out over the open range. Across the peaks of the Rockies that jut up toward the heavens.

This view, wild and craggy, is bursting with color in the early summer—grass a little too green, sky a little too blue, and sun bright enough to wash everything out a bit and make you squint.

After tossing some coffee beans into the grinder to make a fresh pot, I press down on the top to fill the house with the sound and try not to think about what I'm going to do with my kid for the next couple of months. It just leads to beating myself up. Feeling like I should do more for him. Be more present for him.

Basically, it's not productive.

The sound has the added benefit of drowning out the pleasantries that my dad and Summer are exchanging with Lucy at the front door.

Not my house, not my responsibility. We're doing the nanny interviews at the main farmhouse, where my dad lives, because I don't like letting random people into my home. Especially not ones who look at me like this is their ticket into completing some weird little premade happy family fantasy with me.

Harvey, on the other hand, would run a bed-and-breakfast out of this place and enjoy the hell out of taking care of people. Ever since he got injured and handed the ranch over to me, it's like he just wanders around socializing 24-7.

I watch the small grains tumble into the white paper filter in the coffeemaker's top and then swivel to fill the pot with water at the sink.

"Kinda late in the day for a pot of coffee, don't you think?" Harvey strides in, with Summer not far behind.

They have no idea. I'm full up on coffee today. Almost jittery. "Just premaking it for tomorrow morning for ya."

Summer snorts and my dad rolls his eyes. They both know I'm full of shit.

"You weren't very nice to her, Cade," is his next

comment. And now it's my turn to roll my eyes. "In fact, you've been a challenge with this entire process."

Crossing my arms, I lean back against the countertop. "I'm not very nice. And I'll happily be a *challenge* about protecting my kid." I swear my dad's lips twitch when he sits down at the table and crosses a booted foot over his knee. Summer just stands, hip propped against the doorframe, staring at me. She does this sometimes and it's unnerving.

She's smart. She doesn't miss a beat. I swear I hear the gears turning in her head, but she doesn't have a big mouth, so you never quite know what she's thinking.

I like her and I'm glad my little brother was smart enough to put a ring on it.

"You're nice," she says thoughtfully, "in your own way."

I clamp my teeth onto my lip because I don't want to give them the satisfaction of seeing I'm amused by that comment.

She sighs. "Listen, that's everyone we've interviewed. I went out of my way to weed out the applicants who seemed less interested in spending time with Luke and more interested in spending time with . . . you."

"Hoo boy"—Dad slaps the table—"and there were several. Who knew women would willingly sign up to endure your scowls and bad moods? The pay isn't *that* good."

I scowl at him before turning my attention back to Summer. "You didn't weed thoroughly enough. I want someone who has zero interest in me. No complicated shit. Maybe they could be happily married?"

"Happily married women don't want to live in your house for the summer."

I grunt. "What about someone from another town? Someone who doesn't know our family. And all my shit. Someone who hasn't slept with one of my brothers." My nose wrinkles. "Or my dad."

Harvey makes a little choking sound, almost a laugh. "I've been single for decades, son. Mind your business."

Summer's cheeks pinken, but I don't miss the smile on her lips as she turns to peer out the window.

"I could just do it, you know," Harvey adds. And not for the first time.

"No."

"Why not? He's my grandson."

"Exactly. That's what your relationship should remain. You've done enough helping with him for his entire life. Your back, your knees—you need a rest. You can still have your fun days with him any time you want. But you don't need to run yourself into the ground with long hours, early mornings, and possibly late nights. It's not fair, and I'm not taking advantage of you that way. End of story."

Then I turn back to my future sister-in-law. "Summer, can't you just do it? You'd be perfect. Luke loves you. You don't like me. You already live on the ranch."

I see her jaw twitch. She's getting sick of me asking her, but I don't want to leave my boy with just anyone.

He's a handful. More than one handful. And I can't accomplish everything I need to do on this ranch this summer without someone here to take care of him. Someone I can trust to keep him safe.

"I'm also a new business owner, and these summer months are my busiest. It's not an option. Stop asking. It makes me feel bad. Because I love you and Luke. But we're getting tired of bending over backwards interviewing people just to make zero progress with you."

"Okay, fine," I grumble. "I'll settle for someone just like you, then."

Her head quirks in response to that, her body stilling. "I might have an idea." She brings a finger up to tap it against her lips, and Harvey turns to her, eyes full of questions.

He looks so damn hopeful. If I'm tired of the saga that is finding a new nanny for the summer, then Harvey must be downright exhausted.

My eyebrows knit together. "Who?"

"You don't know her."

"Does she have experience?"

Summer stares at me, wide, dark eyes giving nothing away. "She has experience with handling rowdy boys, yes."

"Will she fall in love with me?"

Summer snorts in the most unladylike way. "No."

Her certainty should probably offend me, but I'm not bothered by it. I push off the counter and twirl a finger around. "Perfect. Let's do it up," I tell her as I march out the back door toward my house and away from the cluster-fuck that is finding a capable nanny for a five-year-old boy.

I just need someone to get in and get out. Someone professional and complication free.

It's only two months. It shouldn't be that hard.

~

I count in my head the last time I had sex.

Or at least I try.

Two years? Three years? Was it that one time in January when I spent a night in the city? How long ago was that even? What was that chick's name again?

The woman in front of me shifts, one hip popping out, full ass rounding out her skinny jeans in a way that should be illegal. The under-cheek crease is almost as alluring as the swing of her copper hair as it swishes across her slender back.

She's distracting. Tight shirt tucked into tight jeans. Every fucking curve on display.

I lose count entirely. It's the sight of her in front of me in line for coffee that has me counting anyway.

The takeaway here is I had sex so far back now that I don't even remember. But there's no forgetting why I haven't even let myself consider members of the opposite sex.

A kid I'm raising on my own. A ranch I'm running on

my own. A million responsibilities. Too little time. Not enough sleep.

Time for myself hasn't been a thing for a long time. I just didn't realize how long.

"What can I get you, ma'am?"

The woman in front of me laughs, and it reminds me of the chimes on my back porch when the wind dances through them—melodic and airy sounding.

What a laugh.

It's a laugh I'd recognize. I've definitely never met this woman. I'd remember it because I know everyone in Chestnut Springs.

"Ma'am? I don't know how I feel about that," she says, and I swear I can hear the smile in her voice. I wonder if her lips match the rest of her.

Ellen, who runs Le Pamplemousse, the little gourmet coffee shop in town, smiles at her. "Well, what would you have me call you? I usually recognize every face that walks in my door, but not yours."

Ah, it's not just me. I lean forward a little, hoping to catch the name. But one worker chooses this exact moment to grind coffee. Which just makes me grind my teeth.

I don't know why I want to know this woman's name. I just do. I'm from a small town, I'm allowed to be snoopy. And that's all this is.

When the grinding noise stops, Ellen's wrinkled face lights up. "What a pretty name."

"Thank you," the woman in front of me replies,

before adding, "How come this place is called The Grapefruit?"

Ellen barks out her amusement and grins from her side of the counter. "I told my husband I wanted to name the shop something that sounded fancy. Something French. He said the only thing he knows how to say in French is *le pamplemousse*. It seemed good enough to me and now it's like a little running joke between us." Her eyes soften at the mention of her husband, and I feel a flicker of envy inside of my chest.

Followed by a flicker of annoyance.

The only reason I haven't grumbled about their slow-as-fuck chitchat is because I'm too busy fighting off a public boner over this chick's laugh. Under normal circumstances, it would piss me off that grabbing a coffee is taking this damn long. I told my dad I'd be back to grab Luke—I check my watch—right about now. I need to get back so I can meet with Summer and the person who will hopefully be Luke's nanny.

But my mind is wandering in ways I haven't let it in literal years. So maybe I'm meant to just enjoy the ride. Maybe it's okay to let myself feel something.

"I'll grab a medium, extra hot, no foam, half sweet . . ." My eyes subtly roll back in my head as I tip the brim of my black hat down. Of course, the outsider with the rocking body must have an annoyingly long and complicated drink order.

"That'll be three dollars and seventy-five cents," Ellen says, eyes fixed on the cash register's touch screen in front of her while the woman at the till digs through her oversized purse, clearly searching for her wallet.

"Oh shit," she mutters, and from the corner of my eye, I see something fall from her purse to the polished concrete floor at her sandal-clad feet.

Without even thinking about it, I drop into a crouch and swipe the black fabric off the floor. I see her legs turning and rise back up.

"Here you go," I say, my voice all gravel as a shot of nerves hits me. Talking to strange women isn't a well-honed skill of mine.

Scowling at them? I'm a professional.

"Oh my god," she says.

Standing now, I get a good look at her face. My feet root to the ground, and my lungs stop working. Her laugh has nothing on her face. Cat-like eyes, arched brows, and milky skin.

She's fucking stunning.

And her cheeks are fire-engine red.

"I'm so sorry," she gasps, hand falling across her rosebud lips.

"No need. It's fine," I say, but I still feel like everything is happening in slow motion. I'm having a hard time catching up, still too fixated on her face.

And *fuck*.

Her tits.

I'm officially a creepy old man. My eyes trail down to my fist, the soft fabric poking out from between my fingers.

She groans as my fingers unfurl. And slowly but surely, I figure out why she's acting so horrified over me being a gentleman and picking up her . . .

Panties.

I stare at the scrap of black fabric in my hand, and it's like everything around us goes blurry. My eyes shoot to hers, all wide and green. So many shades. A mosaic.

I'm not known for smiling, but the corners of my mouth twitch. "You, uh, dropped your panties, ma'am."

A strangled giggle bursts from her as her gaze darts to my hand and back to my face. "Wow. This is awkward. I'm really—"

"Your coffee is ready, sweetheart!" Ellen calls.

The redhead's face flips away, relieved by the interruption. "Thank you!" she calls back a little too brightly before slapping a five down on the counter and grabbing the paper cup. Without another glance, she's making a beeline for the door. Like she can't get away fast enough. "Keep the change! See you again!"

I swear I hear her giggling under her breath as she breezes past, clearly avoiding my gaze while murmuring something to herself about this being a good story to tell her kids one day.

I absently wonder what the hell kind of stories this woman plans on telling her future children before I call out to her. "You forgot your . . ." I trail off because I refuse to shout this across the coffee shop full of people I have to face day in, day out.

She turns and presses her back into the door as she

leaves, holding my eyes for a beat, barely contained amusement touching every feature. "Finders keepers," she says with a shrug.

Now, she does laugh, full and warm and so damn amused. Then she exits into the sunlit street, hair shining like fire and hips swinging like she owns this town.

She leaves me stunned.

And when I glance back down at my open palm, it hits me she's long gone. I have no idea what her name is, and I'm still here . . .

Holding her panties.

2
Willa

"Who was he?" Summer's voice is strangled.

"Not a damn clue." I think back on my black underwear plunking down on the floor and how mortification slowly morphed into hysterics.

Only me.

Things like that would only happen to me.

My best friend gasps, rocking forward on the porch swing. "You didn't take them back?"

I smirk and take a sip of my beer. "No. He looked so . . . I don't know. Stunned? Like not offended, but not pervy about it either. It was kind of adorable. I feel like I freed a house-elf or something."

"Did he resemble Dobby?"

I groan and waggle my brows at her suggestively. "If Dobby was hot."

"Willa, that's nasty." She wheezes. "Please tell me they were clean."

"Of course. They're my spares. You know I don't like wearing panties. But now and then, the need arises, you know?"

Summer narrows her gaze in my direction. "I have that need every day."

"To be uncomfortable? No thanks. Life is too short. Bras and underwear are overrated. Plus, now I can lay awake at night and wonder what some rando is doing with them."

Summer just laughs again. "He probably threw them out like any sane person would." She's so happy these days. Since she left her strained family and overper-forming city life. She met a bull rider and ran off into the sunset and now here she is. My best friend. All smiles and freckles and curled up on a porch swing in front of a beautiful, custom-built rancher that faces out over the Rocky Mountains.

Nothing has ever looked better on her.

I like to bug her about living in the middle of "butt-fuck nowhere" but the truth is the view out near Chestnut Springs is breathtaking. Prairie land so flat it almost seems impossible. Dark, craggy mountains rising like a tidal wave, heading right for you.

In the city, we can see the mountains, but not like this. Not like you could reach out and touch them.

"So, what are you going to do about the next several months?"

I sigh. I have no idea. But I also don't want Summer worrying about me. It's kind of her thing. She'll get all worried, and then she'll try to fix things for me when I'd just rather go with the flow.

"Maybe I'll come live with you and Rhett for a while?" I say innocently, glancing around. "The house is so nice now that it's finished. You wouldn't mind, would you?"

She rolls her lips together like she's really thinking about it. Goddamn, this woman has a heart of gold.

"Sum, I'm kidding. I wouldn't do that to you guys." Huffing out a ragged sigh, I gaze out over the fields. "I don't know. When Ford told me he was going to shut down the bar for renovations, I was honestly excited. I figured I'd spend the summer traveling from horse show to horse show and blowing through all my savings. Avoiding coming up with a plan for my life and just being a twenty-five-year-old with nothing except family money going for her."

She tries to interrupt me. She doesn't like it when I'm hard on myself about managing my super successful brother's bar. Or tagging along on my super successful parents' vacations. Or just stumbling through life with zero sense of direction in a family full of overachievers.

I ignore her protests and continue. "But of course my horse had to go ruin all my plans and injure himself just in time for show season. Tux needed surgery and now I'll just spend my summer feeding him carrots and obsessively brushing him."

My best friend just stares at me. I want to reach into her brain and pluck out her thoughts because I know she's chock-full of them.

"I'll be good. It's a first world problem. I'll visit you a bunch. You can brutalize me at your gym, and I'll pick up the odd hockey player or bull rider. Win-win-win."

"Right . . ." Her pointer finger taps against her top lip. "What if—"

"Oh no. Please don't do the thing where you make it your job to fix my life. You help people too much, you know that?"

"Willa, shut up and listen to me."

I press my ass back against the porch railing facing her and reach for the bottle of beer beside me. It's dripping condensation down the side, and the liquid inside isn't even that cold anymore. It's only June and already unseasonably hot. Jeans were a mistake.

Taking a big pull, I roll my shoulders back. Ready to be scolded.

"What if I had a way for you to live out here for the summer? But not with Rhett and me."

That is not what I was expecting her to say.

"I don't want to camp in your yard. I'm not cut out for sleeping outdoors. I may not know what my path in life is yet, but I promise it doesn't include air mattresses and sleeping bags."

She rolls her eyes and forges ahead. "No. Rhett's older brother needs help with his son for the months between school. The woman who took care of him when he was little can't keep up anymore. He's five."

I stare at my friend, beer bottle swinging back and forth between my fingers. "You want *me* to take care of a child?"

"Yeah. You're fun. And high energy. And if you can handle a bar full of drunk guys, then what's one little boy who needs entertaining? You like kids, you always say you do."

I mull the idea over in my head. My first inclination is to say no, but truthfully, I'm dreading these months without work, or competing, or my best friend. I've always liked kids, possibly because I still feel a bit like one sometimes.

"And where would I live?"

Her eyes widen just a little and her throat works as she swallows. "With his brother, Cade. He runs the ranch. His mornings are early and sometimes his nights are late if something goes wrong. But he's got a good crew hired on the ranch to offset his hours. Their dad likes to help with Luke, but honestly, he's not cut out for twelve-hour days either. But he'd tag you out pretty often, I'm sure."

"You look scared? Is this the dick brother or the funny, hot, superhero brother?" I almost feel bad asking because I haven't been great about coming out here and visiting Summer. We often just meet in town rather than driving the extra twenty minutes out to Wishing Well

Ranch. I should probably have met all the members of her future family by now, but I haven't.

"The dick brother."

"Of course it is." I drink again.

She jumps in quickly. "But you won't see him that much! He specifically doesn't want someone who will, um . . . get in his way? Plus, Rhett and I will be around. It could be fun."

When she puts it like that, it does sound kind of fun. More fun than spending the best months of the year in the city alone.

"Can we do boozy brunches?" We always did boozy brunches when we were both living in the city, and I want them back.

Her lips twitch. "Yes."

I toss back the rest of my beer, already knowing what my answer is going to be. I've gone with the flow my entire life. Opportunities pop up and I stumble into them. This feels like another one of those.

Who am I to say no?

"Well then, fuck it. I'm in."

We drive across the farm and pull up in front of the most picturesque red house with white trim. Little hedges rim the yard, and a white gate opens to a dirt path leading to the front door.

I'm instantly charmed.

"I get to live here?" I ask as we climb out of her SUV, unable to tear my eyes from the adorable, perfectly manicured house.

"Yeah." Summer carries on, missing the part where I'm beyond charmed by the whole vibe out here. "I think his hours are so variable that it makes sense. Before we were tag teaming it with his dad and Mrs. Hill but waking up and getting over here at 4:30 a.m. is just too much for them. Cade doesn't enjoy asking them to do it, but if you're living here, you can just keep sleeping and then Luke won't be alone in the house."

Summer saunters up to the front door without a care in the world, and I trail behind, wondering what the hell I've actually signed myself up for.

I don't know shit about taking care of kids.

Or parenting.

Or ranching.

My steps falter as I fall behind, but Summer doesn't notice. She marches up the couple of steps in her flip-flops and cutoff jeans to the front porch, lifts the knocker, and bangs hard.

"Hey, Sum—" I start, reaching out with a hand as though I can stop her when she's already knocked. Thinking that we should talk this through more thoroughly. Hammer out some details.

Maybe my impulsiveness has gotten me in over my head for once. I almost feel like she's rushing. Like she can't wait to wrap this up. And I have questions.

Lots of questions.

But they all evaporate from my mind the minute the front door swings open, and I'm left standing stupidly in the middle of the dirt walkway, gawking at the man from the coffee shop.

The one I left my panties with.

He's still all man, from head to toe. Dark hair, darker eyes under furrowed brows, broad shoulders, the sexiest scruff surrounding a slightly curled lip . . . and a scowl.

He stares in my direction while his knuckles turn white where he grips the door.

"Cade!" Summer starts in, oblivious to the death glare he's pinning me with. "This is my best friend, Willa. Your new nanny."

"No," is his only reply.

"What do you mean, *no*?"

"I mean, over my dead body." Condescension drips from his words.

Her head quirks to the side, and I close the space between us. If he thinks he's going to talk to my best friend that way, he's got another thing coming. I've had her back since we were teenagers. Summer's endured enough shitty men in her life, so this one can fuck all the way off.

"Cade, don't be ridiculous. We've been trying to find someone for—"

He cuts her off. "*You're* being ridicu—"

I step onto the porch, seeing red. No one else in my family has red hair, and I don't know if it's to blame for my fiery side, but I have been known to fly off the handle and hold a hell of a grudge.

I've been known to break up bar fights with a bat.

And maybe I'm about to be known for kicking a hot-as-hell rancher in the balls.

I wave a hand right in front of him to shut him up. "Choose your next words carefully. I don't care if she's about to be your sister-in-law. No one speaks to her with that tone, period."

He turns his dark gaze on me now, eyes starting on my face before trailing down my body in the most critical and unnerving way. When his eyes come back up, the look in them is perfectly flat.

Like he's sized me up and found me entirely lacking.

"And I don't care if you're her best friend. You smell like beer and your panties are still in my back pocket. You're not taking care of my son."

My eyes narrow, and my lips curve up at his misstep. "You saving them for later?"

I wink at him, watching fiery red splotches crop up on the apples of his cheeks and seep out across the immaculate bone structure hidden beneath that beard and scowl.

Summer spins on me, chocolate eyes wide as saucers. She resembles one of those squishy-faced dogs whose eyes are constantly bugging out in the most adorable way. "Cade is the panty guy?"

"I'm not the panty guy," he interjects, but Summer and I ignore him.

"Yeah. And you said that any sane man would have thrown them out. So you know what that means."

We're grinning at each other like crazy people now, and before I know it, a giggle slips from between Summer's lips. And before long, she's doubled over, hands on her knees, gasping for air.

"For fuck's sake." The grump runs a broad hand through his hair in frustration. "I am *not* the panty guy."

Laughter shakes my shoulders, and my eyes water as I mumble, "What are the chances?"

"This is a small town. The chances are rather good," Cade grits out, not nearly as amused as us.

Summer practically howls as she straightens and swipes at her eyes. "Don't worry, Cade. They're clean."

His nostrils flare, and his eyes fall shut as he sucks in a deep breath. Like that might bring him some sort of peace.

"Panty Guy." I shake my head and grin at him. Nanny or not, I'll be spending time around this man for the rest of my life with Summer being married to his brother, so I might as well smooth things out.

"He's not a panty guy! He wears boxers!" A small voice echoes from the hallway as the most adorable dark-haired, blue-eyed little boy comes blasting into view. "Those tight ones though," he clarifies, adding insult to injury.

"Yeah," I deadpan to the little boy who's now wedged himself under his dad's arm. Big eyes regard me with keen interest. "Can't have any chafing."

"What's chafing?" he asks curiously, as his dad holds one broad, tanned hand up to his eyebrows and rubs at them.

"Luke."

"Like when all your junk rubs together," I explain.

You don't grow up around my parents and act shy about this stuff. Nothing is off the table in our family.

"Oh yeah," he nods, appearing wise beyond his years. "I hate it when that happens."

"Luke, back in your room." Cade's broad form has turned to face his son, and I can't help but admire him. The strength he exudes. The ripple in his forearms. The way his Adam's apple bobs. The way his eyes soften as he stares down at his son.

That's the real kicker.

"Why?" This kid has his number though. Sapphire eyes widen almost dramatically, and his bottom lip pushes out ever so slightly. "I wanna go play with Summer and her friend."

He's *precious.*

"No," his dad says, right as I say, "Sure!"

Cade's head snaps around, brows harsh slashes across his forehead, the lines there furrowed as though I've done something to personally offend him.

"Cade." Summer props her hands on her hips. "Just let him come hang out for a bit. Maybe it will be okay. Maybe you'll be pleasantly surprised."

My eyes bounce between the two of them. Summer, all pint-sized and sweet, Cade, all big and growly.

23

"Please, Dad?" When Luke's sugary-sweet voice speaks, he doesn't look so growly. He looks more . . . resigned. Tired somehow?

Cade spins on me. "How old are you?"

I straighten, refusing to cower under his piercing gaze. "Twenty-five."

His throat works as he assesses me again. "Do you have a criminal record?"

"Not a substantial one," I reply honestly. I got caught with pot once before they legalized it. Sue me for being a fun teenager.

"Jesus Christ." One thick hand runs through his closely cropped hair as he shakes his head.

"Do *you* have a criminal record?" I cross my arms and arch an eyebrow back at him. If this is the brother I think it is, the one Summer has told me about, then I'm almost positive he's not some walking, talking angel. And I'll be the one stuck living with him.

He stares at me. Hard. It feels like it lasts forever. Summer looks between us, and from the corner of my eye I see Luke peer up at his dad and tug at the hem of his shirt. "Can I go play now?"

"Fine." Cade glares at me when he says it. "But Summer is in charge."

The little boy squeals and launches off the front porch.

And I just glare back at his dad.

3

Cade

With Luke out of the house, I officially have a little bit of free time. A little bit of time to myself. A little bit of time to relax.

I keep saying I need this, but now that I have it, I'm not so sure I like it.

It turns out that after a lifetime of taking care of people, I'm not great at relaxing. I flick the TV on and try to find something to watch, but nothing appeals to me. I walk over to the bookshelf in my living room, stocked with some classics from my parents and some books I grabbed for myself along the way. Books I thought seemed interesting and then never made the time to read.

I pull one out and flop down onto the couch with it. But when I do, I feel a lump in my back pocket. And then I'm immediately on edge.

Willa.

I don't even know her last name. I don't know much

about her, really. All I know is that she won't be good enough to take care of Luke.

She's nothing like the uninteresting, responsible, asexual nun who also wants to do fun things with an active little boy I've had in mind for the job.

I'm not delusional enough to think that person exists, but I keep hoping for that anyway. And Willa isn't the answer I was hoping for.

Luke's mom did a number on us. She continues to do a number on us—on me.

My trust levels are at rock bottom. I trust Mrs. Hill because I know she took good care of my brothers and me. Same goes for my dad. I trust Summer because anyone who can manage to tie my wild-child little brother down can handle an unruly five-year-old.

But this Willa character. I don't know her. I don't trust her.

All I know is that she makes my dick twitch, she talks too much, and she has a spare pair of underwear in her purse.

I sit up and pull them out. It's not like they're anything offensive. A silky nylon type of black fabric. Pretty full cut. I guess. For panties? What the fuck do I know?

I feel like the biggest perv, sitting here on my couch, scrutinizing a pair of underwear that belongs to the woman who is currently taking care of my child.

I should give them back.

I don't want to keep walking around with them.

I also don't want to look her in the eye as I hand them back.

I'm thirty-eight years old and acting like a nervous fucking teenager over women's undergarments.

Agitated with myself, I storm over to the kitchen and shove them all the way to the back of my "stuff" drawer. The one where random shit goes to die because I'm too lazy to think of a proper place to put it. I pride myself on keeping a tidy house, but that one drawer is my secret shame.

It seems fitting that Willa's underwear should end up in there.

I swipe my keys off the counter and stride out the front door. I get the feeling my indecisiveness over the whole nanny thing has irritated my dad, so I hop in my truck and opt to go harass my little brother instead.

God knows he spent enough years giving me the few gray hairs that now mingle with the dark ones near my temples. The least he can do is hand me a beer and tell me more about this Willa person before I write her off and make Summer and my dad hate me.

Because I'm pretty sure if I draw this out much longer, they'll both tell me to go fuck myself for being such a picky bitch.

And I'll deserve it.

It only takes me a few minutes on the back road to reach Rhett and Summer's brand-new house.

I see a red Jeep Wrangler parked next to the vintage truck my brother drives. But Summer's swanky vehicle is gone. My fingers itch to grab my phone from my pocket, dial her up, and demand to know where she is and what she's doing.

Maybe I'm on extra high alert with someone new around my kid. But mostly, I always feel this way. I always feel like I'm looking out for someone. For everyone.

I've had the weight of the world on my shoulders since my mom died when I was eight. I'm not even sure if anyone put that weight there or if I just do it to myself.

Either way, it's ever present. And it's heavy.

I stomp up the front steps of the house and bang on the door, even though there's a bell. Hitting something is just so much more satisfying.

Within a few moments, I hear feet padding from the other side of the door. I can see my brother's form through the frosted glass, and when he opens the door, he's smiling.

Smirking like he knows something I don't.

"Where's Summer?" I ask, cutting to the chase.

"Nice to see you too, jackass. My wife is in town. She had to run to the gym."

I snort. "She's not your wife yet. You aren't married."

He laughs and waves me off, opening the door wider. "Details. She said yes. It's pretty much done in my books. And it just sounds so good, you know?"

I wrinkle my nose and stare back at my little brother. Never thought I'd see him this gone over a girl.

"Is my kid with her?"

"Oh, nah. He's off with Willa. Summer said to remind you that you said she was in charge so she decided Willa would stay with Luke so she could work at her own business rather than as your personal assistant."

I roll my lips together and look back out over the wide-open farmland. That sounds *exactly* like something Summer would say. A loophole in my instructions that she would find.

Rhett holds his hands up in surrender while trying to conceal his amusement. "Her words, not mine."

Propping my hands on my hips, I sigh before shifting my gaze back on Rhett and grit out, "Tell me about this Willa person. And where exactly is she?"

"Come sit out back with me. You look like you need a beer. Or ten."

I shake my head as I step into the house. "I do not need ten beers."

Rhett chuckles as he saunters through the open-concept house to the kitchen, lined with glass doors that open wide onto the sprawling back deck. "Yeah. You do. You look like you could kill someone. It's not good for your blood pressure. You aren't getting any younger."

"Young enough to beat your ass," I mutter as I toe off my boots and follow him through to the sunny deck.

Within moments, Rhett tosses me a can of beer and steers me toward a chair facing the field that functions as their backyard. There is one lone tree. A huge willow with long sweeping branches that dangle all around, giving it an almost curtain-like effect.

I crack the beer and put the cold can to my lips as Rhett sits in the Adirondack chair next to me. Summer painted them bright red, cheerful just like her.

They remind me of Willa's hair.

Fucking lame. I push the thought away. And that's when I hear it.

"I can't do it." It's Luke's little voice, a hint of distress soaking through.

"Yes, you can," the slightly raspy tone of the knockout redhead comes next. And I almost shoot out of my seat to run to the rescue.

"Man, just sit. He's fine. Don't be a helicopter parent. It's annoying."

I ignore the instinct, take a big swig, and strain to hear what's going on beneath the tree.

"You won't climb further than you can handle. You're too smart for that. Trust your body."

"What if I fall?" Luke's voice is thin.

"Well, I guess I'll stand underneath you and you can fall on me so that we both get hurt. Because you're too big to catch. And you aren't going to fall anyway. Just listen to me, okay?"

"Okay," he says, a surge of determination in his tone now.

Rhett glances over at me and grins. "Willa Grant is good shit, brother. If she's offering to take care of our boy for the summer, you'd be an idiot to turn her down. I don't know many people more loyal than her. She's got a big heart."

30

I feel like there's a story there I don't know. But I also know my brother wouldn't blow smoke up my ass when it comes to Luke and his well-being.

Her voice trails out from the tree again. "You're going to move your right foot down to this branch." A pause. "Attaboy. Then your left hand here. Then you should be able to sit on that branch and jump down."

I can see her sandaled feet and tight jeans behind the branches as she moves around pointing things out to my son. Soon, small sneakered feet plunk down beside her, followed by little hands catching in the grass.

"I did it!" Luke shoots up, still oblivious to the fact that I'm here.

"Of course, you did. You made this tree your bitch."

Rhett snorts beside me and I glare at him.

"Oh, come on! You think he hasn't heard the way you talk?"

"I've spent years instilling good manners in that kid."

He chuckles and shrugs. "Well, if that's true, then you've laid a good foundation, and one summer with a fun nanny won't ruin him."

I just grunt and take a sip.

Maybe.

"How high can you go, Willa?"

I expect her to shut him down. Or appease him with some line about how adults don't climb trees. But she wipes her hands over the round globes of her jean-clad ass and says, "I dunno. Let's see."

I hold my beer suspended in midair—frozen—as I

watch an adult woman climb the thick trunk. "Is she nuts?" I mutter before taking another drink.

Rhett snorts. "A little. But in a good way."

Luke's feet bounce excitedly as he watches her. "Don't go too high! What if you get stuck?"

"You'd save me," Willa calls back from what sounds like much higher up the tree than I thought she'd go.

"I'm too small. But my dad would save you!"

Her raspy laugh reaches us at the back deck. It's still as disarming as it was earlier today. "I don't know about that. He might be happy to leave me up here, Luke."

I press my lips together. She's not entirely wrong. My life would be a lot less complicated if she hadn't waltzed into Chestnut Springs this morning.

My dick would be a lot softer too.

"Oh never. He helps everyone," my son replies, making my heart twist in my chest. Sometimes I wonder how I must seem to him, how I look in his eyes. And this one gets me right in the gut.

"Sounds like you've got a pretty great dad," Willa replies instantly, sounding a little breathless now. "How lucky are you?"

"Yeah . . ." Luke trails off thoughtfully. "No mom though. She moved away and doesn't visit."

My brother sucks in a breath from beside me, eyes darting in my direction. "Goddamn, kids just say whatever comes to mind, don't they?"

I swallow thickly and nod. I've worked hard to shield

Luke from the reality of his mom, of the choices she's made—the type of person she is.

I never want him to feel unwanted.

Willa drops to the ground, brushes her hands against each other, and crouches in front of my son. Her head tips up to look him in the eye, hands stroking his upper arms as she smiles at him.

"Sounds like her loss, because you might be the coolest kid I've ever met."

She doesn't use a sad voice, or a baby voice, she just talks to him like a normal human being.

"Fucking hell," I curse under my breath because she just practically hired herself.

4

Willa

I swallow hard when Luke pushes his soft little fingers between my own. I also swallow down the agitation I feel at the thought of someone—a mother, no less—not coming to visit a kid like this.

The universe blessed me with two badass parents. Ones who would crawl through glass to get to me. I want to be that kind of mother one day. Fierce. Fearless.

Sucking air in through my nostrils, I remind myself that it's not my business. That I don't know the full story. That maybe there's a good reason for whatever's going on with his mom. But his voice is so sweet, and his hand is so chubby, and he's been cracking my shit up since he announced his dad wears boxers and not panties.

I don't really consider myself a kid person, not in the mushy, heart-eyed kind of way. Haven't spent enough time around them to know for sure if I am. Usually I just talk to them like tiny adults. But after years of bartending, I know *people*. And no matter what his age is, Luke is a cool person.

Giving his hand a quick squeeze—that he almost instantly returns—I pull back the curtain of branches, only to find Rhett and Cade sitting in two red chairs staring at us.

The similarities in their body language are impossible to miss. But where Rhett is all smiles, Cade is all scowls.

All thick arms and broad chest and furrowed brow. Dirty boots. Muscular thighs.

Cowboy porn with a frown.

"Dad!" Luke calls, darting toward the deck. "Did you see me? Did you see Willa? She climbed *so* high. I wanna learn to climb that high. Uncle Rhett, how high can you climb?"

"Can we not ask the daredevil in this family that question?" Cade mutters, but he doesn't look at his son. No, his eyes latch onto me.

Rhett pushes up to his feet beside me. "I don't know, pal. Why don't we go see?"

Luke bounces in place. "Really?"

"Absolutely, little man." Rhett sets down his can of beer and pads across the deck barefoot while Luke turns and races back to the tree. "Let's go! Gotta let the panty bandit here chat with Willa."

"Jesus Christ. They already told you about that?" Cade grumbles as a laugh rumbles in Rhett's chest.

Cade's eyes snap to mine, and I bite down on my

bottom lip to keep from smiling as I continue to walk toward him. Then his gaze drops, and it's like he can't peel his eyes away from my mouth.

I push my teeth down until it almost hurts and drop his intense stare.

Within a few more steps, I'm folding myself down into the seat beside Cade. "I'm not sold on you, really," I start, even though I'm almost positive this man doesn't give a flying fuck what I think of him, "but your kid is something else."

I peek out the corner of my eye and can't help the twitch of my lips as I take in his deep frown.

"Thanks," he eventually grumbles, clearly irritated by me, but not enough to be rude after I pay him a compliment. It doesn't take a rocket scientist to tell that Cade Eaton's favorite thing in the world is his son.

My immediate connection with Luke seems to give me brownie points by proxy or something.

I dip my chin, still watching Rhett and Luke across the yard. I don't want to let my eyes linger too long on Cade Eaton. He's so bitchy looking that I might laugh, or I might stare longer than is appropriate. Because you'd have to be dead to not enjoy staring at him.

He's got an intimidating vibe about him. Like a hot, mean teacher.

"I'm out of work for the summer," I say casually, noting the way the veins in his hand ripple when he tightens his grip on the beer can. "My show horse is rehabbing from an injury and needs a few months off.

My best friend in the world fell in love with a cocky cowboy and moved away. My brother got famous almost overnight and is a full-blown workaholic. And my parents are retired and gallivanting around the globe."

I chance a look up at the dark, foreboding man beside me. Even sitting, he seems tall. One dark brow arches at me while his facial expression remains impassive.

A quiet beat turns into an awkward silence. And I hate awkward silence.

I flip a hand over as though I'm showing him something. "So I'm free."

He just glares at me.

"If you need a nanny. I could help."

He continues to glare, and I can't help but roll my eyes. "Good God. Does it hurt if you smile? Or say something polite? What happened to the *ma'am* guy from the coffee shop?"

"You'll keep him safe?" His voice is all gravel, his eyes like lasers tracing my features. And if he weren't such a grumpy asshole, this whole overprotective dad vibe would totally do it for me.

I nod. "Absolutely."

His gaze, full of questions and devoid of warmth, roams over my face, searching for something. "Will you teach him how to knit?"

My nose wrinkles. "Is that . . . is that like a requirement? Can I outsource it? I'm uh . . . not really big on knitting."

I swear I see a cheek twitch.

"What will you do with him?"

I blow a raspberry and flop back in the chair. "I mean, the options are endless. I'm never bored. Does he ride yet? I could give him riding lessons. I could show him my guitar. Does he like music? I love music. Play-dates with some other kids? Cooking? Ooh! I love to bake. How about garden? I bet you could grow some killer veggies out here."

All I get is a small bob of his head.

"You would send me frequent text updates. I leave early in the morning but like to be home early enough to spend time with him in the evenings. I will do my best to give you weekends off. I know you're young and prob-ably want to maintain some sort of social life."

I shrug and chuckle. I started bartending at eighteen. Seven years later, my desire to go out and party is pretty much shot.

I'll take a boozy brunch with my bestie and a dirty book in bed by eight for a thousand, Alex.

"Not especially."

Cade gazes out over the back yard, laughter bubbling from under the big willow tree. "Okay."

I sit up straight. "Okay?"

He nods once, decisively.

"Is that okay like, *Willa will you please come help me this summer because I would appreciate it so much?*"

He rolls his eyes like I exasperate him. And I'm pretty sure I do. I might even be trying a little bit. I like the way the muscle in his jaw pops, the way his Adam's apple bobs beneath tawny, tanned skin.

I even like the little shimmer of silver strands dusted throughout his dark hair.

Older guys. They've always done it for me.

Cade glances my way now, all raspy, rugged voice and resting bitch face. "I would appreciate your help this summer, Willa. But—"

I hold up a hand. "No buts. That was very polite. Excellent work. I'll be back tomorrow and can start then. The way I understand it, you need someone right away, yes?" I push to stand, knowing I shouldn't overstay my welcome or let him get too many demands in.

I can already tell he's *that* type of man. Exacting. Specific. Knows what he wants and expects you to deliver.

"Yes," he bites out, eyes perusing my body critically.

I give him a cheery thumbs up, not sure what to make of him. Not sure it matters since I'll spend most of my time with his son anyway. "See you tomorrow, then. I'll get your number from Summer and let you know where I'm at." I turn to leave, mentally running through all the things I need to do to get ready. For some people, uprooting their life at the drop of a hat would be stressful. They'd need lists and plans.

But not me. I've always flown by the seat of my pants. No idea where I'm going, just kind of . . . along for the ride. Life is more exciting this way anyhow. Jobs, men, material shit, none of it seems permanent for me yet.

My dad says I'm unsettled. My mom says I just haven't found a place I want to settle down yet. And I think she's right. Plus, the pressure of succeeding the way everyone else in my family has is downright crippling.

Undecided seems easier than failing.

Right when I get to the back door I hear, "Willa." Cade says my name like it's a demand. "You need to wear proper undergarments while you're at work. You can't be dropping them out of your purse around a child."

I swear my feet grow roots and my jaw drops. *The fucking nerve.*

If I didn't actually kind of want this gig, I'd march over there and lay into him for being an overstepping, presumptuous prick.

Undergarments. What year even is this? And why would they traumatize a kid?

He might technically be my employer for the next couple months, but I'm the one doing him a favor. I don't need the income; I just need a purpose. So I opt to do what will piss him off even him even more.

I rise above.

Well, sort of.

I plaster on the sweetest smile I can muster and turn to look back over my shoulder. "I'll be ready for your inspection tomorrow, boss."

Then I wink and saunter away, feeling the weight of his gaze on my body and knowing he's probably wondering if I'm wearing any *undergarments* right now.

5

Cade

Summer: She's going to be great. You're going to love her.

Cade: No. I'm not. I'm going to tolerate her.

Summer: Po-tay-to, po-tah-to! Just be nice.

Cade: I am nice.

Summer: No. You're kind of an asshole.

Cade: With family like you telling me things like this, I just can't imagine why.

Summer: Don't worry though. It's part of your charm.

Cade: I'm a charming asshole?

Summer: Exactly!

I wish I could pretend I'm not standing on the front porch waiting for her. But I am.

She grates on my nerves, sure. But my kid seems to like her and I'm still a gentleman at my core.

I pull my cell phone out of my back pocket and check the time. My countdown is on. She seems like the type of person who would be late. Scattered. Disorganized.

Or maybe I just want her to be so I can be justified in not liking her. If she's late the first time we make an agreement, I'll be able to show everyone that I was right. That she isn't responsible enough to take care of Luke.

Truthfully, I don't know who is. I don't trust easily. Especially not women.

She has six minutes.

I smile to myself, prop a hip against the banister, feeling like there's a good chance I'll be right.

And it's at that moment the crunching of gravel draws my gaze up.

It's at that moment I'm proven wrong.

Because Willa's red Jeep is rolling down my driveway five minutes early.

She pulls right up beside my black truck and hops out. I stare at her feet, starting at her Converse sneakers, letting my eyes trail up long, slender legs to simple denim cutoffs topped with an oversized, distressed Led Zeppelin shirt. There's a hole in it near her stomach, and I can see a little peek of milky skin through it.

Big Ray-Ban aviators sit on her nose, and her coppery hair is wild and wavy around her shoulders. It frames her delicate face like dancing flames. A wisp of it blows across her lips.

The lips that are all glossy and tipped up in a smirk.

"You're early," I growl, because I don't know what else to say. I can't peel my eyes off of her, even though I want to. Even though she's not at all my type at this point in my life.

She has city girl written all over her. She has wild child written all over her. She's not some sweet, small-town girl.

She's the girl who told me she'd be ready for me to inspect her undergarments and didn't think twice about it.

She has temptation written all over her.

But she doesn't act like it, instead she shrugs and pulls her sunglasses off her face, pinning me with her emerald eyes. The kind of eyes that stop you in your tracks.

If nothing else, Willa Grant is a stunner.

Too young for me. Too unpredictable for me.

But a stunner all the same.

"I was excited to get out here."

I blink at her because, well, what am I supposed to say to that? I'm here counting all the ways in which she's a problem for me, and she's just excited to be here and take care of my child.

Maybe I am the asshole everyone tells me I am.

"Willa!" Luke comes tearing out of the house like a bat out of hell, socked feet straight down the dirt path and onto the gravel driveway. He knows better but hasn't stopped talking about Willa since she left yesterday. Poor kid is so starved for female attention that all someone needs to do is climb a tree with him and he has them up on a pedestal.

He comes to a screeching to a halt in front of her. "I'm so glad you're here."

Willa laughs, all pretty and sexy, with a little rasp—like she smokes or something. And I'm wondering if she does. I didn't ask her if she smokes.

She crouches in front of him and ruffles his soft hair. "I'm so glad to be here. We're going to have the best summer."

"What are we going to do?" His eyes go all sparkly, excitement pouring off him.

"Everything," she replies, waving a hand in a wide arc. "All the things."

My brows furrow from their own volition. I want Luke to have fun, but not *too* much fun.

She reads my expression because her eyes twinkle with amusement. "Cliff diving. Bull riding. I'll even teach you how to shotgun a beer."

I shake my head at her as my lips flatten, already seeing my peaceful summer swirling down the drain.

She's going to drive me up the fucking wall.

Luke's nose wrinkles. "Beer is gross."

She just laughs again. "Smart answer, kid. I'm just

joking. But I have lots of fun ideas. Help me get my suitcase inside?"

"Of course!" my son's sugary voice exclaims as he slides his hand into hers without hesitation.

I groan and stride down the stairs, covering the ground quickly to reach the back of her Jeep at the same time they do. Holding a hand up to stop them, I grumble, "I've got this."

"Very chivalrous. Thank you, Mr. Eaton."

I bite down on the inside of my cheek. *Mr. Eaton.* That makes me feel like an old perv.

Or like my dad. Which is possibly the same thing.

But I don't correct her, because the old perv part of me likes it. Instead, I open the back hatch and pull out her massive suitcase.

"I want to show you my room!" Luke says, like an excited squirrel with a nut that can't figure out where to put it.

It's honestly kind of endearing.

I heave the suitcase out just in time to watch them walk hand in hand into my house, and for some reason, I stop and watch. Unable to look away. Lots of people have walked through that front door.

But somehow this feels different.

~

"In bed by eight."

Willa nods, face perfectly serious even though I'm

pretty sure there's a part of her that's mocking me. "Okay."

We're sitting across from each other at the white oval table in my living room, facing off now that Luke is asleep for the night. Willa has crossed her forearms over each other, and I'm still trying to steal glimpses of her skin through the hole in her T-shirt.

"No sugar after dinner."

She rears back, eyes widening. "Not even dessert?" She sounds like I've just told her I kick puppies or something.

"Not on weeknights."

"You rule with an iron fist, Daddy Eaton."

I groan, cheeks pinching up in distaste. "That's what we call my dad."

A silent puff of air slips from her lips, the bottom one more full than the top. "Daddy Cade it is."

I'm not sure what I did to deserve this torture, but it must be something terrible. I like to think I've lived a straight and narrow sort of life, yet I've been handed heartache after heartache, challenge after challenge. It seems like the universe could have granted some sort of reprieve.

But it granted me Willa fucking Grant.

"No."

She smirks and tilts her head in challenge.

"You'll send me text message updates throughout the day so that I don't worry. Keep me apprised of your activities."

"Is this something his teachers do for you while he's at school?"

I lean back, scanning her up and down. I feel the sneer touch my lips before I can stop it. "No. But I trust them. I *like* them."

Willa blinks slowly, staring at me almost blankly. The silence stretches as her stare shifts into what I'm sure is more of a glare.

Maybe it was a dick thing to say, but I'm not known for giving people the warm and fuzzies. Every time I've done that, I've walked away a little less whole than I started.

Never again.

I've got nothing left to give if Luke wants a dad who can be happy and present.

"I know you didn't just say that to me."

I lift one shoulder carelessly. "Sure did."

The smile she gives me is flat, her eyes dull—all traces of playfulness evaporated. "Well, in that case, I'll be going."

She scoots her chair away efficiently, pushes to stand, spins on a heel and leaves me sitting at my table, staring at her perfect ass.

"Willa."

She deposits her glass of water in the sink but ignores me.

"Willa."

She ignores me and turns to head down the hall toward

the guest bedroom where Luke so happily helped her get settled a couple of hours earlier. I could hear him chattering away at her. Asking her about her horse. About her guitar. About what her favorite type of snake was. Like that's a normal question you ask when getting to know someone.

If I didn't think it would wake Luke up and upset him, I'd raise my voice right now. But I'm stuck whisper-shouting "Willa" and she's not fucking listening.

With a growl, I stand and stride after her. Past Luke's room and right to the door of her bedroom that veers off the long hallway before it would lead to my master bedroom at the very end.

"Willa." I catch the door just before she can quietly close it. Obviously, she's trying not to wake my son as well, something I appreciate, because he doesn't need to be a part of this conversation.

I stand on the hardwood floor of the hallway, and she stands on the carpet in the bedroom. A brass divider shines on the ground between us like a line in the sand. Me versus her.

"What are you doing?" I ask.

"Leaving," she deadpans.

"Why?"

Her eyes roll as she turns away from me and starts setting things back into her barely unpacked suitcase. "Because I'm not spending my summer living with a woman hater who doesn't trust me and will be an over-the-top control freak the entire time I'm here."

I lurch back a little like she's slapped me. "I'm not a woman hater."

She bends over to grab a pair of pink, fluffy slippers. The kind that would melt into plastic in the heat of a fire. I try not to fixate on the way her shorts creep up the smooth skin on her thighs. "You should try harder not to look at me like you hate me, then."

It's not the first time people have told me this. But it's the first time I've faced the reality of how it might make them feel. It's not intentional. I'm pretty sure it's just my default facial expression now. My smiling muscles have lost all their tone.

"I don't hate you."

She rises, a wry laugh twisting her features as her copper waves fly around her neck. "Could have fooled me."

"I'm sorry."

Her chin juts out, and she holds up a hand to her ear. "Pardon? I think I misheard that."

"I'm. Sorry." I bite out. "I'm having a hard time letting him go."

I watch her shoulders fall as she hisses out a sigh. "That's fair. But there's no amount of money in the world you could pay me to stay here and be your punching bag all summer."

I fucking love the pair on this girl. If I weren't so irritated by how attracted I am to her, I'd be cheering her on.

I glance over my shoulder toward Luke's room, where my entire world is sleeping. The little boy who is excited at the prospect of spending the next couple of months with the firecracker in front of me.

"Stay," I mutter, holding a hand up to stop her and staring down at that line on the floor. The one stopping me from storming in there and dragging her back out to the table and forcing her to listen to me.

She stops shoving stuff into her bag and turns to face me, crosses her arms beneath her generous breasts and cocks a hip. If attitude were a person, she'd be it.

"Beg."

"Pardon me?"

"You heard me." Her lips don't even twitch. She's not joking at all. "Beg."

My cheeks heat against my will. My heart thunders in my chest. She's got me so on my heels it's not even funny. I can't allow it to last. But can I suck it up for the sake of making her turn her ass around?

Maybe.

"Please stay."

She doesn't react other than to arch an eyebrow.

"Don't leave."

Her lips roll together in the most distracting way.

I sigh, propping my hands on my hips and staring up at the stippled ceiling above me.

"Luke is everything to me, and I want him to have a fun summer. Proper fun. Sometimes he's stuck out on this ranch with a bunch of adults, and I worry he doesn't get enough attention from me because I work such long hours. And I need *help* because it's all just way too much. I'm fucking exhausted." My chin drops, and I look her in the eye. "I really need your help. Please stay."

The column of her throat shifts, and her eyes take on a slightly glassy quality. With a few soft steps, she comes to stand right in front of me. She smells like citrus and vanilla. Like some fancy pastry at the coffee shop in town. I can't help but lean in just a little bit.

She draws close. It almost feels too close in the dimly lit room. Too intimate in the quiet house. It feels like the kind of moment where you could make a mistake and no one would ever know.

And maybe I already made a mistake tonight, or maybe I'm about to make one. Usually I'm so sure of myself. But in this instance, I'm struggling to tell right from wrong.

"Fine." She sticks her hand out to me, and I instantly let my palm meet hers. I can feel the dainty bone in her wrist against the pads of my calloused fingers. "I will send you texts. I will keep him *mostly* sugar free. But if you act like a dick, I'm going to call you out on it."

"I have no doubt you will, Red."

We're still shaking hands. It's a handshake that has lasted longer than is proper. It's a threat or a promise— I'm just not sure which.

6

Willa

Willa: I just got up.

Cade: Okay?

Willa: I'm making coffee.

Cade: Alright.

Willa: I'm getting dressed for the day. Panties? CHECK.

Cade: Too much information.

Willa: Luke is now awake.

Cade: Oh good.

Willa: He peed.

Cade: The bed?

Willa: No. In the toilet. Sounded like a big one. Like when Austin Powers comes out of being frozen or whatever.

Cade: Why are you telling me this?

Willa: Just keeping you apprised of *everything we do!!!*

Cade: I already regret telling you that.

Willa: Oh, I'm just getting started.

Cade: Willa.

Willa: Remember that time you BEGGED me to stay?

"Let's just put some back in the bag!" Luke says, standing on a chair beside me at the kitchen counter as we stare into the bowl of pancake mix.

The pancake mix that is now more chocolate chips than batter. I'm no mathematician, but I'm pretty sure this ratio is off. I forgot that children's motor skills aren't super refined and handing Luke a bag of chocolate chips to put in might not have been the most strategic plan I've come up with in my life.

"Dude. We can't put them back in."

He shrugs, not looking sad about it. "I guess we'll just have to eat them."

I try not to laugh. If I didn't know any better, I'd think he did it on purpose. "Guess so."

We move his chair over to the stove, and I read him the riot act about hot elements, telling him that his dad will bury me in a hay field somewhere if I let him get burned.

He giggles and tells me I'm hilarious.

I've never felt cooler than I do hanging out with a five-year-old.

Especially when he sits across from me at the table, pats his belly with sticky chocolate fingers and exclaims, "You might be better at cooking than my dad!"

I point my fork at him. "I cannot wait to tell him that."

His little blue eyes go comically wide. "You can't tell him that. He'll be sad."

"Don't stress, little man," I reply, trying not to melt over how sweet it is that he's so worried about his dad. "Your dad will be able to handle the loss."

He sighs deeply and gazes at me expectantly. "What now?"

"Anything you want." I grab my plate as he picks up his and hands it to me.

"Anything?"

I peer down at him, one brow shifting up. "*Almost* anything."

"One of the kids at school said that he and his dad drove really fast down the back roads and threw heads of lettuce out the window and watched them explode on the road."

I stare at the little boy, all earnest and genuine. It's like he doesn't even realize what majorly hillbilly shit he just asked me to do.

Goddamn, small towns are weird.

"It's day one. Are you trying to get me fired?"

"You can't get fired. We like you too much!"

"Who is we?" I ask, loading the dishwasher. And I freeze momentarily when his response is, "My dad and me."

I will not burst his bubble by telling him that his dad does not, in fact, like me. He just needs my help and is stuck between a rock and a hard place.

A hard place where I'm literally his last and only option.

I shrug. "Okay sure, why not?"

Hillbilly shit it is.

～

I take the top off my Jeep, and we cruise to the grocery store blasting some of my favorite '80s hits. Luke cackles maniacally from his seat in the back when I do my best Billy Idol imitation.

I rolled my eyes when I saw the booster seat already installed in the back seat. I told Cade I could handle it, but he went into my vehicle while I was sleeping and did it anyway.

Control freak.

In town I easily find the grocery store. I took a bit of a detour on my way out to the ranch and gave myself a pep talk. I considered turning my ass around and heading back to the city where I could stick to what's comfortable, but I've never been one to say no to new experiences. So I pulled myself up by the bootstraps and got a lay of the land so I wouldn't be totally useless without someone showing me around.

"How many are we getting?" I ask Luke, who is strutting through the grocery store like a tiny king. Cowboy heir to the deer antler throne. Or something equally rustic.

"Ten," he replies decisively.

"Ten? That's a lot."

"It's just the right amount."

I stare at the section of iceberg lettuce before us. If we take ten, we're clearing out more than half of what's here. "Five."

His head shoots in my direction so quickly, little brows furrowing. He instantly looks like his dad. "Seven."

I press my lips together so hard it almost hurts. This kid is too smart. "Five, final offer."

A little spot on his jaw pops, and I am dying. He is a miniature Cade. Take away eye color and the resemblance is uncanny. Hilarious. "Fine."

"You're going to be bored after three," I supply, while reaching for the first head of lettuce.

"I am not!"

I turn and quirk a brow at him. "Luke. I may be new here, but I'm going to tell you what I told your dad. Mind your tone. You and I aren't going to talk to each other like that. Or I'll put you back to bed for a nap."

His baby blues widen. "Naps are for babies."

"Agreed. But if you act like one, I might get confused."

He sighs heavily and offers me a brief nod before reaching for another head. "I'm sorry."

"Thank you for apologizing. That was very not-baby-like."

A smile touches his lips and I mirror the expression. I feel like the two of us just came to some sort of under-standing.

When we turn to leave, I'm met with a far less friendly glare.

"Who are *you*?" a woman asks, hand propped on her hip with a grocery basket in the opposite hand. The way she draws out *you* reminds me of the caterpillar in *Alice in Wonderland* puffing out smoke O's. But all she's blowing at me is bad breath.

Not a fan of the way she's glaring at me either. Up and down with a little sneer on her face, like I'm yester-day's roadkill.

Regardless, I smile sweetly—a little too sweetly—and say, "I'm Willa."

The woman sniffs, the tip of her nose wiggling. I'm having a hard time placing how old she might be. The mini skirt and rhinestone sneakers make me think young, but the heavy makeup flaking in the creases on her fore-head makes me think older. It's a fascinating dichotomy.

"What are you doing out with Cade's boy?" She bends down a bit to address Luke. "You okay, honey? Do you need my help?"

An earnest and confused look is what Luke gives her back, followed by, "Yeah?"

He rears back a little, and I think it might have to do with her breath. To be fair, I'd like to get as far away as possible too.

"You sure, baby? Is this woman taking you somewhere you don't want to go?"

I roll my eyes. "If I were kidnapping a child, I wouldn't stop at a grocery store to buy five heads of lettuce first. I'm his nanny."

Her eyes narrow, but she turns them back on me. "I applied for that job." She sniffs again as she straightens.

"Yeah, and my daddy said he'd rather roll around in the manure pile than hire you."

My eyes nearly pop out of my head right as my hand slaps over my mouth to contain my amusement. This is a moment where I need to behave more grown-up than I'm feeling inside.

The woman blinks rapidly, heat rising on her neck. I honestly feel bad for her. I mean, we can't be offended by the things a five-year-old says . . . but we *can* be offended by the things men who are pushing forty say.

"I'm so sorry." I scoop Luke's hand into my own and give her an apologetic look. "I, uh, I hope you have a lovely day." Smiling brightly, I drag Luke toward the till, feeling so grateful that I'm off to a good start in this small town.

Dropping my panties and insulting the locals. And it's only day two.

I keep that smile plastered on my face throughout the checkout. It feels like people are giving us weird looks. I swear I can feel their eyes on me. Their judgment. Maybe it's in my head. Maybe it's not real at all.

All I know is that I can't get out of there fast enough. I'm not used to living somewhere that everyone recognizes you. I'm sure it's why my parents travel so much. To get away from the people who stop them and ask for autographs all the time. To just *be*.

"Okay, get in, little man." I open the back door of my jeep and toss the bags of lettuce in the front.

"Did I do something wrong?" he asks, climbing into his seat.

I sigh, watching his little hands pull the strap down over his shoulder and then struggle with the buckle. I reach across him and lend a hand, pulling away when I hear the telltale click. "Yes and no. Sometimes there are things we don't say out loud."

No point in beating around the bush.

I round the vehicle and hear his confused, "What do you mean?" through the open top.

"What I mean," I start, getting into the vehicle and buckling myself in, "is that there are things we think in our heads or say to other people who we know and trust that we don't share publicly. So like when you run into people like we just did, we might think about it, but don't say it. It's a bubble thought."

"What's a bubble thought?"

I feel like he's missing my point here.

"Ever read a comic? Or see one in the newspaper? Your dad seems like the type of person who reads the newspaper."

"Only on the weekends," Luke supplies as I back out.

Figures.

"Okay, so comic book characters sometimes think things that they don't say out loud. And that's drawn as those little bubbles coming out of their head. So sometimes—bubble thoughts. That way, you don't hurt anyone's feelings when you say it out loud. Got it?"

"When you called my dad a woman hater, was that a bubble thought?"

Shiiiiitttttt.

Called out by a five-year-old.

I'm teaching a kid about bubble thoughts when I haven't mastered the concept myself.

I swallow and peer back at him in the rearview mirror. "Yeah. It was a bubble thought. Sometimes they slip out on the best of us."

"What do you do when that happens?"

I groan and stare hard at the road in front of me as we cruise down the main street toward the empty fields that head back to Wishing Well Ranch.

"You apologize," I say, feeling like a heaping pile of trash for saying what I said. Made even worse by the knowledge that his son heard me.

"My dad will accept your apology. He likes you."

"How do you know he likes me?" He's mentioned this twice now, and honestly, I'm downright confused.

"Because he hasn't said a thing about rolling around in the manure pile."

I snort. Because that's the bar. If Cade Eaton "likes" you, you'll know because he won't mention his preference for rolling around in horse shit.

Within minutes we're on a back country road and our serious conversation turns to squeals of joy as the wise-beyond-his-years kid in the back seat tosses heads of fucking lettuce out the window and laughs hysterically.

I laugh too.

7

Cade

Willa: I'm sorry I called you a woman hater.

Cade: It's fine.

Willa: Do you know what the first thing I did this morning was?

Cade: Willa, I'm working. If everything is okay, we don't need to chat.

Willa: I put my panties on.

Willa: Are you ignoring me?

Willa: I figured you'd be proud. Day one and I'm knocking all the rules right out of the park.

Cade: If I pay you more, will you stop texting me about this?

Willa: Probably not. I don't need the money. I'm just easily bored, and poking the bear is fun.

"How was your first day?" I ask as Willa cuts into one of the chicken breasts I whipped up for us the minute I got in the door.

It was a strange transition. It's like she didn't realize she was off the clock as soon as I walked in the house. She offered to cook dinner, and I shot her a death glare. I love cooking dinner; it's how I unwind at the end of the day. It's when I get to spend time with Luke.

I think I expected the glare to send her scurrying to her room, but all she did was roll her eyes at me.

Offering to help with dinner isn't a crime, and I need to get over this idea that I'll just be able to snap my fingers and have her disappear when I walk in the door.

It's an unfamiliar feeling walking into a house in full swing. One where I can hear my son's giggles and Willa's soft, raspy tones.

"We had a great day, didn't we, Luke?" She grins over at him, and he grins back.

He's smitten.

When I got home, they were playing dinosaurs outside. I can honestly say I've never heard a woman make the noises that Willa was making. Some combination of a goose honking and a donkey braying, intermingled with that light, charm-like laughter.

She was stomping around with her hands folded up in front of her like those tiny T. rex arms.

She looked insane and carefree.

And fucking beautiful.

"Other than playing *Dinosaur Ranch*, what did the two of you get up to?"

"Nothing," Luke says altogether too quickly, and I see a flash of shiny copper hair as Willa's head flips in his direction. One perfectly manicured eyebrow arching at him.

Her bullshit detection is well-honed. I suppose that comes with working with children.

Mine is just from wading through bullshit every damn day. Those goddamn cowboys in the bunkhouse. My brothers. Town drama. My ex.

The only person who doesn't exhaust me is my little sister Violet. But that could be just because she moved away to the coast.

"We didn't do *nothing*, Luke." Willa spears a green bean, and I try not to get distracted by the way she slides it into her mouth.

"We . . ." My son flips his gaze between us. Guilty as all get-out. "Made pancakes! With chocolate chips! Lots and lots of chocolate chips."

Willa winces as she glances back down at her plate. When she peeks up and catches me staring at her, she says, "What? You said no sugar after dinner."

Shaking my head, I turn my attention back on Luke. "What else?"

"Nothing—" he starts, right as Willa says, "We bought heads of lettuce and then threw them out the window of my Jeep."

My lips roll together as I cast a quick glance in her

direction, seeing that she looks entertained and fucking clueless.

"Luke." He looks terrified. It's so hard to give my kid shit when he's this cute. But I don't get the privilege of playing good cop, bad cop with another parent. I get stuck doing all the dirty work. Doling out all the scolding. Some days I worry about how that makes me seem to him, but someone's gotta keep him on the straight and narrow.

Someone's gotta keep him safe.

"Sorry!" he exclaims, shrinking down in his seat while Willa's head swivels between us.

"Why are we sorry?"

I sigh deeply, shaking my head and sawing into my chicken breast with altogether too much force. "Luke has already asked to throw lettuce heads out the window and I told him no."

Luke can't even hold my eyes, and Willa's jaw drops as she stares back at him. "Dude! Seriously?"

His little lips clamp down as he curls in on himself. He's not a bad kid, he's just got a little bit of a rebellious streak. I guess he comes by it honestly as an Eaton boy.

"I thought Dad meant *he* just didn't want to do it." He turns pleading eyes on Willa. "You said you had fun doing it!"

"Luke—" I start but Willa cuts in.

"We both know you're smarter than that, Luke. You tricked me. On purpose. Not cool. I had fun, but knowing that you lied to me about it ruins all the fun."

She says it with nothing mean in her tone, but Luke looks devastated.

I lean back in my chair, crossing my arms over my chest, a little surprised by her taking this seriously rather than laughing me off. And a little relieved that I don't have to lay into him—again.

"I'm sorry." His eyes are instantly shrink-wrapped. He's a sensitive kid. It doesn't take much to put him back in place.

Willa nods, taking another green bean between her lips. "I know you are. You're a good person. But when you trick me, it breaks my trust. And your dad is trusting me to keep you safe, and we need to respect his rules, at least sometimes. Because now we've broken his trust too. Does that make sense to you?"

There's a part of me that wants to jump in and protect Luke. But the fact of the matter is, Willa is right. She's talking to him respectfully, like an adult, and I can't fault her.

I'm also just so relieved to have support, even if it comes in the form of Willa Grant. The redheaded mouthpiece who makes eating green beans look pornographic.

Because my dad just acts like Luke is hilarious all the time—which is fine. In fact, that's why I don't want him to be Luke's full-time caretaker. I don't want to ruin their friendship. I also don't want Luke to turn into Mowgli. A little wild boy raised by a pack of wild men all living together on a ranch.

It's fucking weird if I think about it too much.

"I'm sorry, Dad," Luke says carefully.

"I know you are, buddy."

"I just wanted to have some fun. It sounded so fun! It really was fun!"

"We're ranchers—farmers, Luke. It's a waste of good food."

"I know," he replies, defeated. And then he brightens as he glances up at me. "Next time you cover the Jansen's tractor in toilet paper, can I do it too?"

How the fuck does he know about that prank?

I see Willa's lips twitch, but she keeps her focus fixed on her plate. And then she goes for another green bean, and I have to look away.

This kid is going to be the death of me.

And so is his goddamn nanny.

~

Putting Luke to bed is my favorite part of the night. The cuddles. The stories. The things he tells me in the safety of his dark, peaceful room. He goes all soft and sweet, and we talk about things that don't come up throughout the day. It's why I'll never give up that part of his schedule.

My second favorite part of the night? A hot tub to soothe away the aches of the day. A quiet moment in my most frivolous purchase. Time alone to stare up at the stars and enjoy a little solitude.

Which is what I'm doing, head tipped back, arms draped over the outer edges, when I hear the back door click shut. My lids pop open, and I see Willa's silhouette through the rising steam around me.

"Shit, sorry. I'll leave," she whispers, turning to go, towel wrapped around her tall frame.

A smart man would say, *Yes, please leave. That's an excellent idea.*

I am not a smart man.

Instead, I blurt out, "It's fine." After all, I told her to make herself at home and use whatever she wanted. Truthfully, I can't blame a person for wanting to soak out here after chasing a five-year-old all day.

"You sure? I thought you were in bed." It's hard to hear her because, for once, she sounds a little uncertain. It's hard to see her too through the heated haze rising off the bubbling water. The shape of her is only highlighted by the glow from within the house, seeping through the sliding glass doors.

I should stop using the rising steam as an excuse to stare at her this hard. It's rude. She's in her twenties and I don't want to make her uncomfortable.

I tip my head back again and let my eyes flutter shut. "Wouldn't say it was fine if it wasn't, Red."

I hear shuffling and a quiet chuckle. "Yeah, you'd tell me to beat it."

Fuck.

She's not trying to be forward. But the words *beat it*

out of her mouth in that slightly hoarse voice has the air around me feeling altogether too thin.

Fabric rasps and gentle steps move toward the tub. I squeeze my eyes tighter, refusing to give in to the voice inside my head telling me to peek. To watch her climb over the edge. To see what type of bathing suit she's wearing and if her skin is as creamy as it looked from that glimpse I could see beyond her shirt yesterday.

I ignore the flipping sensation in my stomach.

The gentle sound of water sloshing tells me she's crawling in. Hot water laps at my chest as she settles, and suddenly sharing a hot tub with this woman who I barely know and can't stop eye-fucking feels entirely inappropriate.

Altogether too personal.

"Ah," she hums in pleasure.

I give in and glance across at her. Willa's positioning mirrors mine almost perfectly. Her slender arms drape across the frame, and her face is tipped up to the navy-blue sky. My gaze snags on the exposed column of her throat. The elegant length of it. The way it's positioned, open for the taking. The way it moves when she swallows.

"I'm sorry," she murmurs without moving her head to address me.

"For what?" I rasp back, a little confused as to what she's talking about. "I already told you it was fine for you to come in." Even though I'm not so sure that's true.

Tiny, flimsy straps lay across her collarbones and wrap around her shoulders. So easily ripped away.

"For doing the hillbilly lettuce thing." She shakes her head, and another melodic laugh bubbles out of her, like she just can't quite believe it. "I can't believe I got duped by a five-year-old."

My lips almost tug up at that. *Hillbilly lettuce.* "Well, you've worked with kids. I'm sure you know how to handle it." I'm mentally patting myself on the back for complimenting her—sort of—when she drops a bomb I didn't see coming.

"I haven't worked with kids *at all*."

I go deathly still before pulling my arms down into the water and sitting up tall. "Pardon me?"

She must hear the bite in my voice because her head tips in my direction and her eyes narrow as she sits up too, the water droplets trailing down over her full chest, right into the valley between her breasts. I grind my teeth at letting my eyes follow and snap them back up to hers when she replies with, "Watch your step, Eaton."

Swallowing, I stare at her from the opposite side of the tub, facing off. "Summer told me you had worked with children. She said you have, and I quote, 'lots of experience working with rowdy boys.'"

I watch Willa's expression transform from irritated to incredulous. "She didn't."

"She did."

"Did she elaborate?" Willa scrubs a wet hand over her face and slides it up to the top of her hair, before hitting the twisted knot of her fiery strands. "Did you ask any further questions? God. I should have given you a resume or something. This is so awkward, even by my standards. And it takes a lot to make me uncomfortable."

"So, you have how much experience working with kids?"

She barks out her surprise, strawberry lips parting in the most tempting way. "None. Zero. Zilch. I'm a bartender."

My fingers clench into fists beneath the water. "A bartender?"

"Yeah. I guess I do have lots of experience with rowdy boys, but not, ya know, children. Adult boys?"

"Summer is dead."

Her lips press together and wiggle under the strain of holding back. Laughter erupts from her in the most enthralling way. I shouldn't be charmed but she's so genuinely amused. It's hard to not be at least a little captivated.

Her head tilts back and the notes of her laugh drift into the surrounding night.

"It's not funny," I say, but I don't mean it, really. I mean . . . it's kind of funny. Just not *haha* funny.

"Looks like we both got tricked." Her chuckles slow, and the dim light illuminates the fullness of her breasts, shimmering with dampness.

Scrubbing at my face with my hands, I groan. "Summer was so sick of me being picky that she tricked me into hiring a bartender."

"Listen, if you want a resume or a criminal record check, I won't complain. But I still think I can do this. I still think Luke and I can have fun this summer. I grew up with great parents, so I must have learned something from them."

"Oh yeah?" I say from behind my hands, partly to hide my frustration and partly to give myself a break from how fucking stunning she looks sitting across from me in my hot tub. "What do your parents do? Do you come from a long line of bartenders?"

When she's silent for too long, I move my palms back into the water. Willa's lip is wedged between her teeth, and she's eyeing me critically.

"Cat got your tongue?"

"No. I'm just not convinced that the answer is going to make you feel any better."

I roll my eyes and huff out a harsh breath before tipping my head back again. There is definitely going to be a criminal record check. "Try me."

"Okay. My mom is a sex therapist."

She has to be kidding me.

"And my dad is the lead singer for Full Stop."

I sit up straight. "Come again?"

"Do you need to get your hearing checked? My dad had to get hearing aids pretty young after going on tour and playing too loud."

Mouthy.

"I heard you. I just . . ." I shake my head. "A sex therapist and a famous rock star raised you and this somehow qualifies you to take care of my kid?"

"Why not? They're exceptional parents. Don't get all weird now. People always get weird when they find out Ford Grant is my dad."

I glare at her.

"You're not some psycho superfan, are you? I had you pegged for a Garth Brooks kind of fella."

My jaw ticks.

"Songs about your truck breaking down. Your dog dying. Your woman leaving you for another man."

She laughs, oblivious to the fact that she just ripped open the stitches of a wound that has been painfully slow to heal. And not because I miss Talia, just because there are only so many hits a man's pride can take.

It only takes a couple of moments for a sober, awkward silence to stretch between us. I'm not doing a great job of keeping things friendly. It's not my forte.

I'm not playful, I'm responsible. That's all I've ever been allowed to be. That's what my family has needed me to be.

Green irises glowing, she looks at me in the most unnerving way. "How far down my throat is my foot right now?"

"You're pretty much digesting it at this point," I deadpan.

"Well, shit. It's going to be hard to chase your kid around all summer like this."

I huff out a gravelly breath, grateful that she isn't

pushing for more information about the hot fucking mess that is my personal life.

"Do you want me to leave? I would understand if you did."

"No," slips out a little too quickly, and I'm not even sure why. I should want her to leave, but I don't. Luke already likes her, she's already here, and we've already had it out. Plus, she's substantially less annoying than almost any other option available to me. "It's fine. Just get me an autograph to make it up."

She blinks at me. "Was that a joke?"

"No."

Her foot slides across the vinyl bottom of the hot tub and brushes against mine. "That was a joke."

"It wasn't." I bite the inside of my cheek to keep from grinning. Maybe I should be madder about this. Maybe I should send her home. But the thought of going back and undoing everything that's already been done feels exhausting.

There's something freeing in just . . . letting it go.

"It's fine. I won't tell anyone you made a joke. I'll get you an autograph *and* keep your reputation as The World's Grumpiest Rancher completely intact."

"Willa, you're making me regret hiring you."

She points at me. "Yes. Exactly. What joke? No jokes here."

She's carefree. She's funny. She's got a smart sense of humor that I like even though I refuse to show it. And she spends the next twenty minutes telling me stories about growing up as the child of a household name. She talks and I listen. And now and then, when one of us shifts in the small hot tub, our feet brush.

It's innocent contact. Or at least it should be. We don't look at each other when it happens. I'm afraid to look at her too closely if I'm being honest.

But it still sends sparks up my legs.

And when we get out, I do the gentlemanly thing and offer her a hand so that she doesn't slip.

But that's just before I do the distinctly ungentle-manly thing where I let my eyes ravage her tight body. I soak up every curve and try to burn it into my mind so that I never feel the urge to devour the sight of her like this again.

I imagine her wearing those simple black panties that are still in my kitchen drawer.

My dick swells fast and hard enough that I wrap a towel around myself and disappear inside without saying goodnight.

Because I'm just so fucking gentlemanly.

8

Willa

Willa: I can't believe you didn't tell Cade I'm a bartender and not some professional Mary Poppins.

Summer: He was being insane about the entire process. You're perfect for the job. Luke is gonna love you.

Willa: OBVIOUSLY. I'm very loveable. Unless your name is Cade Eaton. Then I'm the object of all your exaggerated scowling.

Summer: He has different scowls. Haven't you figured that out yet?

Willa: That's insane. I'm not paid enough to decipher a man's scowls. Here's the new deal. If your shitty version of matchmaker doesn't work out, you're the new nanny. End of story. And you're going to do it with a smile. They need help.

Summer: Adorable. You're already protective.

The screen door bangs shut loudly, which means Cade is home. Crabby Cade stomping in after a long day of doing god knows what with a bunch of cows and cowboys.

"Welcome home, Master Cade," I announce with a flourish as he walks into the kitchen, shooting me a scowl. An annoyed scowl?

"What are you doing? And why are you calling me that?" Cade's voice rumbles dangerously.

"Stirring the spaghetti sauce that the young Padawan requested, I am." Ask stupid questions, get stupid answers. He can clearly see that I'm moving a spoon around in a pot full of Bolognese sauce.

He glowers at me like I'm the least funny person he's ever met. "And I'm talking like this because it's hard to get out of character after playing Star Wars all afternoon."

"You're not supposed to cook dinner." His fingers rap against the marble countertop, but his eyes stay fixed on the pot. Lately it's like he totally avoids looking at me.

"The force is just too strong with me in culinary arts. Young Luke has announced that my cooking is superior to yours." I smirk at him, getting far too much enjoyment out of needling him, especially since I know he loves to cook and is damn good at it.

The manly man across from me just scoffs, finally lifting his eyes. "He did not."

"He did."

His arms cross petulantly. "I don't believe you."

I smile prettily. "Okay, Darth Cade."

At that moment, Luke blasts into the kitchen from washing up. "No! I want dad to be Jar Jar Binks!"

Cade's forehead wrinkles and he appears genuinely confused. "What the hell is a Jar Jar Binks?"

Luke and I dissolve into a fit of giggles. Cade ignores us and removes the spoon from my hand, dips it in the pot, before lifting it to his lips for a sample. His only reaction is a low grumble. Which is practically a five-star review coming from him.

~

"What is all that laundry doing on my bed?"

It seems like every day I do something helpful around the house, and Cade finds a way to complain about it, like I've gravely offended him.

I pop a chip into my mouth and don't bother looking at him from where I'm sprawled on the couch. I already know he's scowling. I practically see that expression on the back of my eyelids every night when I try to fall asleep.

"I did a couple of loads today and wasn't sure where it all went."

"You're not supposed to do my laundry."

"Well, you're not supposed to interrupt me watching Gossip Girl reruns. But here we are."

"I don't need you to do my laundry."

I sit up with a deep sigh. "Okay. We're really fixating on that? It was some towels and a few sweaters. Not your *tight boxers*. So let's just cool our jets, yeah? They were already in the basket, and I'm not lazy, so I tossed them in the washer. Not a big deal. No need to put me on death row over it."

He stares at me, but rather than scowling, he appears a little perplexed. "No one has ever done my laundry for me."

"Probably because it's not worth facing the electric chair over."

He just glares at me.

"Imagine if I dropped a red sock in with your white towels? Oof. *Brutal*. End of days."

More glaring.

I pop another chip into my mouth. "Is this where you try to melt me with the power of your mind because I had the gall to help you with a chore?"

"Anyone ever told you that you're rude?" is all he comes back with.

I grin at him before turning back to the TV and cranking the volume. "Says the guy who still hasn't given my panties back."

"Willa!" I hear Cade calling from inside the house. But Luke and I are hiding outside on the back porch, waiting to jump out and scare him. "Where are you guys?"

"Luke?" His footsteps march through the house with authority. It feels like I might be in trouble for something, but I always feel that way with Cade. "You hungry, pal?"

We don't move an inch.

"What the hell," he mutters, drawing nearer now. Probably in the kitchen.

Luke is behind me, and I peer down at him, his palm clamped across his mouth to hold back laughter. I raise a finger up to my lips, reminding him to keep his shit together and stay quiet.

The fridge door creaks open. A bottle cap hisses as it pops open. I can imagine Cade's throat working as he takes a deep pull of a what I assume is a beer. He's close now. He must be staring out the screen door.

Luke presses in against my hip, and I absently wonder what Cade is thinking.

"This fucking woman is going to be the death of me."

Okay. So that's what he's thinking. I take a strange sort of pride in his statement.

The door swings open, and he steps out onto the porch, which is right when Luke and I jump out from behind a planter.

"Boo!" I shout, as Luke yells, "Chipmunks!"

Cade flies back, and I glance down at Luke, wondering what the hell would inspire him to randomly scream *chipmunks*. But I don't think about that for long, because when I look back up Cade's stern face is the color of a tomato and he's wearing his beer down the front of his fresh T-shirt.

Oh yeah. We got him good.

All I offer is a lame attempt at a joke. "Wet T-shirt contest?"

And all I get back is a scowl.

~~~

"Willa, how has your first week been?" Cade's dad, Harvey, smiles at me from across the table. It's my first family dinner at the ranch, and I'm downright enamored. It's so . . . wholesome?

When I walked into the dining room, Cade pulled a chair out and stared at me until I figured out he meant me to sit there. After I did, he tucked me into the table and one of his calloused hands brushed casually—mistakenly—over my bare neck.

But it flustered me all the same. Sent gooseflesh out over my arms all the same. The simplest touch has taken up residence in my mind for no good reason.

I finish chewing and return Harvey's smile, but it's Cade's dark eyes I feel on me from beside his dad. The similarities between them are insane. It's like I can see how Cade will look in twenty some-odd years.

Which is to say, *good.*

"It's been great. Luke and I have had a lot of fun. Haven't we, Luke?" I tilt my head to gaze down at him.

He insisted on sitting beside me, even though he hasn't seen his dad since last night. We came up to the main house early and Cade met us here.

The little boy beams up at me. "Sure did."

Cade scowls. It's what he did when Luke moved across the table, away from him.

"The most fun!"

Harvey's kind eyes turn back toward his grandson. "What have you been doing?"

Luke peers around the table, grinning at everyone. He's the kind of kid who flourishes under attention rather than crumbles under it. And everyone is here. Both of Cade's brothers, Rhett and Beau. Summer, of course. Even the hockey player, Jasper Gervais, who everyone loses their mind over—apparently, he grew up here on the ranch.

I'm just snoopy enough to wish I knew more about his story. Where his parents are and how he got to where he is. The fact he hasn't said a damn word throughout dinner has me even more curious. He smiles at people from behind the brim of his team cap. Little smirks and winks. He seems nice enough. He seems like he requires more investigation.

Beau, on the other hand, has barely stopped talking. Except for now. When Luke talks, everyone listens.

"We threw lettuce out the window while driving really fast down the back road!" For a kid who seemed suitably chastised a few days ago, he sure is hamming it up now.

"Goddamn. That sounds like fun." Beau shakes his head and spears some lettuce, a look of nostalgia touching every feature.

My eyes snap to Cade's, who is scowling at his brother. I absently wonder which scowl that is. Irritated? Scolding?

Through the salad in his mouth, Beau adds, "I'm gonna do that with you when I get back from this deployment, Lukey. We'll do watermelons instead."

"Yes!" Luke shoots up in his seat, like he's forgotten the conversation we had earlier this week.

"You sure as shit are not." Cade pushes the salad around his plate even harder. Hard enough that the tines of his fork screech across his plate. This guy needs to work out some goddamn tension.

My mom would say he needs some good sex.

I'm not so sure she'd be wrong.

"Luke and I have had some good chats about food scarcity this week," I pipe up to defuse the conversation. "That not everyone is as fortunate as he is. We dug out a garden and today we planted our lettuce seeds, didn't we?"

He nods enthusiastically at me, and I'm relieved I wasn't a total buzzkill. Five isn't too young to hear some truths about the world, but I'm wondering if I overstepped.

When I peek over at Cade, though, his scowl is less irritated. Possibly an appreciative scowl?

I mean, fuck my life. How did I get to the point

where I'm analyzing the way a man scowls at me?

Beau chuckles. "Well, you know. Boys will be b—"

"No," I cut him off. Because that saying is straight trash, and years of bartending have given me plenty of time to see boys being boys. Which really is just boys being shitheads. "Boys will be gentlemen." I point my fork at the big army Ken doll sitting across from me.

It's then that I hear a huff of air in the otherwise dead silent dining room, and I almost drop my fork when I figure out it came from the least likely person.

Cade is still moving food around on his plate—like barbecue ribs require a fork or something—but the corner of his mouth slants upward. The angle of his face and the darkness of his beard make it hard to see, so I squint a tad, jutting my chin at him to get a closer look. I'm not sure I can call it a smile.

An amused scowl?

The hockey player clears his throat, not hiding his amusement at all. "Well, Harvey, what have you been up to this week?"

He chuckles and wipes a weathered hand across his mustache. "Thanks for asking, son . . ."

I find myself glancing between him and Cade, wondering how Cade might look with a mustache. A joke about free mustache rides pops into my head, and I blink rapidly to clear it.

I glance around the table to see if anyone noticed I was thinking about riding Cade's face. Thankfully, that would be impossible, and everyone has fixed their attention on the head of the family, who's running down what he's been up to this week while I've been thinking about how Cade's beard and tongue would . . .

Then I feel it. The scowl. My eyes shift, and Cade is staring right at me, bulging arms crossed over his impossibly broad chest. Biceps straining against his signature black T-shirt. And my cheeks heat for no good reason other than my body is a traitor and I'm probably ovulating.

I stare back at him across the table, refusing to look guilty. Trying to stretch my consciousness back to whatever the sweet patriarch of the family is talking about.

" . . . Today I got to tidying up around the property a bit. There were leaves everywhere, so I gave the yard a good blow job."

Cade's eyes widen. Comically wide. Playfully wide. And I can't help the hysterical little giggle that bubbles up out of me. I slap a hand over my mouth to cover it.

Rhett chokes on a piece of his food, and Summer slaps his back and coos at him like he's a baby choking on applesauce while trying to suppress her giggles.

"I'm sorry, Dad," Beau says with a playful glint in his eye. "You're gonna have to explain that one to us again."

Harvey shakes his head and rolls his eyes. "You not wearing ear protection at the shooting range? I said the yard was a mess. Next time you can make yourself useful and blow it yourself, Beau."

My god. Is Harvey Eaton a sheltered simpleton or a comedic genius? He's got the entire table stunned speechless, struggling to hold in their laughter, and he's just munching away at the food on his plate, looking oblivious.

"Do you have a special technique he should know about before he gives it a go?" I don't have a clue how Jasper is keeping a straight face after delivering a line like that. Is this something they teach you in the NHL? Because I'd like to have that training.

"Excuse me for a moment," Cade bites out in a strained voice before pushing away from the table and heading toward the front of the house. I can't make out his facial expression. Not even a little bit. Is he sick? Is he pissed that this conversation is going on in front of his kid? Am I fired for not instantly giving Luke earmuffs?

"Hey, Luke," I say, my voice strangled, "why don't you tell everyone about our guitar lessons this week? I'm going to go check on your dad."

I smile as politely as possible, refusing to glance at Summer. Because if I meet my best friend's eye, I'm going to get the giggles.

Uncontrollable giggles. Totally impolite.

I can see her from my periphery, craning her neck to catch my eye, but I just toss the cloth napkin on the table beside my plate before following the same track as Cade.

I walk through to the other side of the house, admittedly not really knowing where I'm going. Where Cade's house is bright and airy with a cottage-type vibe, the main house almost feels like some sort of hunting lodge—wide floorboards, dark wood beams beneath vaulted ceilings, brass hardware, and dark green walls. I peek down a hallway and see nothing, so I continue toward the front door, seeing that it's propped open.

There's a long, wide deck with raw log banisters that face out over the long driveway and a full copse of poplars.

Cade is standing there, Wranglers hugging his strong legs, the muscles in his back bunched beneath soft cotton. His close-cut black hair is slicked back neatly, and his trimmed beard gives the impression he made an effort tonight. I've grown accustomed to seeing him waltz in after a hard day's work looking all dirty and sweaty and, well, fucking hot, to be honest.

I stand for a moment and watch him, trying to decide which look I prefer.

His wide palms are propped on the railing and his chin is tucked into his chest.

As I approach, his scent sneaks up on me. Crushed pine needles and sunshine. I don't know how else to explain it. It's that warm earth that I associate with digging in the garden on a sunny day. There's nothing manufactured or store-bought about his scent—it's pure outdoor masculinity.

But it's the shaking of his shoulders that draws my gaze now.

He's crying or laughing, and to be honest, both seem equally unlikely from what I know of this man.

"Wanted to come see what a well-blown yard looks like, huh?" I ask.

"Willa—" He can barely get my name out. It's a breath. It's a wheeze.

I smile and lean against the post several feet away from him before turning my gaze on the yard. "It does look great out here. Your dad could suck the chrome off of a—" With one hand held up to stop me, his head drops lower and his shoulders shake harder. "I wonder if he's sore. He really put his back into it." I snort as I say it. Honestly, I'm barely holding it together. I am a child.

Cade gasps and stands up straight, turning his attention to me. There are tears in his eyes, and I'm sure he's smiling—he has to be—but he has a fist held up over his mouth.

He seems younger when he's laughing. Lighter somehow. It makes me laugh too, and before I know it, we're both standing there, regarding the clean, violated yard, having a chuckle together.

And for once, Cade Eaton isn't scowling at me.

"Man, my dad is such an asshole, making a joke like that. It's just to watch us all get uncomfortable too. And then Jasper has to go from saying shit-all to delivering the killing blow without even breaking a sweat."

I smile and marvel at the man beside me. I've seen him every day for a week and not once has he looked even close to this happy.

"Eaton. You grumpy motherfucker. You just laughed," I blurt.

"Yeah, Red. I did."

He turns to me and offers the most devastating smile.

One that makes my stomach flip and my lips pop open in shock.

It's like I just put glasses on for the first time and am seeing him in a completely different light.

And I can't look away.

9

Cade

I hold the door open and usher Willa back into the house. She flashes a look over her shoulder as she walks through the front hall. One that's all smug and satisfied. One that says she thinks she's in on some sort of secret.

And maybe she is. The secret is that even though I try to act like the tough, mature big brother and dad, I'm dying inside over blow job jokes.

I've just been spending all these years faking that I'm ultra-responsible, hoping that I can fake myself into believing it. Most days I do, but moments like tonight I wonder what I've lost in the process.

I wonder if I'm still applying what responsibility looked like to me as a child to the life of a full-grown man. Because that's what I was when I stepped up in the wake of our mother's death—a child.

Maybe that's why I allow myself to eye-fuck the hell

out of Willa Grant as we walk back to the dining room. Her round, apple ass, the confident sway of her hips, the spot where her waist nips in—the thought of holding her there.

The feeling of following her brings out something primal in me.

Like, under different circumstances, I'd chase her. I'd take her. And there wouldn't be any blowback because she wouldn't be Luke's nanny. And the fact that I'm this much older than her wouldn't matter because I wouldn't give a fuck.

"Wow, Harvey," Willa announces as we walk into the dining room. "It looks fabulous out there. You blew the hell outta that lawn."

I scrub a hand over my face as the table erupts into giggles. Harvey included. *Bunch of children.*

My dad is grinning so wide, his eyes twinkling at the gorgeous redhead currently pulling out her chair next to my son, who's peering around the room, genuinely confused by what we're all losing it over.

I shove away a spark of jealousy over the way my dad and Willa are smiling at each other. Because that is *insane*.

She was just so excited over me laughing. Over me smiling. She smiled back. It felt good. And now she's in here giving that megawatt grin to other people, who are grinning back at her. And I feel like I want all her smiles for myself.

How hard would it be to smile more, to laugh more, if it made her look this happy?

"We're going out." Beau points at me, using that military voice that hedges no debate. Or at least he thinks it does. "Dad's taking Luke for the night. I want some fun before I deploy again."

I frown. "No." This little fucker has never been able to tell me what to do, and I'm not about to let him start now.

"Yes." His thick brow arches at me.

I'm about to fight back, but Willa turning her strawberry lips up at me stops me in my tracks. "Come on. It will be good for you."

My brows knit together as I stare down at her.

The nanny.

The nanny. The nanny. The nanny.

The nanny shouldn't look this fucking good to me. The nanny shouldn't know or tell me what's good for me.

And I shouldn't listen.

But I'm an idiot, so I respond with, "Fine."

Luke cheers and runs over, flying into his grandfather's lap. Probably because he knows they'll eat food that rots their teeth and stay up too late watching movies that I'd never approve of.

The small smile on Willa's angelic face catches my eye, and without even thinking, I give her a small one back.

We walk into The Railspur, the best bar in town. It used to be the only bar in town before Chestnut Springs started growing with city folk moving out this way to live the country lifestyle or some cheesy shit like that.

And I'm pretty sure Honky Tonk Sundays are designed just for them. It's the night when they all play cowboy dress-up and line dance or two-step, and just generally pretend they aren't high-rolling city slickers.

If I weren't so annoyed by it, I'd find it funny.

It feels like everyone in our group is a local celebrity of some sort. Rhett the retired rodeo king, Beau the military hero, and Jasper the hockey sensation—even though he avoids attention like the plague.

I'm just the brother who runs the ranch, the one whose woman left him with a child and more responsibility that he reasonably knows what to do with.

It's the nudge of Willa's shoulder against mine that keeps me from diving into a huge well of self-pity. "This place is so cool."

I thought she'd take off with Summer. The two of them had a serious case of the giggles in the back of my truck on the way over here. I'm pretty sure I heard Summer say something about peeing a little, and that's when I tuned them out.

"Yeah, I guess." I survey the bar as we make our way

toward our favorite spot at the back. The one with big green leather couches and a roaring fireplace.

What do people call this? Cowboy chic? That term has always amused me. Cowboying has never seemed all that chic to me.

The place is warm, all dark woods and fireplaces, ornate chandeliers. It's changed a lot since the days when I'd come here more regularly. Now I only ever come when my brothers drag me out.

"Do you come often?" Willa asks.

"What?" My brain takes that question in a different, sex-starved direction.

Her lips roll together, not missing a goddamn beat. "*To this bar?* Do you come *here* often? God, I don't know if that's really any clearer. I mean come like c-o—"

I close my eyes and say a silent prayer for patience and a flaccid dick, holding up a hand. "I know what you mean and the answer is no."

When I open my eyes again, she's smirking. We come to stand in front of the couches. Everyone files in and she watches them carefully, eyes assessing where everyone sits. As always Jasper takes the back corner seat facing away from the rest of the room and Beau takes up position across from him—always facing the room.

Willa doesn't even glance at me when she murmurs, "You don't come often?"

"Not here," I bite out.

She peeks at me from behind a silky curtain of her copper locks. "Yeah, no. That would be rude."

95

I opt to glare back at her. Because my wish for a flaccid dick is not being granted with this line of banter. Or are we flirting? I don't even know what flirting looks like anymore. "Willa, sit down."

I point at the only spots left. A love seat facing the end of the low-slung table. She moves effortlessly, with an inherent grace. There's something kind of . . . magical about her. Her laugh, her voice, the fluidity of her movements. It's not sexual, it's just an appeal I can't quite put my finger on.

An appeal I'm now going to be stuck sitting beside all night. And living with all summer. I absently wonder if putting up with one of the other applicants who didn't catch my eye at all would have been preferable, even if it meant putting up with their overt advances for a couple of months.

Our server, Bailey, swings by once we're seated. The girl works her ass off here and at the hospital as a porter. It's like every ounce of focus and drive that could be shared by her family was all just packed into her. The Jansens own the farm next to us, and she's the youngest of them. The best of them. The only one without a criminal record, most likely.

"I'll have a Guinness," Willa says, surprising me by ordering a thick, dark beer. And maybe I'm a dick for expecting something else. I had her pegged as a prissy city girl who'd order some frilly *Sex and the City* drink.

"I'll have what she's having." I hike a thumb at Willa and give Bailey a terse smile. Bailey blushes and drops my gaze. I'm not sure how the hell she works here. She's young and painfully shy.

Willa elbows me, before leaning close and whispering in my ear. "She gets smiles. You should go for it. She's cute."

I glance at Bailey's retreating form and shake my head. "Nah. No way. Bailey's way too young. I just like her."

Willa's eye twitches, her lips flattening as she looks around the bar. She seems like she's all bravado and bluster, but I get the sense I just hurt her feelings. Not so much by what I said, but by what I didn't say.

I bump my elbow back at her. "I like you too, Red. I just feel bad for Bailey. Her family is shit but she's a sweet girl. She gets a bad rap around town."

She rolls her eyes while staring out across the room. "You don't like me. You tolerate me."

I mull that over. Is that how I come off to her? I guess she has no way of knowing it's a struggle for me to keep my eyes off her when she interacts with Luke, even harder to keep her image from popping up in my mind when I fist my cock in the shower. Both things I don't intend to tell her, so I opt for, "The way I see it, I like you a little more every day."

Because that much is true. The girl is growing on me, like a vine wrapping up around an old oak. And for once, I'm not sure I mind.

Willa's head turns slowly, with intent, and her eyes

scour my face. I feel like I'm being analyzed, decoded—it's fucking unnerving.

"You trying to put a spell on me, Red? Some sort of city-girl voodoo shit?"

"City girl voodoo shit?" She smiles, still staring at me hard. Amused. Glowing. She's goddamn breathtaking. The rest of the bar fades away, and with a little shake of my head, I give her a reluctant smile and drop her gaze.

She laughs and flops back against the couch, watching Bailey approach with a tray full of drinks. "Daddy Cade, you're a whole lot prettier when you smile."

I can't help but snort. "You're insane." Usually a woman's attention makes me squirm. It's too intense. There's too much pressure. But with Red, she toes the line of joking. Truthfully, I can't make heads or tails of her. If nothing else, she has my attention.

She grins up at me, gently tugging at her long, straight hair. Like that's an answer.

I'd like to tug on that hair too, is what I'm thinking when I feel a hand clamp down on my shoulder. "Cade, buddy, how are ya?"

The smile comes easily now. My high school friend, Lance Henderson, is towering over me, grinning like the fucking loon he is.

I stand, reaching out to shake his hand in a firm clap while slapping at his shoulder. It's our kind of equivalent of a hug. "I'm doin' alright. How about you? What brings you out this way?"

"Rodeo nearby. Thought I'd take a detour through the old stomping grounds."

"Yeah?"

"Heck yeah." He nods at the table. "Look at you all. The entire Eaton clan. What is this? Some sort of family reunion?"

"Nah, that's next month."

His eyes drop, and I catch him eyeing up Willa, who is pretending to pay attention to everyone else in the loud bar, but I can tell by the angle of her head that she's eavesdropping. Snoopy little thing.

When I glance back at Lance, it's almost impossible to miss the appreciative way he's looking at her.

And it fucking bugs me.

I take a step over, blocking Willa with my body. "This isn't the grocery store, Henderson. Whatchya looking for?"

His head tips back and he barks out a laugh. "That your girl, Eaton?"

I scowl back at him. "No. She's my nanny."

He arches a brow at me from beneath his tan cowboy hat. "*Your* nanny?"

I sigh like I'm exasperated with him, but no chance am I backing down on this. "You heard me, dickhead. How long you in town for?"

His eyes are twinkling, but he doesn't push the Willa thing any farther, and I drop my shoulders, tension easing out.

Pathetic.

"Just one night. Was actually hoping to get in touch with you. Couldn't find ya on social media."

"Why would I need social media?" I deadpan.

"I don't know. To stay in touch with friends like me?"

"Once every five or so years in person is perfect for me. Too much of a good thing and all that." I like Lance but me sharing photos with him and hearting his status updates—never.

"I need a partner. My guy is out with a broken collarbone. We're close to qualifying for the national finals."

"No."

"Why not? You're one of the best penners I've ever seen. It's a shame you never continued."

People don't get it. Traveling around rodeoing was never an option for me. No one ever asked me if that's what I'd *like* to do. Because I would have loved to do it. I am a good fucking cowboy. But duty called, and that duty was here at home. The ranch. Luke. Family.

I was never granted the privilege of doing whatever I wanted, and being reminded of it smarts.

"I rope and pen all the time. For work. Not show."

"Good, then you're not out of practice."

"Lance, it ain't gonna happen." I cross my arms over my chest, hearing the buzz of conversation behind me, but I can feel Willa shift closer toward the midline of the couch.

"Why not?"

"Because I've got the ranch. I've got a kid. I can't just

take off for days at a time. I can't hang at your place and practice. I have responsibilities."

"What about the nanny? We can wing it without practice, or I can trailer in." His eyes drop, and my chest puffs as I shift to block his gaze.

"She gets the weekends off."

"We can figure someth—"

"I don't mind working a couple of weekends." Willa's body presses beside mine as my head snaps in her direction.

"No," I grit out.

She shrugs. "Calm your tits, Eaton. I'm just offering."

Lance laughs and smiles at her, all cowboy charm. It's fucking annoying. It's even worse watching him shake Willa's hand. Her smiling back at him. They're both sunny and happy. They suit each other well and I hate that it bugs me.

"Lance Henderson."

"Willa Grant. Pleasure to meet you."

His smile transforms into a smirk I recognize well from watching him pick up buckle bunnies when we were younger. "Oh darling, the pleasure is all mine."

I like Lance. He's a good guy, and he's charming as all get out, but I don't like him charming my nanny.

Which is why I say something I never thought I'd hear myself say. "Willa and I were just about to dance. But it's been nice seeing you, Lance." I give him a tip of my chin and grab Willa by the elbow before dragging her out onto the dance floor.

"I think I missed the part where we were *just* about to dance?" she teases as I pull her into a two-step position, trying to just plant my hand at her waist rather than sliding it over her ribs the way I want to.

"It was an excuse to get away from that smiley motherfucker."

She casually drapes a hand over my shoulder as my fingers wrap around her dainty hand and we easily fall into step to the upbeat, twangy song. I make a point of staring over her shoulder rather than at her.

It's *hard*.

She's got some pretty pink dress on. It's simple, but it hugs her curves, skims her knees, and is altogether too low cut. The way she's paired it with a pair of white Chuck Taylors makes her look too fucking young.

Where Summer is all pencil skirts and high heels, Willa is bright colors and sneakers.

"So . . ." I peek at her and notice the way she's watching other people on the dance floor. People who are definitely watching us. Because grumpy Cade Eaton never dances. When I come here, I nurse a beer and glare at any woman who comes my way.

It's worked well for me so far. But Willa Grant is shaking my shit up.

"You come here often?" she asks.

"Willa." My teeth clench.

"If I make a blow job joke, will you laugh again?"

My teeth grind. "No."

"What's the best thing about a blow job?"

"Good lord, woman. Just stop." I turn my chin down at her and try to give her my most intimidating expression. Just hearing her say the words *blow job* is too much for a guy who hasn't gotten one in years.

But, as usual, Willa isn't the least bit deterred.

Her fingers pulse in mine, and she does that light, sparkly laugh that makes my dick twitch. "No, wait. You're going to love this one. It's so you."

She leans into my ear, and her breath fans across my neck as she huffs out a small snort before composing herself enough to finish the joke. I bite the inside of my cheek to contain whatever expression might pop up on my face. "The ten minutes of silence."

I have to look away across the room. I can feel her body shaking, laughing at her own joke.

No shame.

"I got you. I saw that. Are your cheeks bleeding, Eaton? Does it hurt to hold in your laughter like that? I hear it can give you erectile dysfunction."

"You kiss your mother with that mouth, Red?"

She blows a raspberry, highly amused. "Oh yeah. She'd love that joke."

"The joke's on you though. I wouldn't last ten minutes and just because you'd be quiet doesn't mean I would be."

We both go still, and I watch her eyes widen while I beat myself up internally for letting a snippet of my old self tumble out, woken up by the beautiful redhead in my arms.

"Who said anything about me and you, Cade?" She blinks, her thick lashes making her appear a lot more innocent than I'm thinking she is.

Young? Yes.

Shy? No.

It's a dangerous combination for a man like me.

The song changes, and before I can reply, some guy who works at the bank cuts in and asks if he can have the next dance.

I nod and step away graciously, even though it kills me. The thought of letting someone else dance with her makes me see red, but I also need to get the fuck away from wherever that conversation was heading.

10

Cade

Beau: Dude. You look like you're trying to kill someone with the power of your stare.

Beau: Do you have a special superpower I don't know about?

Cade: Why are you texting me from the same table?

Beau: Because you're too terrifying to talk to.

Cade: I hope our nation's enemies don't find out what a pussy you are.

Beau: That's rude. I think I'll go dance with the nanny. She seems nice.

Beau: Yikes. Is that face special for me? Wanna go outside and blow off some steam like when we were kids?

Cade: No. You act like a chucklehead, but you know how to kill people with your bare hands. I'm not dumb enough to fight you.

Cade: Stop grinning at me like that. It's weird.

I spend the next ten minutes hating myself for walking away. Approximately four songs fit into a ten-minute window, and watching Willa dance with four different men is four men too many.

Ten minutes too long.

She's all smiles and swagger. I watched her lips move almost the entire time. The bottom one is a little fuller than the top. If she wasn't smiling all the time, it would give her a pouty sort of look. But there is nothing pouty about Willa Grant.

She's a spark in the dark. Dancing flames against a midnight sky. She shines brighter than almost anyone in this entire place with her glossy hair, bright dress, and twinkling green eyes.

And she's the fucking nanny, which means I shouldn't be counting songs and minutes like some sort of possessive psycho, when all I've been to her for over a week is a grumpy asshole.

Doesn't stop me from breathing a sigh of relief when she shakes hands with whatever asshole just stole two and a half minutes of her life and waves goodnight to him.

When she gets back to our table, I can see the rosy blush on her cheeks, a little perspiration shimmering at her temples, a wayward strand of copper hair sticking to her glossed bottom lip.

Summer says something to her, but it's hard to hear over the blaring music and constant chatter. Her laughter draws my gaze right as she plunks down beside me without sparing me a glance.

She sits closer this time though. Teasing that center line of the couch. I'm reminded of that night I followed her to her room and stared down at the line on the floor.

Lines I shouldn't cross. Lines I shouldn't even be spending this long staring at.

She reaches forward for her beer, and as she does, she places a palm on my thigh to catch her balance, and all those lines blur in my mind. Because all I can see is how petite her hand is on my leg. And all I can feel is the roil of heat seeping into my muscles. The slow swell in my pants.

Suddenly I'm not measuring time. I'm measuring inches, because her hand is mere inches away from feeling just how much I don't dislike her. Not even one bit.

Then her hand is gone and I'm stuck staring at her lips. The way her throat works as she takes a deep swallow of beer.

With a sigh, she leans back, appraising the bar before her, and announces, "This place is fun."

I clear my throat, grasping for something to talk about. "Is this like the bar you work at?"

She smiles so easily. It just rolls off her like she doesn't even think about it. It's incredible. "No. Not at all. I actually manage my brother's business. It's this old theater that he turned into a live music venue downtown. Cleared out the seats. Spring loaded the dance floor. And we book in all sorts of awesome bands. If there's no show, it's just a regular bar—a quiet night for the regulars."

I can one hundred percent see Willa in a setting like that. "And why aren't you working there now?"

She rolls her eyes. "Brother blew up. He started a record label and picked some good nobodies. Turned them into somebodies. So he decided to renovate the venue even though he's never there anymore."

"That doesn't mean he gets to stop paying you."

She waves a hand and takes another sip. "Oh, nah. He didn't. I'd pull his pretty-boy hair if he did. But that place is also basically my social life. Truthfully, I was lonely in the city. It's nice to be around people—your family."

It's fascinating to me, listening to someone so uninhibited talk. Someone who says what's on her mind without concern, who laughs so freely.

It's addictive having her attention on me. I wonder if Luke feels like this too?

"Yeah. They're alright." I look over at my brothers, watching Beau and Rhett and Jasper joke together, like they have since they were teenagers. I'm always sad when Beau leaves on tour, even though I don't tell him. He always says it will be his last mission—that he'll leave the military when he's back. And then he goes again.

I think that's *his* addiction.

"I'm close with my family," Willa says. "Closer than lots of people. But we all live parallel lives now that my brother and I are adults, whereas you guys are all up in each other's business. It's charming. I can see why Summer loves it out here."

"Yeah. She fits in. That's for sure." We both glance over. Summer is in Rhett's lap, and everyone is listening to Beau tell a story, his hands moving animatedly as he does. Everyone except Jasper, who to the average onlooker might seem like he's listening, but I know better.

He's slipped into the past. Eyes and head somewhere else entirely. Sometimes he still looks like the devastated little boy we took in. I wonder if he relives that day as often as I relive our mother's death?

My head steers in Luke's direction, and I wonder what he's doing. If he's happy. If he's warm. I know he's with my dad, but the anxiety around keeping him safe is real for me. I often ponder whether he worries I'll abandon him like his mom did.

I worry I'll leave him the way our mom left us. Suddenly. Tragically.

Now I don't feel like being out at all. I want to be home, with him tucked in safely in the room next to me or—as still often happens on weekends—in the same bed as me. Because for all his wildness, Luke is a cuddler. Softhearted beneath it all.

"I think I'm gonna head out," I say to Willa. "You okay to catch a ride with the others?"

She starts at my change of subject, but she also doesn't miss a beat and slides her pint glass onto the table, this time touching my knee as she does. "Nah. I'd rather go with you."

I know she doesn't mean it the way I'm thinking. That she'd literally rather spend time with me than out with everyone else.

But it's kind of nice to dream about all the same.

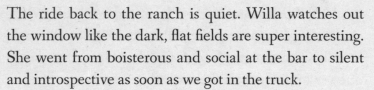

The ride back to the ranch is quiet. Willa watches out the window like the dark, flat fields are super interesting. She went from boisterous and social at the bar to silent and introspective as soon as we got in the truck.

I wish I had the balls to ask her what she's thinking. But I don't.

I'm worried she'll bring up what I said to her on the dance floor. I'm worried she'll ask me about us again. I'm worried my attraction to her is becoming all too obvious. And I don't want to become the creepy dad hitting on the babysitter.

Even though she's twenty-five and clearly isn't doing this because she needs the money.

"Hey . . ." I say, examining the dark road in front of me harder than is necessary.

Her head quirks in my direction, and in the truck's dark cab, she's all creamy skin and soft hair.

"Do you mind if we check in at the main house and make sure everything is okay with Luke?"

I don't want to sound like some insane helicopter parent. I try so hard not to be, even though I'm freaking out internally ninety percent of the time, hoping I'm doing this whole parenting thing right, often wishing I had someone to do it with, to explain my fears and failings to. Instead, I just close my eyes and hold on for dear life. Say a prayer that I can keep him alive into adulthood.

Her features soften, not a stitch of judgment on her face. "Yeah. Of course."

"Sorry. I know it's your weekend now. You're probably sick of dealing with him."

She chuckles and toes off her shoes before putting one bare foot on the dash. My eyes leave the road for a moment, noting the pink polish on her toes and the delicate bone in her ankle. "Actually, no. I have fun hanging out with Luke. Kinda missed the little fella tonight."

"Yeah? You'd rather play Dinosaur Ranch than go out with friends for drinks?"

She shrugs, looking out the window again. "Yeah. I mean, I've been working in a bar since I turned eighteen. The allure isn't what it once was. I feel like I'm ready for something new. I'm just not sure what."

"Did you go to college?"

She turns, offering a saucy wink. "Just the school of life."

I snort. "Same. But you seem like the post-secondary type. Smart. Wealthy. Well-connected."

Her head quirks as she assesses me. "That's funny, in like, a very judgmental sort of way. But I've never really enjoyed school. I'm sure if I'd applied myself, I could have done better. But I was always more interested in riding my horse. Or being on the road with my parents. Or learning to manage a bar with my older brother. School is always there if I want to go back. But I'm a firm believer that learning doesn't always happen in the classroom."

"I like that," I reply gruffly, nodding. "And sorry. I didn't mean it like that." Because she's right. I've done nothing but judge her since the moment I first saw her.

And that's a real dick move.

One she doesn't deserve.

"Luke and I had a lot of fun researching which plants we could grow this week. I think he learned a lot. I did too. Guitar was a huge hit. Do you mind if we do some horseback riding next week?"

My chest warms at the thought of her planting in the yard with him, showing him an instrument. Skills and memories that will last a lifetime. Giving him undivided attention that he deserves. "Yeah. Of course. He'd love that."

A pleased smile touches her lips, and she lets out a little humming noise.

"He's been invited to a birthday party in a few weeks too," I tell her. "It starts earlier than I can get there. Do you think you'd be okay with taking him and then I'll come right after work and tag you out?"

"Yeah. For sure. Just let me know where I'm going." We turn into the driveway and pull up to the house before she adds, "Or leave me a trail of lettuce and we'll just follow it."

I shake my head and stifle a laugh as I hop out of my black pickup and bound toward the front door of the sprawling farmhouse. There's still a warm glow inside, and I see the flicker of the TV through the front porch window.

I open the door and peek in.

"You're not even going to knock?" Willa asks from behind me. I start, thinking she'd have stayed in the car, and her hand falls to the middle of my back. But this time, I don't even freeze. I flex my shoulders back, kind of liking the familiar way she touches me. I've seen it with Luke too. She's just an affectionate person.

A hugger, probably.

"And risk waking him up? Hell no." Craning my head and taking a step forward, I try to focus on what's going on in the house, but find myself entirely wrapped up in the way her fingers feel trailing down my spine when I step away. The way I shiver under her touch when I'm not cold at all.

My tongue darts out over my lips as I enter the house, all too aware of her body pressing in close behind mine to peek over my shoulder into the living room, where some cartoon movie is still playing.

To where my dad and Luke are curled up on the couch together. Asleep.

A bowl of popcorn is on the table, along with a tub of ice cream that is now more of a milkshake than anything else.

"How precious are they?" Willa whispers behind me.

I can't help but smile. Looking at Luke always makes me smile. It has since I felt that first little kick. Since I could see the little bulge of a foot pressing out on Talia's stomach.

She complained it was uncomfortable, and maybe I wasn't attentive enough to that. Because all I can remember thinking is that it was incredible.

"Precious," I husk, walking forward to get a blanket from the basket in the corner. After our mom died, I never got attention like this from my dad. He did his best, but he wasn't present for a long time. And by the time he was, I didn't want his attention in this way anymore. I'm glad he and Luke are getting it though.

I cover them carefully and hear some shuffling behind me. I turn to see Willa tidying the table and then sauntering away toward the kitchen. Hands full of the mess they made, hips swaying happily. Like this is no inconvenience to her at all.

As if a stunner like her wants to spend her Friday nights with a washed-up single dad, cleaning up the mess a kid and his grandfather made.

My lids fall shut as reality comes crashing back in. It doesn't matter how good her hands feel on my body.

The divide between us is too much. It's too wide. She's out of my league, and I'd be an asshole to drag her down into mine.

But when we hop back into the truck and she peeks over at me and says, "You're an amazing dad. I hope you know that," I want to drag her down right on the spot.

11

Willa

Summer: Did you leave with Cade?

Willa: Yeah.

Summer: You could have stayed with me! We're getting a cab.

Willa: Nah. Cade's hotter. Went home with him instead.

Summer: Lol.

Summer: Wait. Are you joking? I can't tell.

Willa: Save a horse, ride a cowboy.

Summer: I still can't tell.

"We have to stop meeting like this," I rasp as I see Cade's imposing form step onto the deck. The sight of him standing above me, looking down on me in the hot tub, makes my stomach flip. He's downright mouthwatering with swim trunks riding low on his hips, framed by a cut V-shape that disappears beneath them.

A V-shape my fingers itch to trace.

I press my thighs together at the intense expression on his face. If it's a scowl, it might as well be the hot one. Because the look is sizzling. Maybe it's in my head. Maybe it's wishful thinking.

Maybe I have a crush on an older man.

Again.

It's pretty much part of my personality now. I've always had a thing for older men. I like to bug Summer about her dad being hot—but I'm not really joking.

I need therapy.

"I can leave." Cade's deep voice rumbles through the cool night air, the smell of freshly mowed grass mingling with the light tang of rain. I heard thunder but didn't see lighting, so I figured I'd take my chances with staying submerged in the hot water.

"Don't be ridiculous. It's your house, I'll leave." I push to stand as he approaches, failing at not checking out the imposing width of his shoulders, the way his scruff dusts down over his sharp jawline and throat, the muscles in his thighs.

When I go to step out, Cade's harsh voice lances through the silence. "Please. Sit down."

I glance up to see where the bite in his voice came from, but his eyes are trained on my chest. On the unpadded one-piece swimsuit I'm wearing.

On the way my nipple piercings press against the fabric.

With a small squeal, I fall back into the water and sink down. It's not like I'm embarrassed about my piercings—I actually love them—but I don't typically waltz around advertising them to employers.

I see his jaw pop as he avoids meeting my eyes while he climbs into the sunken tub, holding a hefty glass of amber liquid in his hand.

"Did you, uh, build this deck?" I offer lamely, mind racing with how I must be the naughty girl who drops panties and flashes her pierced tits at him.

But then he's the man who suggested he wouldn't be quiet while I gave him a blow job. The one who ran away when I questioned it.

I berate myself internally. *He's the man who signs your paychecks, you horny fool.*

"Because it's a really nice deck. The way you worked the hot tub into it? Top tier."

He settles in across from me, arms slung the length of the hot tub, chin dipped just slightly as he glares at me from beneath his lashes.

This scowl has him looking like a predator.

Not a grumpy rancher.

Not a sweet single dad.

Like someone who has a lot more experience than I do staring me down in an unnerving way.

"I made it, Red."

Red. It's not the first time a person has taken to calling me that. Usually it's regulars at the bar. Usually it's a casual nickname.

But with Cade, it feels different. I *like* it. Feels like he has a special name for me.

I'm so lame.

"You did good," I reply, rolling my lips together and admiring the deck. I'm not lying, it's a great deck. I just feel like a bumbling idiot bringing it up. It's probably worse than talking about the weather.

"Would you like a drink?" His voice isn't harsh, but it's strained.

Hell yes. A drink would be excellent for this situation. "Sure."

He shifts and stares down at his lap before stretching one long, muscled arm in my direction, a crystal tumbler held between strong fingers, forearms rippling in the dim light. The veins like an enticing path. My eyes can't help but wander up to his biceps.

To his chest and the dusting of black hair there.

To that little dip between his collarbones.

The man is a walking, talking wet dream and I'm not even sure he realizes it.

I take the glass from him, trying to ignore the zing of electricity that shoots up my arm when our fingers brush.

I drop his glare, focusing on the glass—on not dropping it. "Thanks."

When I peek up at him, he's still glaring at me. And I'm not sure what I've done to make him mad.

"You're welcome."

"What is it?" I take a sip, grateful that I can hide behind the rim of the glass for a minute and try to find my composure.

"Bourbon."

The sweet burn of it warms my throat, and I lean into that, trying to let it soothe my nerves, the ones that are rioting under his stare.

More often than not, his scowls make me want to flip him the finger, but I feel a bit like we turned a corner tonight, and now the glare is making me feel self-conscious.

While I lick the remnants off my lips, I slide through the water to hand it back to him. His eyes follow my tongue in the least discreet way. The brush of it more sensual than I anticipated. The weight of the water pressing on all the best places.

I've never reacted this way to a man simply looking at me. Years in a bar with men giving me covetous looks, and none had me fumbling around like a nervous virgin.

I should hate him for it. But I'm intrigued. "Want to play a game?" I ask, pushing backwards across the space toward my bench. My foot glides against his calf as I go.

He quickly pulls his leg away. "I'm a little old for games, Willa."

I quirk a brow, hiding my arms under the water to cover the gooseflesh popping up in response to his words. "Never too old for truth or dare."

He stares at me, fingers pulsing around the glass propped up in his hand.

Having Luke out of the house is making me bold. It's just us and what feels like an endless stretch of land behind me. "Truth or dare, Cade?"

He takes a swig, eyes almost coal black in the night. "Truth."

"Where are my panties?"

His lips slope up, a sly expression hitting his face. "In the garbage."

I giggle, tipping my head up to stare at the stars overhead. "Good. Your turn to ask."

A deep rumble hums in his chest, and my eyes drop to the definition in his pecs. "Truth or dare?"

"Truth." No way am I picking dare. He'll dare me not to talk for a week or something.

"Why did you have underwear in your purse?"

I push forward to snag the glass of bourbon out of his hand. My knee brushes his, but this time he doesn't move. I take a small sip, eyes shifting to meet his. "Honestly, I don't like wearing underwear. They're uncomfortable, they ride up, they leave panty lines that I hate. They're just a nuisance, so I carry a spare pair." I point at him. "Clean ones. Just in case of emergency."

"A panty emergency?"

I shrug, pressing the glass back into his fingers and

giving them a squeeze around the glass to make sure he doesn't drop it. "You just never know," I reply as I move to his bench rather than across from him.

It will make sharing the drink easier.

That's what I tell myself.

"Why do panty lines matter? If people know you're wearing underwear, is that . . ." His face scrunches kind of adorably. "Is that a bad thing? Everyone wears underwear."

I laugh. "Well, that's true. I guess it shouldn't matter." I hold up an imaginary drink in his direction for a fake cheers. "Thank you, patriarchy."

"You know I'm right."

"You might be right, but I still hate them."

His lips work against each other like he's really chewing on something. "Every morning when you text me you've put them on, are you lying?"

"You just had your turn, Eaton. Don't be greedy with the questions. I thought you didn't like playing games?"

"Fuck my life," he mutters, taking another long pull of the alcohol.

"Truth or dare?"

"Truth."

"What's the story with Luke's mom?"

The blank stare he gives me is unnerving, but I don't back down. I'm probably being snoopy, but I also spend all day with this kid. I'm supposed to attend a birthday party with him. It seems like something I should know. The bare bones of it, at least.

"Did I go too far?"

"No. It's fine."

"Her and I knew each other since high school. She was always around. I knew she liked me. Hell, everyone knew. She wasn't subtle about it. My mom died when I was eight—giving birth to my little sister—and Harvey struggled with losing the love of his life, having a newborn and three little boys to raise all on his own. So I stepped up. I grew up fast and did more than most eight-year-olds should ever have to do. I look at Luke . . ." His eyes trail away, past me, out into the pitch darkness behind me. "I wonder how the hell I did what I did. How everyone just let me. I did school, pitched in around the ranch, cleaned, cooked what I could, and helped every-where possible. Because that just seemed like what needed to be done."

My chest aches uncharacteristically. Our fun, playful game took a more serious turn. I try to imagine a little Cade. A boy not really getting to mourn his moth-er's death because he just threw himself into doing what *needed to be done* rather than doing what he wanted to.

"I spent years living that way. It's a hard role to shake off. And I don't know that I would have if I could have. And then one night Talia was there. She was willing. I was drunk and so damn tired of being responsible. And that was all it took. One little plus sign and I did what needed to be done. I went from rolling my eyes at her antics to get my attention, to irrevocably stuck with her. We got married. And while the chemistry was lacking,

I'll admit I liked having her around. The company. I guess I was so busy working the ranch that I missed the part where she was miserable. Where she was off sleeping with other people."

He chuckles now. "Or maybe I noticed and just didn't care."

"Jesus," I mutter. Because I don't think this man has ever strung so many words together and directed them at me. I don't think he's ever told me anything personal, and then he goes and unloads all that. And I soak it all up raptly, loving getting to know this man who's been a mystery wrapped up in an enigma. Loving that he feels comfortable enough to share it all with me.

"And then she left. I came home from working one night and there was a note. Luke was with my dad. And that was that."

"How old was Luke?"

"Two." He takes a deep swig, the column of his thick throat working as he swallows.

"Does she ever visit?"

"Whoop." His index finger pulls off the glass, and he points at me. "You've already asked two questions in a row, Red. My turn."

My lips press together and I nod. "It's admirable, really. Everything you've done for your family." He doesn't respond, so I just clear my throat and forge ahead. "Your turn."

"I bet you're too chicken to pick dare," he taunts, eyes looking a little glassier than they did when he first walked out here. The heat. The bourbon. The walk down memory lane.

He looks different. Lighter somehow.

"Dare." I'm not going to let him figure me out that easily.

He swirls the glass and studies me like he's weighing his options. With one more swig of liquor, he says, "I dare you to sit up on the edge of the hot tub for the rest of this game."

I blink slowly, hearing the rush of blood in my ears. The pounding of my heart.

He thinks he can make me put a stop to this game. But I'm not sure Cade Eaton knows me all that well. If he wants me to sit where he can watch me while he drinks bourbon, then I'm all in.

I'm not going to fold.

Pushing myself across the tub and out of the water, I hold his dark eyes, lips parting on a labored breath. I don't look down and neither does he as I slide my ass onto the edge of the hot tub, leaving my legs dangling into the water.

It's a test of wills, which one of us is going to look down at my chest first. And this time it's not just the metal barbells causing a scene. My nipples are pointing straight at him.

"My turn," I rasp.

He nods, still holding my gaze. "Your turn."

"Truth or dare, Cade?"

"Truth." A muscle in his jaw twitches.

"Wimp." He doesn't even react to my jibe. "If you're really good at rodeo stuff, why wouldn't you go do those events while I'm here to help you?"

The weight of his gaze has my entire body humming. The intensity in his eyes. I feel like he's trying to light me on fire with his glare alone.

I lean back on my hands, waiting for him to answer.

But instead, he claims his prize. His eyes rake over my body, and I *feel* it, like the tip of something cool and pointed. There's no distaste on his face this time. It's pure want. And that's a look I can recognize.

My core throbs and I feel too hot, even with the cool night air hugging my skin.

I sit, watching him. Watching his expression. Watching him devour me with his eyes.

I do the same. Unable to tear my attention from the beautiful, intense man before me. The way the skin on his throat throbs over his pulse point. The subtle shake of his head as his tongue presses into the side of his cheek.

"Because it's frivolous. I have responsibilities that I can't overlook." He's talking to me, but he's staring at my breasts.

"We all need to do something frivolous sometimes. Even you." I absently wonder if we're talking about rodeos at all right now.

"Careful, Willa. You don't know what you're talking about." His jaw pops as he glances up at me.

I reach out to him, pulsing my fingers, silently asking for

what's left of the drink in his hand. Needing a little liquid courage of my own. He moves forward, handing it over and hovering before me. Indecision tracing his every feature.

"You're a giver, Cade." I take a sip before I stare down at him and delicately wipe my lips. "What if you took something for yourself for once?"

"I can't," his voice cracks as he looks at me imploringly.

"You should let me help you. You deserve to enjoy yourself too."

Now I *know* we aren't just talking about the rodeos. We're toeing a line. A line between employee and employer. A line between an older man and a younger woman. A line that may well differentiate appropriate from inappropriate.

"No." He grabs the glass and pushes himself across to the opposite side of the square, leaning back to feast on my body. I chance a look down at myself now, seeing the outline of my nipples battling against the fabric and the thin nylon at the bottom of my swimsuit lewdly wedged between my pussy lips.

Something that hasn't escaped his attention based on the way his eyes snag there before slipping back up to the dark sky above us.

A little part of me wants to hide in the water, but the bigger part of me gets off on sitting here on display for him. Knowing he likes what he sees but won't let himself touch. Knowing he *wanted* to see it.

Knowing his cock has got to be rock-hard under the water.

"Truth or dare," he bites out.

"Truth," I reply, not sure I can handle another dare or where it might take us.

His brows furrow and his eyes narrow on mine. "What are you thinking right now?"

"That I like sitting here with your eyes on me."

"Fuck," he groans, running a wet hand over his face and through his dark hair before tossing his head back and polishing off the dregs of the bourbon.

"What are you thinking?" I push. Wanting to know. Wanting to hear him say he likes what he sees.

"I didn't pick truth, Willa."

I bite my lip, regarding him. Wondering if I'm going way too far right now and wondering if it matters. Watching him struggle to hold himself back, watching him put himself through hell to keep things appropriate.

"Truth or dare?" My voice is full of undisguised desire. I've used this voice before to get what I want. It's worked for me with other men. But never has it resulted in the expression of distressed pleading on Cade's face when he glances up at me and says, "Dare."

His expression doesn't say crawl onto my lap and ride me. It says *help me*.

And so that's what I do. But probably not in the way he saw coming.

"I dare you to do those rodeos and let me take care of Luke while you do."

The look he gives me back is dark and fathomless. It's confused and thankful all at once. Disappointed and relieved in the same beat.

When I hear his low, "Okay," I smile softly at him and swing my legs out of the water onto the deck, not oblivious to the way he's blatantly watching my every move now. I feel momentarily self-conscious, like he might see something he doesn't like.

But I shake the thought away. The lighting is dim, and it doesn't matter if he sees the dimples on my ass anyway.

Away from the steam of the hot water and the buzz of the bourbon, things look a whole lot clearer. And what Cade Eaton thinks of my body is of little importance.

I wrap a towel around myself, turning only when I hit the back door. "Good night, Cade." He drops his head back and stares at the blanket of stars. "Thanks for . . . the game."

He doesn't turn to look at me when he rasps, "Goodnight, Red."

12

Cade

Cade: Fine. I'll do it.

Lance: Yeah?

Cade: Yeah.

Lance: Fuck yeah, buddy. Let's do this!

Cade: But I want to win. No mediocre shit. I don't want to waste my weekends losing.

Lance: Deal. You need to borrow a horse?

Cade: No. Mine knows her job better than any of your shiny show ponies.

Lance: LOL. Kinda forgot what a dick you are.

I groan when the first splash of coffee hits my tongue. I need it because I've been up all night trying to will away the world's most persistent hard-on.

Thanks to Willa fucking Grant.

I could hear the rustling of her blankets in the room next to me and wondered what she was doing. Tossing and turning? Sliding a dainty hand between those pretty thighs?

Thinking of me?

And I refused to relieve myself. I wrapped my palm around my thick shaft and gave it one firm tug while I laid there. Then I stopped. Because blowing my load while thinking of the twenty-something nanny sleeping on the other side of the wall just felt fucking gross. Daring her to sit on the edge of the hot tub, when we both knew why, was bad enough.

God. What was I thinking?

I lean back against the kitchen counter and swipe my hand over my mouth. Out of control, that's what I am.

It's like I didn't break enough rules when I was younger—I was too busy being serious—and now that streak is cropping up on me.

It's perfectly natural. Willa is a smoke show. She'd make a priest crumble. And I'm no man of the cloth.

"Good morning." She waltzes into the kitchen like I summoned her just by thinking of her. All wild copper hair piled on top of her head and fresh-faced, which is making her look awfully young.

But when my eyes drop to her chest, all warning thoughts of her being too young grow wings and fly right the fuck out of my head. Her perky tits are teasing me through a soft, white cotton concert tee.

I couldn't tell you which band it's for, because all I can see is outlines of those goddamn nipple piercings.

Taunting me. Reminding me how that pretty, pale purple swimsuit wedged itself between her pussy lips.

Jealousy of a bathing suit is a new feeling for me.

"Good morning," I bite out, madder at myself than her. But I lash out all the same. "Are you averse to bras as well?"

Her laugh is airy as she rises on her tippy-toes to reach the top of the cupboard where I keep the coffee cups. My eyes are drawn to the way her calves flex, toned legs disappearing into a pair of baby blue short-shorts, her bare feet on my floor. There's something intimate about having Willa in my space like this. And Luke isn't even here to make a good reason for it.

"Here, I'll grab that." It only takes me one step to stand directly behind her and reach into the back of the cupboard. I guess I don't normally go through mugs this quickly when I'm the only one using them.

"Thanks," she breathes, shrinking back down onto the soles of her feet, brushing the curve of her ass along my front as she does.

I step away quickly, placing the mug on the marble

countertop and willing my cock to not pop up and make a special appearance, outing me as the world's biggest creep.

As she pours herself a coffee, she says, "Not at all averse to bras." Her lips tip up. "But I don't normally sleep in them. Just grabbing coffee."

She leans against the countertop, all smug with herself.

"Do you normally walk around like that when Luke is here?"

Her hands wrap around the mug, and she takes a tentative sip, eyeing me over the rim as she does. "No. I normally wait until I hear you leave. Then I get up and make my cup of coffee."

I grunt, feeling like a dick for policing how she walks around. Luke wouldn't even notice. I'm the fucker with his head in the gutter who can't handle it.

"Then I go back to my room and put my panties on," she huffs out quietly, peering up playfully from behind her mug.

"Wait. Did you just say that you wait for me to leave and then make coffee?"

Her brow arches. "Smarter than you look, Eaton."

"But I'm up at 4:30."

She shrugs. "Yeah. It's kind of nice. I sit on the front deck and read my dirty books. It's peaceful. I like the morning, and since I'm not out until three a.m. working, I can actually enjoy them. I hate sleeping in. I always feel like I've wasted my day."

"Why do you wait for me to leave?"

She gives me a face that says she thinks I'm an idiot. "Because if you're this grumpy midmorning, I'd hate to see you first thing. Those cowboys down at the ranch must be terrified of you."

I grunt. They are. And that's just how I like it.

"Do my nipples bother you, Cade?"

Coffee sprays from my mouth.

I get most of it back in my mug, but not all. My hand is soaked, and I can feel the droplets of it in my beard.

Willa blinks at me innocently, and my heartbeat thunders in my ears.

Fake innocence. She knew what she was doing when she asked that question.

"No." I wipe at my face, turning to put my coffee back down on the countertop. I need to pick my next words carefully so I don't come off like a condescending asshole.

I know I often come across that way, and I don't want to with Willa. It's an unfamiliar feeling, *wanting* someone to like me. "It's just that—"

"It's funny. I thought about you telling me panty lines aren't something we should worry about people seeing, and I'm feeling the same way about my nipples."

I blink at her.

Hell. No.

"We all have nipples, right?"

I swallow, at a loss for how to reason my way out of this. She's trapped me in a box of my own logic.

134

"For example . . ." Her bright green feline eyes drop to my chest. "I can see yours right now."

My chin snaps toward my chest, and sure enough, my nipples are giving me away.

"And they don't bother me at all." She licks her bottom lip slowly, with intention, before one cheek hitches up in a lopsided smirk.

Then she turns and walks back toward her bedroom, holds one fist up above her head, and says, "Fuck the patriarchy."

And I'm left standing there. Watching her. Wondering if she's wearing any panties under those soft, loose shorts I could so easily pull to the side.

~

"You can't put your fingers there, pal. Or you're going to cut them clean off."

"I know what I'm doing, Dad." Luke rolls his eyes and continues to chop a cucumber in the stupidest way imaginable.

I grab the knife and lift it up. "Listen. You're going to hold this properly or risk giving me a heart attack. I want you to know how to do this properly. You said you'd listen to my instructions."

The trade-off was that I have to listen to his terrible pop music on the speaker. The stuff that all his little friends have indoctrinated him with in only one year of school.

It's Sunday night, and I'm making a full-blown gourmet meal. Luke is helping me cook because I refuse to raise a man who doesn't know how to hold his own in a kitchen. Feeding the people I care about is how I tell them I care without having to say it out loud.

Because saying it out loud makes it a little too real for me.

"Fine," he huffs out, dramatically shrugging his shoulders.

"Your dad's right." Willa appears out of thin air, reaching in and swiping a coin of cucumber and popping it into her mouth. "If you cut like that, all you'll be left with is a thumb, and how will I teach you to play guitar?"

"Willa!" Luke turns on the chair he's standing on and launches himself into her arms. "We missed you!"

She laughs, squeezing his ribs and spinning him in a little circle. They're equally dramatic.

"She spent *one* night in the city, Luke." I cross my arms, trying to hide how adorable I find it that he likes her so much.

Willa winks at me over Luke's shoulder. "I missed you too, you little psycho. I'm not so sure your dad missed me though."

"Pfft." Luke's head rolls as she places him back onto the chair. "He did. He told me so."

Willa looks visibly shocked by that. "Oh, yeah?"

"He said the house feels silent without you here."

Her lips twitch as she tries to hold back her laughter.

"I think that just means I talk too much or play my music too loud."

"No way." Luke sighs. "I love talking with you. And playing music with you."

There's a beauty in children his age saying what they mean. They don't wonder how it will come off, or if someone might read too much into it. If it's in their heart, they say it. I know Luke loves talking with Willa, and it makes my chest ache.

Especially when she gives him the full, megawatt smile that lights her up head to toe, ruffles his hair, and says, "I love talking with you too, buddy."

"We're cooking you dinner," Luke announces.

"We're cooking *dinner*," I clarify. "Of course, you're welcome to join us."

I don't want her thinking I'm downright obsessed with her.

I don't want her knowing I did kind of . . . notice her absence. It's only been a couple of weeks, but I've gone from being annoyed by her presence when I get home from a hard day's work to smiling as I kick off my boots and listen to her and Luke laugh or talk together.

Music to my fucking ears.

"You boys are amazing chefs. Count me in."

I go back to peeling potatoes in the sink beside Luke but say, "Let's put some different music on for Willa." It's the perfect opportunity to get rid of whatever this happy, danceable shit is.

Horrified, Luke asks me what's wrong with "Watermelon Sugar", but before I can answer, Willa tilts her head at me and says, "Yeah, Cade. You got something against Harry Styles?"

I glance over at their wide eyes. One set offended, the other amused. "It's just so . . . pop-y."

"I have an idea." Willa's hand snaps up, and then she strides out of the kitchen.

I try not to stare at her ass in the denim cutoffs she's wearing.

I fail.

Then I'm back to the potatoes, skinning them aggressively while trying to monitor Luke's precious little fingers. He's focusing so hard that his tongue is captured between his lips, eyes narrowed.

He looks . . . grown-up. I know he's not yet, but he's also not the fully dependant toddler he once was. He doesn't wake me up multiple times a night. He can get his own cereal out for breakfast.

It's terrifying.

The music shuts off, and I turn to the kitchen table where Willa has pulled a chair out for herself and has a beautiful, ornate acoustic guitar slung over her lap. "What should I play?"

Luke shouts for her to play "Watermelon Sugar" before he drops the knife and sits to watch her.

I can't blame him. She's practically glowing.

I groan dramatically, just picking on him now. Feeling alarmingly relaxed. Better somehow, knowing that Willa is here under the same roof rather than out in the city or whatever she and Summer got up to on their *girls' weekend*.

Perfectly normal outing for two young women, I'm sure, but I've never been good at turning off the protective streak. The one that's constantly worrying about everyone's safety.

"Pick something easy, like 'Twinkle Twinkle.' We don't know if Willa is any good."

"Dad!"

Willa laughs and shakes her head, before dropping her gaze to the strings that her fingers and pick hover over, a curtain of warm copper hair shielding her face like she's a little bit shy. Her long lashes flutter shut for a moment, and her knee bounces.

Then the smooth hum of the strings fills the kitchen. I immediately recognize it as a slowed down acoustic version of the song that was just playing.

I stop and put down the peeler in my hand. I'd be the first person to confess that I leave my radio tuned to the country station. I'm no connoisseur. And when I'm out in the pastures, the soundtrack is the snorts of our mounts and the thrum of the cows' hooves against the land.

Truthfully, silence doesn't bother me in the least.

But she's impossible to look away from. I figured she'd have some basic knowledge of the guitar, but this is impressive. Or maybe it's just because it's *her*.

There's something soulful, something that warms me to my bones as I watch her.

"Wait! You missed the part where you sing!" Luke's tone is accusatory.

Willa peeks up, timidly pushing her hair behind her ear. "I don't sing, Luke. I just like playing guitar."

"You sang during our dance party the other day."

She drops her eyes, lips pressing together, cheeks flushing the prettiest shade of pink. "That was just for fun."

"Sing! Sing! Sing!"

A deep laugh bubbles up out of me. Luke is so damn persistent.

Willa's eyes widen on mine, and I cross my arms with a shrug. "Sing, Willa. Let's hear it."

Her blush deepens, crawling down her neck onto her chest. It's how she'd look with beard burn on her.

My beard burn.

"Fine. But I don't have a good voice, so no making fun."

"You do too!"

She points at Luke. "This was supposed to be background music while you cooked, not a concert."

"It sounds so good, Willa. I want to play the guitar as good as you."

The shy smile that touches her lips as her head dips down has me softening toward her. She's so brash sometimes, and then there's this sweet side. This bashful side. This insecure side.

And she has no business feeling that way at all.

"It's beautiful, Willa," I add, hoping to reassure her, but her cheeks go darker.

What I want to say is wholly inappropriate.

You're beautiful.

How was your night out?

I'm sorry I haven't been leaving enough coffee for you in the morning.

Words that lodge in my throat. Turn to cotton batting on my tongue. Words and feelings I don't know what to do with anyway.

She pulls the hair back down to cover her a little and starts the song again from the beginning. A tiny part of me thinks I should turn and keep peeling, but a bigger part of me can't take my eyes off her smooth legs bent under the guitar. One bare foot propped on the lower bar of the chair. Slender ankle flexed, the curved arch of her foot somehow sensual. I run into this problem where she's concerned a lot.

The most trivial little details have me obsessing over her.

The tune sounds just as good as it did the first time. Sultry and slow. It's like she took some teenybopper song and made it sexy.

Her lean fingers move across the string seamlessly, stretching and flexing with every note she strums.

And then her voice kicks in, and it's a shot to the gut.

Raspy and sweet, all at once.

Shy and sure.

Quiet and strong. Just like her.

The first line is something about strawberries and summer evenings, which is fitting, because her strawberry red lips move, and I'm entranced.

Luke sways to the song, happy and oblivious. But not me. I can feel my precious control slipping where she's concerned. And who knew some stupid song would be the thing to do it?

She peeks up and her voice breaks ever so slightly when she catches me staring her down.

She doesn't look away though.

The lyrics talk about breathing in and breathing out —which is a great reminder for me at this current juncture.

My stomach bottoms out, and I worry about what's written on my face. My carefully practiced poker face is slipping, like she's peeling it back, piece by piece. All the armor, all the protection.

I'm not ready to be laid bare. Not by her. Not by anyone.

Luke's mom may not have been the right woman for me, but she was *a* woman for me. And I did my best to keep her happy. I tried to love her. And in my own way, I did. It wasn't cinematic but I was faithful. I provided for her. I worked myself to the bone to build us a good life.

And she left.

It wasn't enough. Even today, I don't have much more than I did then.

And at the end of August, Willa will leave too. Back to her city existence. Back to bars and famous musicians.

Back to an exciting life that doesn't include a moody rancher with a chip on his shoulder.

Maybe it would be fine. Maybe I could let her go and move on.

Luke will be sad either way. But he'll be devastated if I let him think there's more here than a seasonal arrangement. And his heart isn't one I'm willing to gamble.

So, I turn my back on her and get back to peeling potatoes.

I listen to every note, hang on every word, and feel grateful that she can't see my face as I do.

"Again! Again!" Luke exclaims, and I just shake my head. I won't say no because I'm enjoying it way too much to stop her.

"How about another song?" she asks him.

"What song?"

"A song your dad will know."

"He doesn't know any good music," Luke provides very matter-of-factly.

My shoulders shake as I laugh silently. "It's true," I call over my shoulder.

"He's too old!"

I turn and narrow my eyes at him jokingly.

"He'll know this one then." Willa's fingers strum a few chords, and I instantly know the song.

I turn my fake dirty look on her, and she grins back. Who doesn't know "Dust on the Bottle"? It's a classic.

Her voice is thick with amusement, her posture

straighter when I smile at her. She lights up when I laugh.

She sings about dust on a bottle and how the contents just keep getting better with age. It's funny, she's poking fun at me and she knows it. The night flows from there. Conversation, jokes, good food. And after that song Luke has resorted to teasing Willa and me about being old. He's dubbed us "Grandma" and "Grandpa."

"Pass the mashed potatoes please, *Grandma*." He dissolves into a fit of giggles, the golden evening rays glinting off of his dark, shiny hair, cheeks rosy from summer days spent in the sun.

I feel alarmingly . . . at ease.

"You're a weird kid, you know that?" Willa picks up an unevenly cut piece of cucumber and pops it into her mouth. "A *total weirdo*."

Weirdo is Luke's favorite joke insult right now, and he laughs so hard that he gasps for air. Willa laughs too, looking at him with so much affection that my heart twists in my chest.

"No, Willa! You're a weirdo! I've seen you dance. You're the biggest weirdo in the world!"

Her hand falls across her chest, and she leans back dramatically. "How *dare* you, Luke Eaton. That's just cruel. I dance beautifully."

"Show my dad! Show my dad how weird you dance!" Amused tears glisten in the corners of his eyes, and he wipes at them with pudgy little fingers.

"Okay, fine. He can be the judge. Got that, Cade? Luke and I are going to dance, and you'll decide which of us is the bigger weirdo."

I lean back in my chair and cross my arms over my chest, wondering why I ever disliked her. How can a single person not like Willa Grant?

She's fucking enchanting.

"Okay?" Her head quirks, and her silky hair tumbles around her shoulders.

I give her a small smile, chuckling at the absurdity of their competition, but too entertained to stop them. "Okay."

"Good." She grins at me, moving over to the countertop to hook her Bluetooth up to the speaker. "Let's do . . ." She glances over her shoulder at me as her thumb presses down and the first few notes of "Summer of '69" filters out through the sound system.

I shake my head. But can't help the smile stretching across my face. *She would.*

Willa starts off with a terrible moonwalk, before moving into a horrendous sprinkler. She may have been shy playing guitar, but she isn't shy about dancing. She's fun. She's funny. And Luke loves it. He doesn't even dance. He just jumps around laughing at her, spindly arms and legs flailing wildly.

She does some shaky, twerky move that I'm sure the kids these days have a name for, and eventually grabs his hands in hers to make him dance with her. He jiggles his hips and smiles up at her so widely that my cheeks hurt just watching.

I realize they hurt because I'm smiling that hard. The back of my throat aches as I watch Willa spin my little boy around the kitchen on what's meant to be her day off.

"Do you see how weird she is, Dad?" Luke calls to me.

"Yeah. Super weird," I agree as she turns to give me a fake scowl over her shoulder.

The only weird thing is what I'm feeling about a woman I've known for mere weeks.

It's not just weird.

It's fucking absurd.

"Okay. Now Grandma and Grandpa dance!" Luke giggles, pulling Willa over to me.

I scowl at them both.

Willa holds a hand up to her mouth and whisper-shouts toward Luke, "I think he might be the weirdest."

Luke cackles, and even I can't turn him down. Bryan Adams isn't so bad, and they both look totally irresistible standing in front of me with wide smiles, bright eyes, and rosy cheeks.

"Let's go, Grandpa." She reaches a hand toward me, eliciting another round of manic laughter from Luke, who is clearly beyond exhausted based on how bad he has the giggles.

I wrap my hand around hers with a groan, like I'm annoyed, even though I'm not.

Not even a little bit.

I stand and spin Willa in a quick circle, telling myself that I've already danced with her before at The Railspur.

This is just in my kitchen.

There isn't much left in this song anyway.

"I'll be right back!" Luke tears out of the kitchen, cackling like the Joker as he goes.

I spin her again, feeling my boxers grow tighter at the light laughter that crests her perfect lips. When the song ends and the beat of silence slips into a softer, slower melody, I should step away.

But I don't. Instead, I pull her close, not missing the tiny, shocked gasp she breathes out as I do.

"Should I stop?" I drop my voice, letting my eyes linger on her lips.

Her response comes fast, without hesitation. "No."

I pull her closer, lining our hips up and feeling her hand slide across the expanse of my shoulders.

As we sway, I take my time trailing my fingers over her rib cage. And I don't miss the way she shivers when I do.

"You're a hell of a dancer," I husk.

She smiles up at me. "Yeah. A total weirdo."

I chuckle, rubbing a thumb over her lower back. Her hand feels clammy where it's gripped in mine.

"Pretty good at guitar, I might add."

"Ah, well, when Ford Grant is your dad, it's pretty much mandatory."

"What about the voice?"

"What about it?" Her eyes roll, suddenly shy again.

"Your voice is beautiful." I say it because it's true and I meet her eye when I do. She's strangely uncomfortable with being complimented, always deflecting or making a joke. We sway quietly to the song, listening to the words.

It goes on about a stranger's heart that has no home—smiles covering your heart. It's haunting and beautiful, and I find myself straining to listen. "What song is this?" I ask, entranced. "Her voice almost sounds like yours."

Her eyes dart away, and my hand tightens on her waist. I let myself imagine my calloused hands gliding over her smooth skin. Worshipping every inch of her. Sinking into her.

"The song is 'Fade into You' by Mazzy Star. It's one of my favorites," she rushes it out quickly before the compliment leads her to changing the subject entirely. "Thank you for trusting me with Luke. This is already the best summer I've had in a long time."

"You're welcome. Thank you for making him laugh like that. Best sound in the world. You missing anything about the city?"

"No. Just riding."

She steps closer, and I feel the press of her against me. The heat. The friction. My hand splays on her back. "I'll find you a horse to ride."

"You're a good man, Cade Eaton. Quite possibly one of the best." Her voice is so soft that I barely hear it.

The hair on the back of my neck stands on end as I drop my head toward her. Everything around us fades away. I don't know how she has this knack for telling me the things I crave. Tracing my insecurities the way she does. Soothing the hurt she doesn't even know exists.

I trail the tip of my nose up the side of her neck and wish I could swallow the small moan that escapes her. I want so much more than one stolen dance in the kitchen while my son is off doing god knows what.

"You guys are both the biggest weirdos!" Luke mocks us as he runs back in wearing his too-small Batman costume from last Halloween. We both startle, pulling away quickly, realizing we were altogether too close just now.

And maybe Luke's not wrong. There's definitely something weird happening.

13

Willa

Willa: Hi, Lawyer friend. Can I ask for some legal advice?

Summer: Do you need me to come bail you out? Just send the address. I'm there.

Willa: Is it illegal to bang your hot boss?

Summer: Are we talking about your brother or Cade?

Willa: Fucking gross.

Summer: Dude. I've had to listen to you make hot dad jokes for years. Shooters gotta shoot.

Willa: I'm never coming to you for advice again.

Summer: My legal advice is to be very specific when you ask a question.

Willa: OK, FINE. Is it illegal to bang Cade?

Summer: You'd have to ask him. Haven't seen him with a woman the entire time I've known him. Maybe he thinks it's illegal?

Willa: He *is* a stickler for the rules. Maybe I'll break them and see if he spanks me.

Summer: Fucking gross.

~

Once I hear the door click shut the next morning—so Cade doesn't have to be scandalized by my nipples—I peek in through Luke's slightly open door to see him sprawled wide in his bed, looking adorably exhausted.

Smiling to myself, I pad through the quiet house toward the kitchen. The sun is up, but barely, and the light in the house is blue. The birds sound so damn happy, trilling away outside. I can't wait to sit on the front porch with my book and a hot cup of coffee.

I stop in my tracks when I get far enough into the kitchen to see that there is still a sizeable amount of coffee left in the pot.

As I draw closer, I see a Post-it note on the counter, written in a choppy scrawl.

Red,

The coffee is for you. Starting some two-year-olds today. If you feel like getting your back broken, meet me at the barn and you can sit on one.

- C

I snort. Oh, I feel like getting my back broken alright. By him.

Not a horse.

He's also left a mug beside the coffeemaker. I trail my fingers over the rounded handle, remembering the feel of him pressing in behind me as I reached for a cup the other morning. The feel of him pushing his hips into mine as we swayed in the kitchen.

I pour myself a cup, and it tastes better just because he made it. Just because he left everything out, knowing I was waiting for him to leave. Because he listened to what I told him.

Cade is the embodiment of actions speaking louder than words. He wasn't about to fall all over himself apologizing for not making enough coffee for me. Instead, he just made more and left me a mug, knowing that it would make me feel good.

And a Post-it note addressed to Red.

Maybe I'm an idiot but it feels sweet. Coming from Cade, it *is* sweet.

The morning passes calmly until Lukeasaurus Rex wakes up and makes me run away from him like I'm terrified.

I feed him a suitable dinosaur breakfast, and then we head down to the barn to see what starting a two-year-old horse is like.

Or in my case, to check out Daddy Cowboy.

I park my Jeep near the main barn, and we follow the sounds of hooting and hollering to the other side, walking hand in hand.

"There he is!" Luke shouts, pointing at his dad.

My mouth dries out on the spot. I do show jumping —fancy white pants and horses imported from Europe— so while I know horses, cowboys are still a new ball game for me.

But *goddamn*. What a ballgame it is.

Cade sits on a dark horse, speckled with gray—a beautiful blue roan color with black mane and tail— which perfectly matches his black cowboy hat, signature bicep-hugging black T-shirt, and black leather chaps over worn jeans.

He's seated comfortably in the saddle. Leather-gloved hands on the horn of his saddle, hip popped comfortably, with a toothpick hanging out the side of his mouth and an amused smirk on his lips.

He's so fucking hot.

He's always been hot, but I wasn't so sold on his personality. A shit personality can really ruin an otherwise hot dude, but there isn't anything wrong with Cade's personality. He's just slow to warm up. A little chilly.

But I'm finding I like a lot about him. I'm finding he doesn't make me feel chilly at all. He makes me feel hot and bothered.

"Dad!" Luke rushes forward, and Cade's head flicks in his direction, that smirk morphing into a full-blown smile.

One that makes my heart stutter-step.

"Hey, bud." He swings a leg over his horse and slides

down just in time to catch Luke in his arms. The same greeting they do every night.

"When do I get my own horse?" Luke eyes the group of youngsters in the holding pen, glancing at the round pen where a cowboy sits on a horse doing its best to buck him off.

"When you actually take an interest in learning about them. They're a serious commitment, and the only thing you're committed to right now is dinosaurs."

"I want Willa to give me riding lessons, not you," Luke announces, hands on his hips.

Cade looks at me, rolling his eyes playfully. Is Luke a smidgen obsessed with me? Possibly.

"Hi, Red."

I startle as the cowboy behind him gets turfed onto the metal fence panel. Other men sitting around have a good laugh at the guy, who spits on the ground and shakes his head. "Goddamn fucking asshole!" he exclaims.

"Gotta be smarter than the horse, Lee," Cade calls. "And watch your fucking mouth. There's a child and a city girl in our midst."

"Sorry, boss."

Luke giggles at the f-bombs flying left and right. And I feel it then. All eyes swivel in my direction, the men straightening or clearing their throats, like I've never heard a swear word in my life. Leave it to Cade to make me seem like some fragile princess.

I wave in their general direction and offer a friendly smile as I drawl, "Nice to fuckin' meet y'all."

Luke barks out a laugh. He's so good for my confidence, always approving of my jokes. "Bad word, Willa!"

A couple of the guys press their lips together, trying not to show their amusement. Because if I can feel Cade's scowl, no doubt, so can they.

"Nice to meet ya, city girl!" one guy calls from where he's seated atop a fence, waving one dusty hand in my direction.

When one domino falls, so do the rest. Within seconds most of the guys are laughing and Cade is shaking his head at me.

He does that a lot where I'm concerned.

I wink at him. "Thank you for the coffee. I'm ready for you to break my back."

His face pales, like he realizes how I could have interpreted his note. "I meant you could ride if you wanted to."

"Oh, I want to."

Heat flares on his cheeks. I shouldn't prod the bear like this, but it's just who I am. I like to watch him squirm.

"A horse. You can take mine." He hikes a thumb over his shoulder.

"Nah, I think I'll take one of the young ones."

"No chance." His jaw hardens.

"Why not?" I quirk a brow.

"I don't want you to get hurt." He says it so simply, like it should be obvious to me.

"But I thought that's what the note meant? Unless the note really meant . . ." I trail off and waggle my eyebrows at him.

"You're insane."

"I know," I smile back brightly. "I'm a redhead. No takesies backsies, Eaton. A couple of hours ago you were fine with me getting on a youngster and now you're not?"

"I changed my mind. My ranch. My rules. It's possible you don't ride all that well anyway. Plus, you need to be in one piece to take Luke to that kid's birthday party today."

I quirk a brow at him. *Dick.* Is he trying to bring out my competitive side? Leaning close, I whisper in his ear, "I dare you to let me sit on that one." I point at the leggy youngster standing in the middle of the round pen, giving the foul-mouthed cowboy total stink eye.

"That one is rank. I'm pulling you something good-natured," he says, walking away with his horse in hand, Luke following to see the others. Like his choice is final.

There must be at least ten horses in that pen, but it's the sorrel horse in the round pen that has my attention. The one who chucked that cowboy good and hard.

I feel kindred with that one, and I didn't wear my jeans and paddock boots in the middle of summer so I could stand around in the sun, sweating.

While Cade's back is turned, I march in the opposite direction and duck under the fence post of the round pen. I feel eyes on me, but the men say nothing to stop me.

They must be smarter than Cade.

The little horse's nostrils flare with each breath, wary eyes looking around a little. But honestly, I'm not worried. I ride well. I know I do. I haven't been handed easy horses my entire life. I haven't had grooms and trainers do the dirty work while I sat on the sidelines. I grew up with more money than most of the other girls at my barn, and yet I was always the one that had to work for things.

My dad often joked that none of the money was mine. It was his, and he wasn't going to spoil me with it.

Both my parents value a good work ethic. Hard work and making something of yourself are what they value most. They never forced my brother or me into post-secondary educations. They followed our leads, and while I thought it was unfair at a younger age, I get it now. I get not bankrolling your children's lives. I get not micromanaging their choices.

And I'm glad they haven't. However, I'd have taken a *little* more pressure.

Maybe I wouldn't be a directionless bartender if they had set more expectations. Who's to say?

With that in mind, I take the reins and slide a hand over the young horse's shoulder.

"Boss is gonna kill ya," one cowboy mutters from the opposite side of the fence panel.

I just smile to myself.

No, he's not. Cade Eaton is out of his depth with me.

I push my hand into the stirrup, shifting the saddle across the horse's back, watching her ears flick back and forth. "Easy, baby," I murmur.

Her head inclines toward me slightly, big round eye assessing me. I decide she likes me. I decide she's smart.

These guys all think they're tough and can outmuscle a horse, but they're wrong.

I put my foot into the stirrup before pressing down, and she still doesn't move.

"Red, don't you fucking dare."

I shake my head, but don't look behind me at Cade. He's only sort of my boss.

He doesn't feel much like a boss lately. And I'm difficult to boss around at the best of times—ask my dickhead brother.

With one deep breath, I swing a leg over the filly's narrow back, sinking gently into the saddle.

"Woman."

I snort. Cade just *womaned* me. I want to laugh, but I can feel the horse's back curled up beneath me.

She's standing still—but not for long. She's coiling all that energy to go straight up, so I open one rein wide, turning her head in toward my leg and give her a firm kick before she can bunch up any further.

Instantly, she's hopping and kicking, but I squeeze my thighs and drop my heels, keeping her in a tight circle so she can't explode.

"What a good baby," I coo at her, even though she's

tossing herself around like a total fool. But not enough to loosen me off her. I refuse to fail in front of these guys. I especially refuse to fail in front of Cade.

He'll be all annoying and *I told you so* about it and my ego honestly can't handle that type of blow where he's concerned.

I urge the filly forward, driving with my seat, to send that momentum ahead of us rather than up in the air. And in under a minute, she's dropped the shenanigans and is cantering around the round pen.

It's not pretty, but it's not a bronc show either. I hear the hoots and hollers of the guys around me—the whistles and the "yeehaws"—but I keep her going, letting her tire herself out. Letting her run until she settles and drops her head.

It takes my all to not turn to Cade and stick my tongue out at him.

You're twenty-five, you're twenty-five, you're twenty-five.

He turns me into an idiot. A bold, drooling, showboating idiot. He's a challenge and look at me—I love a challenge.

Eventually the filly breaks to a trot, and then a walk, and I reach forward to run a hand up her sweaty neck.

"Not bad, city girl!" One of the guys calls out, and I peek up, grinning in his general direction, before hopping off.

"Better than any of you fuckin' dress-up cowboys

managed," Cade bites out, seething from beneath his cowboy hat.

He looks pissed, and the flutter in my stomach at how imposing he is has me wishing he'd take some of that frustration out on me.

"I'm gonna ride like Willa when I grow up!" Luke has climbed up to the top panel of the fence and leans over, eyes glowing with excitement. "She made that filly her bitch!"

"Luke!" I say right as Cade barks, "Lucas Eaton."

The little boy's eyes widen as he drops off the fence, like he knows he's stepped in it now. He takes off into the barn, tiny cowboy boots thumping against the dirt road, without a backward glance.

"You taught him that." Cade points at me as I lead the filly over to one of the guys.

"Yeah?" I quirk a brow and head toward the man I started out not liking but who I now can't stop thinking about.

Fantasizing about.

From my side of the fence, I lean close, dropping my voice. "I'm pretty sure of the two of us, you're the one with the filthy mouth, Cade."

His hand shoots between the metal panels, fingers hooking through my belt loop to hold me still. To keep me there, as he breathes down on to me. The whoosh of each exhale caresses my cheek. "You have no fuckin' idea, Red."

With one little tug on my jeans, he jostles me and

then steps away, spinning one hand up above his shoulders and shouting at the guys. "Let's go assholes. Break time is over. You've been shown up by a prissy city girl. Now prove to me I shouldn't fire your useless asses."

I snort. The man really has a poetic way with words.

As I scoot through the fence near the barn where I saw Luke run, one man exclaims toward my retreating form, "God fuckin' damn. The view out here has never been so good."

My lips quirk, and I turn to give him a wink, but with two easy steps Cade's arm darts out and shoves him off the top of the fence where he'd been sitting. The cowboy lands on his knees with a loud bark of disbelieving laughter.

Cade's not laughing though. "Eyes on the dirt if you plan to keep your job, cowboy."

I just turn away and smile to myself, because Cade is seething. It's almost like he's jealous.

And I think I like that.

14

Cade

Willa: Panties? Check. Bra? No check.

Cade: You're going to a children's birthday party. Try again.

Willa: Right. Let me try again.

Willa: Panties? No check. Bra? Also no check.

Cade: The town is talking about you enough as it is.

Willa: Oooh. What are they saying?

Cade: That your panty lines are very defined.

Willa: My god. Did you just make a joke?

Cade: I'll be there at 6 tonight. Please don't embarrass me.

Willa: Oh boy. Is that a challenge?

Cade: Bye, Red.

Willa: I do this with Luke when he behaves badly too. Just ignore him. I don't think it's going to work on me though.

I pull up in front of the sizeable newly built house where the birthday party is being hosted. Truthfully, I hate this shit.

Showing up at kids' birthday parties as a single dad in a small town feels like being locked in a cage full of hungry lions.

Or is it cougars?

I shake my head, stepping out of my truck. Droplets of water rain down the back of my neck, because I rushed out of the shower to get here so Willa wouldn't be stuck in the cougar den by herself.

I'm not oblivious to how snoopy and pushy people in this town can be. Especially around my family, who they've always treated a little like royalty. Like ticks who crawl up out of the shrubs to catch a ride.

Talia happened once and that will never happen again.

I snag a cap from the back seat and fit it to my head before spinning the brim to the back.

The happy squeals of children and the sound of splashing water draw me around the side of the house. I reach over the wooden gate and pull on the hidden string.

City folks.

It's like they think no one knows this string is there.

I step into the heavily landscaped backyard, taking in

the in-ground pool and the parents milling around while children run around in their swimsuits.

But it's the sight of Luke crying in soaked clothes while Willa crouches in front of him, rubbing at his arms at the poolside that gets my heart pumping.

The kid puts up a good front. He plays it tough. But right now, he's borderline inconsolable.

I can see the tension in Willa's body, the heartbreak in her eyes. And it makes me like her even more. She doesn't care about the rest of the party buzzing around her. She's only got eyes for my son.

And when she pulls him in for a hug, soaking herself in the process, I melt.

Luke whispers something in her ear and points at another kid. I should recognize these kids and parents, but I usually pawn this shit off on my dad.

Forced socialization with adults I don't like is its own special brand of torture, and I guess there are limits to what I'll do for my kid.

Willa stands and glances over her shoulder at the boy sucking on a lollipop, standing with his back to her. I think he's the birthday kid, but I'm not entirely sure. His mom, whose name I also forget, is standing with two other moms chatting.

A quick glance back at Willa has me walking across the grass, because her expression is pure fire. Rhett told me she was loyal, and I recognize that look on her face. Because when someone shits on a person I care about, I make it too.

In just a few strides, Willa is bent over by the birthday boy, who stares up at her and laughs with a little shit-eating grin on his face.

"Excuse me!" his mom trills, her white wine spritzer swirling in the glass.

Willa isn't touching the kid, but she's right in his face, and I can see her lips moving slowly like she's carefully enunciating her words.

"Did you hear me? Stop talking to him!"

"Somebody needs to explain right from wrong in terms he can understand," Willa says over her shoulder to the red-cheeked mom. "Or did you miss the part where he pushed Luke into the pool and held his head under water?"

"It was a joke! You're out of line, and you will not speak another word to him."

Luke's tear-stained face tells me he wasn't in on the joke.

Willa rises slowly, almost predatory in her movements, as she turns and arches a brow at the woman. "Oh, no?"

"Not another word."

"Fine." Willa smiles but it's a scary smile. And then, with one well-placed hip check, the birthday boy goes flying into the water.

"Sebastian!" His mother's spritzer sloshes on her hand as she rushes forward.

Luke is suitably shocked. The mom's mouth is

moving, but no sound is coming out, just like when you pull a trout from the lake.

Willa crouches at the pool's edge, smirking at the boy, who is already standing in the shallow water, angrily wiping his eyes. "Life lesson, shithead. Careful who you pick a fight with. Someone insane might love them."

"You need to leave! Now!" The mom points toward the gate, and her arm shakes with fury.

I'm almost to them, but the sight of Willa knocking a kid into the pool stopped me in my tracks.

She really is insane.

Possibly in the best way.

"Gladly." She stands, brushing her hands. "Contact a professional if he starts killing bunnies or something."

"Willa," I bark, back in motion now.

"Oh, good," the mom says. "A *real* parent is here."

I should know her name for the number of times she's tried to chat me up at the grocery store or school pick up, but I don't, so I take a guess at what sounds close and pray I'm right. "Hi, Bunny."

She blinks at me. "It's Betty."

Should have prayed harder, I guess. "Oh, sorry. My mistake. Slip of the tongue. Is there a problem?"

"Yes. Your *nanny* is the problem."

I don't appreciate the condescending way she says nanny, so I offer back, "Willa is a friend, actually."

Willa blinks. Betty blinks. Luke walks up and wraps his arms around Willa's waist, while the shithead kid pulls himself out of the pool, looking suitably chastised.

"She pushed my son into the pool."

"I tripped." Willa smirks, wrapping a protective arm around Luke's small body.

Betty's blue eyes narrow, and her voice is shrill when she stomps her foot and sort of squeals, "Leave!"

"Let's all be polite here." I give Betty a pointed look before Willa goes even further.

"Of course. Thank you so much for having me, *Bunny*." Willa winks before turning to Luke. "I'll see you back at home, buddy."

Home.

She says it so easily. Like it's true. That our home is her home. She also said she loves Luke, and I don't know what to make of that.

I should be more pissed at someone about something right now, but I'm altogether too busy trying to wrap my head around the firecracker in front of me.

"No! I want to go with you." I watch Luke's knuckles turn white where he grips at her clothes, practically clinging to her, tears still shimmering on his pudgy little cheeks.

I turn, squeezing one hand on Willa's slender shoulder while running the other over Luke's hair. I bend down and press a kiss to the crown of his head.

When I straighten, Willa's confident air has melted away. She has a pinched forehead, and her eyes are a little glassy. Her voice is hushed and cracks when she says, "That kid held him under water." Her blinks turn rapid. "I had to pull him out. And they all just laughed like it was a funny prank."

The papa bear in me roars at the story she's recounting. My protective side. The one I've been honing for decades. I slide my hand up to the side of her neck, rubbing a thumb over the pulse point there, as I hold her bright green gaze with my own. "Go. I'll meet you back at home. I got this."

Her head tilts ever so slightly into my touch. And then she nods.

I watch for a few beats as she departs with Luke leaned into her as if she's the most comforting thing in the world. I absently wonder how he'll handle her leaving when school starts back.

Poorly, probably.

I wonder how I'll handle her leaving next month.

Just as poorly I bet.

"That Willa character needs a leash," the mom sniffs from behind me.

My chest puffs up when I turn my attention on the bottle blonde across from me. "Betty, I like to think I'm a gentleman, but I'm only going to tell you once. Keep her name out of your mouth if you're going to use that tone. Let's talk about your kid instead."

One manicured hand falls across her chest, and she rears back, like she's totally scandalized.

Joke's on Betty.

I'm just getting started here.

Willa might drive me insane. She might deserve a

little pushback. But if Betty thinks she's going to be the one to push back at her, she's got another thing coming.

Willa might be a bit of a psycho—after all, she did just push a child into the pool—but the more time I spend with her, the more I feel like she's *my* psycho.

~

When I get home, the house is empty, which suits me fine because I walk to the kitchen, pull out my favorite bottle of bourbon, and take a deep swig before putting it back in the cupboard and propping my palms against the counter.

I'll find Willa and Luke after catching my breath and sorting my thoughts.

Head falling low, I try to shake off the mental image of Luke struggling under water.

I kept my conversation with Betty fairly contained. It's a small town, and there are only so many bridges you can burn. Everyone will talk about this anyway. Particularly with the way Willa went off.

I shake my head at the memory. The way she'd called her *Bunny* even after Betty corrected me. The girl has a real pair on her—I'll give her that. Especially after watching her on that filly this morning.

The sound of delighted giggles draws my attention out the open kitchen window toward the back hay field where the first cut bales are stacked. When I see a flash of copper hair, I know they must be out there.

Playing. Laughing. I let my eyes flutter shut and listen to them.

"Ready or not! Here I come!" Luke shouts breathlessly.

It's perfect.

I smile to myself and then open my eyes, knowing the only place I want to be right now is out in the field with them—even if I am dead on my feet after working all day and dealing with small-town-mom drama.

Within minutes, I'm stepping into the huge maze-like structure made of big round bales, the dark passageways between them almost too narrow for me to pass through.

"I can hear you giggling, you little goose."

"A goose?" he shouts.

"A silly goose!" she calls, voice back to the light singsong version I first noticed, all traces of the earlier anxiety gone.

I run into Luke first as he hunts Willa down with a serious expression on his face. He instantly holds a finger over his mouth, signaling me to be quiet, like he didn't just totally broadcast his location by calling out to her.

Crouching down, I pull him into a quick hug, needing to feel him—the beat of his heart, the little whoosh of his breath, his chubby cheek against my stubbled one.

"I love you, buddy," I rasp out, feeling emotional.

"I love you too, Dad." He pats my back. "But you're going to make me lose."

I chuckle. I'm sure Willa knows where he is. What he doesn't know is he's only going to catch her if she wants him to.

It seems crazy that I ever thought she wouldn't be able to keep him safe, and now she's done nothing but. Sure, his nannies and babysitters always watched him, but I don't know if they'd have gone to bat for him the way Willa did today.

The way I would have in that same situation.

"I'll go that way, see if we can track her down together. Divide and conquer."

He bobs his head. "Yeah. Yeah. That's a good plan."

I give his hair a quick muss, pressing one more kiss to his head before he turns and darts away. I know we need to talk about what happened today, but now's not the moment. I'm sure it will all come out when I lie down with him at bedtime.

I turn into the bales, heading in the opposite direction, the dry points of stray pieces scratching at my arms as I move in toward the center of the structure searching for Willa.

I hear the dull thump of small feet around me, Luke winding his way up and down the rows. Every sense feels elevated in here, the hay providing a sort of sound-proofing, a privacy. The walls of it press in around me. It smells comforting.

It smells like nostalgia. I'm taken back to days when Beau and I would chase Rhett and our little sister Violet through here. Same field and everything.

To my right, I see a flash. Daylight blocked out for a moment before it shines through again. I turn and follow, knowing I've got her now.

My strides lengthen as I veer right, catching sight of her creeping along carefully.

"Red," I whisper-shout.

Her head flips in my direction, her eyes twinkling. Because, if nothing else, Willa Grant is a shit disturber, waltzing into my life and complicating it without even trying. Looking all pleased with herself over it.

With a wink over her shoulder, she shoots off, running from me.

And something primal in me roars to life.

I chase her.

Luke is way over on the other side of the bales, and while I wouldn't say that I've forgotten about him, it's Willa who has my full attention right now.

I jog as best I can in the cramped space, my mind laser-focused. All I see is her, and all I hear is blood pumping in my ears.

She veers again, and I hear a small, gasped giggle when she glances over her shoulder and sees that I've gained on her.

One turn left has her heading in Luke's direction. And while I told him I was going to help him catch her, the truth is . . . I want her to myself for a moment.

I can't explain it. It's instinct.

My arm extends in front of me, and my fingers wrap around her delicate wrist, clamping down and yanking her back to me before she can cross paths with my kid and put a stop to this dangerous game of cat and mouse we seem to be playing.

Air whooshes out of her lungs as she stumbles back into me, shoulder blades thumping against my chest.

"Jesus Christ." She chuckles, not moving away from my body. In fact, she leans into me, glancing over her shoulder. "Relax, daddy. It's just a kid's game."

I turn, pulling her back in toward the center of the maze. "Running pretty hard for a woman playing a kid's game, Red."

She laughs, not taking me seriously—in typical fashion.

"And stop calling me that."

"Why?" she asks breathlessly as I turn a corner before pressing my back into the hay, giving her a tug that has her stumbling into my chest.

She catches herself by splaying one hand on my pec. We both look down, transfixed by where she's made contact. My shirt might as well not be there because it feels like she's touching my bare skin.

My cock twitches, clearly not differentiating at all.

"Because I don't like it," I bite out. The nickname makes me feel creepy.

That just makes her smirk. "But I'm pretty sure you're about to scold me like one."

My brow furrows as I raise my chin to get lost in her emerald eyes. "Scold you?"

Her eyes roll. "Look, I know I shouldn't have

knocked that kid into the water, but I was really mad. He was just so *mean*. And not accidentally. I got picked on like that as a kid and it was always my brother who stepped in and saved me. But Luke doesn't have a big brother to kick someone's ass for him, and I just . . . snapped."

I soak in the woman before me, a fucking knockout. "Why did *you* get picked on?"

"I'll show you pictures sometime. Taller and skinnier than everyone. Big buck teeth. Crazy red hair. Can I blame assaulting a seven-year-old on my hair color? I've always flown off the handle kind of easily. Or like"—her lips roll together—"I don't get mad easy, but when I do it's really, really bad. And Bunny sucks. Eye-fucking you like that at a child's party."

I blink at her, frantically explaining herself like she's in trouble with me when she's not. The only people in trouble are the assholes who picked on her. I don't care if it's been a decade. I want names and addresses so I can set them straight.

She carries on, oblivious to the way I'm looking at her and the hard-on growing in my pants. Oblivious to the way her fingers absently stroke my chest.

"I know there's this whole weird, small-town vibe happening where everyone knows everyone else's busi-ness. And that bottle-blonde bitch was spitting mad. I imagine I'd be mad if I found out my kid was a raging loser too. But I don't really care what she thinks of me, you know? So if you need to blame it on me to save face as the town's grumpy prince, that's fine. I won't hold it against you."

I just stare at her. She must think I'm a real dick if she's assuming I wouldn't come to her defense on this.

Her tongue darts out over her lips, wetting the full bottom one and making it shimmer in a way that I can't peel my eyes away from.

"God. Why do you have to wear a backward cap too?" Her voice is softer now. Raspier. Breathier.

I swear she's leaning closer.

"What?" She's a confusing woman, talking a mile a minute. We've gone from a scolding to teenaged trauma to small-town drama to my hat in under a minute.

She really is kind of insane.

"The cowboy hat." She groans and lets her eyes roll back in her head. "Is so good. I mean, I feel like I'm living in some made-for-TV movie with a hot cowboy. But then you clean up and style your hair, and you give these hot, debonair older-man vibes."

I'm so confused.

"Sorry?"

Her fingers curl into the fabric of my shirt, and I feel the scrape of her nails against my chest. I love the way it looks; her pale skin gripping at the black fabric. I imagine lying her down in my bed, getting lost between her pretty milky thighs, and making her come so hard that her fingers curl in the same way.

"But then, you go and turn a cap backward and give me the full rough-around-the-edges country-boy experience. Do you know how hot that is? I can't even explain it." She laughs lightly, like she didn't just say something that broadsided me. "Hat forward. Cute." Her free hand mimics grabbing the brim of a cap and turning it backward. "Hat backward? Game *on*. It's like a switch."

I shake my head at her, watching the blush in her cheeks, the fire in her eyes. The trace of shyness on her face.

"Well, that was altogether too much information. The backward cap is melting my brain cells. Gotta go!" She startles me when she pushes away and runs down the compressed path. I hear Luke's voice taunting her, but he sounds far-off still. Her strides cover the ground but not the way mine do. The urge to chase her and hold her down consumes me. It has me feeling wild and untethered.

Which is why with one sharp turn, I capture her arm at her elbow and push her against the prickly hay. Pressing her into it firmly, my hips lined up with hers. My hard cock against her flat stomach.

"Game on?" I rasp out, as all my reservations about touching the nanny fly out the goddamn window. I don't need them—definitely don't want them. Not with the way she's staring at me right now, eyes fixed on my lips while I grip her elbow and prop another hand against the wall of hay behind her.

Her lip is still wet when she whispers, "Game on."

I want to shove her back and devour her—leave her struggling to breathe—but I hold that side of myself back.

Because more than that, I want to thank her.

I want to thank her in a way that my words won't let me, so rather than mauling her like a teenager, I take a ragged breath and let myself drink her in for a moment. The pert tip of her nose. The thick fringe of her lashes. The heartbeat in her temple, just in front of where that beautiful copper hair starts.

I release her arm and trail my knuckles over her skin, starting at her shoulder, slowly dragging them down to her wrist. I'm fascinated by the spray of goose bumps that crop up in the wake of my touch.

My fingers slide between hers, her palm fitting so perfectly in mine.

"I don't know this game," she whispers, and I drop my hand from above her head, pressing into her body with the full length of mine. My free hand slides into her hair, and I watch as I slowly comb through the strands, the burnished tone of it matching my tanned skin so well.

"Me neither, Red." My eyes stay glued to her hair. Truthfully, I don't know what the fuck I'm doing. All I know is that I want to savor this.

Savor her.

Because I have a sinking feeling that when we step out of these bales, things will look a lot different. The dusty, grassy smell will drift away, and reality will seep back in.

The reality where I know better than to go after a girl like Willa Grant.

A reality where I'm still too fucking wounded to trust someone.

"Are you gonna make a move, Eaton? Or just stand here petting me?"

My head shakes and my chest rumbles as I chance a look at her eyes. Clear and certain, so bright.

I feel safe when I'm scowling, but it's getting harder and harder to look at Willa Grant without smiling.

It's with a smile on my lips that I lean in and press my mouth to hers. She's soft and willing. She parts for me with such ease. Welcomes the kiss.

Takes me.

When I groan, she whimpers into my mouth, and I swallow her sweet little sounds. Wanting to keep them for myself, memorize them for a rainy day.

It's been years since I've been touched like this, and my chest cracks open at the feel. The contact. The closeness. The intimacy. Hands sliding up over my chest, pressing up over my neck before gripping either side of my skull. Dainty fingertips behind my ears.

I didn't even realize how badly I missed the attention of a woman. And not just any woman. The woman I've glued my attention to from the moment I saw her.

The woman who's thawed my icy heart in a matter of weeks.

Heartless. That's what Talia called me in her letter. And I believed her.

I still do.

But it's hard to deny the feeling in my chest right now. The ache. The heat.

It's especially hard to deny the bulge in my pants. The one I'm grinding against Willa.

That part does have me feeling like a teenager.

She moans, hiking a leg up at my waist, opening herself to rub back against me, and I take that opportunity to swipe my tongue into her mouth, to shape my fingers into a fist in her hair.

To go with the intensity of the moment, even though I thought I could keep it sweet and slow. That's the thing about Willa. She doesn't strike me as the sweet and slow type of girl.

Every time I draw away, she pushes harder. Every time I glare at her, she prods, hoping for a reaction. And now she's getting it.

"Willa—"

"Don't stop." Our teeth clash as she talks against my mouth. What started off reverently is quickly turning frantic. A well-crafted facade coming apart at every seam.

I take a handful of her round ass, squeezing hard, before picking her right up and pulling her toned legs around me so I can rut into the denim covering her pussy like the sex-starved caveman I am.

"Yes," she hisses when my fingers trail over the torn hem of her shorts.

She smells like oranges and warm grass, refreshing and comforting all at once. She feels like heaven in my hands. And she looks just as wild as I've always known she is.

But there's something about seeing her wild for *me*—giving in for *me*—that makes me feel more desired than I have in, well, ever.

"Don't stop." Her hips swivel against mine as my fingers inch dangerously close to where I might find out if she's actually wearing panties.

I imagine inspecting her every morning. Bending her over the kitchen counter. Flipping up some flimsy sun dress that's just her silent way of begging me to fuck her.

"You're desperate for it, aren't you?" I husk against her ear, lost in the daydream.

My tongue glides against hers, gently probing her mouth. The same way I'd slide a finger into her slick pussy.

She whimpers the way she would when I add a second finger. And then a third.

"Fuck," she hums against my lips, because my hands are moving of their own fruition, fisting her hair and plumping one full breast.

It's all too real. Too much.

Too fucking easy to imagine.

By the time I realize how far down into this fantasy I've disappeared, I'm throbbing in my pants. Leaking in my pants.

Like a teenager.

Heat shoots through my groin, and I bite back any

sign of what just happened. Willa is clueless, still soft and desperate in my hands.

And clearly more than I can handle, which is why I step away panting. Needing some space. Needing to hide from my skyrocketing levels of intense humiliation.

"I'm sorry. I shouldn't have done that," is what I come up with. A douchebag thing to say, no doubt. But it's all too much in this moment.

I need my solitude, and I need to get away from Willa. Because staring at her all mussed, lips all puffy and pink, matching the stain on her cheeks while her full chest heaves and her eyes go glassy and wide, has me hardening again.

I turn and stride away, hoping to get a grasp on my dignity somewhere between the hay bales and the back door of my house.

Yeah, I run.

Like a fucking teenager.

15

Willa

Summer: Come for dinner tonight. Bring the boys!

Willa: I can promise Luke and I will be there.

Summer: What about Cade?

Willa: Who knows?

Summer: Trouble in paradise? Did you bang him?

Willa: I wish. He barely even looks at me.

Summer: Flash him.

Willa: I've tried. He's too mature. He just rolls his eyes and walks away.

Summer: Wait. Did you really flash him?

"Why do you keep looking over there?"

"Over where?" I reply, really sucking at playing stupid.

"At the guys?" Summer's big brown eyes are scanning my face like I'm a barcode that she can easily read. Bitch doesn't miss a beat.

"Just keeping track of the bocce score. Making sure no one cheats."

We're at Summer and Rhett's house after another family dinner. Apparently, Harvey is driving across the country with Beau back to wherever he deploys from—according to Cade, this is something their dad does every time.

I don't know Beau well, but I can't imagine packing Luke up to go do what he does over and over again.

"Bulllllllllshit." Summer cackles and leans back in her chair, sipping daintily at her glass of white wine with the golden sun shining behind her.

Nothing gets past her. She knows damn well I'm sitting here checking out Cade like it's my last moment on earth. Ever since that goddamn kiss, things have been *weird* between us. And not the typical grumpy-dick-mode weird.

"We kissed and now everything is weird," I blurt. Summer and I have always told each other our deepest, darkest secrets.

"You kissed!"

"Sum! Shh. If you announce it like that, the entire

town will know, and they already hate me. Last thing I need is the bitch brigade to think I'm waltzing in here stealing the town's most eligible bachelor."

"Hm." When I peek at her, she's nodding thoughtfully, bare feet propped against another chair. "Figures."

I roll my eyes and take a large swig of my wine. "That's all? I'm always full of good advice for you, and I get a thoughtful hum and snarky one word shot?"

"I'm thinking."

"Think faster."

She chuckles and rolls her head along the back of her chair toward me. "Weird how?"

I sigh and stare out over the expansive backyard at the big willow tree that Luke and I first hung out under. Rhett, Cade, Jasper, and Luke are out there playing bocce, throwing around balls and tossing back beers.

"Well, first he started off crabby, then he started coming around a bit. And I mean, okay, there was some sexual tension—but it was friendly enough. We talked at dinner or in the hot tub."

One of Summer's dark eyebrows arches in my direction. "Hot tub? What is this, high school? Has anyone told you that you can get pregnant in there?"

"Shut up. But now he talks in grunts. The only way we converse is via text message or the Post-it notes he leaves around the house."

"He leaves you Post-it notes?" Her lips pop open in surprise.

I shrug. "Yeah. He'll walk in when Luke and I are

cleaning up after making a batch of cookies and say nothing about it. Just talk to Luke. But then in the morning he'll leave a note by the coffee that says, *Best cookies I've ever had.*"

Summer laughs.

"Summer! Stop laughing and help me. What does that mean?"

Her head tips back, and I catch the guys glancing up at us. "It means he loves your cookies, Wils."

I snort. "Of course. My cookies bring all the boys to the yard."

Summer laughs harder, her wine sloshing in her glass as she does. "He did it all for the cookie," she wheezes.

"Good lord. Can we please stop quoting awful songs and talk about my actual problem?"

She wipes at the tears on her cheeks as she straightens. "Okay. *Okay.* I'm honestly still just trying to wrap my head around this. Did you kiss him? I know you're forward. Did you freak him out? He's very . . . stern?"

"Way to take his side!"

Her eyes roll. "There are no sides. Tell me more about the notes."

I sniffle and shoot her a dirty look. "Sure feels like it. Oooh. Poor innocent Cade who pushed me up against a hay bale and kissed me stupid."

Summer rolls a hand, urging me to get over it and tell her more.

"Things like, *Luke told me about his guitar lesson*

185

today. Thank you. Or, *Please don't paint the front porch.* I don't know how to take that though."

"You painted the front porch?"

I scoff. Cade is such a stick in the mud sometimes. "We used paint to add details to the banisters. It looks cute. You'd swear I painted his front step Barbie pink or something."

She eyes me like we both know I should have said no to Luke's idea. But whatever. We can paint it over. It's not like we killed someone or threw heads of lettuce out of my car.

"Basically, he comes home and we silently cook together. We eat dinner, and he mostly talks to Luke, avoids looking at me, says, *Thanks,* and then gets to work putting Luke to bed. I assume he's exhausted after that and passes out. Truthfully, I don't know how he does it. It's way too much for one person to handle all on their own. But if I cook dinner, he gets all crabby. If I clean, he gets crabby. Oh! When he told me to stop doing laundry the other day, he said that I'm *just* the nanny, not the maid. So who the hell knows? Then he left me a note on the dryer that said, *Thank you for your help.*"

"It's really kind of sweet. Like . . . for Cade?"

"Ugh. Is it though? *He* kissed *me* and then pulled away and said he shouldn't have done that. He *apologized.* I'm trying not to be offended."

"Have you tried *talking* to him?"

I blink at her. "Talking?"

"Yes. You know . . . where you use your mouth to

create words that describe what's going through your head."

"Sounds weird. Sounds *awkward*. Don't like it. Not approved by me."

She gives me a disapproving look. I imagine it's one she'll use on her future children.

"Why can't we just have sex for the next little bit and then high-five each other at the end?"

"And spend the rest of your lives running into each other because of me and Rhett?"

I turn my nose up. "We're adults. I'm head over heels for Luke. Do you know how cool that kid is? It'll be fine."

Summer stares wistfully out over the field, spinning the engagement ring on her finger. "Adults who won't talk to each other."

She says it kindly enough but I know it's a dig. And I know she's right. I know I fly by the seat of my pants with little regard for where I'm going. Planning stresses me out.

That's why *go with the flow* is my motto.

Too many ways to fail. Too many ways to fall short. And in a family of wildly successful people, I'd rather be the flighty wildcard than the failure.

"You coming to the rodeo next weekend?" I change the subject entirely, actively sidestepping the thoughts bubbling up inside me.

She nods. "Of course. You?"

"Yeah. I told Cade I'd take care of Luke that day. We'll go watch him."

"Working the weekends, huh?"

I shrug. "Spending time with Luke doesn't really feel like work."

In fact, it feels like the most natural thing in the world.

⟶

I should have known when Luke asked, "What does it feel like when you get carsick?" that something was wrong.

Instead, I kept bobbing my head to my favorite Broken Bells song and said, "Just like nauseous, buddy."

We had a fun day at the spray park in town—our new go-to spot on hot days. He gets to see a bunch of friends from school, and I get to mean mug the psychopath birthday boy and his mom who will forever live on in my head as Bunny.

They stay away, looking at me like I'm an escaped convict, which works just fine for me.

I even spend time together with a couple of moms that I actually like. Ones with nice kids and good senses of humor. I feel relieved that not all the moms in this town are Bunnies.

But I'm not feeling relieved anymore.

Because Luke just sprayed vomit all over the back of my passenger's side seat.

I pull over on the country road. We're only five minutes from the ranch. So close, and yet so far away.

After running around the front of the Jeep, I whip the back passenger's side door open and take in the barf-covered boy before me.

"You okay, little man?"

His eyes are wide and watery. "I'm so sorry, Willa."

"Oh, sweet boy. Don't be sorry."

"I barfed in your car."

"It doesn't matter." I reach forward and run a hand through his wet hair.

"It's a mess!" He's crying now and I want to hug him, but we all have our limits. I've handled my fair share of vomit as a bartender, but hugging a barf-covered child is where I draw the line.

Instead, I unbuckle him, whip his shirt off, and *then* squeeze him to me. Sobs rack his little body.

"I-I'm s-s-so sorry!" He's wailing now.

"Shh. Luke. Luke. It's just a car. It doesn't matter. You're what matters. I don't care about the car, babe. I'm more worried about you." I pull away, looking at him, trying hard not to glance down. Because I *know* there is barf on me. The last thing I need to do is start heaving too.

He nods tearfully at me. "Willa?"

"Yeah?"

"You have throw up on you. I can still see a strawberry."

I pop my lips open and opt to mouth breathe so I stop smelling it, focusing on his wide blue eyes. *I'm an adult, I'm an adult, I'm an adult.* "That's okay. Everything can be washed. I'm going to buckle you in and drive the rest of the way. If you feel like you need to barf again, just tell me and I'll pull over for you. Got it?"

He nods, looking determined.

And God bless his determination because we stop twice more on the way back to the ranch.

The first thing we do is strip down outside. At least all pieces of barfy clothes. Which for him is everything, and for me is just my tank top over my bikini.

The shower proves a challenge because he can't stop retching.

I've never felt more helpless. I've never felt teary watching someone get sick—usually I'm just annoyed—but watching his little body heave so violently has the back of my throat aching and my eyes watering.

He's finally clean, seems relatively empty, and just looks totally exhausted standing in the middle of his room.

"When will my dad be home?"

I check my watch. "In about an hour. I'm going to call him and get our clothes in the wash. Take a quick shower. How about you lie down?"

He nods, standing in front of me, like he doesn't quite know what to do with himself. "I want to sleep in my dad's bed."

"Yeah, of course." I know he often sleeps there on the weekends, but weekdays are tough because Cade wakes up so early. We'll figure it out later. "Let's go." I hold my hand out to Luke, but he just nods again, clearly out of it.

I touch his forehead and it feels hot. But maybe that's from the shower? Fuck, I don't know. I'd ask Harvey for help, but he isn't back yet. Rhett is on the road. Summer is at work.

I opt to scoop Luke up, propping his chin on my shoulder. His little arms wrap around my neck and my arms fold under his legs so that I'm carrying him like a koala.

He sighs when I press a kiss to his hair without even thinking. I don't know what's appropriate anymore. I know he's not my kid, but he feels like mine in some little way. He feels like mine enough to comfort him when he's sick.

I carry him down the hall, trying not to stress at how heavy he feels in my arms. He's just tired. He has a tummy bug. Kids get sick. He's not on his deathbed—or at least that's what I keep telling myself.

I nudge Cade's door open with my foot and take in his room. The door is always closed, and I feel like I'm invading his privacy, but I'm also insanely curious. Like the rest of the house, his room is warm and airy, a total contrast to the main house where his dad lives. The walls are a creamy yellow, framed by big crown moldings painted a high-gloss white. The oak bed frame is stained a yellowish tone, and in most cases I would say it's dated —but something about it works in here. Topped with a cream and navy plaid duvet set, the space is still masculine without being dark.

It's honestly not what I was expecting.

Once I gently slide Luke onto the king-sized bed, I peel back the duvet and tuck him in. He's already half-asleep, but he groans when I fold the blanket in tight around him.

Peeking over my shoulder, I see the door to a small en suite bathroom. With a few steps over, I push it open, deciding this setup is ideal.

The bathroom is tight quarters, just a toilet and a sink and vanity. It's clean, and it smells like Cade's signature pine smell mixed with something spicy and sweet.

I momentarily wonder if it would be weird to just hang out in here for a few minutes.

A small whimper from the bed draws me from my thoughts. I flip the toilet seat up—marveling at a man existing who puts it down in the first place—and head back out.

Bending over a slightly delirious Luke, I whisper, "If you feel sick, you just go straight into your dad's bathroom, okay?"

He offers me a small nod without opening his eyes, and I run a hand over his forehead. Still hot.

"I'll be here if you need anything." Then I press another kiss to his feverish temple and pad softly out of the room, already reaching for my phone and dialing as soon as I'm in the hallway.

"Red." Cade's voice has a bite to it today. I'm sure some people would flinch, but I just roll my eyes. "Now isn't a great time."

"Okay, it's just that—"

"If this is about your panties, save it for your morning text."

Dick.

"Luke is sick, so get your head out of your ass and talk to me for once."

"Is he okay?" His tone changes instantly.

"He threw up on our way back from a day at the spray pad in town. And then he threw up a lot more. He's clean. He wanted to go in your bed, so he's sleeping there. It's close to a toilet, so that's a bonus. But I know you wake up early for work, so I'm sorry about that too. I'm worried he's too hot. Do you have a thermometer? What do I do? Do I make him drink something? I'm really worried I'm fucking this up. Also, I kissed him on the forehead and I'm feeling like I need to tell you that because I don't know if that's okay. I know he's not my kid, but he just seemed like he needed comforting and—"

"Willa," his voice is soft now.

"Yeah?"

"Take a deep breath."

"I don't want to. There's barf on me and it smells terrible." My voice cracks and I don't know why. It's like getting everything out of my brain and sharing it with Cade has me all up in my feels.

"Everything is okay." Who knew such a simple sentence could put me at ease so instantly. "He always spikes a solid fever when he gets sick. You're doing great. We're lucky to have you here helping us. Luke loves you. You'll never catch flack from me for comforting him."

"Okay." The words come out watery and I blink hard, trying to regain my composure.

"Here's what you're going to do. Are you listening?"

"Yes." I sigh, already feeling relieved at having Cade take control of the situation. He's so sturdy—there's a dependability about him that I love. He's practical. He works hard. He's decisive.

It's a relief to have him on the other end of my phone.

"You're going to go take a shower before you do anything else." Under different circumstances, the prospect of Cade ordering me to shower would excite me. "Then you're going to go into the hall closet. There's a digital thermometer in there so you don't even need to wake him to check his temperature. Just aim it at his forehead. There is also children's Tylenol in there. It might be hard to keep down, so you can always use the syringe and just give him a little when he wakes up and see what happens. Water or ginger ale—small sips."

"What do you mean when he wakes up? Aren't you coming home soon?"

I swear he growls. "We've got a fence down by the highway and are rounding up cows. I'm going to be late. Any other day I'd already be on my way, but I can't leave them out by the road."

"What if I mess this up? Luke isn't a martini I can just toss out and try again with."

The deep rumble of Cade's laugh filters through the receiver.

"You are not laughing at me right now!"

"Willa. You will not mess it up. You need to believe in yourself. You're smart. You're capable. You're determined. I know you are because you made me like you when I swore I never would."

"Is that supposed to be a compliment?"

"You got this. I'll be late, but I have total faith in you."

"Well then, you're stupider than you look," I mutter.

"That supposed to be a compliment, Red?" is all he says before I sigh and hang up.

16

Cade

Cade: How you holding up, Red?

Willa: Got some Tylenol down.

Cade: Good. But how are YOU?

Willa: Tired. But okay.

Cade: Did you shower?

Willa: Yeah . . .

Cade: Good. Go to bed. You don't need to worry. I'll be there soon.

B y the time I pull up to the house, the sun has set behind the Rockies. I can hear crickets, and there are a few lights on in the house.

I'm in a foul mood. The cows I can handle. It's the cowboys that piss me off—sometimes I think I'd be more efficient running the ranch entirely on my own. I wouldn't have time for a kid or family, but at least I wouldn't have to listen to a bunch of yahoos wax poetic about my hot nanny.

I told Bucky that if he kept wagging his jaw, I'd break it.

Assholes just laughed and shifted to making fun of me for having a crush on her. *Cade and the nanny sitting in a tree.*

Assholes.

I told them they were all fired, and they just laughed more.

Closing my truck door as gently as possible to keep from waking them up, I head toward the front door, wishing away my agitation. My worry. My confusion. I don't want to step into this house as anything other than what they need.

I'm halfway expecting Willa to be up when I step inside. That wobble in her voice on the phone has haunted me all night. It boggles my mind that a self-possessed woman like her can doubt herself so thoroughly.

She's all swagger and confidence ninety-nine percent of the time. But now and then, I get this flash of insecurity. It leaves me shaking my head.

After toeing my boots off, I walk through the house on socked feet, desperate for a shower, but more desperate to check on my son.

Willa too.

I head to my bedroom first, absently wondering if it will be weird if I pop my head into her room to check on her.

But those thoughts come to a screeching halt when I step into my darkened room and see copper hair floating across *my* pillows. The light from the hallway illuminates her creamy, pale arm wrapped around Luke's tiny body.

My heart seizes in my chest. Stops right in its fucking tracks. And I can't look away. I let myself stare, shoulder propped against the doorframe, arms crossed against my chest—my only armor against the intense feelings the sight of Willa snuggling my son stirs up in me.

I soak them in.

I think about her saying she loves him.

I think about the moment he reaches for her hand, the way he looks up at her—just a little uncertain that she'll want his hand in hers.

I think about the curve of his lips and the way his tiny shoulders drop on a sigh when she effortlessly wraps her fingers around his, like it's the most natural thing in the world.

I stand here and think way too damn much as I stare at them curled into each other. I let myself imagine things that I have no business imagining. Things I'm not sure I could ever live up to.

With a shake of my head, I tiptoe into the room, hovering over them carefully as I reach out and lay the back of my hand over Luke's forehead.

Blissfully cool, which means either the fever broke, or she managed to get enough medicine into him.

I sigh shakily and just before I straighten, her eyes flutter open.

"Hi." Willa's voice is soft and sleepy.

"Hi," I whisper, and I can hear the smile in my voice.

"Oh God. I'm sorry. He wanted me to lie with him. He got sick again. He got sick . . . a lot." Her head turns as she takes in her surroundings. "I didn't mean to fall asleep in your bed."

I like you in my bed.

It's on the tip of my tongue, but I bite it back, opting for, "It's okay." I reach out and run a hand over her silky hair, gently pressing her head onto the pillow. "Just go back to sleep." Luke is crashed out on top of her arm anyway.

"Where will you sleep?" She blinks groggily.

"In Luke's room." I should take my hand off her, but I stroke her hair.

Soothing her or myself? Of that, I'm not entirely sure.

"I'm sorry."

"Don't be. Thank you. You were a godsend today."

"That's overkill, Eaton," she mumbles, nuzzling her head into my pillow to hide from the compliment.

I wonder if she can smell me there.

Thumbing some of her hair, I push it back behind her ear, letting my fingers trail over the line of her jaw.

"You need to learn how to take a compliment, Red. A simple thank-you is all it requires."

"Oka—"

I press my thumb against her lips, entranced by how supple they feel under my touch. "Red. Just take the thank-you. Now shut up and go back to sleep."

Her lips press together and she gives a firm nod. The motion makes Luke stir, but rather than waking up, he turns over and nuzzles into her chest, small hand splayed on her arm.

I watch Willa blink down at him, like she's still trying to wrap her mind around where she is and what she's doing. And when she looks up at me, uncertainty painted all over her pretty face, all I can do is smile.

Willa Grant looks way too good in my bed.

~

"I think I watched a porno like this once."

My head snaps up from where I'm scrubbing the upholstery in the back of Willa's Jeep. "Pardon me?" I pop around the open door and take her in, sitting on the top step of my front porch, wearing black leggings and a black tank top.

She looks good.

There is not a single place in this house this woman doesn't look good.

I can see the outline of her nipple piercings, but more than anything, I'm entranced by the way her pale skin contrasts against the dark fabric of her clothes. The way her fiery hair seems even brighter.

"The grumpy mechanic guy with bulging muscles. A girl who can't pay her bill. A tale as old as time."

"The shit that comes out of your mouth sometimes." I dry my hands on a piece of torn towel. It's a pale pink. Like Willa's lips.

"It's the backward hat." She points at me with a light chuckle. "You flipped the switch."

"Have you ever been told that you use humor to cover up being uncomfortable?"

"Oh, yeah. All the time." She smiles, and I shake my head at her in wonder. "My mom's a therapist, remember?"

"I told you that you didn't need to clean my house or do laundry."

Her head quirks, the morning sun glinting off her smooth skin. "Have you ever been told you're terribly particular?"

"Willa." My arms cross.

"Cade." She mirrors my motion with her arms. Except it creates a shelf beneath her full tits and I lose my focus. The scowl melts off my face. "I wasn't about to hang out in a house with barf laundry just sitting around. That's plain gross."

"You cleaned the bathroom."

"There was barf there too."

"The floors?"

She grimaces. "Barf."

"Jesus." I take my hands over my hat, pressing down at the brim over the back of my neck. When I peek up, I don't miss the way Willa is eyeing my arms.

There's a part of me that gets off on it. But there's another part of me—the adult part with all the baggage—that knows I need to put a stop to whatever this tension is between us.

Probably not kissing her and grinding into her until I blew in my pants would have been a great start.

Or not making her sit on the edge of my hot tub so I could eye fuck the way her bathing suit violated her.

"I don't mind. It's"—her hand waves around in front of her—"whatever. I felt bad for Luke. You work hard all day. You didn't need to walk into a barf-covered house."

"You're not a maid, Willa."

Her lips quirk up and her eyes narrow. I've noticed this look. It comes right before she says something inappropriate. "I was a sexy one for Halloween one year."

I scowl at her. Internally I'm scowling at myself because my first two thoughts were:

1. Does she still have that costume?

2. How do I track down and kill every guy who saw her wearing it?

She snickers and I ignore her. It's what's best for both of us. "You cleaned my entire house but left your own vehicle saturated with vomit?"

Her head wobbles from side to side. "Well, yeah. It seemed like a problem for another day. I'm going to get it detailed. It's not a big deal, so you can stop reenacting that porno anytime now."

"I'm almost done, Willa. It seems like the least I can do for you," I grumble, ducking back into the Jeep, needing to stop staring at her and seeing her lips part on the word *porno*.

"Cade, stop. It's seven a.m. and you were home late. What time were you up? Don't you have work?"

"I don't sleep in, Red. And I'm taking the day off to take care of you guys."

She doesn't respond. I hear the front door shut and let out a sigh, relieved she walked away. I get lost in shampooing the seat, watching the bubbles form and turn into a white foam.

It's a pleasant escape. Manual labor has a peculiar way of stilling my mind, easing my worries—keeping me on track and focused on the things that matter.

I'm lost in thoughts of things that matter when I feel a soft hand press against the center of my back.

I squeeze my eyes shut—hard—because I know who I'm about to face and I need to play it cool.

But when I turn to Willa, I feel the pads of her fingers trail along my ribs. And then she's standing before me, holding a steaming mug of fresh coffee. Wide green eyes look up at me—a hint of confusion in them. So many questions. And a softness that I want to pull out and wrap myself in.

She holds the cup out to me. "Here. Seems like the least I could do."

And I realize that taking a moment with my eyes closed to give myself an internal pep talk will not keep me away from Willa Grant at all.

I need to try harder because she's quickly becoming one of those things that matter to me. And I'm not sure I can handle more responsibility.

17

Willa

Luke has managed to keep water, ginger ale, and some soda crackers down over the course of the day. He's also snuggled the hell out of me on the couch, and I am living for it.

At first, I wasn't sure. Because with Cade around, I felt he should be the one soaking up the cuddles. But he's kept himself busy, and I've caught the occasional soft look he's given us on the couch.

Luke's propped against the end with his legs slung over my lap as he leans into my shoulder. He's been twiddling my hair in his pudgy fingers for a while now— reminds me of his dad.

We're watching some cartoon, and I wish I could say what it was about, but I'm altogether too aware of Cade puttering around the house. Cleaning. Fixing stuff.

He literally washed the baseboards.

I've never known a man to be so tidy. But he's also

driving me insane. Sitting around while he works makes me twitchy.

When he pulls all the food out of the fridge to wipe things down, I break.

"Cade, you're giving me a headache. Please come sit and watch some silly, mind-numbing cartoon with us."

"Hey!" Luke pouts up at me like I've just insulted some sort of Oscar-worthy performance rather than something that only holds children's attention because it's bright and flashes non-stop. It's the music that kills me. It's *so* bad.

"You saying my mind could use a little numbing, Red?" Cade grumps from the kitchen without even glancing up at me.

"Yes. You're giving me anxiety."

"I'll cook you something. You're always less peppy when you're full."

I snort. "Dick."

The sizzle of something in a pan hits me first.

Then the smell of butter.

Then the feel of Luke's weight against my stomach.

I breathe through my nose, trying to focus on the terrible TV show. How cute Luke is. How hot Cade is.

Anything to rid myself of this growing sense of nausea.

It's when Luke leans close and puts one clammy hand on my cheek that things go south.

"Willa, you have the prettiest hair," he murmurs

sweetly. But his breath is all crackers and ginger ale and damp heat and I can't stay here anymore.

I clamp my lips together and start fumbling with prying his legs off me. "Thank you, baby. But I need out."

His brow furrows. He looks mildly offended, but not as offended as he'll be if I barf on him. I catch a flash of Cade's concerned face as I literally jog down the hall toward the bathroom. The seat makes a loud clanking noise as I flick it open and empty myself with *the most* unladylike roaring noise.

When the urge ends, I flush and peer up to find Cade and Luke standing in the doorway watching me. As if hearing me barf wasn't bad enough, the two boys are standing there staring like they've never seen a person get sick.

"At least you got yours in the toilet," Luke says with an earnest look on his face.

I can't help but laugh as I look back into the bowl, the sound of my chuckle echoing against the porcelain.

"Luke, go back to the couch."

I see his small form departing from the corner of my eye, but Cade doesn't move, still standing in the doorway. He's staring at his toes and the brass room divider where the hardwood floors swap to tiles.

"You going to stand here and watch?"

"I'm sorry," he mumbles without glancing up.

"For watching me barf? You should be. I don't know how I'll look you in the eye anymore."

He scoffs. "That you're sick."

"Well, it's not like you did this to me."

His head raises slowly. "No, but you were here taking care of Luke. You stayed with him all night. You helped him, and now you're paying for it."

I hum at that, reaching for a piece of toilet paper to wipe my mouth, because if Cade Eaton sees me with barf on my face, I will dive headfirst into this toilet bowl and flush myself down it. With a small shrug, I glance over at the man standing in the doorway—tall and broad and imposing, with the sweetest expression of concern on his face.

"He's worth it," I say, with a watery smile.

Sadly, smiling makes me feel nauseous again and within seconds, I'm frantically waving a hand at Cade, hoping he'll just leave me to be sick alone.

He does.

But only briefly.

He's back with some sort of war kit, and I watch him place things on the counter. Thermometer, Tylenol, water, ginger ale and . . . one of his T-shirts?

"What are you doing?" I grumble as I wipe at my watery eyes, no doubt smudged with mascara.

"Taking care of you," he replies without even looking my way. His tone says that I just asked him a stupid question.

"That's fine. I can take care of myself."

"I know you can, but you don't have to because I'm here to help." He says it so matter-of-factly. Like doing this for someone is the most obvious thing in the world. And I wonder if, for him, maybe it is.

He stepped in to take care of his siblings in the wake of tragedy. He stepped up to be a single parent to his son.

Barfing babysitter? That's a perfect job for him too.

At his core, Cade is a caretaker. Selfless. With such a big heart I almost can't wrap my head around it.

He turns now, lips tipped down and brow furrowed. I've started thinking of this expression as *resting scowl face*—it's just his default.

I startle when he holds the thermometer gun to my forehead where I'm kneeling on the floor.

"I'm just taking your temperature." His face softens.

"I know." I push my hair off my face. "It still feels like a weapon to me."

He clicks the button. When it beeps, he frowns. "101.4—it's red." He turns to show it to me, like I don't trust his ability to read or something.

"Okay."

"Did it come out of nowhere?"

I shrug. "You're neurotic cleaning really was giving me a headache. And then it was Luke's weight on my stomach and the smell of his cracker breath."

A deep rumble rolls around in his chest. "Well, if Luke is anything to go by, it seems short lived. The bad news is—"

"I'm going to be barfing my brains out for the next several hours?" I ask.

His head tilts as he swipes the T-shirt off the counter

beside him, takes one step toward me, and crouches down to look me in the eye.

Really look me in the eye. In a way that makes me realize he's been avoiding my gaze or turning away when I meet his. But not right now. Right now, it's all dark chocolate and warm caramel streaking across multi-faceted irises. I note the fine lines beside his eyes. On anyone else, they'd be laugh lines, but on Cade they lend to his rugged sex appeal.

He smiles, making them crinkle even further. "No, Red. The bad news is that you have some barf on your shirt."

I close my eyes and groan. "This is my go-to style these past twenty-four hours."

"It's okay." His voice is like velvet dragging across my skin. "No one has ever looked better than you do with barf on their shirt."

Popping one eye open, I regard him warily. "Are you hitting on the barfy girl, Eaton?"

He grins and reaches forward, fingers stretching for the hem of my shirt. "Let me help you, Red," he says quietly.

There's nothing sexual about the way Cade takes my shirt in his fingers, but it doesn't stop my pulse from racing or my breath from quickening as he peels my shirt up, exposing my bare stomach and plain sports bra.

He's such a gentleman, he doesn't even glance down. He keeps his eyes on my face, even after I lift my arms and let him pull the shirt over my head. I will the nausea away, hoping upon hope I can hold it together.

But even the beautiful man in front of me can't distract from the feeling at the back of my throat, the smell of my shirt as he moves it away.

"Sorry," I groan before I turn back to the toilet, gripping the shiny edges as another wave of sickness hits me.

It racks my body and I moan, which is right when I feel Cade's calloused fingertips at my neck, gently lifting my hair away from my face. I spend the next minute of my life hugging the toilet while Cade fists my hair and smooths gentle circles on my back.

I've imagined Cade taking my hair in his fist—but not like this. This is humiliating in a way I'll never recover from. The magic is straight *gone*.

When the urge subsides, I quickly flush again, wiping my face before turning back to the sexy-as-sin man who just held my hair and rubbed my back while I emptied my stomach.

He continues caressing my back and, like the saint he is, doesn't even look horrified by me. "It's okay, Red. I got you."

I got you.

There's something about being sick that turns me into a child again. Helpless and pitiful. And the fact Cade is here and not annoyed is the biggest relief.

I nod and he pulls his T-shirt off the countertop again before carefully sliding it over me in a wave of cool fabric. It's massive but it smells fresh. It smells like him—

pine. And that's not a smell that's making me nauseous at all.

"You okay?" His expression is concerned but not panicked. There is something comforting about the fact he is so unflappable.

"Yeah. I might just . . ." I wave a hand around the bathroom. "Camp out in here for a bit. My dignity would appreciate a little privacy. Don't quite know how I'll repay you for holding my hair back while I got sick." I shake my head and let my eyes flutter shut.

He laughs but it's a gentle one. I hear him pull away, and I let myself slump against the wall behind me. The sound of him opening and closing drawers fills the small room, but I'm too tired to bug him about cleaning again.

Neat freak.

I feel the warmth of him as he approaches again. "Sit up, Red."

"Can't. Too tired." Why is barfing so exhausting?

"You can do it," he coaxes with one hand on my shoulder.

"I'm going to get you sick," I whine, still not moving.

"I never get sick." His thumb rubs sweetly across my collarbone, and I force my eyes open to look at him. "Come on, lean forward a bit."

I don't know why he wants me to do this, but it seems like he's not leaving until I do, so I comply, even though the rebellious part of me wants to lean back and say, *Make me.*

It would seem nausea easily quells the rebellious part of me.

"That's my girl." His deep voice vibrates through my bones, and then his fingers are in my hair, gently combing it back into a ponytail and wrapping a soft silk scrunchy around it. One he must have fished out of my drawer.

I moan at the feel. At his words. *My girl.*

God, I must be delirious. I chance a peek up at his stubbled jaw and stern features, while he carefully pulls my hair back. I want to melt into a puddle, and I'm certain that has nothing to do with the stomach bug.

Grumpy Cade is hot.

Sweet Cade is irresistible.

With my hair secured, he meets my gaze, face lined with concern. He runs a wide palm down the side of my head, resting it at my neck. "I'm going to leave you alone now, even though I don't want to. If you need me, I'll be out there." He lifts his chin toward the door.

I'm not sure what to say to that. To him. To this. So, I just nod stupidly.

And stare at his ass as he walks out of the bathroom.

~

"Okay, up we go."

I'm faintly aware of the most masculine smell and the feel of gentle hands shaping my waist.

"Come on, Red. I tried to be a gentleman and respect

your wishes, but your wishes are bullshit. I stayed out of here as long as I could, and it drove me crazy to do it. I'm not leaving you sleeping on my bathroom floor."

That comment has my eyelids dragging open as awareness seeps back in that I am indeed still in the bathroom. It's no longer light out and the kink in my neck is causing more discomfort than any actual sense of nausea.

Cade's hands slide into my armpits and lift me. I go with him, leaning into him once I'm standing. He wraps an arm around my waist to support me without even blinking.

"Let's go," he whispers. I can feel the rasp of his beard against my ear, and suddenly I'm wide awake and intimately aware of the fact I have not brushed my teeth.

"Go where?" I blink at him, groggy and still trying to get my bearings.

"My bed."

I blink with more intention now. "Come again?"

"It's closest to a toilet if you need it. Don't be weird about it. It makes sense."

His logic isn't flawed. It's the same reasoning I used last night with Luke. "Okay, fine. But I need to brush my teeth."

He rolls his eyes and I watch his jaw work. "I don't care about your breath, Red. I'm not taking you there to make out."

I laugh, but my biggest question is, *Why not?*

While I brush my teeth, he stands in the bathroom

doorway, arms crossed, glaring at me like I'm an inmate and he's a warden or something.

When I finish, he holds out a hand to me, and I take it, letting him lead me through the quiet house toward his bedroom. I tug him to a stop outside of Luke's room and peek in at his little body rolled up in a blanket with plastic sticky stars glowing on the ceiling. I can't help but smile, relieved that he seems to be resting comfortably.

"Was he feeling better?" I ask, before glancing up at his dad.

"Yeah. He's going to be fine. Fever broke and everything. It's you I'm worried about now. You two are giving me some extra grays today."

I smile and drop my gaze. "Ah, well. They look good on you."

He says nothing, but as he pulls me the rest of the way down the hall toward the master bedroom, his thumb rubs soft circles on the protruding bone in my wrist.

"In," he orders, pointing at the enormous bed.

"Aye, aye, Captain." I salute, but it's weak and tired, and I feel overwhelmingly relieved to be crawling into his bed.

"Did you keep anything down?" He clicks on the bedside lamp and pulls the blanket over me.

"No." I sigh.

He grunts and then turns, striding out of the bedroom. Within moments he returns with liquids and meds.

He cracks open the can of ginger ale and holds it out to me. "Small sips."

With shaky hands, I take it from him, eyeing the way his arms go back to crossing over his chest. "You just gonna stand there and glare at me? I feel like I'm in trouble."

He blows out a loud sigh and runs a hand through his hair. "I'm sorry. You two had me worried."

I take one small sip, not loving the taste of it mixing with the leftover mint flavor from my toothpaste. "You're a big softy, Cade Eaton. Sit down."

"Here?" His brows knit.

"It is your bed." I pat the spot beside me. "Just keep me company for a few minutes, and then I'll go to sleep. I bet I'll be fine tomorrow."

"Maybe," he grunts, skeptically assessing me while taking a hesitant seat.

I let my head rest against the bed frame as the fizzy liquid settles in my stomach. "Tell me how Luke was tonight."

"Seriously?"

"Yeah. Of course. Did he seem better? I was so worried about him."

Cade stares at me, like he can't quite believe what I'm telling him. "He was worried about you. He wanted to make sure that I gave you this bed. He peeked in and saw you sleeping sitting up—which he didn't tell me until I was already lying down to put him to sleep."

I laugh a little at that because I can totally imagine

him sneaking a peek. "My little troublemaker," I murmur, taking another sip.

Cade hums at that, staring at me even harder. "You sure you've never worked with kids before?"

"Positive."

"Huh." He folds his hands awkwardly over his kneecaps, as if he doesn't quite know what to do with them. Like he's uncomfortable sitting here talking to me in the silent room. "You're good at it. Maybe you should become a teacher or something."

A whoosh of air rushes from my nose. "Yeah. Maybe. That sounds fun, actually. I don't know though. It just all feels so daunting."

"What does?"

"Jobs. Careers. Life. Being a grown-up?"

"Do you like bartending?"

I roll my lips together and regard my boss carefully. "Not especially. It was fun when I was younger. It felt like getting paid to be social. But going back to it will be hard. I like it out here."

His throat bobs and he stares down at his hands, not responding to what I just said.

"Do you like ranching?" I ask, trying to coax him out of whatever caused his silence.

His lips slowly tip up. "I love it. I love being outside. I love the long days. I love how tired I am when I crawl into bed at night. I act like the yahoos in the bunkhouse piss me off, but I even love them in my own way."

"Unless they check me out." I point at him, taking another sip.

He chuckles. "Yeah, Red. Unless they check you out."

"That must be a good feeling. To be so sure that you're doing the right thing in your life."

Cade nods, fingers tapping on his knees, corded forearms flexing as he does. "Do you think you'll keep working at the bar? Or try something new?"

I settle back a little, enjoying Cade's comfortable bed and the perfectly supportive pillows. Has any bed ever felt better? "I don't know. New sounds scary. It sounds like failure." I scoff. "I mean, look at my parents. Insanely talented meets insanely educated. And my brother? Just had to have all that plus be insanely driven. And I'm just over here being insanely flighty."

His teeth grind. "You're a lot of things, Red. But flighty is not one of them."

"Well, I'm too intimidated to try something new and too scared of failure to commit to anything more than a string of short-term relationships and the same job I've had since I turned eighteen. Everyone keeps telling me I can be anything I want to be and do anything I want to do. And I'm just . . . paralyzed by it all." I snort out a sad laugh. "I sound flighty to me."

"Knock that off," he grits out, staring at me with fire in his eyes.

"What?" I quirk a brow at him, noting that after my

bathroom floor nap, I feel well enough to give him back a bit of attitude.

"Putting yourself down like that. Avoiding compliments. You're young. Your life is far from over, and we all get to make mistakes and come back from them. Look at me. I've made my fair share of them, and all I can do is try to be better—to do better."

"You had a lot of relationships since Luke's mom left?"

He huffs out a breath. "No, Red. I said *try* to be better. I haven't totally figured out how to come back from that one."

"You know what you need? Some no-strings-attached sex with the nanny." My tone is teasing, but I think we both know I'm not joking. Saying something for shock value isn't unusual for me, but this was really my flippant way of making the offer.

His knuckles turn white on his knees as he stares at his hands. He gives his head a shake as he reaches for the bottle of pills on the nightstand. I watch raptly as his fingers twist the top off and he empties one onto his palm before putting the bottle back.

Finally turning to look at me, he holds the pill out, and I open a hand for him in response. The tension between us is like a living entity in the wake of what I just suggested. Something we both know is there but are choosing to ignore.

When he drops the gel capsule into my palm, he wraps both his big, strong hands around mine and then leans in close. Electricity zings between us. I want to lean forward and bunt on his facial hair, beg him to stay here with me. To just think about it.

His breath fans across my cheek, and his eyes hold me captive. "That's the thing, Red. There are too many fuckin' strings with you. Enough to strangle us both. So we're going to be responsible and ignore whatever this is between us. Because a month from now, we'll be parting ways. You're going to live some fabulous, wildly successful life in the city, and I'm going to be here, taking care of this place for the rest of my days. We're on different paths, you and me."

The smile he gives me is flat, but his hands squeeze mine before he pushes to stand. "Take the Tylenol and get some rest."

"Where are you going to sleep?"

"I'll take your bed," he says over his shoulder. "I can wash the sheets tomorrow."

And then, he's walking away, leaving me holding a pill, a drink, and the tattered remains of my ego. In a bed that smells like him and makes me wish he were here with me.

"Cade?"

He stops just as his hand wraps around the door handle. "Yeah?" he replies without even looking at me.

"Will you stay?"

His body goes eerily still. No part of him moves. If I didn't know better, I'd think he was dead.

Actually, come to think of it, I wish *I* was dead after

blurting that out like some dork with a crush on the hot, grumpy single dad who just told me I'm too complicated for him. I should have more pride and shouldn't put him in such an awkward position. But here I am, asking him to stay.

He turns, brow low, expression tight. "Stay?"

"Yeah . . ." I bite my lip, crumpling a little under the intensity of his scowl. "Just for a bit. Just to chat. Or something."

He stares at me for a few beats, a glimpse of shock darting across his hard features. He did not expect me to ask him to stay.

But with a firm nod in my direction, he takes quiet steps back to the bed.

And he stays.

18

Cade

Lance: Can I swing by and practice with you one day this week?

Cade: Sure.

Lance: Wednesday?

Cade: Sure.

Lance: Will the nanny be there?

Cade: Fuck off, Lance.

Lance: Lmao. So angry all the time. See you on Wednesday!

◦～◦

"Tell me about young Cade."

I'm sitting as far away from Willa as I possibly can. If I could build a wall of pillows down the middle of this bed, I would. Not that it would stop me from dragging her underneath me.

Terrible, horrible, no good, unbelievably bad idea.

Even her questions I don't want to answer aren't helping distract me from the nearness of her. The smell of her.

The fucking temptation of her.

"Um." I clear my throat. "I dunno. Not much to tell." Propping my hands across my stomach, I chance a peek over at her.

She's a little pale, the dark circles under her eyes highlighted only by the dim glow of the bedside light.

She's fucking beautiful.

All sloping lines. Her neck. Her nose. The bottom line of her jaw. There's an elegance about her. Willa Grant is classy. She's got fancy written all over her, yet she walks around in old concert tees and is just crazy enough to knock a kid into a pool for revenge.

She's so much more than meets the eye, and sitting in a dark room with only a small stretch of soft mattress between us, I have to admit to myself that the way I want her is about so much more than how she looks.

She captured my attention the first time I laid eyes on her, and I haven't been able to look away since.

It's goddamn distracting.

"Come on. Were you this serious as a kid? Or were you like Luke?" She says it lightly, but I can see the way her eyes have started to sag.

"I was nothing like Luke. And I don't want Luke to

be anything like me either. My mom dying changed too much."

She nods solemnly but doesn't start dithering over me, which I appreciate. For someone who grew up privileged, there's an inherent practicality about Willa. Something in the way her mind works. I see it when she talks to Luke. She's not prissy or high maintenance. She's down to earth, and I love that about her. Even if she is delusional about accepting compliments.

"I watched her die that day. I watched my dad hold her. I watched him sob." My teeth grind, and I drop my eyes for a moment. "I think my childhood kind of died that day too."

I glance at her wide green eyes, a little shiny now. Her strawberry lips slightly part, and she nods again. I appreciate she doesn't fill the silence with meaningless words.

"Maybe I was practical from an early age. Strategic?" I sigh and stare up at the ceiling. "I don't want to sound like a martyr or something."

"You don't." Her reply is soft and firm.

"But I saw a need, even as a child. Our family needed help. And I opted to help. I guess I never stopped. Duty-bound or something. I don't regret it, but I also didn't get lazy, goofy summers. When I came home from school, I took care of my brothers so my dad didn't have to come in early from work. The neighbors pitched in. Mrs. Hill helped with Luke until she was just too old to keep up. But I didn't want him to spend his summer working around the ranch or getting dragged everywhere with me. It's fun for a day. Not for two months."

"Enter, me." I see her lips lift as she gives me a little wink. "The fun."

I huff out a breath. "You are pretty fun. He worships the ground you walk on."

Staring down at her nails, she tries not to laugh. "As all men should."

Chuckling, I fully turn my gaze on her. "What were you like as a kid?"

The tip of her nose wiggles as she considers her answer. "I wish I could tell you I've changed a lot, but I'm not so sure I have." There's a self-deprecating hollowness to her voice. "I've always been the fun girl. The carefree girl. My dad was on the road a lot when I was younger. My mom worked all the time. We had nannies too. Or family that helped. Come to think of it, it wasn't so different from the community Luke has around him. So don't worry, he'll turn out great. Just like me."

She says it like it's a punch line to a joke, and I just don't get why she's this hard on herself. Why does she see herself as some sort of failure when all I see is a smart, funny, self-possessed young woman? One who made me *beg* her to stay.

I shrug. "I'd be very proud of him if he turned out like you."

When she tilts her head, one soft tendril of hair slips out and caresses the side of her face. "Really?"

"Yes, Willa. What more could I want for him? Intelligent, independent, a solid sense of humor, a good head on his shoulders."

"Do you think he'll proposition his nanny for no-strings-attached sex though?"

"Jesus Christ, woman." I stare at the ceiling again.

She laughs and it's so pretty. Like chimes in the wind. One of the first things I noticed about her that day in the coffee shop.

"Well, if we can't joke about it, things will get awkward. I figure we're stuck together for the rest of our lives with Summer and Rhett." That reality hits me like a wrecking ball. "One day, years down the road, we'll be gray-haired and soft in the middle section, drinking an enormous glass of spiced rum and eggnog around the Christmas tree. I'll make some joke about the night I offered friends-with-benefits to you. Rhett will howl. Summer will roll her eyes, because I'm going to tell her tomorrow, and she'll think I'm ridiculous for bringing it up so many years later. Your small-town wifey will throw a hand over her chest"—Willa imitates the motion—"and act scandalized all night. In fact, she'll give me the cold shoulder for the rest of our lives. And I'll outlive her, so that's fine. Joke's on her. I win. And my husband will be accustomed to my antics, so he'll just roll his eyes and continue drinking."

It's funny and I should laugh. But I'm caught on the part where she's married to some man who rolls his eyes at her. A man who isn't me. And I have somehow failed to wrap my head around the fact that I'm going to be connected to this woman for the rest of my life.

"Red, don't marry a man who rolls his eyes at you."

"You roll your eyes at me all the time."

Fuck, I need to stop doing that. She deserves better.

"Don't marry me either."

She shrugs and carries on, undeterred. "He'll go back to obsessively checking his investment portfolio, and everyone will hear us fight about it later that night. Christmas morning will be awkward because he'll leave, and everyone will talk about how obviously the third time is *not* the charm, because Willa's third marriage is about to fall apart."

I laugh now, a fist over my mouth, shoulders heaving under the strain of not waking Luke. "Red, you're nuts. But I like that about you. You're like a goddamn hurricane."

Her mouth curves, sinfully wicked. "Sometimes I feel like that. Out here though? I don't know. There's something about the endless stretches of land around me that's just . . . soothing? Like there's nothing else that needs doing. I feel very settled for the first time in a long time."

"The eye of the storm," I say, allowing myself to study her.

It's hard to meet her gaze. Her eyes are so green. Her lips so tempting. No wonder I can't stop thinking about her. She's looks like a doll and cracks jokes like a cowboy.

Even working cows in the middle of a scorching afternoon, she pops into my head.

That's always been the wildest thing to me about having a kid. I'm never without him. Never stop thinking about him. Worrying about him. And somehow, in a matter of weeks, Willa has implanted herself into that same space.

"The eye of the storm," she repeats softly, eyes scouring me intensely before glancing around my room. "Maybe you're right."

When she turns back to me, her eyes twinkle and her lips look soft and damp.

"Willa." I say in warning, because I'm old enough and wise enough to recognize the expression on her face.

"Yes?" She rolls up onto her knees, facing me.

"What are you doing?"

"Looking at you."

I resist the urge to roll my eyes. She has a hard enough time taking herself seriously without me adding to that insecurity.

"Why?" I husk.

"Because I want your attention when I thank you."

"For what?"

She lets out an exhausted sigh. "Taking care of me."

I shrug and look away, unable to handle the weight of her stare.

"You're a good man, Cade Eaton."

Her compliment has my skin crawling. Maybe I'm

just as bad when it comes to accepting praise. But for her, I can be better.

"Thank you. And you're an exceptional young woman." I hold her gaze. The air hums between us and everything inside me says to reach for her. To crush my lips against hers, run my fingers through that silky copper hair.

"It sounds like you're writing my report card." She leans closer.

But I draw away. Because she's too damn close, and I'm too damn old—carrying too much baggage.

A report card. I almost feel like I could be.

Swinging my legs over the opposite edge of the bed, I turn my back on her and run my hands through my hair. "Glad you're feeling better. Get some rest."

I head for the door and it's a Herculean effort to walk away from her. One quick turn over my shoulder confirms the disappointment on her face. Resignation.

Two offers in one night.

Two offers turned down.

When the door clicks shut behind me, I realize I'm shutting the door on my chance with the girl sitting on my bed. Because her pride won't let her ask again. And I'm still too fucked-up over the shit Talia put me through to let myself have her. Too scared to want something that badly, too scared to care about something that deeply.

Too scared to get my heart broken again.

What heart? I chide myself.

I walk straight to her room and crawl into her bed,

the zesty scent of her orange body lotion wrapping around me like the sweetest torture.

I take a deep breath and press the heels of my hands into the sockets of my eyes.

And then I lie here, staring at the ceiling, replaying that look on her face.

And feeling sick to my stomach.

~

"I'm so excited! Luke exclaims as we pull up to the rodeo grounds a few towns over.

"Me too." Willa turns a smile into the back seat of my truck. She rode with us today because Luke begged for us to all drive together. He's oblivious to the tension between us, the slight pang of heartache and missed chances.

In another lifetime, we might have worked. Or we'd have had a fling. But I know I can't have her and not keep her—it's just not the way I'm wired. And I know she doesn't want to be kept.

We've been dancing around each other for over a week. Polite but slightly uncomfortable. Professional and friendly but less playful somehow.

She hasn't texted me about her panties, and I wish she would. She spent the weekend at Summer's, and I wish she hadn't.

I'm a fucking mess. And now I have to do cowboy-showboat shit because I played a stupid game of truth or dare with Willa and was too dumbstruck by the outline of her pussy to say no.

"You're going to win, Dad!"

I snort. Probably not, but I don't tell Luke that. "Thanks, pal. With a fan like you, it'll be hard not to."

I pull into a spot where it'll be easy to unload my horse. My *ranch* horse that Willa and Luke spent all week grooming like she's a show pony. Her dark, speckled coat is glistening. There's not a tangle to be found in her mane, not a burr in her tail. I think they even put oil on her hooves. I'm not sure that Blueberry has ever looked this good in her life.

With my rig parked, I risk a glance at Willa. "You good?"

Her lips roll. She doesn't mean it to be seductive, but every little thing she does feels like a missed opportunity now. *Those lips should be mine. On mine. Wrapped around my cock. Moaning my name.*

"Yup. All good. We'll"—she hikes a thumb over her shoulder—"head out and look around. We'll be back in time to watch your run."

I nod before gazing at the sea of people, thinking of how my life might have been if things had gone differently. Would I be here? On the road? Penning and chasing buckles?

"Can we get ice cream?" Luke calls as he flies out of the back seat.

"Yeah, we're getting every sugary thing we can find because it's still before dinner," Willa deadpans as she gets out of the truck, and I know she said it just to pester me.

"Score!" Through the window, I see Luke leap, a fist shooting up into the air over his head. The motion knocks his cowboy hat off, straight into the loose, dusty dirt.

Willa's head tips back on a laugh before she crouches down and scoops it off the ground, dusting it off while saying something to Luke I can't make out. Whatever it is, it makes him giggle.

She squats and places the hat on his head, giving it a little tug at the same moment the corners of her mouth pull up into the most infectious smile.

I find myself smiling at them from where I'm still sitting behind the wheel. Luke is grinning even wider. When Willa reaches forward and boops the tip of his nose, I see his smile soften and go a little wistful. He boops her back and they take a moment to just smile at each other.

Something in my chest cracks wide open as I watch them together. Kindred spirits in so many ways.

They turn to leave, and Luke slips his hand into Willa's. They're cute together. He's dressed like a tiny cowboy, and she's wearing a white, old-school Pepsi T-shirt, a belt that looks more like a chain, and her hair in loose waves down her back.

I imagine her wearing that belt and that belt only, but then my eyes travel down over her torturously tight jeans. The ones that display her ass like it's the star of the show. The ones that flare out over a pair of snakeskin cowboy boots she borrowed from Summer.

I'm going to tell Summer to keep those on lockdown, because they look too fucking good on Willa.

She looks too fucking good. Period.

And I want to punch someone. Because based on all the turning heads, I'm not the only one who's noticing how good she looks.

19

Willa

Rhett: Where you kids at?

Willa: Working on ruining our blood sugar. You?

Rhett: Jasper and I just pulled up. Wanna meet near Cade's truck?

Willa: Sure, we'll head your way.

Rhett: I'm supposed to tell you to be careful.

Willa: Of what?

Rhett: I think my brother's words were: she's clueless that a bunch of dumbass cowboys keep humping her leg when she walks past.

Willa: Cool, cool, cool. I'll try not to trip while they do.

I wasn't lying when I told Luke we were getting all the sugar. Being around Cade makes me want to drink, but that's not an option when you're taking care of a child. So I lean on sweet, sweet sugar.

"I can't decide which flavor I like better," Luke announces from beside me as we weave through the crowd.

"Why choose? Cinnamon sugar and brown sugar don't need to compete. Mini donuts are a win, no matter what." I stick my hand out to Luke as we press into the thickening crowd. "Stay close, bud. It's busy."

Cowboys as far as the eye can see, right when I've realized I've only got eyes for one. Over a year of me making jokes to Summer about saving horses and riding cowboys, and I don't even want the rest of them. I was *fine* until he took care of me. Held my goddamn hair up and rubbed my back.

I still refuse to accept that people normally do that for their employees. And the fact he did has me over-thinking things something fierce because, if I'm being honest, getting turned down is a new phenomenon for me. And I'm a little bit pissed about it. A little bit embarrassed.

A little bit wounded because Cade is such a good man. I'd want more than just sex, and he doesn't even want that. It's a rough blow to what I'm realizing is my already fragile ego.

I've never considered myself self-conscious, but the

other night Cade made some points I keep turning over in my mind. Things about myself I've never realized.

"There's uncle Rhett!" Luke shouts up at me, knocking me off the winding path I got lost on in my mind.

Rhett's hard to miss with his shoulder length hair and cocky grin, one that morphs into a wide smile when he hears Luke shouting his name and sees me getting dragged behind the boy.

"Hey, little psycho." Rhett picks up Luke and tosses him onto his shoulders, giving him the best view in the house. He turns to me and nods his head. "Willa."

"Hi." I return his smile. I like Rhett Eaton. I especially like him for my best friend. It's the worst when your friends date someone you can't stand, but that's not the case with Rhett. They're perfect together, and I can't wait to see their insanely beautiful babies one day. That is, if Summer will ever hammer down a wedding date. Because she'd never do things out of order.

"Hey, Willa." Jasper pops up beside Rhett, several inches taller and looking like he wishes he were anywhere else but here.

I crane my neck back to meet his blue eyes. They aren't bright and sparkly, they're deep and dark, almost navy. "Good lord, what are they feeding you Grizzly boys? Somehow, I missed you being this tall." He must be at least six foot four.

He smiles, but there's something pinched about it.

"Seems to be a thing for goaltenders these days. I'm lucky I fit the bill, I guess."

His self-deprecating response reminds me of something I'd say—chalking my skill up to luck or my hard work up to genetics. The difference is, he's an NHL player and I'm a bartender.

"Let's head to the bleachers and get a good seat." Rhett claps Jasper on the back and gives me a nod, and I follow him, Jasper hanging back closer to me. I feel like I'm being escorted by bodyguards. People get out of the way when these guys walk through.

They also stop and stare. Some even say hi.

When we turn up the bleacher steps, Rhett's head swivels, scanning for a spot. Luke is still on his shoulders, pointing somewhere. Jasper moves ahead of me, long legs taking every other step. But when he glances back and sees me falling behind, he stops on a landing and then opts to take each step. He doesn't say anything, but I know he's acutely aware of us all staying together. It's busy and these country boys are protective as hell.

Only proven further by the way Rhett moves down a row and Jasper sends me in first, opening one arm wide and gesturing me through before following behind me. When we're seated, Luke is beside me and we're flanked by two tall men.

Worse things have happened to me in my life.

Luke immediately tells Rhett how he's going to ride bulls when he grows up. Rhett and I exchange a look, knowing that Cade would probably keel over if this ever really happened.

"Do you know much about this team penning stuff?" I ask Jasper, tipping my chin down to the ring.

He nods. "Yeah. I'm actually not bad at it myself. We all practiced a lot as kids."

"Really?" My brow quirks.

"You don't grow up at Wishing Well Ranch and not learn how to pen and rope and cut and toss a lasso."

"Well, shit." I lean back a little, wrapping my hands around one knee. "Color me impressed, Jasper Gervais."

He chuckles, eyes crinkling at the sides—which does nothing but remind me of Cade.

That's where the similarities end though. Jasper is quiet, but there's a gentleness about him. He's introspective. There are things that weigh on him. Years behind a bar has honed my eye for people who carry invisible weight. He strikes me as . . . sad, maybe?

"Do you know anything about it?" he asks, eyes focused on the big dirt ring. There's a pen with a bunch of cows at one end and a smaller pen nearby.

"Not a damn thing. I ride fancy jumping horses."

"Okay, so basically a team of three will ride in. Those thirty cows all have numbers on them—three sets of ten—and the judge is going to call a random number. Then they're going to separate the three cows with that number out and herd them down into the smaller pen on the opposite side."

I nod and turn my lips down. "Okay."

Jasper huffs out a soft chuckle. "It's the rider's job to predict how they might slip away. Bet you're thinking that doesn't sound so hard. But cows are pretty smart, and they like to stick together. Trickier than they look."

I laugh at that. The cows look pretty cute to me with their big wide eyes and round wet noses.

"You'll see them in real action when Cade pulls the cows up in a couple of weeks."

"Oh?" I tilt my head.

"Yeah. Did Cade not tell you? It's like a big family get-together at the ranch. We work all the cows. Get them vaccinated, check them over for fall—even though Cade is out there checking on them almost every damn day. Then there's a big meal. Music." He shrugs, staring back out over the ring. "It's fun."

"That sounds fun. Too bad Beau is away."

A smile tugs at Jasper's lips. "Yeah. It's never quite the same without the class clown. But I think Violet is coming back. I don't think you've met their sister yet. You'll like her. She's a fancy racehorse jockey. But it's a surprise for Harvey, so keep that on the down-low."

I wink at him. "We'll unite in our fanciness, then, huh?"

Rhett must have overheard us because he says, "Jesus. You and Summer and Violet all together is going to be terrifying. Toss in Sloane? It's going to be a mess."

Jasper freezes for the briefest moment. "Sloane is coming?"

"Yeah, Vi told me the other day. She's picking her up at the airport."

Jasper covers whatever that physical reaction was with a chuckle. "Yeah. That'll be quite the combo."

"Who is Sloane?"

"Our cousin," Rhett says right as Jasper says, "Their cousin. My friend."

"Dude. You're my brother. She's our cousin. Don't be weird about this. We're too old for that shit." Rhett shakes his head.

"We've stayed in touch in the city. You know that. I'm not related to her. She's a good friend."

Rhett rolls his eyes. "I don't care about your last name, Jas. You're an Eaton boy, like it or not."

Jasper's cheeks flush a little and his lips curve up. "I like it just fine, little Eaton."

My head flips between them as they snipe back and forth. "Good god. You guys are adorable together."

"Sloane is really pretty," Luke announces when he surfaces for air out of his giant bag of mini donuts.

"Oooh." I nudge my shoulder at him. "Does someone have a crush?" The boy rolls his eyes but his cheeks flame.

I bite back the laugh threatening to slip out. Luke doesn't need me making fun of him about this, no matter how badly I want to.

The guys poke at Luke's little shoulders until his ears turn red.

"She's pretty, Lukey. No one denies that. Right, Jas?"

A little tendon in Jasper's jaw twitches, but he nods and smiles all the same.

"Look!" Luke points to the area behind the metal gates. "There's Dad!"

And there he is . . . warming up and looking sexy as hell. Shoulders held tall. Black hat. Black shirt with silver snaps. Black chaps. Black boots. Even Blueberry matches him.

"I wonder if he has a favorite color?" I ask to a chorus of laughs.

"He looks like Cowboy Batman," Rhett says.

"Ooh. I like Batman," Luke agrees while nodding.

Jasper chuckles. "He looks nervous is what he looks like. I told him I could show him some mental exercises I like to do before a game, and he told me to"—his fingers pop up in quotations—"take my soy-boy-woo-woo shit back to the city."

Rhett cracks up. But I find myself feeling a little defensive of him, even though I know they're joking. Even that does sound like something dickish that Cade would say.

"He's got this," is all I offer back with a firm nod.

"Wonder if Blueberry will hold her own against these horses? She's seriously outclassed with the fancy penning horses Lance hauls around," Rhett wonders out loud.

I toss an elbow in Rhett's ribs. "Hey! We cleaned her up! She looks beautiful. Stop picking on them."

"I heard Dad tell Grandpa it doesn't matter how

much money Blueberry is worth because she's the biggest bitch he's ever ridden, and her mean attitude already makes her a winner."

I drop my face into my hands, body shaking with barely restrained laughter.

"Jesus, Luke. You gotta stop eavesdropping on people," Rhett scolds, but the big grin on his face kills the intimidation factor.

Jasper pulls at the brim of his hat again, and I'm pretty sure it's to hide his misty eyes.

My gaze finds Cade again, sitting so tall, chin held so high. He oozes confidence, and I can't help but wonder if he actually feels it.

A cowboy says something to him, and his head tips back on a full laugh, reins held in one hand while the other rests casually on his leg. It's nice to see him having fun after years and years of being responsible.

I don't regret my dare at all.

Do I wish I'd dared him to take off my bathing suit instead? Sometimes.

But he needed something for himself more than he needed that. Something where he gets to be Cade Eaton, the individual, and not just Cade Eaton, the single dad and tireless rancher.

I must have a stupid smile on my face as I stare back at him because I feel an elbow nudge against mine. "It's nice to see someone looking at Cade like that. Defending him like that," Jasper says. "Like they can see him for who he is rather than the man circumstances forced him to become."

"Getting kind of deep for a rodeo," I whisper, not wanting to involve Rhett in this conversation because it will just turn into a big joke.

Jasper shrugs. "Wouldn't be where I am today if it wasn't for him. Would be nice to see him happy."

I nod because I agree. It *is* nice to see him happy. "Where would you be without him?"

Jasper continues staring out into the ring, watching the first team ride in on their horses. He sighs deeply, and without sparing me a glance, he says, "If not for the Eaton boys, I'd probably be dead."

When Cade enters the ring, you wouldn't know he hasn't taken part in a rodeo in years—possibly decades. He looks like a king sitting on his horse. Thick, round shoulders and veined forearms. Like everyone around him should fall to their knees in his presence.

My core twinges at the thought of falling to my knees for Cade. I wish he were less responsible. That he'd shirk all those pressures and just take me.

I'd get off on watching someone as steady as Cade completely lose it.

The judge calls out the numbers of the cows from their table, and Cade and his team members assess the cattle. When a buzzer sounds, time starts counting down and the three men on horseback jump into action.

There's something mesmerizing about watching Cade. He knows what he's doing. So sure. So cool and collected. He's insanely capable, and I've never found that as attractive as I do now.

Capable in the ring.

Capable at the ranch.

Capable around his house.

I can't help but let my mind wander into the gutter, wondering if he's just as capable in bed. I decide he *must* be. No man walks around unaffected by people's opinions of him unless he knows he packs a serious punch.

It's that quiet confidence that has me crossing my legs and squeezing my thighs together, gripping the edge of the wooden bench beneath me.

His forearms ripple in the sun when his gloved hands squeeze on the reins. The tendons in his tanned neck flex as Blueberry cuts and dekes, her head drawn low, eyes laser-focused on the cows trying to get past her.

She has a mean expression on what is normally a sweet face.

It's hard to see Cade's expression from under the brim of his hat, but I suspect it's a mirror image of hers. All focus.

I'm not familiar with this sport, but I am familiar with other equestrian sports—enough to know that nothing about Cade and Blueberry looks outclassed.

They're living proof that working a ranch every day

is all the practice they need. Watching him work gives me goose bumps and has me brushing up and down on my arms, even though it's warm out.

Before I know it, they have two cows squared away in the pen and just the one is left swerving around Lance.

Cade reaches forward and swoops a hand over Blueberry's muscular neck before loping to his aid.

And I want to be that horse. I want his hands on me. His weight on my back.

It's pathetic to be jealous of a horse—but here I am.

I need to get over this. Stat. Pining is not my MO. Especially not over a guy who doesn't want me.

"Oh! There she goes!" Luke squeals and shoots out of his seat, pointing down into the ring where Blueberry cuts low, haunches braced as she spins, her mane trailing in the air she quickly left behind.

"Get 'er, Cade!" Rhett shouts, up on his feet too.

I watch Cade. He's poetry in motion—smooth and balanced—as Blueberry heads off the cow and guides it straight into the pen with the others.

I don't know how the scoring works, so I don't know if it was good or not, but I'm impressed, and that's good enough for me to shoot up and cheer with Luke. The little boy beams up at me, beyond excited for his dad.

"Wasn't he good, Willa?"

"Luke, he was the best! And did you see Blueberry? She's perfect! We did good." We fist-bump, and I catch Rhett tossing a questioning look at me, but I ignore it. I don't know how much Summer tells him, and I don't need everyone and their dog knowing I'm head over heels for Luke and well on my way to being the same for his dad.

"Can we go back and see him?"

"Of course, we can. You guys coming?" I ask Rhett and Jasper.

"For sure," Rhett says. "Let's go give the old man some ass pats for putting on such a good show."

"He's probably going to need a massage tomorrow," Jasper tosses back.

"Willa can do that for him," Luke slides in casually.

And we all freeze.

Rhett looks like a goddamn dog with a bone. "Oh yeah? Have Willa and your dad been swapping massages?"

"No. Just beds."

I make a choking sound, and Jasper holds a fist up over his mouth.

"I got a stomach bug and Cade gave me his room for one night so I'd be near a bathroom," I explain.

"Yeah. But wasn't he massaging you that night you guys danced in the kitchen?" Luke says it so innocently, but my eyes bug out all the same.

"It's . . . that's . . ." I stare down at Luke.

"What?"

I feel my chest flush as I wrap a hand around Luke's shoulder and turn him away from his uncle, who is enjoying this far too much.

Moving my hand to cover Luke's ear, I lean toward Rhett. "Watch it, Eaton. I know where you live."

"Yeah? What are you going to do? Come over and drink a bottle of champagne on my back deck? Braid your hair and have a pillow fight with Summer?"

"I'll braid your hair. Then I'll cut the braid off and wear it as a necklace for you mocking me."

He chuckles. "You're vicious, Willa. I like that about you."

I shake my head and turn away, trying and failing to restrain the smile on my lips.

We cut down the bleachers and follow the fence line to the staging area. The guys are still on their horses, but beers are cracked and they're all chatting and chuckling.

The minute Luke catches sight of him, he surges forward. "Dad!"

Cade's face breaks into the brightest smile as he reaches down and hauls his boy up into the tack in front of him. He gives him a tight squeeze, and my heart clenches in perfect synchronicity as my eyes fall to the swell of his biceps and the way they flex.

"Great work out there," I say, offering a small wave to the other guys.

Rhett and Jasper stride in behind me, offering handshakes that clap with their force and back slaps that appear borderline painful.

"You all coming out tonight to celebrate our win?" Lance asks with a smile.

"Nah. Sorry, man," Cade replies, with a brief nod toward the back of Luke's head.

"I can take Luke," Rhett offers. "I need a night in after traveling so much."

Cade shakes his head, clearly not wanting to go out and using Luke as an excuse.

"How about you, Red?" Lance says, and I visibly flinch because I've come to associate that nickname with Cade. It somehow feels like that's *his* name for me.

When I peek up at Cade, his jaw is set, teeth working with a grimace on his lips.

I wave the cowboy off. "Nah. I'm good."

"It's supposed to be your day off, Willa. You should go," Cade bites out.

I rear back a little as I stare up at him. It feels like he just slapped me. Like he's trying to pawn me off on someone else. But he doesn't look pleased about it either.

He's an awful lot of work some days, and the rush of annoyance at him has me shaking my head in disbelief.

It has me feeling reckless. A little spiteful. I'm not necessarily proud of this facet of my personality, but it's here all the same. I get mad *and* I get even.

"Thanks for the permission, Cade," I snip, watching Jasper fidget with the brim of his hat again while Rhett stares back with wide eyes. I turn to Lance. "Since the boss gives it his stamp of approval, yes. Let's go out."

He smiles back, giving off sweet, boy-next-door vibes. "Alright, cowgirl. Off we go." He points one lanky arm in the direction of the trailers parked in the back.

I swallow a big gulp of dry prairie air and observe the way his body moves in the tack. Not my type at all.

Because apparently my type is a broody asshole cowboy whose handsome face I would currently like to stomp with the heel of my boot.

But then I'd want to kiss it better too.

It's only when I walk toward Lance that I glance over my shoulder. Cade is still sitting on Blueberry and his eyes are laser-focused on me.

I wait for a beat. Hoping he'll say something. Tell me to stay. Ask me to go home with him instead. I love it when he says home like it's *our* home.

But he doesn't.

So I go.

20

Cade

Cade: Be a gentleman.

Lance: Lol. Cade. Relax. You know I'll take care of your nanny.

Cade: One hair out of place and I'll kill you.

Lance: What about multiple hairs?

Cade: Are you fucking kidding me right now? You got a death wish?

Lance: You're the idiot who let her go.

⁓

I hate myself. I want to take it back and throw Willa over my shoulder and drag her home with me.

Where she belongs.

But I pushed her off on a perfectly *nice* guy because

I've convinced myself that fucking the nanny is out of bounds.

It doesn't take a psychologist to know I'm the issue. My insecurities are the issue. If I couldn't make a small-town woman—who was my age and desperately wanted me—happy, how the hell can I make a woman like Willa happy?

When Talia left, it was a blow to my ego. I wish I could say I missed *her,* but it was more about the fact she chose other men over me. That I *lost* somehow. That I didn't measure up. My heart wasn't in it, but I tried my ass off anyway.

But with Willa, my heart is in it. I don't want it to be, but it is.

God, I tried so hard to dislike her, because liking her would lead to enjoying her. And after weeks stuck in the same house, watching her be the closest thing my son has ever had to a real mother, I'm worried enjoying her has turned into caring about her.

And I have no clue what to do with that. I've never properly loved a woman before. Never wanted one like this.

"I'll give her one more chance at water!" Rhett calls as he stalks away with a bucket.

"Thanks!" I mumble back before letting out a ragged sigh and checking inside my truck. Luke is already asleep in the air-conditioned cab. Clearly, the excitement of the day caught up with him. Willa always keeps him so active that he's dog-tired at the end of the day.

Willa is too good to us.

"You were killer out there today." Jasper leans against the side of my trailer, staring at me with a small smirk on his lips. "Didn't even look that old from where I was sitting."

I shake my head. "Just wait until you start sucking at hockey. I have so many old-man jokes stocked away for you. And for Beau, when he finally retires."

"You heard from him?" Jasper asks, looking hopeful.

"Nah. Nothing lately. Wish I knew where that doofus was."

"Yeah. Not knowing is the worst part." We share an anxious look. Sending Beau away never gets any easier on any of us. My dad included.

"You're really dumb, you know?" His eyes flit up as he rapidly changes the topic of conversation.

I scoff. "Is this the opening line of another old-man joke?"

"Not unless getting older means sending away one of the best things that's ever happened to you with another man who isn't too dumb to see it."

I feel the tightness in my chest and the ache at the back of my throat. I don't know if that ache means I'm angry, sad, or if it's just the spot where all the words I want to say get caught in a stranglehold.

"Got something to say, Jasper?"

His head tilts, his blue eyes taking on a slightly vicious expression. The one I only get a peek of from behind his goalie mask. The one that made me want to get up at five a.m. and drive his pimply teenaged ass to practices, because a man with a look like that in his eye doesn't lose.

He was special and I knew it.

I needed another sibling to take care of like I needed a hole in the head, but Jasper was meant to be with us, not his shit parents. And I wouldn't have it any other way.

"The only thing I'm going to say is that you've spent the last, what, thirty years making sure everyone else is happy? You've been dutiful beyond compare. Reliable. Selfless. Responsible. You deserve to be happy too, Cade."

Responsible. That word follows me around like the plague. It haunts my dreams at night.

Fucking responsible.

He turns his massive frame and ambles away to whatever fancy SUV he drives now.

"You coming to the reunion?" I call out, not totally sure what to say to him. The guy is quiet all the time and then hits me with that shit.

"Wouldn't miss it!" he calls back without even looking at me.

"You roping?"

He lets out a deep, amused hum. "Nope, I would never do that."

Every year he refuses to admit that he's going to rope. Something about riding horses being not allowed in his contract. Along with motorbikes, sky diving, and using fireworks.

But every year, I saddle him a horse, and every year he gets on. No one talks about it, but the kid can still throw one hell of a lasso.

Rhett waters Blueberry and then gives her a kind pat. "Way to show up the fancy horses, Blue. That's the Eaton way."

I watch through the window of my trailer, but Rhett catches me. "You're lucky she tolerates you." He chucks his chin at me as he says it.

"Blue?" I ask.

My brother shakes his head and turns away to toss the bucket of water out of the trailer while I latch up the doors. I'm still waiting for him to respond to my question but the asshole doesn't.

For all the years he's spent running his mouth, he's got nothing to say to me right now.

"See you at home?" I call out as he heads over to Jasper's vehicle.

"Yup." He waves over his shoulder.

"Tell Summer to keep those goddamn snakeskin boots to herself!" I call, hoping to engage him. I'd rather argue with Rhett than get his cold shoulder. He's spent his entire life bitching at me, and I want him to keep going.

When he gets to the passenger's side door, he turns and glares back at me, a faint tip to his lips. "I don't tell Summer what to do. Wouldn't listen if I tried. That's the best kind of woman if you ask me." He winks and hops in with Jasper. They peel away with a wave, and I'm sure they'll gossip like little biddies about me on their drive back to Chestnut Springs.

The ladies in town have nothing on them.

Assholes.

Luke is still asleep when I hop in the truck, which means it's just me and my vicious thoughts on the drive.

Me and my regrets.

Luke wakes when we hit the gravel roads and begs to spend the night with Grandpa, like a psycho toy that got plugged in for an hour after running out of batteries and is now charged and ready to terrorize more adults.

I drop him off. Love him as I do, I'm not in the mood to play and be fun.

When I get home, there's no laughter. There's no music. There's no Willa and Luke dancing and singing in the kitchen while cookies bake in the oven.

It's quiet. And I'm lonely.

Deeply lonely.

And angry I sent her away. Angry she's having fun with another guy right now. Multiple guys probably.

I drop my bag and start cleaning to busy myself, scouring corners that no one will ever see. Scrubbing to take out my frustration, to keep away the jealousy that is scorching me from the inside out. It's raging through my veins, searing every nerve ending.

It's fucking consuming.

When my hands hurt, I stop and take a shower. My

dick is hard, but I'm too pissed off to jerk it, so when I get back out, I'm more agitated.

Stomping around my house, I opt to pour myself a bourbon and go sit on the front porch. I know why I'm going there, but I refuse to admit it. I tell myself the view is good from here, but when I take a seat on the top step and glance to the side, I see little doodles painted on the railings. Suns and stars. Happy faces and XOXO.

And hearts.

Willa drew hearts on my front porch, and now I'm stuck sitting here, drowning in the thought that the real reason I'm out here is that I'm waiting for her to get home.

I'm too sick with jealousy to do anything else.

21

Willa

Summer: Are you okay?

Willa: Yeah. Why?

Summer: I just got a text from Cade asking.

Willa: You can tell Cade I'm getting railed by ten dudes at the best gangbang of my life.

Summer: Oof. Even I'm not that brave. I'll let you tell him that yourself.

Summer: He seems stressed, Willa. Just letting you know.

Willa: Good.

I sigh in relief when the cab hits the gravel road. *So close.* I want to be home like nothing I've quite felt before.

It felt wrong being out with Lance and all his cowboy buddies without Cade there. Objectively I had fun, but my head was somewhere else.

My heart was somewhere else.

And as mad as I wanted to be that Cade thought he could check in on me through my best friend when he has my number and could easily have texted me himself, the thought of him being stressed about my safety left a pit in my stomach.

I guess that's why I pulled the Irish goodbye and snuck out like a chicken. All the guys were perfect gentlemen, but they were heading for a level of whipped up in celebrating their win that I just didn't want to be.

The bar scene exhausts me now, and as the cab lights up the dark country roads, I realize I'm torn between wanting this summer to be over because I need the space from Cade, and never wanting it to end because I don't want to go back to my life in the city.

We cross under the big wooden posts that mark where the Wishing Well Ranch land begins.

"Just down this road and then veer left," I direct the driver, who responds with a simple hum. I'm grateful that he hasn't been the chatty type of cab driver because I'm all chatted out for tonight.

When the lights turn into Cade's driveway and shine

at the picturesque rancher, my body sags with relief. This isn't my home, but . . . I feel like I'm home.

I tap my card on the cabbie's machine to pay the obscenely expensive total and step out. Cade is sitting on the front step, glaring at me. His elbows are resting on his knees and he's holding a glass tumbler in his large hands.

There's an energy about him. He looks dangerous tonight, and well, I'm in the mood for a fight.

As the cab pulls away, I poke the bear. "Waiting up for me, Daddy?" I bat my eyelashes and hike my purse up on my shoulder.

I swear he growls. "It's late. You could have let me know when you were coming home. It's still *my* house you're living in."

"I guess I should stay at the main house on the weekends then, just so I don't inconvenience you," I snipe back, even though I don't want to stay at the main house.

I want to stay with him.

"Maybe you should just act like an adult and report back so that I don't have to worry . . ." he trails off before adding, "about you waking Luke up."

The fucking balls on this guy.

"Not wanting to wake Luke up is the only reason I'm not reaming you out right now, Eaton. And if we're going to talk about acting like adults maybe you should text *me* instead of my best friend."

He stands, brushing his hands over the ass of his pants—looking annoyingly good as he does—before he turns his back on me. Then he tosses out over his shoulder, "Luke's with my dad, so you can go ahead and have your tantrum over that if you need to."

My jaw drops and my voice rises. "You're worried about me coming home late and waking him up, but he's not even here?"

He continues walking, but I dart after him, jogging up the steps as I toss my purse on the deck near his bare feet. "Cade! I'm talking to you. Which is lucky, considering you just handed me over to your friend, like I'm some sort of goddamn toy to share."

That stops him in his tracks, the muscles in his back held taut. Everything about his body screams predator. It screams get away from me, but I'm too impulsive to heed a silent warning like that. I step closer, closing the space between us, letting his pine scent wrap around me—letting it intoxicate me.

"You think I'm just some bimbo you can pawn off on friends?"

He spins now, all fire and brimstone. "I think I can't get you out of my head, no matter how hard I try. I think you're too damn tempting and that I'm too damn complicated. I think you smell like *him*, and I can't fucking stand that."

I blink, letting my eyes scan his red cheeks, the flare in his dark eyes, the way his nostrils rise and fall under the weight of his labored breathing.

"The *gall*. The absolute gall to complain that I smell like the man you shipped me off with, who was nothing but a gentleman. The man who, under different circumstances, I might have had fun with because he's a fun fucking guy. But instead, I spent all night stewing over *you*, Cade Eaton. You and your grumpy fucking face, and your stupid broad shoulders, and round Wrangler ass. So . . . fuck you." My finger pokes him in the center of his rock-hard chest. "And double fuck you for being jealous when you have no right. If I smell like him, you smell like bullshit."

I spin away, but Cade is faster. His hand shoots out and wraps around my arm, stopping me in my tracks. I jolt around to face him, my body drawing into his so naturally.

"Keep talking like that and I'm going to fuck the filth right out of your pretty mouth."

I arch a brow at him as goose bumps break out over my body. The air between us sizzles. "Excuse me?"

He swipes the back of his hand over his mouth, like he's pulling away the filter that's been there all along. "You heard me, Red. You keep barking at me like that and I'm going to put you on your knees, open those strawberry lips, and fuck your face just to shut you up."

My mind whirs. The man before me is not the same man I've been living with this past month. This is another version of him. A version he's hidden. A version I can work with.

A version I *like*.

The words sound harsh, but I know Cade well enough to know his words are often frustrated, but his hands are always gentle.

Elsie Silver

Holding his burning glare, I slowly drop to my knees in front of him, tipping my chin up to see every flicker of emotion in his eyes. "I fucking *dare* you."

A muscle in his jaw pops. I know he's standing on the precipice, but he's holding himself back. I'm not some virginal little girl. I know when a man wants me.

And Cade Eaton *wants* me.

He just needs to let himself take me.

So I give him a nudge. I lick my lips and open my mouth wide, tongue held flat, eyes melded to his. The most brash invitation in the world.

"*Fuck,*" he mutters and steps forward with authority, all shreds of restraint seeming to snap and fall around us. My core clenches, and my chest almost vibrates with anticipation. When he runs one broad palm over the back of my head while standing above me, I hum with pleasure.

"You are fucking torture, Willa Grant." He drops the glass on the deck behind him, and it lands with a heavy thud, miraculously not breaking against the wood. And then the pads of his fingers are on my lips, tracing, touching, pressing.

I've served myself up on a platter to him, but he's not diving in yet. He's savoring. And based on the bulge in the front of his pants, he likes what he sees.

"Fucking torture." He slips two fingers into my mouth, running them along my tongue, just to the edge of where I feel like I might gag. "A man can only take so much before he snaps."

My lips wrap around his digits in response as my palms flatten against his jeans for balance, eyelids dropping slightly as I do. I'm feeling a little too vulnerable, a little out of my league—a little *shy*. But this is what I wanted.

I wanted him to snap.

"Suck, Willa. Prove to me you're good enough for the job and maybe I'll give you my cock."

I moan, his words both drugging me and angering me. The challenge in what he's said is clear, and I've never been one to back down from a challenge.

I take it and brace against his muscular thighs, sliding my lips up and down the length of his fingers. I can almost *taste* the bourbon on them.

"Eyes on me, baby. Let's see it."

Heat crawls along my cheeks as I force myself to look up at him. His gaze is downright magnetic. He steals the breath from my lungs and takes it for himself.

His fingers tangle in my hair, stroking at my scalp while I slide my mouth up and down his fingers.

When he murmurs, "That's my girl," while looking me in the eye, nothing in the world has ever felt more right.

My girl.

I swirl my tongue around his fingers, and he groans, before gripping my hair and working my head the way he wants.

Setting the pace.

I give myself over to him, going soft in his hands, feeling my saliva build around my lips as I do.

"Fuck. *Willa*." My name sounds so good on his lips, the way he growls it—feral and possessive.

The boards of the porch bite at my knees, even through the jeans I'm wearing. And when he pulls his fingers from my mouth with a lewd pop, the last few threads holding him together snap before my eyes. I can almost hear the pinging of them flying apart like a popped guitar string.

I smile like the goddamn Cheshire Cat.

Because above me, Cade is breathing heavily and frantically unbuckling his belt. Fumbling with his button. Ripping at his zipper. And when his thick cock tents the fabric of his boxer briefs, my hands free it.

Right in the open, on his front deck.

He pulls his shirt off one-handed, and all at once, I'm licking my lips and running my palms over smooth, hot skin. Almost reveling in it. Sighing at the feel.

"Fuck, Red. You're desperate for it, aren't you?" His hand is back to combing my hair, and I can feel my wet saliva on his fingers as his opposite hand traces the bottom line of my jaw.

I swallow audibly and lick the bead of pre-cum glistening on the head of Cade's cock. Cade's *massive* cock. My eyes shimmer with anticipation. Like Christmas morning. Like I'm going to get to play with a whole new toy. "Yes." I press a kiss to the tip. "But only for you."

His head tips back on a groan, exposing his throat and all the dark stubble over his Adam's apple. I think he needed to hear that, and I didn't even realize it was true until the words left my mouth. His hands are still on my head, holding my skull reverently, as I wrap my lips around him for the first time. Smooth skin, soft musk, fingers tangled.

It's sensory overload as I slide my mouth down his length, tortuously slow, breathing through my nose and taking him as far back as I can.

When I think I can't go any further, I swallow and take just a little bit more.

"Jesus, Willa." I smile at the breathless state of his voice. Cade Eaton is about to learn that the trick to a good blow job is enjoying giving them. And I *love* it.

I don't care if I'm the one on my knees while he towers above me. The power is mine right now. The power to make him fall apart is mine. And I'm drunk with it.

My tongue swirls as I bob slowly, one hand twisting at the base of him while the other slips back to cup his balls, fingers working in tandem while my lips suction hard.

I moan on his cock, and his grip tightens in my hair. "Careful, baby. It's been too long, and you feel too good. I'm trying to make this last." His barely restrained voice husks with a light tremor.

I love the sound of it. It urges me on. If he thinks this is a one-time thing, he's confused. I'm realizing his ex did a bigger number on him than I first imagined. I wonder as I take him further back into my throat if he's a lot more insecure than he lets on.

I wonder if I can *show* him how irresistible he is to me. I take one hand and trail it over his hipbone, dragging a nail over the line that cuts just below where his abs start. Moving up the trail of hair toward his abdomen, I splay my hand over his stomach, feeling all the lines and ridges there.

When I glance up at him, his hooded eyes are locked on my hand. As he catches me watching him, his eyes soften and he brushes the pad of his thumb over my cheek. "You look so fucking pretty like this, Willa."

I groan and my lashes flutter as I feel a surge of wetness between my thighs.

"A mouth full of my cock." He guides my head in a rhythm he likes, and I remove my palm from his base, opting to explore his body. He seems to like that, and more than anything, I want to make him feel good.

I want him to want more.

"You've been dreaming about this, haven't you?"

I stare up at him and nod, sucking him even harder.

"That's why you've spent every single day here under my roof, driving me absolutely insane. Teasing me with that perfect ass, those goddamn nipples, and your silky hair. Even your laugh makes me hard. Did you know that?"

I moan, loving hearing that I drive him crazy. Gliding my hands over his ribs, I slide them behind him and trail over his muscular ass the way I've wanted to for a long time.

I squeeze and he picks up the pace, fingers gripping

my scalp as his palms cover my ears. A soothing white noise fills my head, and I stare up at him, turning myself over to the wild look in his dark eyes.

He said he was going to fuck my mouth, and that's what he does. I hold on for the ride, but it doesn't last long. Soon his thrusts turn longer and harder, rather than fast and frantic. His pinched eyes remain laser-focused on mine.

"Willa, I'm going to . . ." He huffs out a breath as he trails off, trying to pull away from me. Trying to pull out. But I yank him closer, stretch my neck and give him a little shake of my head as I widen my eyes at him.

His mouth pops open, ever so slightly, and I watch the tip of his tongue dart out over his lips. "Fuck."

And then I get to *watch* him come apart. *Watch* him give in. And it feels like winning.

His cock jerks and pulses in my mouth, and I swallow as it does. I keep my eyes on his face, even when his flutter shut. Even when his hands go soft in my hair and switch from gripping to stroking. To gentle touches.

When his eyes flick open again, I draw away, feeling him soften and hearing his breathing even out.

"Christ, Willa," he breathes as he pulls his pants back up and I wipe at my lips.

He crouches down, lifting me up with him, and crushes his mouth against mine, clearly not caring about where it's been. Because the kiss is searing. Heartfelt. His lips are soft against mine, and when I tangle my hands behind his neck, I can feel a damp layer of perspiration.

He pulls away and rests his forehead against mine. "I'm sorry," he whispers against my lips.

"You don't need to apologize for that. I think I had almost as good of a time as you." I chuckle quietly, feeling his breath against my damp lips.

His forehead rolls along mine. "No. I'm sorry I let you go out tonight."

My eyes roll, but neither of us moves. Still standing out in the open on the front porch. Still trailing our hands over each other. "You don't *let* me do anything, Eaton." I arch a brow at him, and he pulls me into a hug, his steely arms wrapping me up tight.

And it feels so damn good.

"I'm sorry I didn't beg you to come home with me."

I nuzzle against him, thriving on that specific type of apology. "You do beg well," I joke.

He turns his head and presses a kiss into the crook of my neck. "I don't know what I'm doing."

"Welcome to my life," I joke again, trying to lighten the mood or just quell the slight pang of discomfort.

Cade squeezes me tighter and presses a kiss to my shoulder. "I promised myself I wouldn't cross this line with you. That I wouldn't complicate things. That I wouldn't tangle us up like this when you're leaving so soon."

A pit forms in the bottom of my stomach, and insecurities leap like fish out of water, because standing in his arms doesn't feel cozy. It feels like a cage. It feels like an apology. And all my walls shoot back up. I felt like a goddess two minutes ago, and now, there's a sense of dread creeping in.

I pull away, giving him a flat smile and sort of patting at his shoulders. "Well, let's just not complicate it."

He gives his head a little shake, seeming surprised by my response. I turn and walk toward the front door.

Am I being dramatic? Maybe. Probably. But my pride can only take so many hits where Cade Eaton is concerned. He can only turn me down so many times or make excuses about why this can't happen before I take it personally.

Complicated.

I think the only thing making this complicated is him.

Once I reach the privacy of my bedroom, I shut the door and step into the space, sucking in a big breath.

Flicking the bedside light on, I let my mind wander to stupid Cade Eaton. Big-dicked, strong-biceped, fucking handsome-faced, complicated asshole that he is.

The door bursts open behind me. I turn and see Cade standing there, hands fisted at his sides, in unbuttoned jeans and still no goddamn shirt, which is really just the cruelest kind of joke. His shoulders take up almost the entire doorframe, and his expression is one I recognize as his angry scowl.

"What do you think you're doing?" he barks out.

I sniff and look away because he's intimidating right

now. "Making sure things don't get *too complicated* for you. Obviously."

"Woman." He always sounds so snarky when he calls me woman. "Are you insane? You think I went three years without laying my hand on a single person to break my streak with one as exceptional as you and then let you just walk away?"

Three years?

"I—"

"No." He holds up a hand. "I'm going to talk. And you're going to close your mouth and listen. Because if you'd let me finish what I was saying out there, you wouldn't have spent a single moment in here thinking I don't want to complicate things with you. I said I *promised* myself I wouldn't complicate this with you. You're young, you're restless, and I'm truthfully too fucking jealous to do anything casual with you." He runs a hand through his hair, giving the ends a frustrated little tug. "I've watched you with my son. I've watched you, period. I've *longed* for you. I went crazy tonight thinking of you out with Lance. I know in my bones that I won't want to let you go at the end of the summer, but I'll take what I can get. Because you're too fucking special to pass up. Fuck my promises, that's what I was going to say."

My throat tightens as he stares down at that brass line separating my space from his. Arbitrary and yet, symbolic. Like when we cross that line we're not going back.

"I . . ."

He holds a hand up again. "No. I don't want to talk anymore. Unless it's to hear you explain why you think I'd let you suck me off and then not return the favor. What kind of assholes you been dating, Red?"

My lips roll together as I watch him cross that line into my space.

It feels like our space.

"Now, get on your back. I want to watch you squirm while I taste you for the first time."

22

Cade

"So you're allowed to talk, but I'm not?" Her arms cross over her chest, but there's a small smile on her face. That's the look I like, not the stricken one she walked away with moments ago.

For a girl with so much attitude, she has a serious case of self-doubt on her hands. One I intend to clear up for her.

"I love listening to you talk, Red." I prowl into her room, not missing the way she's squeezing her thighs together. I smirk because I know she got off on giving that blow job. Best blow job of my life because no girl has ever been *that* into giving one. "But when you say things that aren't true, I get pissed off. Things you make up in your pretty head and toss around in there long enough that you believe them."

She steps backward, eyes flaring as I follow her into the room. "You think you don't do that too?"

I ignore her question. I do that too. The difference is I realize I'm doing it. "You have no idea how special you are. How insane you make me feel. How I haven't stopped thinking about you since the moment I laid eyes on you."

She rolls her eyes at me, and I point at her. "That right there. Don't do it. The only appropriate response is, *Thank you.*"

Her legs bump into the bed, and she drops to sit, biting at her lip in the most distracting way. I step between her legs, sighing at the nearness and the heat of her body against mine. After so long, it feels so fucking good to be this close to someone.

Especially to her.

"Let me hear it, baby. Say thank you."

She clears her throat, eyes darting away. "Thank you."

"Good girl." I grip her chin and turn her face up to me. "That's what you're going to say to me all night. Every time I tell you something good. Are we clear?"

A shiver runs over her, even as I see that spark of defiance in her eye. The one I admire. I want to turn that spark into a whole damn fire so this girl goes out and does what she wants with her life.

"Fine."

I let a smile touch my lips as I stare down at her. "Good."

"Why are you smiling? It's creepy. You never smile."

I shake my head at her. "I smile. You just miss them

because it's when I'm staring at your ass. And I'm smiling now because I'm really looking forward to this."

One of her shapely brows arches, and her glare moves down my torso to my crotch. "Yeah. I can see that."

"I think you meant *thank you*." Sliding my hand along her cheek and into her hair at the base of her neck, I crouch down and kiss her, tipping her head up to me. A deep rumble emanates from my chest when I feel how soft she is in my hands. How willing. How eager.

Her plush lips are supple beneath mine, and her warm hands are tentative as she brings them back to my torso and starts exploring.

Gooseflesh erupts over my skin everywhere she moves them, and I revel in her touch. In the years I've spent abstinent, I didn't imagine it ever feeling this electric, this deeply necessary—natural, like I don't even have to try with her. There's just this spark. One we can't see, but it's been burning between us from day one.

"Thank you," she murmurs against my lips, and I take that opportunity to slip my tongue into her mouth. To claim her and take my time with it. Not like the frantic kiss in the hay bales that ended in embarrassment. Not like the blow job edged in frustration on the front porch.

Just a private room and a full night ahead of us. Exactly what I need—what *we* need.

Our kisses are languid. No teeth clash, neither of us fumble. It's been a long time since I kissed someone, but I remember early kisses being awkward, having to figure out a rhythm, the give and take that didn't quite match up right.

But with Willa, that's not the case.

Everything feels right. Except for . . .

"You're wearing too many clothes, baby," I say, pulling back to rest my forehead against hers as I reach down to the waistline of her jeans and pluck at the cotton shirt tucked in there.

In response she leans back and lifts her arms up above her head, staring me in the eye like this is some sort of challenge. I give her a small grin, liking the way she looks with her lips all puffy and wet. Her cheeks all pink. Her hair all mussed from *my* hands in it.

Fuck, another man touching her hair tonight was something that specifically crossed my mind. I don't know why I got hung up on the image of someone else's fingers trailing through her shiny copper strands. Someone with softer, more manicured hands. Someone with more money to their name. Someone with more to offer her.

I drop my gaze to where my hands are touching her, where they wrap around her waist, right on that milky skin I was trying to catch a peep of the first day she stepped on my property. "Is this okay?" I ask, wanting to be certain I'm not doing something stupid.

"Yes," she hisses out almost desperately.

As I push my hands up her torso, the shirt bunches. It's like unwrapping a present, revealing silky skin followed by a simple nude bra with a lace overlay, tits round and firm above the line of the cup that cuts across them. I peel the shirt over her head and drop a hand to flick the clasp on her bra, pulling it away and tossing it on the floor beside us.

I take a step back to appreciate her. She's propped her hands behind her on the bed and is gazing at me with wide green eyes, a little intoxicated looking—but not on alcohol. Her breasts are full and heavy, dusky pink nipples erect and pointing right at me. Little silver studs adorn either side, sparkling in the light, and I want to fucking play with those.

I want to play with everything.

If Willa is the playground, I want to fucking play. Period.

"You are *beautiful*." My eyes race over her form, illuminated only by the warm light of the small lamp beside her bed. "Fucking perfect. I knew you would be. But goddamn, Willa. You're almost too much."

The blush on her cheeks spreads down her neck and onto her chest. Being naked in front of me doesn't make her uncomfortable, but hearing my words does. I click my tongue at her and when she looks back my way, I pin her with a scowl.

"Thank you." Her voice wobbles, but she gets it out all the same, looking fiery, chest heaving under the weight of her slightly labored breathing.

I smirk at her and she rolls her eyes but her lips tip up.

With a deep chuckle, I drop to my knees in front of her and reach for the chain belt looped into her jeans. "You want me to keep going?"

She scoffs playfully. "How many times does a woman need to proposition you before you know she wants you to keep going, Eaton? Like, do you really need to hear me keep saying it out loud?"

My eyes drop, and my hands shape her waist, sliding up to the base of her breasts. I breathe deeply around the heavy thud of the blow she just unknowingly delivered. When someone else chooses other men over you, I think you do need to hear it. At the very least, I *want* to hear it. Because Willa wanting me seems wholly unlikely. Totally crazy. Plus, hearing her say she wants it might be the sexiest thing in the world.

I lift my chin and gaze into her bright emerald eyes. "Yeah, Red. I really need to hear you say it out loud."

Her lips pop open, and realization flashes in her eyes as she sits up straighter, hands reaching for me. When her fingers curve behind my ears and her palms rasp against my stubble, my eyes flutter shut.

Touching her feels incredible. But being touched? Fuck. I didn't realize how badly I was missing this.

Her nails rake against my scalp, and this time she bends down to kiss me, so gently, so carefully.

Until she bites down on my bottom lip, squeezes my head in her hands, and says, "Cade Eaton, if you stop undressing me, I will absolutely lose my mind and hide in my bedroom every night touching myself while thinking about how fucking hot sucking your cock on the front porch was."

"Jesus Christ, woman." I pull back to look her in the eye with a little skip in my heart. "I won't stop. But can I come watch that show sometime?"

The apples of her cheeks go round as she smirks back at me. "Definitely." And then she's kissing me again, ratcheting up the urgency. Her hands grip my neck, while mine work over her breasts. They're soft and firm all at once, a reminder of her age if I let my head wander that way—but I don't.

Instead, I just enjoy the little mewling noises she makes when I brush my thumbs over her nipples. When I pinch them, I push my tongue into her mouth and enjoy the way her hips rock in my direction, like she just can't get enough.

It's empowering. It's like a fucking drug seeing how badly she wants me. And I break the kiss only because I'm not done playing with the rest of her body.

I know I'll have lots of time to kiss her because I don't plan to stop so long as she's willing to let me have her.

"These fucking tits have featured in my dreams for weeks," I say, sliding my mouth down her throat, pressing kisses to the little indent at the base of it and working my way along her collarbone. A lick to her slender shoulder sends a shiver through her entire body, and I smile to myself because her reactions are just so damn satisfying.

"Thank you." Her head tips back, which makes her

breasts press out in my direction like some sort of special offering.

It feels like everything is dialed up a zillion notches. Every reaction is stronger somehow. Every feeling magnified. I can't explain it and maybe I don't need to. Maybe the lesson here is that I just need to relax and let myself enjoy something for once.

Because I fully intend to enjoy Willa Grant.

My mouth latches onto one nipple, and she cries out instantly. "Ah! Don't stop doing that, Cade."

I suck harder and her body writhes. My opposite hand thumbs at the other nipple in a steady rhythm, the metal piercing adding a weight to it. My cock surges painfully against my jeans, and she's not even totally naked yet.

"I'm a fucking goner for you, Red. Watching you squirm? Listening to you moan my name? What am I supposed to do now?" I trail my tongue across her sternum before latching onto the opposite breast, strumming at her wet nipple.

"Fuck me. You're supposed to fuck me." Her words are breathless, edged in desperation, and I love the sound, the vibration in her chest that I can feel against my lips.

I drop my hand and press it against the apex of her thighs. Even through her jeans, I feel the heat. I know when I peel all these layers back, she's going to be fucking soaked.

For me.

"Is that so?" I lean back a little and press my thumb hard against the denim. "Right here, Red?"

"Yes." She throws her head back, her tits glistening with my saliva, fingers fisted in the sheets.

I rub firm circles on her jeans, chuckling darkly at the way her hips gyrate against the pressure.

"Cade," her lips part on my name, her tongue darting out to wet them. "God."

"He's not here right now, baby. It's just me. And I'm done asking nicely. I'm ready to take." I pull one nipple into my mouth, swirling my tongue around the metal before clamping down on it. Her corresponding whimper is light and airy, just like her consuming laugh.

I wrap her loose hair around my fist, pull her close and whisper against her ear. "I'm going to peel these skin-tight jeans off of you and enjoy a taste of what I already know is going to be a perfect little cunt." A tremor racks her body, but I keep going. "Make you come in my mouth. And before you've even recovered from that, I'll shove my cock into you, make you scream my name loud enough they'll hear you one town over."

Willa's eyes flare in surprise and she nods.

"Is that what you want, Red? Let me hear you say it."

Challenge blazes in her eyes, her chin jutting out stubbornly. "Take it then, Cade. Taste me. Fuck me. Fuck me so hard I'll forget my own name. I've never wanted anything more. I'm yours tonight."

My chest rumbles in satisfaction, and my hands work

at the button on her jeans. "And when I'm finished, what will you say?"

"God," she breathes out so quietly I almost miss it, her eyes fixed on where my hands are now making quick work of her pants. "I knew you had big dick energy, but this is something else."

I yank at her jeans and she eagerly lifts her hips. "What are you going to say, baby?"

"Thank you," is her breathy response.

"That's my girl," I grit out as I peel her pants off, dusting kisses down her thighs, feeling gooseflesh pop up under my lips where I drag my stubble across her tender skin. When I get her jeans past her knees, they catch on the tall snakeskin boots she's wearing.

"These fucking boots," I grumble, moving back and grabbing them at the heel to remove them. And then I stop.

"Do you like them?" She does that little signature arch thing with her eyebrow. I fucking love when she does that. A silent challenge.

"I'll like them a whole lot better when I get them off so I can see you naked and spread out for me."

She hums. "Summer told me they were good luck when she lent them to me."

I toss one boot behind me and reach for the other as I shake my head. "You women are witches. I don't even want to know where these boots have been. Get them the fuck off."

Willa giggles, never put off by harsh words. She

points her toe, and the boot slides off, which is good timing, because her naked and laughing is an aphrodisiac.

The jeans are gone.

The socks are gone.

"You're wearing panties," I grumble, staring at her nude lace full-cut booty shorts. Perfect curves. My cock twitches.

She nibbles at her lip. "You keep telling me to."

"Red, me telling you to do things"—I reach forward and tug at the top so they wedge between her pussy lips and sit high on her hips—"has almost never worked."

"Some days I do. Some days I don't. Gotta keep things interesting. Plus, I keep waiting for you to check. Kind of hoping you'll dole out some discipline if you catch me without them."

"Fuck." I roll my lips together, eyes caught on the fabric disappearing into her slit. My hand trembles when I reach forward, and I still it by rubbing my fingers over the wet fabric that separates us. I groan when she sighs and spreads her thighs wider, palms still propped behind her on the mattress. "Lie back, baby. I want you to relax."

"I don't know how I'm supposed to relax with you between my legs, Cade," she says. But she also flops onto her back.

"Is that a thank-you, Red?"

She chuckles, but it's all raspy. Deep in her throat, right where I was not so long ago.

"I should pinch myself for how unbelievable this is."

My opposite hand grips her ankle, where I press a kiss to the protruding bone. Even her fucking ankles are pretty. "How unbelievable you are." I prop that foot on the edge of the bed and push her leg open.

"Thank you," she says, hips lifting urgently as she does.

"You still want me to fuck you, Red?"

"Yes." Her hands roam her tits, plucking at her nipples.

"Beg for it, baby." I press my thumb to her clit and watch her head pop up over the hills of her breasts.

"Pardon me?" Her eyes go wide.

It wasn't so long ago she told me to beg in this exact room. This time, I'm running the show. Not her. "Beg, Willa." My thumb trails down, and I press into her just slightly, seeing her legs tremble as the lace rasps over her soft, wet pussy lips.

Her head flops back down and her fingers twist on her nipples. "Please take me, Cade."

Her back arches, and I drag a finger along the lace that's skimming the edge of her pussy while continuing to press my thumb in, soaking the fabric.

Legs spreading even further, her body shudders. "I need it. I need you." I throb painfully against my jeans at the way she emphasizes the word *you*. "I need you so badly, Cade. Please. Please fuck me."

I lean down between her legs, taking a gentle bite of her flesh through the fabric, drawing a whimper from her lips. "And whose name are you going to scream when you come?"

"Yours." I internally beat my chest when her response comes so quickly.

I pull my wallet from my back pocket, ready to pull out what is probably an expired condom. But she grabs at my arm. "No. I need to feel you."

Fuck. I want that too.

"You sure?" She moans when I drop my head, tongue darting out to get a taste through the soaked fabric.

Her hips swivel and she gasps. "I'm on the pill."

A deep groan rumbles in my chest. A possessive one. A satisfied one. "What a dirty fucking girl you are." I suck her clit through the fabric, feeling her fingers raking across my scalp. "I'm going to fill you up, and you'll thank me for it. But first, Willa"—I reach up and yank her panties down, taking a long look at the pink perfection before me—"I'm starving."

Her hands shoot up to swipe over her face. "Oh god," she moans as I drop back down to take a proper taste.

And then her hands land back on my head and her legs wrap around my shoulders, and I feel like I'm the one who should thank her.

23

Willa

I've died and gone to heaven. I'm sure of it. Because the way Cade wields his tongue is out of this world. He licks me. He sucks me. He *bites* me. And then he makes me thank him for it.

He's reduced me to a puddle of hormones on the floor. Or as the case may be, on my bed, while he kneels on the ground and makes a meal out of me with one rough hand splayed against my inner thigh possessively as he slowly works two fingers into my pussy. I squirm and chant, "Cade," like I'm in some sort of hot-single-dad-loving cult.

I'd be the leader of that cult. *For sure.*

"That's it, baby, wide open for me. Are you clenching, Willa?"

"I don't know," I breathe out stupidly before leaning up on my elbows to look down at him. He's all dark and foreboding, his lips glistening with, well, *me*. "I'm pretty sure I'm having an out-of-body experience."

"Relax. I'm going to take care of you." His thumb strokes along the tendons at the top of my upper thigh, making my head fall back on a sigh, my entire body relaxing as I do.

His fingers slide home and I gasp when they curl up into the best spot. No man should be able to find a clit through jeans *and* the g-spot in one night.

But the one kneeling between my legs can.

"So fucking tight." His fingers work in and out, and when I glance down at him, his gaze worships between my legs. I feel myself stretching as his fingers twist and scissor. "So fucking wet." His coal eyes move up, roaming my body hungrily, appreciating every dip and curve. "I've never seen such a pretty pussy in my life, Willa."

Admittedly, I've never wondered much about the way my pussy looks. It's always served its purpose just fine. She's been a real champ, if you ask me. But I *preen* under that compliment from Cade. He's older. More experienced. If he says it's pretty, well, who am I to disagree?

I lick my lips as I stare down at him. "Thank you." The words come easier every time. The expression of satisfaction on his face is my reward. At first I was a bit fired up over it, but satisfying Cade—seeing that expression on his face—it's quickly becoming a favorite pastime of mine.

"Good girl," he hums, touching my body so reverently that I squirm. He doesn't rush, he doesn't slam into me. His movements are languid as he wrings every ounce of pleasure from every corner of my body, and I've felt nothing like it before. "Now you're going to come for me, baby."

The way his fingers move, his intense stare while he plays with my pretty pussy—his words, not mine—causes everything to build. The sensations. The way the shadows play across his handsome face and chiseled shoulders. The way they flex when he moves his arm. The feel of his fingertips pushing into the soft flesh of my leg.

The sudden way he's sucking at my clit while lazily pushing his fingers into me. He's got the whole movement down pat. The curling and pressing rhythm. He plays my body like it's an instrument he knows inside and out.

And when the pressure winds through my hip, wrapping around the base of my spine, I grip his head and pull his face tight against my pussy, grinding against him as I topple.

"Cade!" I call out, just like I promised him I would, as I come apart. Legs shaking. Toes curling. The arches of my feet cramp, and his movements just continue. He doesn't stop too soon, like so many men do. He's not eager to be done with the foreplay. This isn't a chore for him, and I think that might be the sexiest thing about it.

I smile up at the smooth white ceiling, cast in a golden tone from the glow of the lamp, and feel my limbs go soft. And with that rush of pleasure comes a rush of protectiveness. A rush of rage that someone could wound him so profoundly. That someone could stray the way his ex did.

The resistance. The jealousy. The longing looks. The solitary way he lives his life. It all makes so much more sense now.

And I have every intention of showing him how badly I want *him*.

Pushing myself up, I rake my fingers through his hair, feeling his heavy breathing against my damp skin as I cup my hands around the base of his skull and pull his head up to mine. I link my eyes with his, staring hard into them as my thumbs stroke through the stubble along his chiseled cheeks.

"Thank you," I say simply.

And then I kiss him. I can taste myself on him, but I don't care. All I care about is that he knows I appreciate him. Our tongues tangle and his calloused palms dance over my ribs, somehow making me shiver and my core stir, even though I just finished.

Correction: even though he just finished me.

"That was the best orgasm of my life," I murmur against his wet lips, drawing a chuckle from his chest. "Now lose the pants and lie back on the bed. I want to repay the favor."

His lips trail against my cheek. "You think you're in charge now, Willa? That's adorable."

"Lose the pants, mister." I use a fake authoritative

voice and return his kisses all the way over his stubbled cheek to his ear, where I nip playfully at the lobe.

He huffs out a breath but pushes to stand, fingers working expertly at his jeans, corded forearms rippling. I absently wonder why I was so hung up on his grumpy face when he has a body like this and a sweet, authoritative, doting personality. What the hell was I even on about? I can't remember.

"What are you thinking about right now?" he asks as he shucks his jeans down, impressive cock tenting his underwear. I almost forgot how big it is and that I choked like an amateur when he thrusted hard into my mouth.

"How hot you are. How insane your body is. How sweet you are." When I rip my eyes away from his cock, his eyebrow arches at me as I add, "I think the words you're searching for are, *Thank you, baby.*"

He pulls his boxers down with a smirk, clearly not self-conscious about his body. "You like it when I call you baby?"

I roll my lips together as I regard him. I fucking love it. It sounds so lame and cheesy to me most of the time, but when he growls it and tacks something filthy on to it? "Yes. I love it."

He moves around me, and I turn to check out his round muscled ass—Wranglers hold nothing to the real thing. Every part of his body is bound with strength, and not the type you get from too many hours in the gym. His muscles are real, thick and hard but not overly defined.

His body, his skin, the crinkles around his eyes . . . it's

all just proof of long hours spent hard at work. And I'm not sure I've ever found anything more attractive than a man who works hard.

He sits on the bed and turns, back pressed up against the headboard, chest puffed, long legs stretched out before him like a king.

His fist wraps around his thick cock, and he jerks it a few times. I lick my lips as I watch him, entranced. I think I could happily watch him come just like this.

His gaze heats on mine when he catches me staring. "Get over here and ride my cock, baby."

He doesn't need to ask me twice. I turn and crawl up the bed, trailing my hands over the smattering of hair on his chest as I hike one leg over his waist, straddling him while his hands settle on my hips. I feel the steely length of his cock resting against my bare ass, and I give a little wiggle, moving my hips and feeling his hardness slide over me.

Cade shoots one hand up to my chin, pressing a quick kiss next to my lips. "If you want me to fuck your ass, all you have to do is ask."

I prop my hands against his chest, fingers curling in at his crude words. "You'd probably make me beg for it."

He laughs, deep and raspy, and I feel the vibration of it under my palms. For a man who avoided laughing around me for so long, I can actually *feel* him laughing.

His smile is a shot straight to the heart. "Probably," he replies easily, before kissing me again. "Now take my cock and put it in. I want to watch you."

"Jesus Christ, Eaton. I'm going to be stuck in a permanent state of blushing after getting naked with you." I reach behind myself, running my hand over his length, feeling how wet I am seated across his abdomen, legs spread wide.

He huffs out a breath, thumbs brushing the silver studs on my nipples. I can tell by the way he groans he likes them. A lot. "Works for me, Red. You should see how pretty you look with your cheeks all pink. These perfect tits out. If you don't get to work, I'm going to blow on your back rather than inside you."

"Fuck." My tongue darts out over my bottom lip, followed by a graze of my teeth. I push up onto my knees.

With one hand propped on his round shoulder, I reach down between us, wrapping my fingers around his throbbing length. When I notch the head of him against my entrance, we groan in unison.

It's this moment where everything feels inevitable. It's the anticipation that's almost as good as the real thing. I can feel the dome of his head, just slightly inside of me. It's going to be a tight fit, so before I let go, I run him against my wetness, swiping up and down, pressing him against my aching clit.

"Jesus Christ, Red. Are you trying to kill me?"

"No. I'm trying to make sure it will fit." My eyes are still down, watching the way his cock comes away glistening.

"Baby, it's going to fit. You were made for me."

My eyes shoot up to his, but that's right when his

hips thrust up and he's sinking into me right as I'm sliding down on him. I grip his forearms desperately. The feeling of fullness and not knowing how to respond to that comment draw my eyes back down, and we watch as my body stretches to take him.

"Look at you, Willa. You take me so well," he grits out, voice sounding strained and gravelly.

I moan, feeling the way our bodies throb together. Skin on skin. My hands slide up to his shoulders as I push down the last couple of inches, taking his full length inside of me.

Cade sits up taller to press a kiss to the center of my chest, hands moving around my body to grip the globes of my ass. "Fuck, you feel like heaven. So hot and tight. Just for me."

Just for me. My heart aches, and my arms wrap around his neck. I kiss the top of his head. This strong, stoic, honest, hardworking man—one whose hurt runs so deep that he's lived several years questioning his worth. His value.

I hate it. I hate it for him. So, I rock my hips on him, hug him to my chest and say, "Just for you." My nails graze over his shoulders and down his strong back. I bite on his ear again and nuzzle my cheek against his stubble. I love the feel of it rasping over my skin in perfect tandem with the rough pads of his fingers.

I lift and drop down, taking his full length in one go and hissing against his cheek at the slight burn. "Just for you," I whisper again.

And I think I mean it.

Who the fuck knows what I'm doing? I'm positive that I don't. Or I don't most days. I go with the flow. I take my opportunities.

And God, an opportunity has never felt this right, so I don't question it. I don't overthink it. I give myself over to it.

To him.

I pull his head up to me and kiss him like it's our last moment on earth. The energy in the small bedroom changes. What started off as rough and turned playful, has morphed into something more sensitive. But now we're more frantic.

Our hands roam. He grips my ass, lifting me and pushing me back down. My legs shake and my head tips back. His beard scrapes across my chest. His lips work my nipples. My hands tug his hair.

We don't talk.

But we don't need to. Our bodies do the talking. Our kisses are wet, and messy, and perfectly imperfect.

"Cade," I whimper, as wet slapping noises fill the room, followed by his animalistic grunts. My tits are bouncing. His eyes are glassy. "I think I'm going to . . ." I trail off, hot and breathless and totally out of control. Utterly consumed. But he knows what I'm trying to say. He knows what I need. What I want.

One hand splays over my stomach, and his fingers swipe over my bud. "Come for me, baby," he pants.

"Yes," I hiss. "Please don't stop."

"Never," is his response. And it sets me off, the surety of it striking something in me that causes an eruption.

"Cade!" I scream his name this time. I don't just call it. I let loose, and god, it feels incredible.

We're a tangle of moans and taut muscles. His fingers keep moving, but his hand lands on my shoulder and clamps me onto his body as his cock surges, twitching and throbbing.

He spills himself inside me as he whispers my name against my lips, and there's something intensely personal about it. I'm trying to catch my breath. I told him I'd say thank you, and I want to keep all my promises to him. He's seen too many broken ones in his life.

He crushes me to him in the wake of our orgasms. It feels like he wraps his entire body around me. I nuzzle in closer, with him still inside me, damp chest against my cheek, steely arms clutching me around my back.

I open my lips to say the words he wanted.

But it's him who drops his cheek against my head and rasps, "Thank you."

24

Cade

I wake up hot and hard.

And smiling.

Willa's hair is in my face, and her breath is making my neck feel damp and sweaty. She's sprawled her long limbs over mine and pressed her body so close that all I'd have to do is shift her a few inches and she'd be lying right on top of me.

I'm not especially comfortable. And I fucking love it.

I always kind of chalked up my dry streak to aging, to being past it at thirty-eight. I know I'm not old but I feel old some days. Worn out and lacking the energy it takes to start a new relationship. Too tired to deal with the highs and the lows and the inevitable drama.

But Willa Grant invigorates me.

After having the best sex of my life, I dragged her to the kitchen and fed her. I made us pancakes. We talked. We laughed. But when she smudged a bit of syrup on her lips, I couldn't resist licking it off. And that turned into me getting her on all fours, right on the hardwood floor in the kitchen. Which turned into a shower. Which turned into slamming her into the tile wall until we both came again.

She told me she couldn't take anymore, but when I yanked her into my bed with me, I disappeared beneath the covers for one more taste. And it turns out she's a big fat liar because she absolutely took more.

I should be exhausted right now, but apparently my dick didn't get the memo. Because he's up and ready to defile the twenty-five-year-old sprawled out in my bed. Again.

"Down, boy," I murmur, reaching to adjust myself in my boxers. Willa stirs when I move, but my opposite arm comes around to the dimples at the small of her back, pressing her against me.

I don't care if it's physically uncomfortable. Having Willa close is comforting. It's like having Luke under the same roof. I know everyone is safe.

I wish I could say I felt the same way about Luke's mom. But I don't. The only times Talia crosses my mind are when I'm feeling wounded or insecure. When that bitter taste crawls up my throat and I think about the years I wasted trying to make things work with her when deep down I didn't want them to.

The worst part is, I can't bring myself to regret it because I have Luke. And he's the best thing that's ever happened to me.

Willa moves her head to my chest, sliding her fingers through the sparse hair. "Shh. Go back to sleep. I'm having the best dream."

The thought that Willa is another of the best things in my life crops up, but it scares me. It feels too soon. She feels too young. It feels too . . . impossible.

"What are you dreaming about, Red?" I lift my head and drop a kiss to her silky hair.

I feel her chest shake a little, her breasts pressing against me. Even the metal of her piercings is warm, because of course she sleeps naked. "That my hot boss banged my brains out last night."

I shake my head.

"No, for real. You should see this fucking guy. All dark and broody with a massive dick."

"Willa."

"These big, calloused hands to go with his big, round ass—"

"Woman." I flip her onto her back, the sound of her giggle music to my ears. I lie on top of her, propped on my elbows. She's got this playful smile on her face and creases on her cheek from the pillowcase. She looks like a sleepy, creamy, green-eyed goddess.

I shake my head at her again. I do that a lot. It used to be out of annoyance, now it's more like . . . disbelief.

"Is *woman* how you say, *Thank you for all the compliments, Willa?*"

"Keep teasing me and I'll fill your throat with my cock to shut you up again," I grumble, but it's playful.

And she knows it. She's figured out how to interpret me, rather than being offended by me. She knows when I'm joking, or when I'm grumpy. And when I am, she just rolls her eyes at me or walks away.

I guess that's why she opens her mouth like she's ready to take me there again, but then her eyes widen, and she slams a hand over it. "Oh my God. Morning breath. I'm sorry."

I laugh. After what we did last night, a little morning breath won't scare me off. "Willa, I was with you while you were barfing. Your breath will never be worse than that."

She gasps from behind her palm like she's offended. "Asshole!" And that just makes me laugh harder.

I press a kiss to her forehead before leaning over to whisper in her ear, "Lucky for you, I won't be able to smell your breath with my dick in your mouth."

She laughs silently at that, covering her face with both hands as her body shakes. I flop down beside her and let her infectious happiness take me over.

We lie here—laughing, hands roaming, bodies tangled—but before long, she pulls me back on top of her, slides down my body, and tells me to fuck her mouth.

⁓

"Okay, so like . . ." Willa wrings her hands in her lap as I start the truck. It's like stepping outside of my house has reality crashing down all around us, and she's freaking out. "How are we handling this?"

I should be freaking out but I feel remarkably calm. Something about this is just too right to get worked up over. I live in my head enough to know when I'm losing my shit, and I'm definitely not.

"Handling what?" I reply, as I shift into drive and watch behind myself out of habit. I still check for my old dog, who was always ripping around the farm, burning off his endless energy. The dog Talia took with her. She literally said she wanted "the dog or the kid." I still can't believe those words came out of her mouth. There was no question about that for me. Anyone who put those two on the same priority level was sure as shit not going to be raising my child.

"This. What happened between us. All the sex. Are we doing more of that? Or is it a one-and-done scenario?"

One of my cheeks quirk up. "I think you mean six and done, baby."

"Don't *baby* me right now, Eaton. I'm serious."

"Me too, Red. Should I pull over? We can make it seven and counting."

"I hate you." She crosses her arms like she's pouting. I know better. Willa isn't a pouter.

"Right. But you love my dick."

She sucks in a deep breath and then lets out this adorable frustrated growl. "Weeks and weeks of you being a humorless asshole, and all it took was a few orgasms for you to become Mr. Chucklehead. I should have taken one for the team sooner."

I twist my fingers on the steering wheel, trying to hold back my laughter. "I think you should continue to take it for the team."

Her head whips over to look at me. "Yeah?"

I shrug, keeping my eyes on the gravel road ahead of me. "Yeah. Definitely."

"Why?"

I glance at her now. Her eyes are narrowed, and I can see the insecurity written all over her face. Goddamn, but this girl puts on a good show.

"Because I like you, Willa."

She points at me and tries to correct my statement. "You like to have sex with me."

I stop the truck in the middle of the road. There's no traffic so it doesn't matter. And honestly, even if there were, they could all just fucking wait while I set this woman straight.

I turn to face her, one hand slung over the wheel. My posture might seem casual but my expression is not. She must take notice because I watch her shoulders shimmy as she sits up straighter and scans my face.

"No, Willa. I like *you*. I care about *you*. I didn't go without sex for years just to start it back up randomly. I had opportunities, and I turned them down because I wasn't interested. We don't need to make a show of it, and with Luke around, we probably shouldn't. But I'm interested in *you*. I don't know where that leaves us or what it all means. All I know is that it's going to fucking wreck me when you leave at the end of this summer, but I'm too far gone to care."

Her lips pop open like she's about to say something, but she closes them again. I can see her processing. She's so expressive, nothing is locked up with a face like that. I can read her far too easily.

She doesn't say it, but she looks happy with my response.

What she says is, "Thank you."

I give her a firm nod, put the truck in drive, and reach across the console, palm open. Within seconds she slides her slender fingers between mine, and I wrap her hand up, giving her a quick squeeze as we drive to the main farmhouse in a stunned but companionable silence.

"Dad!" Luke flies around the corner of my father's house like a bat out of hell as I stride around the front of my truck to open Willa's door. I swear this kid never stops running . . . jumping . . . climbing. He's taken years off my life for sure. "Willa!" he cries, when he sees her step out of the vehicle.

"You're not my chauffeur, you know," she murmurs as she takes my hand to hop down.

"I'll add not opening your car door to the list of offenses—that includes not eating your pussy—from past men."

She blushes and drops my hand, stepping away.

Keeping our hands off each other is going to be fucking torture. I can tell by the way her fingers trailed over my palm, like she wanted to hold contact for as long as possible.

Luckily for my ego, Luke launches himself at me first. I pull him up against me, noting how much heavier he's grown. How much taller. He's getting bigger faster than I care for. Growing up way too damn fast.

"Hey, pal. You have a good sleepover?"

"The best!" He smacks a loud kiss on my cheek, and I wonder what age he'll stop doing that.

He pops down and does the same to Willa, except he wraps his arms around her waist. She doubles over, hair fanning around him as she hugs him back and whispers something private to him. Luke giggles, and Willa rubs a hand across the back of his head before dropping a quick kiss to his crown.

I stare at them like a lovesick fool, imagining something I've never let myself imagine. Luke's had plenty of caretakers over the years—teachers, friends—but he's never been as taken with a single person as he is with Willa. He's needed someone like her in his life so badly.

And I guess that makes two of us because I can't take my eyes off them.

"You having a stroke, son?" My dickhead dad calls from the front porch, actually making me jump.

I prop my hands on my hips, giving him my best say-nothing glare.

He's not a stupid man. He's grinning at me like he knows something. And I'm sure he does. I just don't need him making it weird by making some joke about us giving the lawn a blow job or whatever shit he comes up with for entertainment.

I can't wait to be old and retired and say things just to see how people will react to get my kicks. That's the dream right there.

"Just tired," is what I opt to respond with.

Harvey props himself against the post on the front porch with a knowing grin. "That's what happens when you stay up too late partying at your age."

Willa stands up straight now, arm slung around Luke, who is still clinging to her. "I was the one out partying. Cade stayed home to, uh, clean the house. He's very tidy. You did well in that department."

My dad scoffs. "That boy only cleans when he's anxious."

Dick.

"Well then, his anxiety must be off the charts," Willa quips, trying to keep things light. Her bartender banter is on point, but my dad doesn't fall for it.

"He's looking mighty relaxed this morning," he replies, grinning ear-to-ear.

"Jesus Christ," I mutter, kicking at a stone in the packed dirt beneath my work boot.

Willa snickers and looks away. We both know we're busted. Old Harvey's fucking eagle eyes never miss a beat. And that's what I get for staring at Willa like she hung the moon.

It's been all of ten minutes since we left the house, and I'm already failing at keeping things between us under wraps. There's a part of me that doesn't want to, but I also don't want all the pitying looks when she leaves. The throat clearing and the back pats. And if people don't know about us, they won't know why I'm miserable. And that just feels a lot more bearable to me.

"What's the plan today?" I stare down at Luke, opting to ignore my dad entirely.

"Planning my birthday! Willa, you'll come right? Even though it's on the weekend?"

She smiles down at him, giving his small shoulders a tight squeeze. "Wouldn't miss it."

"Will you play happy birthday to me on your guitar?"

She laughs and my dick goes hard. Watching Willa play the guitar is up there for me. All unplugged and stripped down, just her soft raspy voice and the gentle strumming of her dainty fingers, with long hair splayed against the stained wood.

It's almost as hot as watching her sit on a bucking horse and stick the ride.

"I have an even better idea," Willa says. "I'll teach you how to play it too."

Luke's eyes go wide. "In front of everyone?"

"Only if you want to." She ruffles his hair, and my brain snags on *everyone*. Because Luke's birthday is the one day of the year that Talia likes to crawl out of the woodwork.

I glance over at my dad. We spent enough years

working this land together, learned to read each other pretty well, and I see he's thinking the same thing.

I've never wanted to keep Talia away from Luke. I've given her every opportunity to be a part of his life, even if she hasn't taken those chances.

I think it hurts me more than it hurts Luke. For him, she's not a factor. For me, she should have been. I can't wrap my head around missing him growing up, but I'll never shame her for it, and I'll never gatekeep our son so long as she isn't hurting him.

"We need to talk about the reunion, Cade," my dad says. "Come for lunch? You and I can do some planning."

"Willa too!" Luke is already dragging her up to the house, his tiny hand clamped around hers.

"It's her day off, pal," I remind him, seeing the line between everything blur and desperately trying to keep it in place.

She glances down at Luke and over at me. "It's okay. I don't need a day off from you, buddy. You're one of my favorite people in the world."

My heart stutters in my chest, and I suck in a sharp breath. The way Luke smiles, the way he stands just a little bit taller, makes the bridge of my nose sting.

I scrunch it up and give it a wipe before looking away. Then I stride to the house, head down, so no one will see the emotion in my eyes.

But I don't need to look at my dad for him to know. After all, who knows their son better than a single dad?

Before he retired, we spent long days on the range together, so it's damn near impossible to keep anything from each other.

"You've got it bad, boy," is what he says, clapping me on the shoulder as I move past him.

And he's never been more right.

25

Willa

Cade: Just need like ten more minutes.

Willa: Any guesses on whether or not I put panties on this morning?

Cade: I'm sitting with my dad right now. I don't need a boner.

Willa: No panties. My kitty is too sore from riding your massive pole.

Cade: Woman, are you intentionally ignoring my instructions?

Willa: You don't tell me what to do. I thought we'd established that by now?

"Willa! Let's go."

My head whips around at the sound of Cade's authoritative voice, barking at me like I work for him. Like it's not my "day off" and we didn't spend the entire night fucking each other's brains out. I shake my head and widen my eyes down at Luke.

"We should hide from him," Luke says, instantly dropping the sidewalk chalk. We've adorned the entire front driveway with hearts of all different colors, shapes, and sizes.

I nod. "Absolutely we should."

"I know!" He slides his hand into mine, and I try not to think about how sticky it is. Chuckling under my breath, I jog behind him as he drags me behind a big well that sits beside the house. Cement peeks out between the layered stones, and the old wooden beams reach up tall above it. There's a bucket hanging on a rope, but it has the distinct look of being out of use.

It's charming, and symbolic, and it smells like wet flint, or the yard after a rainstorm.

"Helloooo!" Luke pops his little face down into the opening, cackling when his greeting echoes back up at him.

I sink to the ground, yanking him down with me. "Shush it, you little hellion. He's going to hear us."

"Oh, yeah. Right." Luke chortles more. Such a happy, goofy kid, even if his attention span leaves something to be desired.

"Hey, Willa?"

"Hey, Luke," I reply dryly, since the *be quiet* part obviously didn't register.

"Sometimes I wish you were my mom."

I blink at the boy, too stunned to speak, so he continues. "At that birthday party? Where I got held under the water? He told me that even my mom didn't like me."

I want to push that kid into the water all over again.

"Well, I don't just like you, Luke." My voice comes out thick with emotion, but I'm not so sure he picks up on it. "I love you."

"You do?" His smile is shy—tentative.

"Yeah. And that kid is a major shithead."

His hand slaps over his mouth and his eyes go wide before he whispers, "He's a *total* shithead and I love you too."

I instantly pull him close, feeling his tiny body press against mine right where we're kneeling on the ground.

"Luke!" Cade's voice is closer this time. "Willa! Why does it look like Valentine's Day threw up all over the driveway?"

I clap a hand over my mouth to hold in the laughter. Of course, that's how Cade would see it. Fucking pessimist.

"You two think you're funny, don't you?"

I move my free hand to cover Luke's mouth because he has no chill and is going to burst.

Cade's boots move off the paved part of the driveway,

and I can hear them crunching against the packed gravel beside it, drawing closer.

"The worst part is . . . when I find you, I'm going to punish you both."

Luke's shoulders shake harder. He knows his dad is a big softy under that gruff exterior. I don't think he's punished Luke a day in his life.

Me though? I'm not so sure. Bedroom Cade is not Dad Cade. My body tingles in response—I don't laugh at all.

"I bet you're . . . behind the shed!" We can hear him jump and then groan when the spot he thought we'd be in is empty.

I turn and give Luke a warning glare because I feel the little puffs of air escaping his lips. After I mouth, *Be quiet*, he gives me a nod and takes a breath in through his nose.

Cade's heavy footfalls draw nearer. "How about . . ." He's approaching the well, but the opposite side. I give Luke a look and point upward, hoping he understands that we're going to jump.

He nods.

My fingers count down from three.

Two.

One.

"In the well!"

We shoot up and shout, "Boo!"

And predictably, Cade jumps, his tall frame startling as he takes a step back. His handsome face momentarily appears very shocked, and Luke and I dissolve into peals of laughter.

"Gotcha," I wheeze. "No wet T-shirt this time though!"

"You should have seen your face!" Luke points at him.

"Okay, that's it. You're both dead." Cade points at us, spinning his cap backward and hitting me with a wink.

Dick. He knows it kills me when he wears it like that. *Murder me with your dick, please, sir.*

Luke turns and guns it for the main house. Cade lets him get a little ahead before his long strides eat up the ground behind him and he scoops Luke up into his arms and starts tickling him. Luke squirms and his light giggles blend with Cade's deeper baritone.

"Willa! Help!"

"Don't worry, Luke. I'm coming!" I sprint heroically around the well and get my fingers right up in Cade's ribs.

He squeals. He straight up *squeals,* and it is the least manly noise I've ever heard come out of such a manly man. We're all laughing like lunatics, but Cade is stronger, taller, faster—meaner. And somehow, he tosses Luke over one shoulder and hefts me up over the other one.

Luke slaps at his back in breathless hysterics. "Let me down!"

Tossed over the opposite shoulder, I reach down

farther and slap his ass, which just makes Luke laugh harder.

"Giddy up, Daddy!" Luke calls, and Cade's breath huffs out on my bare thigh.

"You two are a pain in my ass."

"How the hell are you carrying us? This isn't normal. Put me down."

"Woman. I can pick up calves, you two are nothing." His finger traces the inside of my thigh, and I squirm.

"Looks like you've got your hands full, son," Harvey calls out, but I can't see him. I don't need to see him to hear the smile in his voice. "Why don't I take the tiny hell-raiser off your hands for a bit longer?"

"Yes! Save me, Grandpa!" Luke screams, thrashing wildly, shaking his dad's body as he does.

Cade grunts and sets Luke down instantly. "Good plan, Dad. Divide and conquer."

I hear Luke sprinting across the driveway away from us as I whisper, "Cade, put me down. I bet everyone can see my ass."

"They can't," he whispers back.

"How do you know?"

"Because I checked. I thought the view might be better than it is. Disappointing, to be honest."

"Dick. Let me down. I'm not a baby cow."

Cade just laughs.

"You kids have fun!" Harvey calls, and it strikes me how blatantly obvious it must be that something is going on with us. "I drove past the other day and noticed your lawn. It could really use a good—"

"Dad, just don't," Cade grumbles and marches over to his truck with me slung over his shoulder like a bag of feed. Or a baby cow.

"Let's go, Red. You're with me today." He claps my ass loudly to the delighted squeals of Luke and a bark of delighted surprise from his dad.

Blood rushes to my cheeks and I cover my face with my hands. I tell myself it's because I'm embarrassed, but deep down, I know it's because this side of Cade is doing something to me.

And that something is going to make leaving when this gig is up damn near impossible.

~

"Why are we trail riding together on my day off?" I ask Cade from where I'm seated on a pretty dun ranch horse. It makes me miss Tux, but I know he's fat and happy in a field right now, recuperating just fine. He'll probably never want to jump another day in his life. He probably thinks he's retired now.

"Because I wanted to show you the land."

I eye Cade skeptically. Blueberry's bobbing head is slung low, totally relaxed as we walk between the sparse bales of hay rolled up behind Cade's house.

"I've seen the land, Cade. I'm feeling pretty familiar with these hay bales too."

"It's been a good year for hay," is his stupid response. He's all serious, shoulders held taut, hands propped on the horn of his saddle. Stupid hat still backward. "Plus, I feel relaxed out here on the land."

"You're acting weird." I give my gelding, Rocket, a little squeeze, urging him forward so I'm even with Cade. "Why are you acting weird?"

"Can't I just take you out on a romantic trail ride?"

My lips roll together as I regard him. "You can. But you haven't spoken a word to me since we got out of your truck. You look like you're trying to disintegrate the leather in your hands, and your mouth keeps popping open like you're about to say something, but then you shake your head and slam it back shut so hard your teeth clank. And I can hear you grinding said teeth until your mouth pops back open again."

He turns and gives me his annoyed scowl. "What are you? A shrink?"

I hit him back with my best cheesy grin. "Nah. Just the daughter of one."

He huffs out a soft laugh and shakes his head, staring out over the flat expanse of land that looks like it shoots straight up into the Rockies. It's beautiful—gold-green grass, gray rock, up to a blue-bird sky.

"It's Luke's birthday next week. The little party we're hosting is the following weekend. It's casual. Just family."

I say nothing because I know where he's going. He

mentioned it once, and I never asked more questions because it wasn't my business.

"His mom always shows up for it."

"As she should," I reply because it's true. "Cade, this is really none of my business. If Luke is happy, I'm happy."

He sort of wobbles his head. "I'm not so sure that she makes Luke happy, to be honest. Nine out of ten times, it's awkward. He doesn't know how to act around her, and she sure as shit doesn't know how to act around him. It's not getting any better with age."

"Okay." It's all I can think to say. I don't really know why he's telling me all this.

"I have a sinking suspicion it's going to be more awkward with you there."

Stiffness permeates my neck as I shift to sit taller. "Are you saying you don't want me there?"

"No." His response is quick and firm. I let out the breath I'd been holding back, ready to keep it together if he'd said yes. "Not at all. If you want to talk about something that would upset Luke—that would be it."

I nod, dropping my eyes to my fingers wrapped around the reins in my hands.

"I want you there too," Cade adds, and I can feel the weight of his gaze on my skin. "She might not like it, though, so I just want to prepare you for that."

My face scrunches as I turn to look at the man beside me. "Why would she not like me there? I'll be there as his nanny."

His jaw works, and I watch his Adam's apple bob when he swallows. "She's . . . I don't know." He chuckles now, scrubbing a hand over his beard. "You know, I try so hard not to say bad things about her, because she's half Luke and I love everything about that kid. But Willa, his mom is a fucking nightmare. I don't know how my biggest mistake brought about my most cherished gift. But here I am."

"You're so mature," I quip. Because really, he is.

He groans and stares up at the sky now. "Talia is oddly competitive. I was a trophy to her. But once she won me, she realized maybe it wasn't the trophy she wanted. I can keep you and me under wraps because that will help keep her claws from coming out. But I can't keep the way Luke loves you under wraps. And that's going to bother her."

I sigh. Feeling way out of my depth with this sort of family dynamic.

"Harvey is hyper-aware of it too. He's not the biggest Talia fan. But he is a huge fan of you."

"Yeah, you did a great job of keeping us under wraps earlier," I joke, thinking back on the way he carried me away like a caveman who just won the hunt.

"Wasn't trying to, Red. Don't want to if I'm being honest."

I snort. "This is weird."

I see his lips tip up when he glances over at me. "Totally weird."

"But I'm not mad at it."

Cade tags on, "I might even be happy about it."

I squint my eyes at him—fuck, but he's hot. It's really just stupid. "Is that your happy scowl?"

He shakes his head and snickers. "Can I tell Harvey that I've adequately prepared you for the party?"

"Yeah, yeah. You don't deal with a bunch of drunken idiots and catfights for years without learning a thing or two about handling shit like that. I'll be fine. Let's just keep it about Luke. Okay?"

He nods, eyeing me like he's checking me for any signs I'm stressed. And truthfully, I'm not. I'm not a drama seeker. In fact, I avoid it like the plague. If I have to smile and nod and fade into the background, then that's what I'll do.

"Okay," he agrees with a firm nod.

"Okay. Good." We stare at each other for a beat until a smile tugs up my cheeks as an idea to kill the tension pops into my head. "Last one to the mountains is a rotten egg!" bursts from my lips before I can stop it, and then I'm urging Rocket up into a canter, glancing over my shoulder at Cade, who's grinning at me like I'm a psycho.

"Git up!" he calls to Blueberry, and her hooves pound behind me.

I lean forward in the tack, coming off Rocket's back to give him some space to gallop, pushing my hands up his neck and giving him slack in the reins. He stretches out, and when I glance back again, Cade isn't gaining on me like I thought he would.

"You scared, Eaton?" I shout.

"No, baby. Just enjoying the view. Your ass looks mighty fine from back here."

We both laugh and joy bubbles in my chest. I don't let up though. He can stare at my ass, but I'm still going to kick his.

"Thank you!" I shout back as a joke. But deep down, it doesn't feel like a joke.

It feels like he's wiggling his way into my heart.

26

Willa

Summer: I feel like we live on the same piece of land and yet, I haven't seen you at all.

Willa: Been busy.

Summer: With what?

Willa: Saving horses.

Summer: Oh, yeah?

Willa: Sum, I've saved so many I might as well open a rescue.

Summer: Good lord.

Willa: Would it be legal for me to have Cade write me a charitable donation receipt to offset my taxes?

Summer: I think he's fucked you stupid, bestie.

Cade's head pops out the back door, and butterflies erupt in my chest. I can tell by the way he scans the backyard that he's been looking for me.

"Hi," is all I say from the far side of the hot tub, steam wafting around me. We're well into the dog days of summer now. It's August and the nights have cooled. The air is fresh against my chest and shoulders, but the hot bubbling water caresses my body, chasing away the chill.

I'm not cold at all. Especially watching Cade step onto the patio, barefoot with thin lounge pants slung low, signature black T-shirt hugging his biceps, and hair all mussed from a shower and lying down with Luke.

"Luke asleep?"

"Yeah." His eyes rake over me hungrily. "I meant to come find you sooner, but I think I fell asleep in there."

"That's okay. I've been keeping busy," I reply, not missing the way his head quirks and his eyes narrow.

"Yeah? Busy with what?"

"Thinking about last night," I reply boldly, stretching my arms above my head and showing him the way my nipples have pebbled beneath my thin, purple bathing suit.

The same one he couldn't take his eyes off of the last time we found ourselves in here together.

Rather than approaching me, he props a shoulder

against a thick wooden beam, still standing under the covered portion of the patio. He crosses his arms over his chest and regards me like he's unaffected. However, when my eyes drop below his waistline, I know that's not true.

"What part?" His voice is a rumble, thunder that rolls over my skin and shoots straight to my core.

"Well, I started out thinking about how I got on my knees for you."

"You do look beautiful on your knees," he replies smoothly. My heart rate ratchets up under his gaze. Recounting last night has every nerve ending firing. "More beautiful when you struggle to take it all. I love watching you work so hard."

A smile twists my mouth.

"Pull the bathing suit down, Red. Let me see those perfect tits."

My thumbs hook under the straps as I lick my lips and swallow against the dryness in my throat. Peeling the wet nylon back, I hold his gaze. It burns like hot coals, following my every movement.

"Good. Now, play with your nipples while you tell me more about last night."

He doesn't move an inch, and I try to gather courage to keep going because, while I've had some good sex in my life, I've had nothing like this.

Or anyone like Cade.

My forefingers and thumbs twist my nipples, and it makes my voice go all breathy when I say, "I liked when you came after me. I'm sorry I stormed off before you could finish talking."

He blinks at me, like he's a little surprised by what I just told him. "You don't need to apologize, Red. I haven't exactly sent clear signals with you."

Pinch. Roll. Swipe. The truth tumbles out.

"Neither have I."

His jaw shifts. "No one would expect you to be the mature one in this relationship when I'm the one who's in his late thirties."

I tip my nose up, refusing to let that comment make me feel childish or young. Cade isn't looking at me that way, so I push the thought away, focusing on another word he used.

My hands smooth over the fullness of my breasts, and he watches, eyes glued to me, his length straining hard at his pants. "Is that what this is? A relationship?"

I realize I want him to say yes—take control of how out of control I'm feeling around him—and tell me how this is going to work. Because I want something to work.

But he says, "It's whatever you're comfortable with, Red. We can let it be gradual. We can skip a label. We can figure it out when the time comes. But whatever it is, it's important to me. *You're* important to me."

My hands stop moving because I feel like this might be a chance to tell him I want him to go full caveman and tell me I'm staying here with him and Luke.

I've flitted around doing whatever I want for years with no real tether to anything except my best friend and my brother. I've enjoyed seeing his career take off, but none of that was for me.

I feel grounded out here. At this house. With Cade and Luke. It's happened slowly, but I feel like I belong here, which seems absolutely insane to blurt out to this man who just very clearly reiterated our age difference or pointed to my maturity as a reason for my behavior.

And he's not wrong. I've always been a little averse to growing up and settling down, but I'm finding I want nothing more. After so much time spinning around not knowing what I want, I think I might have finally figured it out.

"You're important to me too, Cade," is what I settle on, because I know he needs to hear that. He's homed in on my insecurities, and I've homed in on his.

We build each other up. We tidy one another's loose ends. We fit so perfectly.

"Good. But, Red, I don't think I told you to stop playing with those tits." His voice changes, taking on a playful edge as he takes long, casual steps toward the hot tub, peeling his shirt away and dropping it on the brick patio.

"Yeah, but now you're standing out there looking like a total snack, and I want you to come play with them instead," I pout dramatically while my hands move again.

He chuckles and leans his chiseled forearms on the rim of the hot tub. "Fucking desperate," he murmurs, shaking his head.

"Hey, yo—"

"Sit on the edge of the tub, baby. You told me I could watch you touch yourself while you thought about sucking my cock on the porch. And I know you're a woman who keeps her word."

I practically purr under that compliment. Because I *am* the type of woman who keeps her word. I'm fiercely loyal, and that's something I've always taken pride in. I'm trustworthy and a good friend. I might not be a high achiever, but you can count on me to be there if you need to bury a body in the middle of the night.

I do as Cade says, lifting myself onto the ledge, steam swirling off my skin as I rise from the water.

"Fuck." He holds a fist up over his mouth and stares at me like I might be his last meal. "That fucking bathing suit."

"This one?" I ask, pulling it up tight so it squeezes my pussy in the way that drives him wild.

"You almost made me lose it that night, you know?"

"I wish you had."

"I don't." He replies smoothly, and I arch a brow at him. "Don't give me that look, Red. It wouldn't have been the same and you know it. I wouldn't have known you the way I do now. You would have still thought I was an asshole."

"Who says I don't anymore?"

He gives me his disapproving scowl. "Between then and now I've . . ." he trails off, glancing away for a moment, thinking carefully about the next words,

324

"gotten to know you and come to care about you in a way I didn't expect."

"Same," I reply, like an idiot who doesn't want to throw herself across the hot tub and say, *Actually, I think I'm falling for you! Hehehe.*

He stares at me, but like, *into* me. He stares at me like he really knows me, like he could pull out all my deepest, darkest secrets and insecurities. I almost giggle because in a lot of ways he already has.

I wonder if he can tell that I'm losing control where he's concerned.

I decide I don't care, so I widen my legs and pull my bathing suit to the side, baring myself to him, smiling when his eyes flare in perfect time with his nostrils.

"You were so jealous that night," I say. "So angry. Not at me, I could tell that much. But at yourself for wanting me. And I couldn't wait to watch you come undone."

I swipe a finger through my lips, feeling the slippery wetness between them just from having Cade's eyes on me.

"I was too rough," he says, licking his lips, but he doesn't look sorry.

"And I liked it. No. I *loved* it." I press lightly on my clit, teasing myself for him, letting him watch. "Your hands in my hair." He groans as I prop one foot up on the edge, feeling more and more bold. More and more turned on by the way he's looking at me. "Your cock in my mouth. Hard boards biting at my knees."

I tease my slit again, dipping a finger in but only to the first knuckle. "The way the muscles in your legs flexed beneath my hands. I felt like a goddess. And the fact that anyone could have walked up and seen us together? I loved it."

His jaw pops under the strain of holding himself back. I can see the muscles in his forearms rippling as he rubs his hands together. It's like he just needs something to do with them that isn't ripping this hot tub apart to get to me.

"You wanted everyone to know that mouth is mine, Red?"

I nod. His throat bobs. "You looked like a goddess too. You always do. You should see yourself right now. All that pretty copper hair stuck to your shoulders." His eyes trail over me. "Tits out and heaving. Begging to be fucked." His gaze moves down over my torso. "Flimsy bathing suit all bunched up, proving how fucking useless it is at hiding your body."

His eyes flare when they land between my legs, where my fingers are still swiping lightly over my pussy. "That cocktease of a tight little cunt all out on display for me. Begging. Just like every other inch of your body."

A whimper spills from my lips and heat rushes out through every limb. I feel like I could turn to putty for him and his filthy words. Crass words that are reverent at the same time. So full of admiration. Possession.

"Stop fucking around and show me how pretty you look with your fingers shoved inside, baby." His voice sounds strangled as he moves his eyes to mine. There's something on his face I can't quite place. A vulnerability that pops up only now and then.

A look that says he needs me as badly as I need him. In one smooth movement, I slide one finger in, then two. But he doesn't watch between my legs, his eyes stay on my face. A blush rushes over my cheeks.

This should feel dirty, a bit playful, but it feels like worship and he's not even touching me.

"Has anybody ever told you how incredible you are, Willa?" I swallow. "How fun? How smart? How goddamn witty?"

Fuck. His words are like a baseball bat to the chest. Totally out of left field.

My lips pop open, and only a small squeaking sound comes out. I try to cover by saying, "What about pretty? I get that a lot." Because I'm not sure *incredible* has ever really happened.

He shakes his head before stepping into the hot tub, still wearing those lounge pants that skim his body so deliciously.

He drops into the water, toned arms gliding him across to me in one smooth movement. "You're still weari—"

"No. Pretty girls don't make me feel like this." His hand wraps around my calf while the other comes to hold my hand between my legs. He takes control of that hand, making me pump in and out of myself a couple of times.

"Like what?" I breathe, head tilted down, eyes fixed on the man submerged between my legs.

"Totally out of control."

And then he drops his mouth to me. My head tips back, and he makes me feel totally out of control too.

He sucks at my clit. Licks at my lips. Hums like he loves the taste. All while still working my hand with his.

"Keep going, baby," is all he says when he draws his hand away to grip my thigh.

My legs end up wrapped around his neck, one hand propped on the deck while Cade Eaton lays me out and makes a meal of me.

It's the corded muscles in his back, the sight of wet fabric beneath the water—proof that he couldn't hold himself back even a second longer—that has me barreling quickly toward that cliff.

The same one he's been pushing me off for about the last twenty-four hours.

The one he's always at the bottom of to catch me when I fall.

And fall I do.

With my fingers thrusting in and out easily, and his expert tongue working me, I bite out, "Cade! Fuck!" All that tingly pressure inside me explodes. Down my inner thighs. Up my spine.

Straight to my heart.

His hands are all over me, pulling me into the water, sliding over me possessively. My ass, my ribs, fingers trailing up the column of my spine, until he holds me close and whispers in my ear, "Fucking incredible."

I turn and kiss his stubbled cheek, seeing the corner of his mouth lift. But I don't get to see the small smile for long because he's turning us, putting me down in the water while he pushes to stand above me.

He pushes the wet fabric down, letting his thick, proud cock jut up between us.

I lick my lips and he smirks. "No, baby. First, I'm fucking those pretty tits, then you can have a taste."

"Okay, deal," I reply as I quickly draw closer.

A laugh rumbles in his chest. "So eager. I'll add that to your list of admirable traits. Now put my cock between your breasts and push them together. It's my turn now."

"You like to watch, huh, Eaton?" I tease while doing as he told me.

"I like to watch you, Red."

I shake my head, like it might ward away the butter-flies erupting in my stomach. I've never done this before, and it's exciting—his cock on my chest, breasts pushed tightly around his girth, a drop of white glistening on his thick head. I glance up at him and smile. His tongue darts out over his bottom lip, and then both lips flatten in concentration. Arms slung back behind himself, he thrusts. The water lubricates us, and his movements are slow and measured.

His mouth is slightly open, chiseled cheeks slack as he watches himself sliding between my breasts. We don't talk. I think we're both in a bit of a trance—or maybe we've said enough tonight.

Maybe he's feeling just as exposed as I am.

Maybe if I feel like a goddess when we're together, he feels like a god.

Maybe we both just revel in that feeling.

My arousal hasn't abated and watching him slide his cock through my tits is getting me worked up all over again. Every time he murmurs, "Fuck," in that deep breathy voice, my pussy clenches.

"Willa, I'm going to come."

"Yes," I hiss, biting at my lip, propping my chest in the most inviting angle, loving watching him come apart for me.

And then I feel it. Cade goes still and his cock throbs and twitches. His cum shoots out over my chest. One shot hits my chin, and he groans, which turns to a quiet sigh as his hand strokes the back of my head.

I rise and stand before him, dripping with his seed. "That was fun."

Cade huffs out a deep, appreciative chuckle. "God, was it ever." And then his eyes are burning over me, assessing his handy work.

"How do I look?" I quirk a brow and arch my back.

"Like you're mine," he growls.

Those words. My body aches for more. I want him to be mine too. "Yeah? You like this look on me?"

"It would be better like this." He swipes his thumb over my chin and in one smooth movement, paints my lips with the stray shot of cum. He leans back and looks at me with a mischievous grin on his face. "Definitely mine."

"You're a savage, Eaton." I laugh lightly, before darting my tongue out to taste what he put there. "And I love it."

"Good thing, Red." He slips into the water, dragging me down with him to wash us off. "Because I'm going to haul your fine ass to my cave now. Keep you on your back, coming all night long."

Then he scoops me up and carries me into the house.

Like a total savage.

One that keeps me coming all night long.

27

Cade

Cade: Luke's birthday party is on Saturday at 2 p.m.

Talia: Can we bump it to noon? I have dinner plans that night and need time to get ready.

Cade: No, we cannot bump your child's sixth birthday party to accommodate your dinner plans.

Talia: It's only two hours.

Cade: Exactly.

Talia: I forgot what a stick in the mud you are.

Cade: Well, here I am. Refreshing your memory. If you can't make it, please let me know so that I can prepare Luke.

Talia: Don't be so dramatic. I'll be there. I just might be overdressed so I can make it back to the city in time.

Cade: That's fine. Luke won't care.

Talia: What about you? You always did enjoy me in a pair of heels.

Cade: So did every other guy in town.
Talia: Fuck you.

~

"You're acting weird." I glance down at Summer, who is staring out over the back field, assessing it like it's the Met Gala or something. She and Willa have been up since early this morning setting Luke's party up in the hayfield, per his request.

There's a bouncy castle and a tent with some weird fucking guy in head-to-toe khaki sitting under it who apparently brought snakes and lizards to show the kids. There's another tent with a buffet-style table covered in things Willa has been baking for days. I know because I tested the icing by swiping it on her neck and licking it off.

It was fucking delicious.

She's got lemonade with lemons and strawberries floating in it. It's adorable. She's got little plates with poop emojis on them that Luke picked out with her. The tablecloths match. Only Willa could take shit plates and somehow tie them into a beautiful outdoor birthday party for a six-year-old.

I wouldn't have even let him get them, but she just laughed and tossed them in the basket. "Excellent choice!" she said, and Luke *beamed*.

"Yeah. I know," I finally reply to Summer. Because I am acting weird. Willa and I have been sneaking around for a couple of weeks, and I don't want to sneak anymore. I'm trying hard not to scare the shit out of her by being so sure about everything. But the fact of the matter is, I *am* sure.

I've made my mistakes. I've lived with the fallouts. I've spent years thinking about my life and what it would take for me to give someone a chance again.

And watching this woman plan what I meant to be a simple backyard barbecue for a kid and instead treating it like it's the celebration of the century is just the cherry on top.

It feels fast, and yet it doesn't. I wouldn't have given in to this if it didn't feel right.

"Cade Eaton." Summer's dark eyes are sparkling at me right now, and her jaw drops as she scans my face. Sharp as a tack, this one. I told Rhett once that I loved her because she was good for him but hated that she was smarter than me.

And this moment does nothing but prove that statement.

"You're in love with my best friend, aren't you?"

I cross my arms over my chest and look away. *Love.* I was never sure I could love someone in the way everyone talks about it. My heart has taken too many shit-kickings over the years. My mom. Talia. What Talia meant for the course my life took. All the things I missed out on, which I hate to even mention because I have Luke. But I'd be a liar if I said I never thought about what I might have done differently had life dealt me a different hand.

Maybe I'd be rodeoing. Or traveling all over North America, rolling in the cash that comes from selling top-of-the-line horses.

Maybe I'd be training all day and riding buckle bunnies all night.

All those maybes. But as I watch Willa put little weighted clips on the tablecloth so nothing blows away, I know that none of those maybes would have been right.

The hand dealt to me is what brought her to my front step.

"Yeah," I grumble, still refusing to look at Summer.

She makes a satisfied little humming noise, and when I peek out of the corner of my eye at her, she winks and gives me a side hug. She's so tiny that it's awkward. She doesn't have Willa's height or long limbs.

"You should tell her."

"Tell her?"

She shrugs. "Yeah. I think Willa would want to know that."

I snort. "So that I can scare her away?"

Her lips curve up slowly. "I don't think you'll be able to scare Willa away," is all she says before giving me another squeeze and walking in the opposite direction.

She drops a truth bomb casually and then just leaves me to overanalyze the hell out of it.

The party is already in full swing by the time Talia deigns to bless us with her presence. I don't even have to turn to see her because I hear, "My baaabyyy!" in her high, sugary voice.

Her baby. I can't even stop my eyes from rolling up to the sky when I hear it. It's a ridiculous thing to say to a child you see once a year and walked away from without a goodbye.

I catch sight of Willa talking to my dad and some of the other parents. She's wearing an orange dress with little white polka dots and a soft flowing skirt. I want to flip it up and see what's underneath.

But now, watching the way she stiffens and her fingers crinkle in on the poop emoji cup she's holding, I want to throw my arm around her shoulder and reassure her. I want to make her cheeks pink again because they're going pale right before my eyes.

She wouldn't want me to though. She's too fierce, too proud. So I look away, because if I stay eyeing her, I'm going to do it anyway.

Luke gives Talia a stiff hug, kind of patting her on her slender back as she mauls him. I wish she wouldn't waltz into his party late, when she wanted it earlier, and still make it all about her.

If nothing else, it's very on brand for her.

"Let me see you." She's dressed to the nines in a skin-tight dress and high heels that are sinking into the grass as she assesses him. "How did you grow up so fast?"

I hear Rhett snort.

Loud.

Loud enough that she turns a venomous glare at him.

He just smiles back. "Hi, Talia. Long time no see."

Fucking shit disturber. I always bite my tongue about her around Luke because I want him to make his own decisions about his mother. If he wants a relationship with her one day, I don't want him thinking I poisoned him against her. It kills me but I know it's right.

Which is why I bite back my laugh at her brittle smile and the way her eyes pinch. She's like this beautiful mirage on the outside, all sour on the inside. And if looks could kill, Rhett would keel over on the spot.

Luckily, that's not the case, and he raises his poop emoji cup toward her in a silent cheers.

Behind me I hear a snicker that sounds distinctly like my dad. I don't turn, though, because Luke is looking so uncomfortable with everyone watching that all I can think about is getting to him.

"Hi, Talia." I interrupt the awkward moment by striding forward with my hand out to shake hers as I give Luke's shoulder a firm squeeze.

"Oh please, Cade. Are we so far gone that we need to shake hands?" Her giggle trills and grates on my nerves. It doesn't sound like wind chimes the way Willa's did that day in Le Pamplemousse or the way it does when I step into the house after a long, hard day at work. And Luke's doesn't blend in with it at all.

Luke stands there awkwardly, most likely hitting the age where he's piecing these things together, noting the body language and drawing his own conclusions.

I stand woodenly while Talia wraps her arms around me. One hand rubs up the back of my neck, and I instantly reach up and grip her elbow, pulling her arm away, even as she sneaks a kiss against my cheek.

"Oh gosh"—she laughs—"let me get that for you." And then she's standing close to me, licking her thumb and rubbing at my cheek, trying to get the thick layer of lipstick off my skin.

Marking her territory.

It's been years and Talia hasn't changed a bit. She's always playing some game. The difference is that now I see it. I didn't all those years ago. I saw a pretty package and a willing body.

I was horny and stupid, and she was calculated.

"It's fine. I'll get it." I step away as the surrounding conversation picks back up, which somehow makes me feel better. Like our complicated little family isn't the center of attention. I desperately want to turn around and check on Willa, but I also know Talia will pick up on it immediately.

And I'm not subjecting Willa to her shit. Not until things with her and me are solid. Official.

I should have made things official already. I'm

kicking myself now. The pads of my fingers itch to touch her, to run over her neck reassuringly. Possessively.

"Gosh, Cade. You're like a good scotch. You just keep getting better with age." Talia reaches out to run her French-tipped fingers over my shoulder, like she has some sort of right to touch me. Like she's forgotten our text exchange earlier this week. She was always forward, and maybe she's always been like this when she shows up once a year.

Maybe it just didn't bother me before now.

All the same, I take another step back, pulling Luke in front of me and putting both my hands on his shoulders. "How have you been?"

"Good." She glances around the space in the field. "You know, living in the city. Keeping busy."

I realize I don't know what she does, but I also don't care. She showed up with another man one year, pawing at him like it was going to make me jealous.

It didn't.

"In Calgary?" Luke asks brightly.

"Yes, honey." She looks down at him with a big smile. "Handsome like your daddy, but with Mom's blue eyes."

"My nanny is from Calgary!" is Luke's response.

"A nanny! How adorable." She bends down to see eye to eye with Luke. "Is she here today? I'd love to meet her."

Before I can interject, Luke tears away. I can't blame him for wanting to be close to Willa. She's a comfort to him, where this other woman who lives a little over an hour away can't bother to visit him more than once a year.

I turn just in time to see Willa's eyes dropping from my frame down to Luke.

I also see Talia glance over her shoulder and wink at me.

28
Willa

Rhett: You know Medusa?

Willa: Not personally, no.

Rhett: Remember the part about not looking her in the eyes?

Willa: I've always kind of liked Medusa. If I were her, I'd wanna turn men into stone too.

Rhett: Pretend Talia is Medusa. But a version we don't like.

~ e

This bitch is like a splinter I can't get out. The sight of her nails sliding over Cade's neck burned itself into my mind. She's droned on and on about herself, and I've endured it with a level of politeness I'm extending to her only because she birthed one of my favorite people in the world.

And that must count for something.

"You have to be so sick of living out here."

I smile flatly, staring at the squealing kids in the huge bouncy castle. "Not really," I reply while avoiding Summer's eyes. Because the last time I looked at her, she held her hands up beside her head and made little devil horns with an evil scrunched-up face.

"Aren't you bored though? I mean, I grew up here. I know what it's like. Once you've had a taste of the city, it's hard to come back."

"I mean, Calgary isn't exactly Paris," I quip because she's acting like it's some glitz-and-glam place.

"But what do you do all day? I'd go crazy. That's why I had to get out, you know?"

"No, I don't know," is my reply, because my patience is wearing thin, and my personality only allows me to keep my mouth shut for so long. The pressure is mounting and giving into my redhead streak is hella appealing right about now.

"Excuse me?" Her big blue eyes go wide, her pink lips turning down.

Of course, she has to be smoking hot. Cade couldn't have been married to someone ugly to make me feel better about myself. I'd even settle for average looking, but no, she's a ten. An eleven.

"I don't know what you mean," I clarify. "I love living out here. Your son is smart and fun. The land is beautiful. Cade works hard to provide for him. I'm not bored at all."

A wolfish smile spreads across her lips. "Oh. I see."

I refuse to react. "You're going to need to clarify."

"It's okay. Us ladies can have our secrets. We're not so different, you and I." My brow quirks at her, and what I want to say is that we could not be more different if we tried. "I recommend enjoying him while you're here. But don't hold your breath. That man is as cold as they come. I thought getting pregnant might tie him down. And it did."

My mind reels. "Pardon me?"

She waves a hand and carries on. "Birth control, no birth control, who's really to say? You know? But he was still boring. He married me like it was ticking a line off a to-do list. I mean, sure, his dick is big, but that can only make up for so much. You'll see. Robbing the cradle will eat away at his honor eventually." The smile she turns on me is vicious. "Enjoy the ride while you've got it. I'll still always be the mother of his child."

I promised myself I'd be cool around this woman. I stood in the mirror and gave myself a pep talk, and I only do that when I'm drunk and convincing myself to sober up. But I've been telling myself to give her the benefit of the doubt, to not judge her, to not be jealous of her, and here I am doing *all* of those things.

"Alright. Well, that'll do it," I announce, clapping my hands.

She blinks innocently, but there's a pleased curve to

her mouth. Every word she picked was carefully crafted to get under my skin. And I let her. What can I say? I'm a heart-on-my-sleeve type of gal.

"What will do it?"

I give her the fakest smile I can muster as I turn to walk away. "I'm not in hell yet, lady. Don't need to spend my time hanging out with the devil."

A small scoffing sound erupts behind me, but I don't stop. I stride across the field, ignoring the looks I'm garnering as I try to keep a serene expression on my face. I have a feeling I'm giving major serial killer vibes at this current juncture.

The way my hands have curled into fists might also be a dead giveaway.

When I step into the house, the screen door crashes shut behind me with a rattle and my confidence shakes in perfect time. The bridge of my nose burns, and I shake my head to clear away the tears that are springing up in my eyes.

It's the middle of the afternoon at a child's birthday party, and I need a fucking drink so I can process what that she-devil just told me. Or forget it entirely.

I pull a bottle of white wine from the freezer. It slips in my clammy palm when the screen door slams again. I keep my head down, setting the bottle on the counter and pulling the tinfoil wrapper off the top.

"What are you doing?" Cade's voice is concerned. He's so big that he blocks out a chunk of the light filtering into the kitchen.

"Having a drink," I mutter.

I don't have to look directly at him to know that he's just crossed his arms over his chest and widened his stance.

"Why?"

"Because I need one."

"Willa. Look at me." His tone leaves no room for argument, so I plant my hands on the countertop and stare back at him. "Good. Now tell me what's going on."

"That's why I need a drink."

Cade's tongue swipes across his teeth as he regards me. "Tell me what happened, and I'll pour you a drink myself."

"Your wife just told me she got pregnant on purpose," I blurt. "I think her words were *birth control, no birth control, who's to say?*" My voice is shrill and panicked.

And then this man really sends me for a loop, because he fucking *laughs*. "*Ex*-wife."

"Why the fuck are you laughing? I just told you that the smoking hot viper bitch in your backyard tricked you into knocking her up."

His shoulders shake, and one heavily veined hand props up against his forehead to cover his eyes. "Of course, she did." He sounds amused, flabbergasted.

"Is this funny? Aren't you mad? She just admitted to being an atrocious person and you're suddenly Mr. Giggles? She said you were robbing the cradle with me!"

He laughs harder, wheezing out, "Mr. Giggles?"

"Ugh!" I growl in frustration, too worked up to sit here and laugh about her baby daddy entrapment scandal.

"And you had to be married to someone who looks like a Victoria's Secret model," I rave as I rummage the drawers to find a wine opener. "And she's got that stupid, breathy voice that I've only ever heard in porn."

Another drawer. No corkscrew. I spin on Cade, who is giving me his full attention now. "I swear to God if she lays her shiny manicured claws on you one more time, I'm going to cut her hands clean off."

"You're so vicious, Red," he says with a stupid glint in his eye, like this is all just hilarious to him. "Are you jealous, baby?"

I turn away again, not wanting to look at how hot he is and see her with him. I am having a full-on meltdown, and I hate everything about this situation. I've never felt like this before, and it's fucking confusing.

"Yes, I'm jealous. She's had *everything* with you and I'm just the fucking nanny." God, I hate the way those words sound coming out of my mouth. Heat sears my chest. Embarrassment fuses with a heavy dose of envy.

I pull a drawer open and rifle through it to busy my shaking hands.

My fingers run up against something silky in the drawer full of scissors, elastics, clips, and Post-it notes. I grab and pull and peer down into my palm.

The black panties I dropped in that coffee shop all those weeks ago.

Turning back, I dangle them in my fingers. Cade doesn't look surprised at all; he just regards me with his Annoyed Scowl.

"You kept these?" I demand, sounding petulant even to myself. "You told me you threw them away."

"I lied," he grits out.

"Why?"

"Because you've never been *just the nanny*, Willa." My chest lurches as I look back at him, feeling suspended in time. "You've always been more. The woman I wanted but wouldn't let myself have."

"I could really use that drink now," I say, still staring at him.

"No. You're going to stand here and listen to me." He prowls toward me in a way that sets my heart racing. My blood heats in my veins.

When he's standing right in front of me, he tips my chin up and forces me to look into his eyes. "I'm not mad about whatever Talia told you because I don't give a fuck about her and her antics. I have Luke. Wouldn't trade him for the world. How that came about doesn't even matter anymore because I truly just do not care."

My heavy breathing acts as a backdrop to the deep rasp of his voice.

"Do you know what I care about though?" His fingers bite into my skin. "You, Willa. I care about you. You have nothing—and I mean nothing—to be jealous of."

"But she's had everything. Everything I didn't even

realize I wanted, and she just took it all for granted and walked away. And now she's here acting all entitled, and I'm so jealous that my teeth ache with it. I have never, *never* felt like this, and I want it to stop." The last part comes out pleading, like he can take away the ball of anxiety lodged in my chest.

"You don't want what she's had. You want more. You deserve *more*. And I'm going to give it to you. Nod if you understand me."

With a deep sigh, I nod, eyes locked on his. Heart racing in time with his. "But she—"

He cuts me off. "I thought I told you to stop and listen to me?"

"You did but—"

"If you can't stop running your mouth with that self-sabotaging bullshit, I will shut it for you." His hand cups my cheek tenderly. "I love Luke. You love Luke. And the three of us feel *right* together. Tonight she'll be gone and you'll still be here. At the end of this summer, you'll leave, but you'll be back. Because there's no way in hell that this ends here. I won't allow it. We're going to figure this out. You got me?"

I swallow hard, searching his dark, serious eyes, his furrowed brow, the look of intensity on his face. The little voice in my head says he's joking, but I know Cade well enough to know he wouldn't joke about this.

"But—"

In the blink of an eye, he's adjusted his grip to pop open my jaw and stuffs my panties inside. My irises widen as he works the fabric in and I stand stock still, too shocked to stop him. Too turned on to want to.

"There are no buts about it, Red. Now get your palms flat on the counter and bend over."

I still stare at him wide-eyed, a little shocked by how quickly this conversation has flipped. With a gentle hand on my shoulder, he turns me away, and I let my hands slide across the bare countertop.

"That's my girl," he murmurs, pushing down between my shoulder blades so that my torso presses against the counter, the edge of the cool marble biting into my hips. "Teasing me with this dress all afternoon. The only thing I can think about is bending you over and checking what you're wearing underneath."

I moan against the fabric in my mouth, hips shimmying as I arch my back in a silent invitation for him to check.

"Should I check?" His calloused fingers run up the back of my thighs, taking the hem of my favorite dress with them as they go. Goose bumps erupt across my back, and I hear his breath hitch when the soft fabric clears my bare ass and bunches at the base of my back. "Filthy girl. Walking around out there with no panties. You were hoping I'd check, weren't you?"

I press my cheek flat against the cool marble and look back at him, his eyes fixed on my ass. I nod. Because yeah, I wanted him to check. Wanted him to haul me into the bathroom and fuck me against the wall. Fuck the nerves right out of me.

But I'm here, bared to him in the open of his kitchen with a party happening only a few hundred meters away.

His hands massage the globes of my ass, and I lift my head to see out the window and check if anyone might be coming.

"What are you looking for, baby? You think I'd stop just because someone walked in?" His fingers glide down between my legs, and he runs two gentle fingers through my wet folds. "Maybe Talia will catch us, and I can make things abundantly clear for both of you. Because I can promise you, I've never fucked anyone the way I fuck you." I clench and moan.

"You'd like that, wouldn't you?" His voice is all gravel. "I wouldn't care. You're *mine*, Willa. And I don't give a fuck who knows it."

His fingers slide in, smooth and slow. One hand presses down on my back as he leans forward to whisper, "Is that what you need? You need me to bend you over right here and now, then send you back out there dripping my cum down your pretty little thighs to prove it to you?"

My mind races. Fuck. Is that what I want? I barely need to think about it. I want that so badly I ache with it. The pads of my fingers slide on the counter as I glance over my shoulder and nod.

"Good," he bites out, scrambling with his belt. "Because I want that too."

Within seconds he's dropped his pants and impaled me on his cock. And there's nothing soft about it. My body clamps around his steely length the minute he shoves himself into me.

One of his big hands wraps around my hip while the other presses down on my back, holding me in place.

"You look so good on my cock, Willa," he growls as his thighs slap against mine, and I arch myself up, pushing back at his every thrust, feeling just as wild and unhinged as him in this moment.

Like he can read my mind, he leans over my back and grits out, "You want it all, Willa? The house? The babies? The ranch?"

I nod again because it's all I can do. I want all that. With him.

"You want me, Willa?"

"Yes." I cry out against the soft fabric, nodding frantically as he slams into me. I want him so badly it hurts.

"Good. Because I'm sick of holding back with you. You're not going anywhere. You belong here, with me."

He lifts me, arm wrapped around my stomach as he clutches me to his chest. His stubble rasps against the shell of my ear. "Rub your clit while I'm fucking you. Let me tell you how it's going to be."

My head falls back against his shoulder as one hand gathers the fabric of my skirt. The opposite one immediately dives between my legs and rubs circles while Cade holds me tight.

"You're going to spend as much time as you want at *our* house," he says, while thrusting into me slowly. "You're going to work whatever job you want. Wherever you want. But you'll always have a place here. A home here. I'll make you coffee every morning. I'll leave you all the Post-it notes you want. I'll cook your dinner every day. I'll eat your pussy in the hot tub before bed every damn night."

Yes.

I whimper, almost sagging in relief at his confession. I didn't even realize how badly I needed to hear that he wants me. For more than just a few weeks.

His voice is firm and then he stops, pressing a stubbled kiss to my exposed neck while his hands roam my breasts and I focus on breathing through my nose.

"But this pussy is *mine,* Willa." He drags his lips over my skin until I can't even think straight. I press harder on my clit, feeling myself barrel toward that finish line. "Mine to fuck."

Yes.

I rub back on him as he holds me close. Every sensation magnified, more intense somehow. The scrape of his beard. The pressure of my fingers. The light-headedness seeping in.

My teeth bare down on the fabric in my mouth.

I shake in his hold.

"Mine to fill."

Yes.

With that he pushes me onto the counter and unleashes, right as my vision blurs and I convulse, crying out his muffled name. My entire body surges with fire as I come apart beneath him.

We're just energy, and heat, and breath. I've never been so thoroughly consumed in my life. Never had sex with such an edge to it.

"*Mine.*" His growl is downright feral as he explodes inside of me, hands tracing my back reverently. A man of such dichotomies. Hard words laced with love. Rough hands filled with tenderness.

Immediately, he reaches up and removes the fabric from my mouth. I pant and suck in air, which has more to do with the power of my orgasm than the gag he fashioned for me. His breaths are heavy and uneven, our skin is damp.

And even though I don't think I can get any hotter than I already am, when he pulls away and puts one hand on each globe of my ass to watch me drip his seed, I do.

When he adds, "Just like that," I press my forehead to the cool marble and let a quiet, breathy chuckle escape me.

"Jesus."

With a firm slap, he huffs out a laugh, and it's like I can still feel his eyes on the most intimate parts of me. I clearly have no shame because I make no move to stand. "Have I told you that you look perfect like this?"

I roll my forehead against the marble counter, still trying to get my bearings. "No. I think that's a first for me."

A satisfied noise rumbles from behind me, and I feel the soft slide of fabric covering my legs, followed by the gentle press of a kiss against my back. "Feeling better now?" Cade asks, pulling me up gently, hands never leaving my body as he turns me to face him.

"I'm feeling something alright." I smile a little shyly at him. I mean, how can I not? The things that come out of this man's mouth are downright shocking sometimes.

He eyes me skeptically, tracing my face with his gaze.

"I'm feeling better. Just . . . messy?" I glance down at myself. "I'll just go clean up." I reach out to swipe my discarded panties off the counter, but he grabs them first.

He gives me this evil smirk. A playful smirk? Maybe it's a playful scowl? But it's followed by, "No chance. You're putting these on, and you're going back out there like this."

I shake my head at him, amused, as he drops to the ground and lifts my feet gently into the leg holes of the simple underwear. He presses a soft kiss to my stomach and then he's up, moving around the kitchen, like this is all the most normal thing in the world. When I stop blushing enough to face him again, he's poured me a glass of white wine and is waiting by the back door.

"Ready?" he asks with an outstretched hand and a lopsided smile on his face. A dimple I never even noticed has popped up. He looks boyish and beautiful. And like he might be mine after all.

"I'm going to walk out into a child's birthday party with a big glass of wine and bright red cheeks?" I ask, just to clarify. Because it feels insane.

"Don't forget about your freshly fucked pussy. But no one else will see that. I covered it up for you."

"They'll know though." I point at him and walk in his direction.

The other side of his mouth pops up, and he hands me the wine before he leans in close and whispers, "Good," against my cheek.

29

Willa

Cade: Baby, why are you blushing?

Willa: Because I swear people are looking at me like I just got my brains fucked out.

Cade: You did.

Willa: I think these panties are ruined.

Cade: I'll wash them for you. And then shove them in your mouth again the next time you say something rude.

Willa: Fuck off.

Cade: Careful. They haven't even been washed yet.

ight there at the birthday party?" Summer whisper-shouts across the small table at Le Pamplemousse.

I take a sip of my mimosa and wink at her. "I saved

another horse, Sum. I'm practically an animal rights activist at this point."

She shakes her head. "Goddamn. These Eaton boys are insane."

"Right? I'm definitely in my country-boy era. I think I just haven't settled down because the city boys want to talk to me about oil futures and the size of their bank account like that makes up for the size of their di—"

"Willa." Summer's eyes widen. "We're in public."

"You don't even know what I was going to say."

The look she gives me is downright unimpressed.

"I was going to say dignity."

"The size of their dignity?"

I shrug and cover my mouth with another sip from the champagne flute. "Same thing if you think about it."

"Good lord." She laughs and takes a big gulp while looking out the window. "So just an era. Or more? Cade doesn't strike me as the casual type."

I sigh, letting the word *mine* settle into my bones. I spent all night snuggled next to Cade and spent the entire party catching his eyes on me, raking over me in an impolite fashion. When I played "Happy Birthday" on my guitar, accompanied by Luke on the smaller guitar that I gifted him, everything felt so damn right.

And when I looked back up from the song, Talia was gone. I wanted to be relieved, but I felt sad that she left her own child's birthday party without even saying goodbye to him.

"It's not just an era," I reply. "I don't know what I'm

going to do yet—because do I ever? But I know you'll be seeing more of me. It's not a far commute, and I don't know, maybe I can find something to do in Chestnut Springs. Rhett asked me to give him guitar lessons yesterday. Did you know that? And I'll have to give Ford my notice at the bar. I do like watching him get all pissy when things don't go his way."

Summer snickers because she knows my brother and how notoriously exacting he is. "This is big for you, Wils. I can't say I saw this coming when I pushed you into this gig. Kinda thought you and Cade would hate each other, to be honest."

I lean back in my chair. "Wow. Thank you for signing me up to spend my summer living with a man you thought would hate me."

She waves a hand at me dismissively. "I knew you could handle it. Plus, Luke is fun."

I sigh happily. "Yeah. Luke is the best. I didn't know I'd enjoy life with a kid like I am. It really doesn't even feel like work."

"Uh oh. Have you got baby rabies, Willa?"

I groan and lean back in my chair. "Will you take back my feminist card if I tell you I really just want to live in that little house on the ranch, teach guitar lessons, get titty-fucked in the hot tub, and have a bunch of adorable babies?"

Summer's eyes bug out. "Remember the part about being in public? People here listen to *everything*. And also, no. No one is taking back your feminist card if that's what you want, Willa. I can't even tell if you're being serious or joking right now. But raising good humans is important work. If you can raise nice people and put them out into the world less messed up than me or my sister, I'd say you're winning."

"Yeah." I bite down on my thumbnail considering what she's just said, considering if I'm joking or not. Wondering if there's anything wrong with wanting that. "Luke is just so awesome, you know? Cade's done such an amazing job with him. He's just so devoted."

"Good lord." Summer takes another swig.

"What?"

"The two of you. All mushy and in love. It's so weird."

I give her a flat look. "Thanks."

"Weird and wonderful. Just like you."

I consider her words before nodding. "I'll cheers to that."

I cleared out this morning because Cade had Luke helping him dig a walkway to the house that he plans to pave. When Harvey tripped on the edge of an uneven paving stone after a few too many drinks at the after-party, Cade instantly announced that he was putting in a "proper sidewalk."

And sure enough, he was up at the ass crack of dawn, staking it out and plotting the edges. All while wearing that fucking backward hat that made me want to shove him down into the dirt and ride him.

Again.

Instead, I called Summer and told her I required brunch. Brunch is our thing. It has been for years. And with everything swirling in my head I needed something familiar. Some*one* familiar, someone logical, and utterly responsible.

Instead, Summer has sat here and enabled all the crazy shit floating in my head.

~

When I pull back up at the ranch, a smile breaks out on my face.

"Willa!" Luke drops his shovel and barrels toward me the minute I step out of my Jeep, work so easily forgotten.

He launches himself at me like I've been gone for years, and I smile into his hair as I lift him up. "Hey, little nut bar."

"Can we go practice on my guitar?" He's practically vibrating when I set him back down.

Cade huffs out a laugh as he wedges his shovel into the ground with one booted foot. "I think you won the birthday party with that gift, Red."

"I love the drone too, Dad." Sensitive kid he is, Luke spins quickly, clearly trying to reassure his dad, all worried about hurting a grown-ass man's feelings.

"I know, pal. But the guitar is amazing, right?"

Luke's grin is so wide it looks like it hurts. "Totally amazing!" he gushes.

"Why don't you go practice and I'll help your dad with this for a while. Show me what you've figured out when I get in there, yeah?"

Glancing down at him, I see his little fingers moving like they're just itching to play. Kid has the bug, no two ways about it. I'm going to have to tell my dad about him soon—he'll get a real kick out of this for sure.

"Definitely." He grins like a total loon, and then he's off. He literally skips into the house and watching him go with so much joy makes my heart squeeze. But he stops and turns when he hits the front porch. "Hey, Willa, you're not leaving soon, are you?"

I feel Cade's gaze sliding over my body. His motion has stopped entirely. It feels like the entire world is watching. Both these sweet boys staring at me, putting me right on the goddamn spot.

My mouth opens and closes, and I peek over at Cade for some sort of sign that I'm not out of line in saying something here. His gloved hands are slung over the top of his shovel, his tanned stubbled face glistening with a light sheen of sweat.

He's fucking lickable.

Too good to leave behind, that's for sure.

"No, pal. I don't think I am. Not permanently, anyway. I think I'd miss you too much. Is that okay with you?"

His round face softens, hair flopping onto his fore-head as he nods. "Yeah. I'd miss you too. And I think my dad would be really lonely without you." With a sweet little smile, he turns and scampers through the front door, like he didn't just leave Cade and me out here with watery eyes.

"Did you talk to him?"

Cade rubs a gloved hand over his eye. "No. Figured I should talk to you first." He sniffs.

"You okay? Did I overstep?"

"Not at all." He clears his throat. "Just got dust in my eye." He rubs again.

"Cool, cool. Me too," I say, giving him an exaggerated watery wink.

"How was brunch?" He digs again, arms flexing as he does.

I never knew a man digging out a spot for a sidewalk could be an aphrodisiac, but here I am, admiring the way his shoulders bulge against his T-shirt and the tendons in his forearms ripple in the sunlight.

"Good."

"You actually going to stay?" he asks, without looking up at me. Instead, he tosses a shovel full of dirt behind himself and keeps working.

"You really going to keep working while we have this conversation?"

"Yup," is his gruff response.

"Yesterday you were all *Me Cade. You woman. Stay here. Eat pussy every day,*" I say in what is a sad attempt at some sort of Tarzan impersonation.

He doesn't laugh though. "Well, today I'm more

worried you'll be thinking straight and will realize you belong in the city doing whatever fancy shit you do."

"Manage a bar while slinging beer? My glamorous lifestyle truly knows no bounds."

"Listen"—he shoves the shovel into the ground like he wants to hurt it before finally looking up at me—"if all this out here isn't enough for you, I'd rather you just go now. I wasn't joking about what I said yesterday. And it feels like a lot. I . . ." He glances away, wiping the back of his arm over his forehead. "I don't want to live my life scared anymore. But I also don't want to be made a fool of again."

That painful twisting sensation is back in my chest. The heavy rock in my gut. This man deserves so much better than what he's received.

"Cade, look at me."

His jaw clenches, but he doesn't look my way, opting to stare down at the ground he's dug out.

So that's where I go. I sit down in the dirt right in front of him.

"The fuck you doing, woman?" he grumbles as I tip my chin up in his direction.

"Trying to get your attention." I stretch my legs out in front of me and lean back on my palms, feeling the cool damp dirt beneath them. It smells like earth, and flint, and pine needles.

It smells like home.

"You've had my attention since—"

I roll my eyes and wave a hand at him. "Yeah, yeah. Since I dropped my panties at your feet."

"No. Since I first heard you laugh."

That shuts me up.

"In the coffee shop. I was standing behind you and couldn't stop thinking about how incredible your laugh was. All fucking light and warm. It made me want to laugh too."

My tongue darts out over my lips as I regard him.

"I'm—fuck—I'm scared, Willa. I'm scared you're too young. That you haven't lived enough. That you're too far out of my league. I'm scared I won't be enough for you and you'll walk away. And I'll be stuck here in the shambles again. And so will Luke this time." His free hand swipes at his hat, shifting it on his head as he looks away again.

"I'm scared too," I blurt out. "But not too scared to try."

He stares at me. Hard. It's unnerving really. And then he rasps out, "Yeah, me neither."

I beam at him and see a ghost of a smile on his lips before he starts shoveling again.

"I'll call my brother and quit. That will be fun."

"If you need to go back to the city for a while, that's fine. You might want to take your time."

"And what? Pretend we haven't been living together for almost two months already? Should I go live up at the main house with Harvey?"

He doesn't even flinch. "That might give us a chance

364

to date properly. Maybe a little distance is good for you to be sure about everything. Or we could commute."

I roll my eyes and cross my feet. "Shut up, Cade. Stop being so mature."

"Someone has to be," he grumbles, tossing another shovelful of dirt over his shoulder and looking mighty sexy as he does it.

"Hey, you know what this yard needs?" I press my index finger to my lips as I make a show of examining the property.

"What?"

"A real good blow job."

Cade barks out a raspy laugh and shakes his head. "Lord help me, what have I done?"

We spend the rest of the day like that. Him digging. Me making fun of him. And eventually Luke comes out and plays us a song he made up.

For once, I feel settled. Like everything in my life is where it's meant to be.

30

Cade

Willa: Why did you leave me a Post-it note saying, *No panties today?*

Willa: That just ruins the surprise.

Cade: Because I want easy access.

Willa: Cade Eaton. This is a family event.

Cade: Hasn't stopped you before.

Willa: That was a one-time thing.

Cade: No, it wasn't. It was a precedent-setter.

Willa: Luke is going to be able to read these soon.

Cade: Did you change the subject because you know I'm right?

Asmile breaks out on my face when Jasper hops up on a horse. "Thanks for coming out."

He winks at me. "You know I wouldn't miss it. I love sitting on the sidelines as not to violate my contract."

I shake my head. "And we just love having the one and only Jasper Gervais here to grace us with his presence while we work the cattle."

The expression he gives me is dry—sarcastic somehow. No one is more uncomfortable with his fame than Jasper.

"Lighten up. You know this is one of my favorite events of the year. Really is nice to have you out here."

"Did *you* just tell *me* to lighten up?" Shock bleeds into his tone.

That's when a chorus of hoots breaks out along the fence line behind me. Everyone is here. Willa, Summer, Rhett, and other friends from town.

I turn and catch two matching flashes of blonde hair waltzing down to the pen and my dad with an expression that looks like he just saw Elvis Presley come back from the dead.

"Violet! You're gonna give me a heart attack, girl!" My dad wraps his arms around our little sister, and she's so petite that she almost disappears in his embrace.

"Surprise, Dad!"

He holds her back and takes her in. "Aren't you a sight for sore eyes." He turns to our cousin. "You too,

Sloane. Who knew the little barn brats would grow up to be such beautiful young women?"

God, Harvey is fucking gushing. Sloane comes around now and then since becoming some sort of prima ballerina, but Violet has become something of a sensation herself—a world famous racehorse jockey out on the coast, with a whole damn family—so she's not back nearly as often.

I can't help but grin again. Seem to do a lot of that lately.

I ride over with Jasper following.

"Baby sister," I say.

"Big brother." She beams up at me. "Almost didn't recognize you with that smile on your face."

I hop off and frown at her dramatically before folding her into a hug. "Where's Cole?"

"Oh, your man crush?" she quips because yeah, I like the guy. She married a good one. "He's wrangling the tiny humans so I can wrangle some cows."

"Yeah?" I pull back and eye her skeptically.

"Hell yeah." She claps her hands and brushes them together like she's ready for the challenge. "Bet I can still throw a rope better than you."

I just shake my head before turning to Sloane. She's standing beside Violet but has her full attention on Jasper, like she has since she was a kid.

And he's fucking clueless, like he has been since he was a kid.

He says they're "good friends." And maybe they are, maybe I'm reading into something that isn't there.

All I know is that in those early days, everyone looked at Jasper like he might come apart at any moment. But Sloane looked at him like he hung the moon.

"Good to see you, Sloane. It's been a while. Keeping busy with the dancing?" That probably sounds dumb, but I don't know how to put it. Not a big ballet guy myself.

She smiles at me and before she can talk, Violet grabs her left hand and holds it up. "She's keeping busy with wedding planning!"

"Wedding? Well, shit, Sloane. You've been holding out on us." I reach out to give her a hug. "Congratulations. When's the big day?"

"November, I think," is her soft reply, eyes darting back to where Jasper is still seated on his mount.

"This November?" he asks from beside me.

"Yeah." She tucks a piece of hair behind her ear, now keeping her eyes focused on me.

"Who is the guy? I've never even met this person." I cross my arms over my chest, feeling Blueberry nudge me from behind.

"Jesus, you guys." Violet waves a hand in front of us. "Overbearing much? And you all wonder why I moved away so I could date? She's in her twenties. She doesn't need y'all to play bodyguard."

Jasper and I scoff in unison.

Violet's nose tips up and she ignores us. "I'm having dinner with them when Sloane takes me back to the airport on Monday, so *I'll* be the one to pass judgment on him."

It's Sloane who laughs now, smiling and shaking her head a little. "You mean the one to *meet* him? Because you're the one who isn't overbearing? Right?"

Rhett butts in now. "Ooh. Called out. Looks like you aren't so different from us after all, Fancypants."

"Yeah, yeah," Violet waves us all off with a grin. "Just show everyone that massive rock and stop picking on me. It's making Cade smile and that's just weird."

Sloane lips tip up but her cheeks wobble. It's not the way I'd be smiling if I were set to marry Willa in a few short months. She holds her hand out demurely, and sure enough, the stone is massive. Her family wouldn't have it any other way.

A chorus of congratulations ring out around us. Everyone *oohs* and *ahhs* over the ring, and Jasper hops off his horse, giving the girls a soft smile. He ruffles Violet's hair before congratulating Sloane.

She reaches for him, and he wraps her in a bear hug, resting the palm of his hand against the back of her head as she presses her forehead to his chest.

It reminds me of running my fingers through Willa's hair, and I instantly search for her in the group of people. I find her easily, standing there smiling, wearing skin-tight jeans and holding our boy's hand.

And fuck, it looks good.

"Vi, come meet Willa." I don't specify her role. I

don't call her my nanny because that's not true. And I don't call her my friend because that's sure as shit not true either.

"Ooh! Yes! Willa." Violet turns, and a genuine smile breaks out across her face when her eyes land on Willa and Luke. "I have heard so much about you," is what she says as she strides toward them.

"Likewise." Willa grins back at her, and I just know these two will get along famously.

I don't miss the little wink Violet gives me over Willa's shoulder as they hug.

Harvey and his big fucking mouth. Telling everyone and their dog about Willa and me ever since that day I carried Willa off over my shoulder. Like if he tells enough people he'll make it happen or something.

"Okay, we good?" I shout, wanting to get this show on the road so I can kick back with a cold brew. Probably lay my girl out and have a midnight snack too, find out if she followed my instructions.

She probably didn't. And I love that about her.

Shit, I love *her*, period.

You should tell her. Summer's words pop up in my head often. I should tell her but I'm fucking terrified, so I push it aside and get my ass in gear. It's a problem for another day.

Within the hour, everyone is saddled up and we get to work. Vaccinating. Tagging. Shit-talking.

And wouldn't you know it, my baby sister still throws a better rope than me.

I feel the snap when I get slammed into the metal panel. "Fuck!"

"Cade?" Jasper jumps off his mount at the same time as Rhett, and they race toward me.

"Fucking, fuck!" I clutch my hand to my chest and searing pain shoots through it.

Both guys are climbing the fence to get to me.

"Jasper, don't you dare come in this fucking shoot, you crazy motherfucker. If you get hurt, this entire country will hate me." It's an Olympic year. I can't injure our nation's number one goalie.

"Too late, asshole," he murmurs before hopping down while Rhett adjusts the gates to keep the cows away from me.

I hold my hand protectively, hoping if I just breathe through my nose for a minute the pain will pass.

I've been at this long enough to know better.

"Is it broken?" Rhett hollers while Jasper gives me an unimpressed glare that says I need to show him my hand.

"You're a fucking hockey player. Not a doctor."

"I'm smart enough to make an educated guess." Jasper gives me his best bitchy look. And honestly, it's pretty good.

I hold my right hand out with an irritated sigh, pinky and ring finger already looking totally swollen.

"Oh, yeah. It's broken," Rhett announces.

"And you're a retired bull rider. What the fuck do you know?"

He shrugs. "Well, I know what broken bones look like. And you've got them."

"I agree," Jasper tosses in, folding the brim of his cap over his forehead.

"This is like a stupid joke. A hockey player and a bull rider walk into a doctor's office . . ."

"Cade. You need to get X-rays."

I slump against the metal fencing behind me and groan. "It was the last batch. I just wanted a beer and a hot tub."

"No problem, bro." Rhett slaps me on the shoulder hard enough that my fingers ache. "I'll grab you one for the road. Also, Summer told me to never go in that hot tub again. The fuck you been doing in there?"

"Get fucked, Rhett. I use chlorine tabs in there and test the water regularly."

"Is the water pregnant yet?" he tosses over his shoulder while jogging away.

"Dick," I mutter, gingerly holding my hand and feeling my arms shake.

"What can I do?" Jasper asks gently.

"Get Willa," is what I say. Because she's the only person I want right now.

He stares at me with his soulful eyes and nods. He's walking back with her within minutes.

She looks pale, her eyes pinched, but she doesn't fuss

over me. That's not her personality, and I think I love her even more for it.

"Fancy meeting you here, Eaton. You try to be a hero and break some fingers?" She's doing the thing where she defuses her anxiety with humor, but I let her. Her sarcasm is a good distraction right now.

Rhett is back and hands me an already cracked beer. "No. He was trying to be a hero and get that calf's leg out by himself."

I hold the beer up in Willa's direction. "Cheers, baby. You get to play nurse today."

"Oh, yeah?" She draws closer, running a hand over my shoulder and down my arm to hold my hand. As she assesses the quickly darkening digits, she adds, "I think I dressed up as that for Halloween one year."

Jesus. What *didn't* this woman dress as for Halloween?

I groan and let my eyes flutter shut to the sound of my brothers having a good chuckle around me. The last thing I need is a rock-hard dick to go along with my broken fingers.

"Okay, champ. Off to the hospital we go." Willa slides her hand around my back. "I got him from here, boys. The girls have Luke. I think he's in heaven with two blondes paying attention to him."

"Talk about mommy issues," Rhett jokes to a chorus of groans. Leave it to him to say something inappropriate right now.

"Fucking clown," I mutter as I absently press a kiss to Willa's head.

It's eerily quiet for a moment because I realize I just kissed my nanny in front of these two jokers and didn't even think twice about it.

Willa clears her throat to break the silence.

"We'll finish the cows and then come to the hospital," Jasper says.

Rhett scoffs. "It's fucking broken fingers. I think he'll make it through."

I laugh because this sucks and Rhett is certifiable. "Thanks, guys."

Then we're off, silently walking back to the barn where I parked. When I meet Willa's eyes, they're wide and concerned, so I whisper, "Don't worry, baby. I'm going to be fine."

She sniffles and rolls her shoulders back. "I know," she replies, always putting on that tough facade.

"Were you worried?" I ask as I settle into the passenger seat of my parked truck.

"Of course," she replies, voice even as she hops into the driver's seat. "I don't know how well you'll be able to finger bang me with your left hand."

I chuckle and smile the rest of the way to the hospital because there is only one person in the world who could make me laugh in a moment like this.

It hits me hard as we drive in a companionable silence that Willa is that person.

My person.

The hospital in Chestnut Springs is small. Staffing is a constant issue. Wait times are brutal.

I guess having to wait several hours shouldn't surprise me. First, in the general waiting area. Second, X-rays. Last, back to a private room where we wait some more.

Willa holds my good hand the entire time, thumb stroking at the top, and somehow that numbs the pain of my fingers.

Willa's eyes bug out when a doctor walks into our waiting room with her face turned down to the clipboard in her hands. "Winter?"

The doctor's head snaps up, icy eyes widening only momentarily.

"Like Summer's sister, Winter?" I blurt because I've heard stories about this woman. Summer's *estranged* sister. Like major family drama levels of estranged. Rhett told me about the blow up one day over a few beers, and it sounds like it's out of a daytime soap opera to me.

Fucking rich city people, man.

"Yes." Her lips thin, and her heels click against the floor as she shuts the door. "The one and only. I'm sure you've heard only good things," she says dryly before adding, "but I promise your fingers are in excellent hands, Mr. Eaton."

Hoo boy. Another woman who could use someone to

tell her some good things about herself. I watch her tense movements, the way her lips purse when she glances at Willa. She looks like Summer, but also not at all.

Winter and Summer . . . whoever did that to them deserves a kick to the balls.

"Winter, how are you? What are you doing here?" Willa asks, her voice soft and wary as the petite woman pulls on a pair of latex gloves.

Winter ignores her questions. It's like they don't even register on her face.

"Let's see your fingers, Mr. Eaton." She holds her hand out to me and I put it in hers, wincing as I do. Her dainty fingers prod so gently that I barely even feel them. "Both fingers are broken. The breaks are fairly clean, but from what I can see on the X-rays, there are some bone chips floating in there. We could do a surgical repair—"

"I don't—"

She cuts me right back off with a pointed look. "I'm still speaking." Good God, this woman is kind of terrifying. I clamp my mouth shut and widen my eyes to tell her she can go on.

"Like I was saying, we could operate and tidy things up immediately, but my inclination is to avoid surgery when possible. So the other option is to splint these and let them heal. Hope those chips sort of dissolve on their own and see how you feel. If they're still causing issues, we can operate down the road. It's a trade-off. Heal faster now in the hopes you don't need surgery later, or still have issues and be laid out twice. It's up to you."

She's very direct, very matter-of-fact. Some people might think her bedside manner leaves something to be desired, but I kind of like her. She speaks to me like I'm capable of making a decision, and she isn't pushing treatment down my throat.

Her voice is gentler than I expected based on the stories I heard, and her eyes less vicious. They're more . . . sad. Rimmed with dark circles.

"There are physiotherapy options and alternative health options that can help with rehabilitation from an injury like this," she carries on, scribbling on the chart before her.

"Alternative health options?" I ask, scrunching my face.

She pulls her gloves off with a snap to write something down on her chart. "I'd recommend acupuncture to start," she replies without even looking up at me.

"Okay." I glance at Willa, who is still staring at her best friend's sister, almost like she's seen a ghost. "Let's go the more conservative route."

"Great." She smiles but it's pained. "I'll get someone in here to fix you up and then you can be on your way. I'm sure you're tired of waiting." She stands and marches out the door, the picture of unaffected professionalism.

But Willa takes off after her.

31

Willa

Summer: Is Cade okay?

Willa: Yes. A couple of broken fingers. Will need 6-8 weeks to heal. So he'll be an extra grumpy bitch for the foreseeable future.

Summer: Could have been worse. Luke is asleep. All good here.

Willa: Hey, Sum, has Winter responded to any of your messages?

Summer: No. I keep sending them anyway. I know she's reading them. Why?

Willa: Because she's our doctor tonight.

Summer: How does she look?

Willa: Sad.

"Winter," I whisper-shout as I follow her down the beige hallway with a random green stripe down the middle of the wall. Why the hell do hospitals do that? It doesn't make them any more appealing. "Winter, stop."

Summer has been trying to contact her for a year but gets shut down at every turn. I'm not leaving this hospital before I talk to her.

She rounds the corner but stops in a little alcove that plays host to a couple of vending machines.

"What?" she snaps primly, nose tipped up as she stares down at her nails.

I've known Winter since we were teenagers. When Summer was in the hospital, we spent some time together. Winter isn't as bad as everyone has made her out to be. She's been dealt a shit hand.

One that money and education can't undo. What Winter is missing is love.

I stare at her, breathing more heavily than the distance I just covered warrants. "I just want to give you a hug," I say.

Her long lashes blink slowly, and she's forced to look up at me because these sisters stopped growing at like twelve or something. "A hug?"

I realize now how rough she looks. Too thin. Too tired.

"Yes, girl." I open my arms. "Get your scrawny ass over here."

She glances away for a moment, like the bag of hickory sticks in the vending machine is super interesting. And then her shoulders droop and without meeting my eyes, she steps into my arms.

She sighs when she does, and so do I. It's amazing how the adults around you can fuck everything up. That's what happened with Summer and Winter—and I was there to watch it all go down.

I was also there in the hospital, sitting by Summer's bedside, when Winter would sneak out of the house to be with her too. But only if Summer was sleeping. It's an unspoken secret Winter and I have kept for years.

Everyone thinks Winter didn't care, but I know better. She loves her little sister, even though her mom has made her feel like she shouldn't. Even if she doesn't know how to show it.

Their dad, Kip Hamilton, isn't perfect, but he's also not evil incarnate like Winter's mom.

I think of Luke, and how different his life might have been if Cade and Talia had stayed together and been miserable.

He could have been these girls.

"How is life?" I whisper, and she doesn't let me go. In fact, her fingers curl into my jean jacket and grip me like I'm her only lifeline on a sinking ship.

"Everything is fine." Her voice cracks, and I feel her chest hitch when she sighs. "Fuck. That's not true. Everything is a mess. And I lost the baby."

My stomach hollows out and I almost feel nauseous.

A year ago when everything blew up between her and Summer, she was pregnant.

She's still clutching at me as she speaks. "And on one hand, I'm devastated because I tried for so long. And on the other, I'm relieved because I don't have to be tied to *him* for the rest of my life. How awful am I?"

Her laugh is watery and my eyes widen. Winter has never been emotional. She's always icy and reserved—especially in adulthood. I hardly recognize the woman clinging to me.

"You are not awful." And I mean it. No one deserves to live in a world where the only family they have are an unfaithful husband and a manipulative mom. "You deserve so much better, Winter."

She hums, like she isn't so sure.

"Are you still together?" I ask, referring to the living, breathing trash she married.

"Sort of," is her strained reply.

"He doesn't deserve you."

She squeezes me harder. God, this woman needs to be hugged so badly. "I know," is her soft reply. "I'm just glad Summer has you. God knows the rest of us didn't do her any good."

Shocked by what she just said, I pull away and stare back at the woman before me. She's always cool and removed, impossible to get a read on. "What are you doing here in Chestnut Springs?"

She sniffs and rubs her nose before stepping out of my hold. "I took a rotation out here. Seemed like a good way to spend time away from him a few days at a time."

Him. Her douchebag husband. The one she needs to leave and should have left a year ago.

I can't help but wonder if the proximity to her estranged sister played any role in choosing this hospital.

"Summer would love to talk to you. Hell, see you. That door is always open, you know that, right?"

Her eyes roll, and it's like I can see her shields shoot back up before my eyes. "Yes. The constant text messages she sends have driven that point home."

"So? Take her up on it. She loves you, whether or not you want to believe it." Winter scoffs, back to looking at her nails. "You got something stuck under there?" I ask because she's being rude. "My eyes are up here, Winter."

"How am I supposed to do that? Just waltz back into my sister's life after everything that's gone down between us? After the way I've treated her? She must hate me."

"Yes, Winter. That's exactly what you do. Because she does not hate you."

"I'm . . . I don't know how to mend this. I'm embarrassed," she confesses quietly.

"Don't be. We all need a fresh start now and again. Come hang out sometime. Maybe you'll even have fun."

She snorts at my suggestion. "With the two of you? Why would I even try? You and Summer are so tight, I bet you get your periods at the same time. Totally synched up. I remember you two binging junk food every month and complaining about your cramps."

I laugh but stop as I process the words. Pre-period I'm always extra-bitchy. I'm a couple of days into my placebo pills for the month but nothing has started.

The other day, Summer complained about her cramps, and I just tittered like a sex-drunk idiot.

The blood drains from my face. It feels like it pools in my feet and grows heavy there as questions circulate in my mind, questions I haven't even let myself think about.

"Are you okay?" Concern laces Winter's tone.

"I . . ." My palms come up to rest on my cheeks. How did I miss this? "Fuck. What's the date today?"

Winter's eyes scan me, intelligence flashing in every glance. "Oh shit," she says, rearing back a little. "Did you let that cowboy knock you up, Willa Grant?"

~~~

It's dark by the time we hit the road again, which suits me fine because Cade can't see my face as well under the cover of night.

He's tired. I'm tired.

I'm in shock.

Winter tracked me down a pregnancy test while Cade had his fingers casted. It came back positive for a tiny Eaton, and I just sat in the waiting room staring into space.

Winter stayed for a while. She wasn't overly comforting, but it was nice to have someone with me all the same. She was quiet and withdrawn as soon as the test came back positive.

It was awkward.

"You okay?" Cade asks, jolting me from my thoughts.

"Me? Yeah? Fine. Why?" I turn slightly to peek at his furrowed brow and beautifully crafted face. I'm not even mad, I'm not even sad. I'm oddly at peace with the whole thing.

But I am worried about *him*.

"Because you're gripping the steering wheel like you're trying to strangle it."

"Ah," I say with a nod.

"Did Winter say something to you? Do we like her? Do we hate her? Am I supposed to be mad at something with you? Because I will be if you are. Just tell me how to be supportive."

Fuck, he's sweet. His voice is all rough edges and deep grumbles, but I know he means what he says.

I just worry that after being trapped by one pregnancy, he'll feel the same all over again. He'll feel confined. He'll be stuck providing for a woman and a baby that he never really got to be sure he wanted.

Again.

"No," I reply softly, "Winter was great. I'm hoping her and Summer can mend this thing between them. I think they both need it."

"I'm going to be fine, you know." He reaches across the center console for my hand, twining his fingers with mine, forcing a soft sigh from my lips. I always feel better with his hands on my body.

More grounded. More myself. More confident.

I'm more myself with Cade Eaton than I've ever been, and now I'll have to wonder if he feels the same, or if he's going through the motions out of a sense of duty. Again. Our relationship is in its infancy, and as much as I realize I do want a family—with Cade even—I can't say that I saw it playing out quite like this.

"I know," I say, but I don't know if I believe it. And I don't know if things will ever be the same between us once I say this out loud to him. How could he possibly be fine with this happening to him again?

I know I need to tell him. I can feel the words building in my throat the closer we get to the ranch. The more he strokes my hand, the more flustered I get, and the guiltier I feel for sitting here wordlessly for the past fifteen minutes.

We drive in silence, but I sense he knows something is up because I'm not my normal, chatty self. I can see him tossing nervous glances my way, like he's totally out of his depth.

But so am I.

When we pull up at the house, I put the truck in park but stay staring out the front windshield.

"Look, Red, I'm trying not to be a domineering asshole, but I want to know what's going on in that pretty head of yours. I can see the gears turning. I can tell by the way you're sitting. By the tension in your hand. Usually I can't get you to shut up unless I stuff your panties in your mouth. So this?" He gestures between us. "This is weird."

A raw laugh lurches out of me, and tears spring up in my eyes. I pull my hand from his to rub at my face, to bring some circulation back to my head, because I feel like I'm living in some alternate dream world. Like this can't *really* be happening to me.

It feels like the best way to do this is to rip off the Band-aid. Fast, painless—get it over with because I can't handle these levels of anxiety in my body.

"I'm pregnant."

Those two words come out sure and steady. So much surer and steadier than I feel right now.

Cade stares at me blankly. His mouth pops open and closes again, and then he shakes his head, like it might make reality seep back in.

"Surprise?" I add awkwardly. "I'm sorry," I add even more awkwardly.

My head is spinning, and I'm feeling like I could use a moment alone to get my bearings—to process this—because saying it out loud to him feels so much more real. "I just found out at the hospital and have been trying to find the courage to tell you. I'm sorry."

"Why are you sorry?"

"I didn't do this on purpose." He blinks at me. "I swear I'm on birth control, but apparently barfing it up for two days straight isn't ideal."

His hand slides over his stubbled chin as he sucks in

a breath. Oh god, he's not saying anything, and my anxiety is growing exponentially, doubling.

Like cells.

Fuck. What is wrong with my head?

"You're just so young." Not the words I wanted to hear right now.

"Good God. You act like I'm a clueless teenager! I'm twenty-five! Stop treating me like I'm a child. That excuse is insulting." I huff out an agitated breath. "I think I need a night alone to just process this."

He scowls at me and still says nothing, so I just keep talking. "Yeah. Yeah. That's what I need. And you do too."

I'm starting to spin out. I stare down and rifle through my oversized purse to find his painkillers, feeling a full-on freak-out like I've never had coming on. My hand wraps around something long and slender and I pull out . . . a carrot?

My eyes water and panic rises, and I just toss it in the back seat.

"Was that a carrot?" is the first thing Cade says to me since I told him I was pregnant with his baby.

An excellent sign, to be sure.

I finally find the bottle of painkillers Winter dropped in the room before leaving with a gentle goodbye. "Here."

"Why is there a carrot in your purse?"

Jesus. I've really broken his brain. Who can blame him though?

"I'm going to sleep at the main house tonight."

He blinks. "Like hell you are."

I jump out of his truck, taking the few strides over to my Jeep before clambering into the driver's side seat. Am I handling this well? Probably not. But I'm having a moment, and all he's doing is scowling at me and asking me about the carrot.

Cade grabs the door of my Jeep before I can close it and glares at me.

"I'm sorry," I say. "I'm very aware that I'm not handling this well."

"We need to talk," is all he says, and it sounds so foreboding that dread settles in my stomach.

"I need a night alone. To gather my thoughts. So do you."

I expect him to argue, and there's a little part of me that wants him to throw me over his shoulder the way he did that day Luke and I hid from him. He slapped my ass and laughed, but this time he gives me a terse nod, and my stomach sinks.

He slams the door and pats the hood as I woodenly twist the keys in the ignition. I suck in a deep breath before shifting into drive. I pull away, feeling shaky and teary and totally lame for leaving him there after dropping that bomb.

I see his outline standing in the driveway even as I round the corner.

And my last thought before I lose sight of him is that he deserves better than being back here again. Because he's so damn honorable that he'll stick himself with me and this baby.

Even if it's not really what he wants.

32

Cade

Cade: Willa is heading to your place. Can you let me know when she's there safe, please? She'll need the guest room.

Harvey: What did you do to her?

Cade: Why is that the first place your head goes?

Harvey: Because you have a knack for ducking things up.

Cade: Ducking?

Harvey: Duck off. You know exactly what I mean.

Cade: My fingers are broken. Thanks for your concern.

Harvey: My only concern is about possible brain damage since you let your girl walk out. She's here safe.

Cade: My brain is fine.

Harvey: Could have fooled me.

I don't need a night alone to gather my thoughts at all. But I could tell by the expression on her face that she did. I've seen that look before—a deer caught in the headlights.

Willa prides herself on going with the flow, but now she hit the rapids and she's freaking out. A lot has changed for her in a very brief time. I remember this feeling well, but it's different this time around.

I'd rather she freaks out with me, but I also know better than to smother someone as independent as her, which is why I let her drive away.

But I jump in my truck and follow her to the main house, not about to sit at home alone when she and Luke are both under one roof.

Where they go, I go. It just feels right.

I pull up and kill my engine, eyes locked on the guest room window. When the light turns off, I get out and make my way inside through the front door. I should probably be thinking about a new baby—and I will—but right now, all I can think about is Willa. Soothing her. Holding her.

Keeping her.

When I step into the dimly lit living room, I catch sight of my dad in his deep leather recliner, a glass of bourbon in his hand.

And he's grinning at me like a fucking loon.

"What are you smiling at?"

"You made the right decision for once."

I glare at him. "For once? What the fuck is that supposed to mean?"

"Pour yourself a drink, sit down, and drop the asshole act with me, kid. It doesn't scare me one bit."

With a heavy sigh, I head to the kitchen and pour myself a very hefty three fingers of bourbon before heading back to the living room and flopping down onto the couch.

"You made the right decision coming after her. You start storming out on each other this early on and you'll be in for trouble."

"She didn't storm out. She just needed space."

"I can see needing space from you." I scowl at him. "What did you do?" he asks, adding insult to injury.

"Nothing." I pause, tipping my head. "Well, not nothing-nothing. Something came up and I could have reacted better. I froze."

My dad's hawkish eyes narrow as he regards me. "This have to do with Talia?"

I wave a hand and scoff. "No." Talia waltzed in, stirred shit up, and took off again. Flaky as always.

"Well, fill me in. Maybe your old man can help."

My head flops back against the couch, a wry laugh bubbling up out of me. "She's pregnant."

I can feel my dad's stare, see him take a thoughtful sip out of the corner of my eye. "Did I let you watch the bulls get turned out with the heifers too much as a child, boy?"

I groan.

"You got something against condoms?"

"Dad."

"Some sort of breeding kink I don't know about?"

I throw an arm over my eyes. "Never talk to me again. That you even know that term is altogether too much information."

"Why are you sitting out here with me?"

"Because I stared at her blankly and said nothing when she told me. I kept running through all the things I wanted to say to her and then just clammed up. I don't want her to feel trapped by me, or by this." I swivel a finger around, gesturing to the ranch.

"Did you ask her if she feels that way?"

"No. I just asked over and over again why she had a carrot in her purse like a total dolt."

"Listen, I don't want to hear about whatever weird shit you kids are into."

"Holy shit. Please just kill me before you say something else that makes me want to clean my ears with acid."

My dad carries on, undeterred, but I can hear the humor in his voice. He's having fun watching me squirm. "You two need to talk. I know Talia fucked you up, but don't let her fuck this up for you too. If you want that girl and that baby, you need to tell her. If you don't, then you need to work some—"

Rage flashes through my body, hot and sharp at the mention of me not wanting her. "I do," I bite out harshly. "I want that. I want it all."

"Then stop Eeyoring around out here with me, you grumpy dumbass. I'm going to bed. Y'all kids exhaust me."

His glass clanks against the table, and he retreats to bed without another word. And me? I take my drink and pad quietly through the house. To Willa's door.

I drop myself onto the floor and lean against the wall. I plan to wait until she's had the night to herself so I can toss her over my shoulder and carry her back to our house.

She might need time to think about things.

But I sure as shit don't.

~

I wake up when I fall and hit the floor at Willa's feet.

"What the hell are you doing?"

Pushing up on my hands back to sitting, I shake my head to clear the cobwebs and the light ache that too much bourbon has left behind. Scrubbing my palms over my eyes, I stare up into the face of the woman I know I'm going to spend the rest of my life with.

I flop back against the doorframe and stare at her for a minute. Really take her in.

She's fucking perfect.

"Are you drunk?" Her eyes land on the empty glass beside me. "Why are you staring at me?" Her arms cross over her body, and she pops a hip out.

"I'm not drunk." *Anymore.*

"Did you sleep out here?"

"Yes."

"Why?"

"Because I didn't like the idea of you being alone."

"Ugh." Her eyes shut and her head tips back. "That's really romantic."

"I didn't need time to gather my thoughts at all."

Her head snaps down now. "Yeah? Is that why you sat there all wide-eyed, asking about my carrot?"

I laugh because I can't help it. "I do want to know about the carrot. But I was wide-eyed because I was trying to gauge you and see how I should react. I'm sorry I stayed silent. There are a lot of things I should have said."

She sighs heavily and then slides down the opposite side of the doorframe to face me. "You accidentally knocked a woman up once who upended your whole life by pretending she was on birth control, so I can see how the nanny who told you she's on birth control getting pregnant might freak you out."

My brows furrow. "Willa—"

"I swear I didn't lie. I swear I'm taking my pills. Winter said that when I was sick, they probably didn't stay down and that might have fucked it all up, and I didn't even think about it, and even though I've thought about having like a million babies with you one day, I just absolutely did not do this on purpose, even though I'm actually not that sad about it, which sounds awful, because like, I don't want to trap you with me, so like—"

"Willa!"

Her eyes widen dramatically as she leans back a little. I reach forward and plunk her bare feet into my lap with my good hand. "You're going to collapse a lung talking in run-on sentences like that, baby. And there's no one I'd rather be trapped with." She blinks at me, and I rub my thumbs along the arches of her feet and up her ankles.

"I haven't shaved my legs."

I chuckle. "I don't care. Don't you get it? I'm in love with you, Willa. Prickly legs, random carrots in your purse, pregnant, not pregnant. I want *you*."

Tears spring up in her eyes, and her voice is raspy when she says, "But this has happened to you before, and I don't want to be lumped in with that shit. I don't want you being with me out of some sort of obligation. We haven't even told people about us. We haven't figured a single thing out. You've never told me that you love me. But now I'm pregnant and that's all going to happen? It just feels . . . forced."

"Willa." I can hear an edge of panic to the tone I'm using. "Nothing is forced. We were on this track already. We're not two people who were unhappy and now are trying to make something work that wasn't working before. We were happy."

"Yeah. We were. But this is your personality. This is you swooping in to be responsible before you've even processed what this means because your first instinct is to take care of everyone before you take care of yourself."

Elsie Silver

I can only blink at her. This conversation is not going the way I expected it to.

"Willa, stop—"

"No." She holds her hand up. "For all the times you've told me to shut up and listen, it's now your turn, Cade."

She pulls her feet away and pushes up to stand. "I don't want to be another obligation in your life. Another burden. Another reason you're missing out on all the things you always wanted to do. And maybe I'm not. Maybe this is a happy accident. But getting injured, followed by finding out shocking, life-altering news, followed by getting drunk on the floor"—she points at the empty glass beside me—"isn't the right recipe to be rushing into something like this."

Her sigh is heavy, and one stray tear rolls down her cheek. I raise my hand, needing to wipe it away for her. "I'm going to go back to my place in the city—"

My mouth opens to argue, but her eyes narrow and she makes this zipping motion with her hand that ends in pinching her fingers together before she continues, "For a few days. I want to see my doctor and confirm things. And I want you to spend some time thinking. I want to know that this isn't some shotgun relationship built on failed birth control and a stupid stomach bug. So don't follow me. You have options, and you are free to take them. I want you to let yourself consider your options, because no one has ever really given you any options, Cade. And you deserve them."

I can feel my entire body slumping deeper with every word she says. I know in my heart what's right. But the things she's saying about me and my life? They're true. And I've spent so many years working to fix everything around me that I've never just sat here and let myself feel sad about the fact I've never really considered my options.

She crouches before me now, framing my face with her palms. "More than anything in the world, I want you to be happy. You deserve to be happy."

Her lips press gently to my forehead, and then she steps over me, scooping one hand down to pick up the discarded glass before walking away.

Every part of me wants to go after her, but sometimes loving someone means giving them the space they want. The space they need. For a little while, at least.

So instead, I just sit here. Thinking about my options. About how Willa is the only option I want.

And about how I'll respect her wishes until I can't take it anymore.

Then I'm throwing her over my shoulder and bringing her home.

33

Willa

Summer: Dude. Where are you, and why is Cade rage-landscaping his front yard with broken fingers?

Willa: I'm at my place in the city. Is he okay?

Summer: I don't know. There's a lot of sweating and grunting. It seems a little bit like his shovel has done something to offend him.

Willa: Can you just keep an eye on him? I'm worried about him.

Summer: Fuck no. But Rhett can. I'm coming to your place with a bottle of champagne.

Willa: It's not going to be a champagne kind of visit.

Summer: Don't be a downer.

Willa: Sorry. But I'm going to be a downer for approximately the next nine months.

Summer: Oh shit. On my way. I'll grab ingredients to bake cookies.

"**W**hen is the appointment?" Summer mumbles around a mouthful of warm cookie.

"Tomorrow." I can't even eat the cookies I made. I feel sick and it has nothing to do with being pregnant.

"Are you worried?" Concern laces her every feature.

"About what? I'm pretty sure a blood test will only confirm what I already know."

She nods. "I saw your bathroom garbage is full of a bunch of what you already know. How many tests did you buy?"

"Twenty."

"Seems reasonable." She nods, taking another bite.

"I wanted to be sure."

"How did you even manage to pee that much?"

I chuckle at that. Leave it to my best friend to pick out some inane detail and fixate on it. "So much water. I think I'm hydrated for at least a week now. Remember when I drank way too much Jägermeister and got super sick?"

She laughs now. "Yeah. You barfed in the cab and the cabby asked if you'd been drinking Jägermeister because the entire car smelled like it."

I shudder. "I've still never had another sip of it because of that. Anyway, feeling like that about water right now."

"Are you nauseous?"

"A bit," I concede. "But I don't think it's hormonal."

"Is it Cade?"

"Yeah. And Luke. I'm worried about them. I *miss* them and it's been all of a day since I left. I shouldn't be this dependent on him. I should be able to handle a day away from him without missing him so much that it makes me feel sick. I can't even sleep," I growl in frustration.

Summer smiles softly at me, reaching over to push some hair behind my ear. "Wils, welcome to being in love."

I squeeze my eyes shut and flop my head back against the couch. "This is the worst fucking feeling. Why do people like being in love again? Obsessed and emotional and clingy. Overrated, if you ask me."

"I know you're joking because that's what you do when you're upset."

"Jesus. Have you and Cade been conspiring against me or something? Why are you both always pointing this out about me? Just let me have my quirks, okay?"

"It's okay to feel sad, Willa. It's okay to feel overwhelmed. It's definitely okay to need a couple of days alone to digest. But you can overthink this too. You can turn it inside out until it looks like something different than what it is."

I hold my hands over my face, feeling tears leak out against them. "What is it? I don't even know."

Summer rubs my back because she is some sort of

angel sent to planet Earth. A better person than the vast majority of us. "I don't know what it is. But from where I'm sitting, it's two smart loving adults who are navigating a curve ball in the best way they know how."

A sob racks my body.

"It's two people who were both a little lost until they ended up on the same path and walked together for a while."

I drop my head, openly crying now. I think Summer is *trying* to make me weep.

"It's two people who are happier in each other's company than they are alone." Now I can hear the tears in her voice too. "Better together than they are apart."

I turn to hug her now, wondering if I can blame the uncontrollable way I'm crying on my hormones.

"Just don't make him wait too long, Wils," she whispers against my ear. "He is *heartbroken* without you."

The way she emphasizes heartbroken is my undoing. I soak the shoulder of her shirt, because the truth of the matter is I thought I needed space . . .

But I'm heartbroken without him too.

34

Cade

Summer: Hi! Just messaging to see if you'd like to come for dinner?

Harvey: Hi, son. Thinking I could take Luke off your hands for the day.

Rhett: My wife messaged you about dinner. You haven't answered. Don't be rude to her or I'll drive over and kick your ass.

Jasper: Want free tickets to the game tonight? Would love to see you and Luke.

Violet: I was told to message you and see if you'd respond. You're too old to sulk, Cade. Knock it off.

All I wanted from the main house was the bags of cement from the shed. All I need is to get lost in some physical labor. Alone. Away from pitying looks and overbearing family.

But here I am, watching Luke shout "hello" down the well. It should make me smile, but smiling feels hard today.

Smiling without Willa around feels impossible.

"Dad. Do you think there could be someone down there?"

Okay. Creepy. "No pal. Just a bunch of coins."

His head cants to the side curiously. "Coins?"

I sigh heavily, dropping the bags on either side of myself as I trudge toward the well. "Yeah. My mom and I used to toss coins down there and make wishes." I peer down into the black hole, feeling kindred with it somehow. Empty. Echoey.

"Grandma?" Luke knows all about his grandma Isabelle, even though he never got to meet her.

"Yeah. She named this ranch after the well. When they bought the land Grandpa told her she could name it whatever she wanted."

"What would you wish for?" He peeks in again, and I put a hand on his shoulder. Watching him lean over the edge gives me full-blown anxiety.

I scrub at my beard with the opposite hand, racking my brain. I can't remember. That part of my life feels like a lifetime ago. Like another life altogether. "Probably candy."

Luke's head bobs in approval. "Smart. Did your wishes come true?"

My lips quirk at that. He never fails to lift my spirits. Knowing my mom, I'm sure a bunch of our wishes did come true. "Usually."

"Do you have any coins? I want to make a wish."

Weight lands in my stomach and my lungs constrict. Such a simple request, and yet it feels intensely meaningful. I'm doing with my little boy what my mom once did with me.

I pull my wallet out wordlessly, unzipping the small coin pouch.

"Does it matter what kind of coin?"

"No, bud." I press a silver coin into his hand but pause as I'm about to put the leather wallet away. With a little shake of my head, I take one more coin out.

One for myself.

"Okay," I start, swallowing the uncharacteristic thickness in my throat. "On three. Close your eyes."

Luke's eyes clamp shut, and a hint of steel flashes on his face. He's focusing very hard. Taking this very seriously.

I ruffle his hair once, reminding me of silky, coppery strands as I do, and then I close my eyes. "One ... two ... three ..."

The sound of our coins plunking into the water

below mingles with the sound of wind chimes on the back porch.

Eyes shut, I wish for Willa.

A life with her.

A family with her.

Gray hair and more laughter with her.

When I open my eyes, Luke is staring at me with a thoughtful expression on his face.

"What did you wish for?" I ask him, needing something lighthearted. Thinking it will be something ridiculous. Something frivolous.

Instead, he delivers a gut punch.

One soft cheek hitches up, and he glances back down into the dark well. "I wished for Willa to come back."

My eyes burn when I pull him into me, feel his tiny arms clutching at my waist.

And my voice cracks when I say, "Me too, pal. Me too."

35

Willa

Willa: How is Cade?
Summer: Full hermit-mode. Back to hating everyone.
Please come fix him.
Willa: I'm on my way.

~ ❧ ~

With a positive blood test in hand, I get in my Jeep and start the drive back out to Wishing Well Ranch.

As city streets morph into freeways that morph into country roads, I let my mind wander to how things have changed since the last time I drove out here. How I flew out here on a whim, wind in my hair and not a single responsibility on my radar.

Yeah. Things have changed. Drastically.

But I'm oddly at peace.

I've shed tears the last couple of days, and I am not a crier. I've made plans for myself, and I am not a planner. I have fresh perspective. Took the space I needed to process.

I've realized I'm better with Cade than I am without him. And I think he's better with me too. I intend to tell him as much and then watch him roll his eyes at me.

It's going to be so romantic.

As the drive wears on, I get lost in my thoughts and my anxiety grows. What-ifs pop into my head. I listen to the most upbeat '80s music I can find and chew nervously on my nails, hoping that he wants this as much as I do. Hoping I haven't made him feel stuck.

When I reach the long driveway, I put my Jeep in park and take some deep breaths and shift in my driver's seat and start doing the drunk-girl pep talk again. Except I'm dead sober and my concerns are way bigger than if I look sweaty or stumble in front of a hot guy at the bar.

I'm a smart, capable adult. I have family and friends who love me. This is just another opportunity for me to start a new chapter in my life. I'm a hot fucking mess.

Shaking my head at myself, I put the Jeep back into drive and head straight for Cade's little red house.

The little red house with a freshly poured sidewalk out front.

The little red house with a sweet dark-haired boy strumming his guitar on the front step.

The little red house with a man who makes my heart

race and my cheeks heat just by scowling at me the way he is now.

And I have to wonder if it's not a scowl at all. Because the expression is so full of love, so full of longing, that the muscles in my chest seize and I rush to park so that I can be out of this vehicle and breathing the same air as them.

My boys.

"Willa!" Luke's quickly forgotten guitar rests on the step as he tears across the front lawn toward me. "I'm so glad you're back!"

"Me too, pal. Me too," I say as I wrap my arms around him. But my eyes fixate on his dad, who's standing there, wearing a pair of jeans like a second skin, hands casually slung on his hips. Fucking hat turned backward.

A country boy who looks as good as Cade Eaton should be illegal.

But instead, he's *mine*.

"Hi," I breathe, unable to tear my eyes away.

"Hi, Red," he replies but he doesn't move. His son stays latched onto me like a little barnacle.

"How are you?"

His jaw pops as he stares back at me, and I get nervous. Maybe in doing what I thought was best for Cade, I shot myself in the foot.

But when he says, "Better now that you're here," I know that's not true.

Giving Luke a little pat on the back, I say, "Luke, can you head inside for a few minutes? I need to have a private chat with your dad. And I'll know if you're eavesdropping."

The sheepish grin he gifts me has me smiling back at him. His bright blue eyes, sun-kissed cheeks from a summer spent in the sun . . . I've never fallen harder or faster for a single person in the world than I have for Lucas Eaton.

"Okay. But first I want to show you the sidewalk we made." He threads his small fingers through mine and pulls me off the gravel driveway to the freshly poured walkway. Like, I think it might actually still be wet.

When we get closer, the wet concrete confirms my suspicions. I can smell that chalky scent permeating the surrounding air, but it's what's decorating the walkway that stops me in my tracks.

There are shiny stones pressed into the concrete, laid out in the shapes of hearts, running the full length of the walkway.

"Plain was boring. So we decorated! They're like that day we used chalk on the driveway at the main house!" Luke exclaims.

I peek up at Cade. "Like Valentine's Day threw up everywhere?"

His lips twitch and he just nods.

"And then up here"—Luke drags me toward the house—"we wrote our initials inside the hearts."

"I love that!" I exclaim, giving him a firm side hug.

He nods happily, biting at his lip, and looking so damn proud. "And this one is yours." He points at a heart that's right next to one with the initials C.E., except this one says W.E.

"My initials are W.G., bud."

I give him another squeeze and he giggles. Cluelessly. "I know. But dad made that one. I told him the same thing." My head snaps around to Cade, who still hasn't moved but is staring at me like I might disappear if he blinks. "But he said they wouldn't be for long."

A sob that could pass as a laugh bursts from my lips as I blink furiously, desperate to not fall apart right here in front of them. "I love it, Luke. The whole sidewalk is just beautiful." I hug him again, sucking in air through my nose and trying to compose myself.

"Good. I'm so happy you're back! If you didn't come back today, Dad said he was going to drive into the city and get you." I almost chuckle. That's such a Cade thing to say.

After one last hug, Luke bounds up the stairs to the front door. But just like he's done once before, he stops and looks back at Cade and me with a pleased smile on his face and says, "See, Dad? I told you not to be sad. I told you she'd come back. Our wishes came true! She loves us too much to leave."

The screen door slams and he's gone.

And I'm crying, hands covering my face. I'm overwhelmed. Relieved. And, okay, possibly hormonal.

"Hey, hey." Within seconds Cade is reaching for me, gathering me into his strong arms and holding me tight against his chest. "Baby, don't cry. You don't need to cry. I think if you cry, I might cry. And I'm not a crier."

"I'm not a crier either!" I sob, nuzzling against his shirt and taking deep pulls of his pine scent that I missed so badly these last few days. "But I swear I haven't stopped crying since I left this place."

He rocks us gently, like a soft, quiet dance. The only music is the chirping of birds and gentle breeze across the hay field out back. He doesn't talk. He just holds me until my breathing evens out and the stress has melted from my limbs.

Eventually he tips my chin up so that I'm forced to look at him. His chiseled, masculine features are a welcome sight. "You paying attention right now, Red? Because I've spent *days* thinking hard about my life, and I've got some things to tell you."

I nod and press my lips together, a silent promise to listen to him and not just talk *at* him.

With a deep sigh, he starts, "Thank you. Thank you for being the first person in my life to put me first, to give me options. I'm not sure I deserve that gift, but I know that I'll never forget it for as long as I live."

His thumbs stroke along the peaks of my cheekbones, and he holds my head between his palms. Reverently. Delicately. With so much love. "You're right that I did this once out of obligation. But I'm a thirty-eight-year-old man who has taken years to trust someone again. I've had a lot of time to think about where I went wrong. You are not a decision I made lightly. And tying myself to someone I don't love out of some misplaced sense of duty is not a mistake I plan to make twice."

A tear slips out of my eye, and he thumbs it away instantly, stroking at my hair now like he always does. "I'm glad you aren't sad about the baby because I'm not either. But I want to be clear that *you* have options. All the options in the world. And I'll be here with you, no matter what. I want to come home to the sound of you and Luke laughing. I want to listen to you play the guitar while I cook dinner. I want to leave you Post-it notes for a long time. I don't want *you* to feel stuck with *me*."

More tears slide down my cheeks, and he catches every single one. Always sturdy and reliable.

"I do really love your Post-it notes," I whisper.

"Then I'll keep writing them."

"But I still think I'm a better cook." I huff out, and I know I'm trying to cut the tension with humor, it works for me though, and I'll probably never stop.

Cade groans but it's playful. "We'll have to learn to agree to disagree on some things because I'm not letting you go."

"Luke agrees with me," I argue, sliding my hands up his chest.

"I think it's cute when you two team up on me. I'll have to make sure the new baby is on my team though. Train 'em young."

With a deep, relieved sigh, I curl myself back into his

chest and revel in the feel of his arms around me. And I say my piece. "I don't feel stuck with you at all. For weeks I've been dreading leaving. You. Luke. This place. I've never felt so settled . . . so at home. I also never saw my life unfolding this way."

He rubs a hand up and down the column of my spine. "Me neither, Red. That's just life. But you know, I'm not sure I'd have it any other way."

"You're not sad?"

"Not even a little bit," he replies firmly. And I can tell that he means it. "I've watched you with Luke for months now and marveled over what an incredible mom you'd be one day. A mom I wished Luke could have for himself . . ." He trails off before adding, "Are you sad?"

"Not even a little bit," I whisper his words back, and he drops his lips to the crown of my head before pressing my cheek back to his sternum. Right where I can feel the steady, strong thumping of his heart.

"My dad knows you're pregnant."

"Okay."

"He asked me if I have a breeding kink."

My hands come up to cover my face and laughter shakes my body. "No, he didn't."

"He did."

"Jesus." I murmur, but it's still a little thin. A little watery.

"Forget Jesus. Tell me about the carrot. I've been thinking about it for days."

"The woman you've known for all of two months

tells you she accidentally got pregnant and what keeps you up is wondering about the carrot in her purse?"

He chuckles and gives my hair a little tug, tipping my face up to his. "Yeah." He shrugs. "You feel right in my life. In Luke's life. We just . . . make sense to me somehow. And another little person will too. Nothing about that feels wrong to me. The only thing that doesn't make sense is that fucking carrot."

I laugh again, because everything he just said is so quintessentially *him*. He's not flowery or showy. He's matter-of-fact, and he just laid his heart on the line for me. It seems like the least I can do is explain the carrot. "It's just from feeding the horses with Luke . . . I think."

"You *think*?"

Busted. "Yeah, I don't totally recall putting it in there if I'm being honest. It could be from when I still lived in the city."

"But that's months ago." He sounds suitably horrified. I wonder if he's having second thoughts about being with a girl who keeps old carrots in her purse.

"Yeah," I reply lamely, nibbling at my lip.

"Panties and carrots." He shakes his head and lets his hands roam my back as my breathing continues to even out. "I can't wait to see what falls out of there next."

We stand in silence for several minutes, just holding each other in the middle of the front yard, beside the heart he made for me, with my future initials written into the center. Like he's just that sure of me—of us.

Like we're better together and he knows it.

"I love you, Cade," I murmur against his chest.

"I love you too, Red."

Then he just holds me tighter, and I hope he never lets go.

36

Cade

Cade: What are you doing? Braiding your hair?

Rhett: No, polishing my nails.

Cade: We're going to be late.

Rhett: Dude. Your event isn't even until tomorrow. Take a breath.

Rhett: Are you seriously outside my house honking right now?

Cade: Yes. Making people wait is rude.

Rhett: You can't rush perfection.

Cade: Nothing about you is perfect.

Rhett: No. But this sign I made you is.

"I wish you'd just hurry and have this baby already. I am so excited." Summer bounces on her seat in the back of my truck. I can practically see the excitement pouring off her through my rearview mirror.

"Sum. Hold your horses. I'm like three months pregnant," Willa replies from behind me.

"She hasn't stopped talking about it." Rhett laughs as his fingers drum on the passenger's seat door, just above where he's protectively wedged the poster board Rhett created for my event tomorrow. It's sparkly and reads: *Not bad. For an old guy.*

Fucking dick.

"Ugh. It's just going to be the cutest baby though. I'm so ready to be the cool aunt."

The buzz around the new baby hasn't died off at all since we came out about everything. Everyone is over the moon.

But no one more than Luke.

When we sat down and told him, he cried happy tears. And so did I. The bridge of my nose tingles just thinking about the way my life has changed again so quickly. So unexpectedly.

It's a fucking theme for me at this point.

"Dude." Willa punches my brother in the shoulder. "Read between the lines here. Stop dicking around and make it so that our kids can grow up as best friends."

Rhett's face turns serious, and he shakes his head

solemnly—but I see that shit-disturber twitch of his lips. Same one that was a dead giveaway as a child too.

"I don't know what to tell you, Willa. We keep practicing and practicing, and practicing, and nothing ever happens. It's exhausting, you know? I have to wonder if it's all the birth control we're using?"

"Eat a dick, kid." I take my turn, knocking a hand against my little brother's chest.

"No, babe," Summer pipes up, "it's just that you don't have a *breeding kink*." She can't even get the words out without snorting and wheezing.

"I'm never gonna fucking live that down." I grind my teeth to keep from smiling.

What I hear back is a chorus of "nevers" from every single person in my truck. But I also feel Willa's hand slide over my shoulder to give me a little squeeze. I reach up and lay a hand over hers, knowing that, jokes aside, we're both excited about this.

We're surprised and a little unprepared, but happy. So damn happy. Going with the flow has never felt better. Cheesy as it sounds, I've never felt more at peace.

I spent years feeling jilted. Feeling angry. Feeling like everyone around me had everything going for them and I was just stuck in a rut of responsibility.

And then Hurricane Willa blew into town and turned everything upside down in the best fucking way.

I squeeze her hand and pull it to my lips, pressing a kiss to the knuckles of the woman I chose—the life I chose.

"Jesus. Who even are you?" Rhett asks, looking a little shocked.

Now it's Summer's turn to slap the top of his head. "Stop picking on them. It's sweet."

"Why the fuck is everyone hitting me?"

I chuckle as Summer responds with, "Because you deserve it."

With that sentiment, we pull into the rodeo grounds and the chaos of the Canadian Championship Rodeo swallows us all.

~~~

Competing here is a dream that's been long forgotten. Long shut away as a missed opportunity, something I was too old for—too busy for.

Until Willa sat in that hot tub and dared me to take a shot. Turns out our runs were good enough to qualify us for the finals.

Which means I'm not going to let the fact that my fingers aren't completely healed stop me.

Blueberry is taking everything in stride from where I sit on her back. Her prickly personality won't let her be spooked. Every time another horse walks past, she flattens her ears at them, which makes me smile. She's not a warm-and-fuzzy type of mare, but she's good at what she does.

We're kindred that way.

My dad has Luke out in the stands, and the rest of our group is standing beside me in the staging area.

"Are you nervous?" Willa squeezes my leg and peers up at me. The way she glows makes my throat constrict. Her hair is all curled. Her new boots are fuck-me hot and are going to look so good wrapped around my waist later. She's not showing much yet, but her jeans are extra tight around her ass, and I keep getting busted checking her out.

"Nah," I reply, smoothing my hand over her hair.

"I love it when you pet me." She sighs and closes her eyes with a low chuckle.

"Y'all are fuckin' weird," Rhett quips from beside us, arm slung over Summer's shoulders, with a cocky smirk on his face. "I'd tell you not to worry about the buckle bunnies, Willa, but apparently Cade is so into PDA now that he practically broadcasts how taken he is."

Willa stares back at my brother blankly. "What are you talking about, Rhett? I *am* a buckle bunny." She puts her fingers in the shape of a heart and frames the view through them around my face.

"Cade? Lance? Josh?" The ring steward calls our team's names, and with a quick wink down at my girl, we're gone.

Blueberry's easy strides turn into a prance beneath me, a showy little jog as we enter the ring.

And this ring isn't just another small-town fair grounds. This is a proper arena, one with full stands and a rowdy crowd here for a show.

This arena is a dream I never thought would come true.

I glance over my shoulder, seeking that flash of coppery hair. And she's there, smiling, gripping the metal fence panel with one hand, the other slung over her stomach, looking at me like I hung the moon—and for her I would.

I'd do it for everything she's given me in such a short time . . .

A love Luke has never known.

A reason for me to smile again.

A person to talk to after so many years of silence.

A love *I've* never known. One I'm not so sure I deserve, but one I'll spend the rest of my life trying to preserve. But I'll get to that part later.

For now, I turn my eyes back on the pen of cattle and listen carefully as we're given the number. And then I get to work because I'm going to make this lifelong dream come to fruition.

The noisy crowd falls away when the buzzer sounds, and the only thing that exists is what's between Blueberry's ears.

She cuts. She runs. She turns. She drops a shoulder.

The leather of the reins is warm in my fingers, and I feel like I'm just along for the ride. She's never performed so well in her life. It's like she knows this is it. The big show. Our one chance.

In what feels like it took mere seconds, we've squared away the cows and I'm looking around myself like there must be more. Like we must have missed something. Everything feels like it's moving in slow motion, but judging by the way Lance is standing up in his stirrups whooping like a madman, I'd say we've done it and done it well.

When the judges post our scores, they confirm my hunch and I'm left shaking my head, smiling like a loon, and searching for Willa.

She's climbed up to the top of the fence panel and is staring at me with her hands cupped over her mouth, shouting like a crazy person. My crazy person.

Here for *me*.

Summer is whistling louder than anyone in the arena, and Rhett is grinning and shaking his stupid fucking sign in the air.

But it's Willa I can't take my eyes from. I ride straight to her, in the middle of a packed arena, sling an arm around the back of her neck and kiss her.

I kiss her hard. I kiss her to say the things I can't find the words for.

"I love you, Cade Eaton, and I am so damn proud of you," is what she whispers in my ear while her fingers trail up the back of my neck.

"I love you too, baby," is what I get out, just before she pulls the black cowboy hat off my head and plunks it on her own.

Leaning back away from me, she gives me a playful little smirk.

I quirk a brow in her direction. "You know the rule, Red?"

"You wear the hat, you ride the cowboy." She winks at me, looking fucking adorable wearing my hat. I should have put it on her forever ago. I should have put it on her the first day I laid eyes on her in that coffee shop.

With a twist of my lips and a shake of my head, I turn to ride away and celebrate with my team for a moment because that score is damn near unbeatable.

But I don't get far before I hear a whistle and, "Looking good, Daddy!" followed by the most beautiful chime-like laughter, light and airy and heartwarming.

That laugh I heard months ago and was instantly obsessed with. Just like the woman staring back at me from beneath the brim of my hat when I toss a glance over my shoulder.

And I realize in that moment maybe I am heartless after all, because the beautiful girl with the copper hair grinning back at me right now is the one who stole it.

Epilogue
Willa

Cade: I'm going to be in the far west field today.

Willa: Okay. No problem.

Cade: Do you think you should still be teaching this close to your due date?

Willa: To my knowledge, showing people how to play the guitar has not been known to stimulate labor.

Cade: Don't be a smart-ass.

Willa: I'm pregnant. Not disabled.

Cade: Not funny.

Willa: Neither is your breeding kink. But here we are.

Cade: Call me if something happens.

Willa: Are you ignoring my joke?

Cade: I don't want to miss the birth of my child.

Willa: I think after my lessons I'll give the yard a blow job.

Cade: You're insane. But I love you.

Willa: Love you too.

⟋⟋

"Which ones are better?" I ask Luke from across the kitchen island with a wince. I've been having Braxton-Hicks fake fucking contractions for days and have been baking cookies to busy myself. The baby kicks the shit out of me non-stop, and I feel like a beached whale. Whoever said pregnancy is beautiful can die a fiery death, as far as I'm concerned.

In recent days, I've gone from excited to wishing I could issue an eviction notice.

Luke is what's keeping me sane right now. Luke is the one who makes me smile. The minute he jumped off the school bus, we waddled up to the house and I pulled out two plates of cookies.

He currently has white chocolate macadamia in one hand and peanut butter smarties in the other and is taking alternating nibbles like he's a true cookie connoisseur.

And I suppose after these last couple of days, he is. We've been doing an awful lot of teeth brushing to compensate for the sugar intake.

His eyes close, and he holds one finger up dramatically. I can't help but laugh at him. "Smarties," he announces.

"Yeah. Think you're right." I groan as I haul myself onto the stool next to him and take a bite of one.

"Hey, Willa," he says, turning my way.

"Hey, Luke." I wink at him.

"Can I ask you something?"

"Always."

His wide blue eyes take on an uncertain expression, and his lips press together. "What is the baby going to call you?"

"Well, babies don't talk, Luke, so I imagine they'll just babble a lot of random shit."

He gives me a scoff and a little eye roll, looking like a dead ringer for his dad when he does. "I meant once they can talk. Will they call you mom?"

My eyes travel over his face as I chew. I haven't even known him for a year and still find myself marveling at how much he's changed. "I imagine so, yes."

A sigh lifts and then drops his small shoulders as he glances down at his cookie. "Do you think . . ." He peers back up at me now. "Do you think it would be okay if I called you mom too?"

I'm far too hormonal for this conversation right now and blink furiously down at the little boy who's gazing up at me with the widest, sweetest eyes. "My dude, you can call me whatever you want. I know I'm not actually your mom, but I love you like one. Did you know I fell in love with you before I fell in love with your dad?"

His eyes light at that. "You did?"

I nod, pulling him close with an arm around his shoulders. "I did."

His arms wrap around my middle, or what's left of it. I feel like I'm just boobs and belly at this point. "I love you too, Willa. Even though I think you peed your pants."

My head shoots down to follow where he's looking. "Alright. It's time to call your dad."

~

Summer: Are you close? I called Willa's parents. They're booking flights back now.

Cade: Five minutes out. Everything okay?

Harvey: Oh, good. We're all here waiting. Everything is fine.

Cade: All? No. You all need to leave.

Jasper: I'm on my way.

Cade: Why is my child's birth part of a group text?

Summer: Because we're excited!

Violet: So excited! Send pictures!

Rhett: After though. Not during. I don't need to know Willa that well.

Summer: Rhett Eaton. I know you are not texting and driving with the daddy-to-be in your car.

Cade: He is.

Rhett: Red light, Princess. And why are you only worried about Cade and not me?

Summer: TODAY ISN'T ABOUT YOU.

Harvey: Y'all kids give me a ducking headache.

Cade: Rhett gives me a headache. Specifically.

Summer: I just wanna know what you're naming the baby. And if they're a boy or a girl. And who they look more like. OMG I'M SO EXCITED TO BE THE COOL AUNT.

Cade: Just got here. Now everyone fuck off.

~⌐

Cade bursts through the door of the hospital room looking like he's ready for a fight. I almost laugh at the fierce expression on his face as he rushes to my side. With the trauma of his mom's death, I know this has been anxiety-inducing for him.

We've talked about her a lot. Isabelle Emma Eaton. The woman with the beautiful blue eyes who would make wishes down the well with him as a child.

"Red," he breathes, pulling me close and smelling of pine trees and sweat. The manliest combination.

He came straight from the fields. Harvey drove me to the hospital and Rhett got on a quad bike to go find Cade. I've been playing it cool, but having him here eases my nerves.

"How are you? I came as fast as I could." His broad palm strokes the back of my head and my eyes flutter shut. I love when he does that.

"Better now," I say as he kisses my forehead.

"Everyone is in the waiting room. I told them to leave."

I chuckle but a contraction hits me hard. I grip Cade's hand and do my best to breathe through it but make some sort of insane braying noise.

He continues stroking my hair and letting me squeeze his hand hard enough to break it. We walk. I bounce on a ball. I sit in a bath. And when I look up at Cade and say, "I'm sorry if the magic is gone after this," he replies with, "It's okay, I've lived through a lot of calving seasons."

My hysterical laughter bleeds into a contraction, longer and stronger than any of the others, and when it finally finishes and he's helping me into bed, I say to him, "I know you didn't just compare me to a cow."

"I would never," he says with a chuckle. And as much as I want to punch him in the face for that joke, I also want to hug him.

This man, who mere months ago seemed so cold and unhappy, has turned my world upside down and made me value my life differently. In a simpler way, a quieter way. A way that fits me rather than everyone else around me.

But more than that, he gave me a sense of satisfaction in myself that I have never experienced. A sense of pride and belonging that I never saw until he opened my eyes and showed me.

Everything about Cade Eaton has been a curve ball

from day one. Nothing happened in the "right" order, but that has never been the case for him, or for me.

So maybe this order is just perfect for *us*.

I lose my consciousness in a sea of soft whispers, hard squeezes, and mind-bending pain. There are several moments where I seriously regret refusing an epidural.

But with Cade here, I'm focused. He grounds me. And when it's time to push, he whispers in my ear about how much he loves me.

And I don't just know it, I *feel* it.

Our little girl, Emma Eaton, comes into the world healthy. Kicking and screaming and surrounded by so much love that tears trail freely down our cheeks. She also comes into the world with a big softy of a dad wrapped around her tiny finger.

So many things I never knew I wanted are right here in this room. The nurses place her tiny body on my chest, and I stare down at her in wonder.

Light eyes. Dark hair. She's *us*.

"She's perfect," I whisper.

"Both my girls are," is what Cade says as he crawls onto the bed beside me and holds us both.

We stare at her for I don't know how long. Entranced. Happy. And when Luke comes in to join us —complete.

Heartless playlist

 One Of Them Girls
Lee Brice
03.08

 Speechless
Dan + Shay
03.33

Hurricane
Luke Combs
03.42

Watermelon Sugar (ft. Avenue Best)
Maddie & Tae, Avenue Best
02.56

Bluebird
Miranda Lambert
03.30

Summer of '69
Bryan Adams
03.35

Things A Man Oughta Know
Lainey Wilson
03.23

Springsteen
Eric Church
04.23

Yours
Russell Dickerson
03.36

Keep reading for a sneak peek of *Powerless* . . .

He acts like he wants me.
But after years of turning me away,
he's going to need to prove it . . .

Available now at

PIATKUS

Prologue - Sloane

My car door is open before my parents have even put the Bentley in park. My feet hit the gravel driveway before they've even gotten out of the car. My arms are wrapped around my cousin Violet before they've even had a chance to say hello to my uncle Harvey.

"I missed you!" I squeal as Violet pulls away and grins mischievously at me.

"I missed you too."

I catch my mom looking at us, happy and sad all at once. I look like my mom, and Violet looks like hers. Except Violet's mom died, and my mom lost her sister. I always think she likes bringing me out here because she feels close to her sister.

It also makes it more convenient for my parents to travel to their favorite spots in Europe. My dad said something about it being good for me to "see how the other half lives." I'm not totally sure what that means, but I saw my mom's lips clamp down on each other when he said it.

Either way, I never complain because a full month at Wishing Well Ranch with the Eaton family means I get to hang out and have fun with my cousins. The rules are lax. The curfews don't exist. And I get to run wild for four full weeks every summer.

"Robert, Cordelia." Uncle Harvey reaches forward to shake my dad's hand before giving my mom a tight squeeze. One that leaves her blinking a little too quickly as she looks out over the flat farm fields and jagged mountains behind them. "Nice to see you both."

They start talking about boring adult stuff, but I don't hear them, because my other cousins walk out of the big ranch house. Cade, Beau, and Rhett jog down the front stairs, joking and shoving and roaming like a pack.

And then, they're followed by one more boy. One I don't recognize. One that immediately has my attention. One with long, lanky limbs, caramel-colored hair and the bluest eyes I've ever seen.

The *saddest* eyes I've ever seen.

When that boy slides his gaze over to me, there's nothing but curiosity on his face. I jerk my head away all the same, feeling hot splotches pop up on my cheeks.

My mom moves beside me, patting me on the head. "Sloane, you need to remember your sunscreen. You already look too hot, and you spend so much time in the

436

dance studio, your skin isn't used to this kind of exposure."

Her fussing on me only makes me blush harder. I'm almost eleven and she's making me feel like a little kid in front of everyone.

I give my eyes a petulant roll and mumble, "I know. I will," before taking Violet's hand and storming off.

We go inside and up to my guest room, looking for some privacy while everyone else stands around outside and makes small talk.

Violet flops on the mattress and announces, "Tell me everything."

I giggle and push my hair behind my ears, drawn to the window that overlooks the driveway. "About what?"

"School? The city? What you wanna do this summer? Just . . . everything. I'm so happy there's a girl here. This place stinks like boys *all the time*."

Out the window, I see the mystery boy shaking hands with my parents. I note the distaste on my father's face. The pity on my mother's.

"Who's the other guy?" I ask, unable to look away.

"Oh." Violet's voice gets a little quiet. "That's Jasper. He's one of us now."

I turn to her, eyebrow quirked, hands on my hips, trying to play it cool, like I'm not *too* interested, but not really knowing how to achieve that either. "What do you mean?"

She rolls up to sit cross-legged on the bed and shrugs. "He needed a family, so we took him in. I don't know all the details. There was an accident. Beau brought him here one day last fall. I like to think of him as one more stinky brother. You can just think of him like a new cousin."

My head cants as my heart battles with my brain. My heart wants to stare out the window again, because Jasper is *so* cute and looking at him makes it do this weird little skipping thing in my chest.

My brain knows it's stupid, because if he's friends with Beau, he must be at least fifteen.

But I can't stop myself.

I look anyway.

What I don't realize is that I'll be fighting the urge to stare at Jasper Gervais for years to come.

Chapter One -Jasper

Sloane Winthrop's fiancé is a royal douchebag.

I'm familiar with the type. You don't work your way into the NHL without encountering your fair share.

And this guy has the act down pat.

As if the name *Sterling Woodcock* wasn't enough of a giveaway, he's now bragging about the hunting trip he and his dad spent hundreds of thousands of dollars on to kill lions born and bred in captivity, like that will somehow make their dicks bigger.

From the Rolex on his wrist to his manicured nails, he's practically dripping wealth, and I guess it only makes sense that Sloane might end up with a man like him. After all, the Winthrops are one of the most powerful families in the country with what is damn near a monopoly on the telecommunications industry.

As he rambles, I glance at Sloane across the table. Her sky-blue eyes are downcast, and she's clearly fiddling with the napkin in her lap. She looks like she'd rather be anywhere but here in this dimly lit, ornate steakhouse.

And I feel about the same.

Listening to her small-dicked future husband boast to a table full of family and friends I've never met about something that is honestly embarrassing—and sad—isn't how I'd choose to spend a night off.

But I'm here for Sloane, and that's what I keep telling myself.

Because seeing her right now, looking downtrodden mere nights before her wedding . . . it feels like she needs someone here who actually knows her.

I expected her to be smiling. Glowing. I expected to feel happy for her—but I don't.

"You hunt, Jasper?" Sterling asks, looking all poised and pretentious.

The collar of my checkered dress shirt immediately feels like it's strangling me, even though the top buttons are undone. I clear my throat and roll my shoulders back. "I do."

Sterling picks up the crystal tumbler before him and leans back to assess me with a smug smirk on his perfectly shaved face. "Any big game? You'd enjoy a trip like this." People who don't know me nod and murmur their assent.

"I don't know if—" Sloane starts, but her fiancé steamrolls her attempt at adding anything to the conversation.

"We all saw what your last contract came in at, so provided you've been responsible with your money, it's definitely something you should be able to afford."

Like I said: douchebag.

I bite the inside of my cheek, tempted to say I've been horribly irresponsible with my money and don't have a dollar to my name. But as lowbrow as my upbringing might have been, I have enough class to know that finances aren't polite dinner conversation.

"Nah, man. I only hunt what I can eat and I'm unfamiliar with how to cook a lion."

A few chuckles break out around the table, including from Sloane. I don't miss the quick moment where Sterling's eyes narrow, where his teeth clamp, and his jaw pops.

Sloane jumps in quickly, patting his arm like he's a dog who needs soothing. "I used to hunt with my cousins out in Chestnut Springs too, you know?"

I'm tossed back in time, remembering a young Sloane keeping up with the boys all summer. Sloane with dirt under her nails, scrapes on her knees, sun-bleached hair all tangled and free down her back.

"It's more about the thrill, you know? The power." Sterling ignores Sloane's comment entirely.

He looks at me like an opponent, except we aren't playing hockey right now. If we were, I'd be tempted to give him a quick blocker shot to the face.

"Did you not hear what Sloane just said?" I'm trying to be cool, but I hate the way he's treated her through this entire dinner.

Sterling waves a hand and chuckles. "Ah yes. I'm always hearing about Wishing Well Ranch." He turns to her with a condescending tone and a mocking smirk. "Well, thank goodness you outgrew whatever tomboy phase you went through, babe. You'd have missed your calling as a ballerina."

His shitty response is only made worse by my realization that he heard exactly what she said and *chose* to ignore her.

"I can't even imagine you handling a gun, Sloane!" one guy further down the long table exclaims, his nose a deep red from far too much scotch.

"I was pretty good, actually. I think I only hit something alive once." She laughs lightly and shakes her head, bright blonde strands of hair slipping down in front of her face before she pushes them back behind her ears and drops her eyes with a faint blush. "And then I cried inconsolably."

"I remember that day." I glance across the table at her. "You couldn't even eat the venison for dinner that night. We all tried to console you—it didn't work." My head shakes at the vivid walk down memory lane.

"And that right there"—Sterling points at Sloane

without even looking at her—"is why women don't belong out hunting. Too upsetting."

Sterling's overgrown frat buddies guffaw at his lame comment, which urges him to go all in on his assholery. He holds his glass up high and looks down the table. "To keeping women in the kitchen!"

There's laughter and a smattering of people offering "cheers" and "here here."

Sloane dabs the white cloth napkin over her full lips with a prim smile but keeps her eyes fixed on the empty place setting before her. Sterling goes back to gloating with the other guests—ignoring the woman sitting beside him.

Ignoring the piece of herself she just tried to share with him. Ignoring the way he just embarrassed her.

My patience for this night is quickly dwindling. The urge to slink into the background is overwhelming.

Sloane catches my eye across the table and gives me one of her practiced smiles. I know it's fake because I've seen her real smile.

And this isn't it.

It's the same smile she gave me when I told her I couldn't go to prom with her as her date. Taking a twenty-three-year-old NHL player wasn't appropriate for either of us, and I was the asshole who had to tell her that.

I smile back, feeling frustration build inside me over the fact she's about to tie herself to someone who treats her like an accessory, who doesn't listen to her. Or appreciate that she's layered and complex, and not just the polished princess she's been molded into by her family.

Sterling catches the exchange and turns his attention to me once again. It makes my skin crawl. "Sloane tells me you've been friends for a long time. Pardon my confusion, but a gruff hockey player doesn't seem like he'd be friends with a ballerina. Of course, I haven't seen you around much since her and I got together. Something keeping you away?" He drapes an arm over her shoulder in a show of possession and I try not to fixate on the gesture.

"To be fair, I haven't heard much about you either." I say it with enough humor in my tone that anyone missing the way we're glaring might not even pick up on the jab. I lean back, crossing my arms over my chest. "But yeah. I guess I'm not too gruff to bring over Polysporin and painkillers when my friend's feet are too raw from dancing in pointe shoes to even walk."

"I've told you this." Sloane's voice is placating. "He helped me move into my new condo. Sometimes we grab coffee. Simple little things like that."

"Basically, she knows if she needs something, I'll be there," I add, without thinking.

Sloane shoots me a look, probably wondering why I'm acting like a territorial asshole. I'm wondering the same thing, to be honest.

"Good thing you've got me for all that now." Sterling is responding to Sloane, but he's staring at me. Then he suddenly places a palm over Sloane's hands in her lap. The ones still pulling at her napkin anxiously. But the way he touches her isn't soothing or supportive. It's a swat, a reproach for fidgeting.

It sends fury racing through my veins. I need to get away before I do something I'll really regret.

"Well, I'm going to head out for the night," I announce suddenly, pushing my chair back, desperate for fresh air and a break from the dark walls and velvet drapery pressing in around me.

"Better get a good sleep in, Gervais. You'll need it to get things rolling for the Grizzlies this season. After last season, you're probably on thin ice."

I pull at the cuffs of my shirt and force myself to ignore the jab. "Thank you for inviting me, *Woodcock*. Dinner was delicious."

"Sloane invited you," is his petulant reply, clarifying that he does not like me—or my presence.

I stare down at him blankly and hitch one side of my mouth up. Like I can't quite believe what a raging prick he is. I can feel eyes on us now, other people picking up on whatever unspoken tension is between us. "Well, that's what friends are for."

"Wait, but you're her cousin, right?" The drunk guy's scotch spills over the rim of his tumbler and onto his hand as he points at me.

I don't know why Sloane and I have always been so adamant that we're friends and not cousins. If someone tried to tell me that Beau, or Rhett, Or Cade wasn't my brother, I'd write them off immediately. Those men *are* my brothers.

But Sloane? She's my friend.

"Actually, he's my friend, *not* my cousin." Sloane tosses her napkin on the top of the white linen-covered table with more force than necessary.

The people gathered for her wedding stare.

Her wedding *this weekend*.

My stomach twists.

"You gonna be at the stag party tomorrow, Gervais?" the drunk guy continues. He hiccups and grins stupidly, reminding me of the drunk mouse at the Mad Hatter's unbirthday party. "Would love to say I partied with hockey-superstar Jasper Gervais."

Color me surprised that the only reason a guy like this wants me around is to boost his perception.

"Can't. I've got a game." My smile is tight, but my relief is immense as I rise from my chair.

"I'll walk you out," Sloane pipes up, clearly missing the sharp look Sterling slices her way. Or maybe she's just pretending she doesn't notice.

Either way, I hold one hand open and gesture Sloane ahead of me as we begin to weave our way silently across the restaurant.

I go to press my palm against the small of her back to guide her through, but she tenses, and I jerk my hand away at the feel of smooth bare skin burning my fingertips. My eyes find the floor as I shove the tingling hand into my pocket, where it belongs.

Because it sure as shit doesn't belong on the bare back of an engaged woman.

Even if she is just my friend.

It's only as we near the front of the restaurant that I look up again. Sloane's slender frame sways as she strides across the room. Every movement steeped in an inherent grace—one that comes with years of training. Years of practice.

She smiles politely at the maître d' and then walks faster, like she can see freedom through that heavy front door and is desperate for it. Her shoulders drop and she pauses, almost in relief, when she rests both hands flat against the dark slab of wood.

I watch her for a moment before I step up behind her, the heat of her body reaching out toward mine. Then I reach one arm above her petite frame and push the door open, ushering us both out into the cool November night.

I jam both hands into the pockets of my slacks now so I don't grab her shoulders and shake her, demanding to know what the hell she's doing marrying a guy who treats her like Sterling Woodcock does. Because it's really none of my business.

Her toned, bare back is to me as she faces the busy city street, car lights a blur of white and red just beyond her, misty air puffing over her shoulder like she's trying to catch her breath.

"You okay?"

Her head nods furiously before she turns back

around with that weird Stepford wife smile plastered back on her dainty face.

"You don't look fine." My fingers wrap around the keys in my pocket and jangle them anxiously.

"Shit, thanks, Jas."

"I mean, you look beautiful," I rush out, grimacing when I note her eyes widening. "You always do. You just don't look . . . happy?"

She blinks slowly, the edges of her mouth turning down into a slight frown. "Is that supposed to be better? Beautiful and unhappy?"

God. I'm really blowing it. I rake a hand through my hair. "Are you happy? Does he make you happy?"

Her mouth pops open in shock, and I know I'm out of line, or stepping in it, or whatever. But someone needs to ask her, and I doubt anyone has.

I need to hear her say it.

Her pale cheeks flush and her eyes narrow as she steps up to me, jaw tight. "You're asking me this *now*?"

I huff out a breath and run my top teeth almost painfully over my bottom lip, eyes totally fixed on her baby blues, so wide and pale and sparking with indignation. "Yeah. Has anyone else asked you?"

She drops my gaze, her hands planting against her cheeks before pushing back through her collarbone-length blonde hair. "No one has asked me."

The teeth of my car key dig into the palm of my hand. "How did you meet Sterling?"

"My dad introduced us." Her eyes fixate on the black

sky. It's starless, not like at the ranch where you can see every little fleck of light. Everything in the city feels polluted compared to Chestnut Springs. I decide on the spot to drive out to my place in the country tonight rather than spend another night breathing the same air as Sterling Woodcock.

"How does he know him?"

Her eyes meet mine. "Sterling's dad is a new business partner of his. He's focused on making new connections now that he's back in the city."

"And you've known this guy for how long again?"

Her tongue darts out from between her lips. "We met in May."

"*Five months*?" My brow arches and I rear back. If they seemed madly in love I could buy it, but . . .

"Don't judge me, Jasper!" Her eyes flash and she steps closer again. I may dwarf her in height, but she's not the least bit intimidated. She's spitting mad right now. Mad at me. But I think that's just because she trusts me enough to let her anger out, and I'm okay with letting her. I'm happy to be that person for her.

Her voice shakes when she adds, "You have no idea the pressures I live with."

Without thinking twice, I pull her into my chest and wrap my arms around her narrow shoulders. She's all tense and riled. I swear I can almost feel her vibrating with it. "I'm not judging you, Sunny."

Apparently, this isn't the time for childhood nicknames.

"Don't call me that." Her voice cracks as she presses her forehead to my chest, like she always has, and I slide my palm down the back of her hair, cupping the base of her skull.

Like I always have.

I absently wonder what Sterling would say if he walked out here right now. There's a petty part of me that *wants* him to.

"I'm just curious how things happened so fast. I'm curious why I've never met him until now." My voice is quiet, all gravel, almost drowned out by the hush of cars rushing past us.

"Well, it's not like I have a lot of free time with the ballet. And it's not like you've been in touch lately either."

Guilt nips at me, making my chest twist. Our team came off a bad season, and I promised myself I'd train harder than I ever have during the off-season. "I was training and living out in Chestnut Springs." That's not a lie. My brother's fiancé opened a hell of a gym there, and I saw no reason to spend my summer in the city. "And then it was training camp, and I got swept up."

Also true.

The lie is that I was too busy to make time for her. I could have made time for her. But I didn't. Because I knew her dad was back in the city, and I avoid him at all costs.

"I should have told you," she murmurs.

I swoop a hand over her head and give her shoulders

a squeeze, still trying to avoid that warm, bare patch of skin on her back, and reply with, "I should have asked. I've just been . . . busy. I didn't think your life would just . . . happen this fast." And that part is true. Her engagement blindsided me.

Her body relaxes in my arms, soft breasts pressing against my ribs as her fingers dig into my back. But only for a moment before she pulls away. The hug went on long enough that it was more of an embrace. It was toeing the line.

But I still find myself wanting to pull her back in.

"Well, it is." She looks down and brushes at the sleeve of her pale green dress, silky and shimmering in the dark light. "My dad and I agreed it was best to move forward with the wedding in the fall rather than drawing it out."

That comment has my teeth clamping down, because the mere mention of Robert Winthrop sets me on edge. And him taking part in her decision to get married has all sorts of alarm bells going off.

"Why?" My brow knits. I should know better. I should walk away. I should let her be happy.

I shouldn't be this bothered. Maybe if she actually seemed happy. I wouldn't be.

Or maybe I would.

She waves a hand and glances over her shoulder into the restaurant, exposing her elegant neck as she does. "Multiple factors," she replies with a defeated shrug. It's like she knows her time with me is dwindling. I don't get the sense that Sterling is going to be the type of husband that's okay with her and I being friends.

"Factors? Like you just can't wait to be Mrs. *Woodcock*? Because no one wants that as a last name. Or is this your dad pressuring you?"

Her blue eyes flare at the mention of her dad, because Sloane doesn't see him as a snake. Never has. She's too busy being the perfect daughter—and now fiancée. One who looks good on paper and doesn't go hunting. "And what if he is? I'm twenty-eight. My best dancing years are drawing to a close. I need to settle down, come up with a life plan. He's looking out for me."

I huff out an agitated laugh and shake my head at her. Where's the wild girl I remember? The girl who danced in the rain and would crawl onto the roof so I didn't have to be alone on the bad nights?

That girl has been molded into a pawn. And I hate that for her. We've never fought, but suddenly my urge to fight *for* her consumes my better judgement.

"Your dad is an asshole. He cares about himself. His business. *Optics.* Not your happiness."

She lurches back like I've struck her, lips thinning in anger as she flushes all the way down her chest. "No, Jasper. *Your* dad is as an asshole. Mine loves me. You just don't know what that looks like."

She spins on her heel, yanking the restaurant door open with a level of violence that doesn't suit someone so delicate looking.

But I'd rather she show violence than apathy. That means the wild girl is still in there somewhere.

She hurled words at me that *should* hurt. But I just hurt for her. Because my biological dad *is* an asshole. But the man who really raised me? Harvey Eaton? He's the best of the best. He showed me what love looks like, and I can identify it just fine.

Plus, I remember how Sloane looks at a man when she really wants him. And she isn't looking at her fiancé the way she used to look at me.

I'm more pleased about that than I should be.

Acknowledgments

I think that writing a book about a little boy the same age as my own will always hold a special place in my heart. The countless notes in my phone about hilarious things he's said over the past several months will certainly be kept for years to come.

And yes, he did in fact jump out to scare me and yell, "Chipmunks!" And no, I have no idea what was going through his head. But it was just priceless enough to be book worthy.

To my readers, thank you. You've all changed my life. None of this would be possible without YOU. So thank you for spending your precious free time reading my stories. For loving them, for sharing them, for blowing up my inbox with your sweet messages. I love you all.

To my husband, I'm writing this exactly three days before we leave for our "honeymoon." We said we'd finally take a honeymoon when we made it to ten years, and here we are heading to Spain. Time truly flies when you're having fun. Thank you for making me laugh every day—even when you piss me off.

To my son, chipmunks, baby. You crack me up.

Spending time with you is such a blessing. I love you to the Venus and back.

To my parents, y'all told me I could be whatever I wanted when I grew up. Bet you didn't think I'd be writing smutty books for a living, huh?

To my assistant Krista, thank you for listening to my endless voice messages. Thank you for petting my hair on down days. And thank you for keeping me organized. This release really is "our" release.

To Lena, when are you leaving your husband for me?

To Catherine, I'm not sure how I'll ever repay you for everything you've done for me. The support. The advice. The love. You will forever be the first (very excited) call on my phone when I hit number one and I just love that for us.

To Kandi, I don't think I'd have finished this book on time if it wasn't for your cheerleading and early morning sprint sessions. The Spicy Sprint Sluts makes my life and can't wait to write more books with you. #gratitudebombs

To Melanie, you continue to inspire me with your generosity. Thank you for your direction and help from the very beginning. I know that I wouldn't be where I am today without your wisdom.

To Sarah and Jenn from Social Butterfly, you both kick ass. Thank you for your guidance and attention. I'm so grateful to have women like you on my side.

To my beta readers Júlia, Amy, and Krista, thank you for helping me make this book the best it could be. Your notes make me laugh and your feedback makes me a better writer. I'd be lost without you.

To my editor Paula, I don't trust your carrots, but I do trust your expertise. Obviously, you inspire me. But you also are irreplaceable. Your input and your extra time spent helping me never goes unnoticed.

To my cover designer Casey/Echo, why are you so talented? It's honestly kind of insane. You're stuck with me now.

Finally, to my ARC readers and street team members, THANK YOU. So many of you have been with me since the very beginning of this wild ride. And now so many of you are new. Supporting an author in this way might not feel like a big deal to you, but it's a *huge* deal to me. Every post, every TikTok, every review literally changes my life. I don't know that I'll every be able to repay your kindness, but I will do my best to pay it forward in what ever way I can.

The Elsie Silver Saloon

Come hang out in The Saloon on Facebook and interact with Elsie! Early announcements, exclusive excerpts, bonus giveaways, and general book boyfriend chit chat all happens here.

Take me to The Saloon!